Simon Scarrow is a *Sunday Times* No. 1 bestselling author. After a childhood spent travelling the world, he pursued his great love of history as a teacher, before becoming a full-time writer. His Roman soldier heroes Cato and Macro made their debut in 2000 in UNDER THE EAGLE, and have subsequently appeared in many bestsellers in the Eagles of the Empire series, including CENTURION and THE GLADIATOR.

Simon Scarrow is also the author of the novels YOUNG BLOODS, THE GENERALS, FIRE AND SWORD and THE FIELDS OF DEATH, chronicling the lives of the Duke of Wellington and Napoleon Bonaparte, and of SWORD & SCIMITAR, the epic tale of the 1565 Siege of Malta, and HEARTS OF STONE, set in Greece during the Second World War.

Simon has co-written two bestselling novels with T. J. Andrews, ARENA and INVADER.

Simon lives in the historic city of Norwich.

For exciting news, extracts and exclusive content from Simon visit www.simonscarrow.co.uk, follow him on Twitter @SimonScarrow or like his author page on Facebook/OfficialSimonScarrow

Praise for **SIMON SCARROW**'s novels

'A new book in Simon Scarrow's long-running series about the Roman army is always a joy . . . It is heartening for fans of Cato and Macro that their adventures remain as lively as ever' Antonia Senior, *The Times*

'A satisfyingly bloodthirsty, bawdy romp . . . perfect for Bernard Cornwell addicts who will relish its historical detail and fast-paced action. Storming stuff!' *Good Book Guide*

'A rip-roaring page-turner . . . Sturdy elegance and incisive wit' *Historical Novels Review*

'I really don't need this kind of competition . . . It's a great read' Bernard Cornwell

'Tremendous' *Daily Express*

'An engrossing storyline, full of teeth-clenching battles, political machinations, treachery, honour, love and death . . . More please!' Elizabeth Chadwick

'Scarrow's rank with the best' *Independent*

'Scarrow's engaging pair of heroes . . . top stuff' *Daily Telegraph*

By *Simon Scarrow*

The *Roman Empire* Series
The Britannia Campaign
Under the Eagle (AD 42–43, Britannia)
The Eagle's Conquest (AD 43, Britannia)
When the Eagle Hunts (AD 44, Britannia)
The Eagle and the Wolves (AD 44, Britannia)
The Eagle's Prey (AD 44, Britannia)

Rome and the Eastern Provinces
The Eagle's Prophecy (AD 45, Rome)
The Eagle in the Sand (AD 46, Judaea)
Centurion (AD 46, Syria)

The Mediterranean
The Gladiator (AD 48–49, Crete)
The Legion (AD 49, Egypt)
Praetorian (AD 51, Rome)

The Return to Britannia
The Blood Crows (AD 51, Britannia)
Brothers in Blood (AD 51, Britannia)
Britannia (AD 52, Britannia)

The *Wellington and Napoleon* Quartet
Young Bloods
The Generals
Fire and Sword
The Fields of Death

Sword & Scimitar

Hearts of Stone

The *Gladiator* Series
Gladiator: Fight for Freedom
Gladiator: Street Fighter
Gladiator: Son of Spartacus

Writing with T. J. Andrews
Arena
Invader

SIMON SCARROW

EAGLES·OF·THE·EMPIRE

BRITANNIA

headline

First published in Great Britain in 2015
by HEADLINE PUBLISHING GROUP

First published in paperback in Great Britain in 2016
by HEADLINE PUBLISHING GROUP

1

Cataloguing in Publication Data is available from the British Library

ISBN 978 1 4722 3386 8 (A-format)
ISBN 978 1 4722 1330 3 (B-format)

Typeset in Bembo by Avon DataSet Ltd, Bidford-on-Avon, Warwickshire

Printed and bound in Great Britain by Clays Ltd, St Ives plc

Headline's policy is to use papers that are natural, renewable and recyclable
products and made from wood grown in well-managed forests and other
controlled sources. The logging and manufacturing processes are expected to
conform to the environmental regulations of the country of origin.

HEADLINE PUBLISHING GROUP
An Hachette UK Company
Carmelite House
50 Victoria Embankment
London EC4Y 0DZ

www.headline.co.uk
www.hachette.co.uk

To John and Joan Prigent

CONTENTS

THE ROMAN PROVINCE OF
BRITANNIA AD 52

NORTH WALES AD52

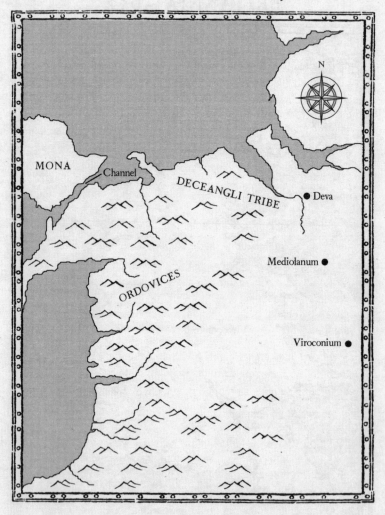

MONA

Channel

DECEANGLI TRIBE

● Deva

Mediolanum ●

ORDOVICES

Viroconium ●

N

THE SIEGE OF MONA
AD 52

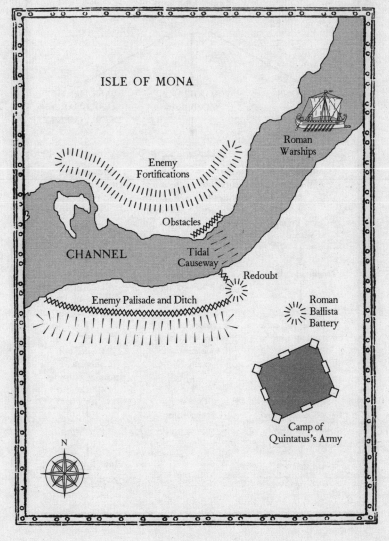

ISLE OF MONA

Roman
Warships

Enemy
Fortifications

Obstacles

CHANNEL

Tidal
Causeway

Redoubt

Enemy Palisade and Ditch

Roman
Ballista
Battery

Camp of
Quintatus's Army

N

THE ROMAN ARMY
CHAIN OF COMMAND

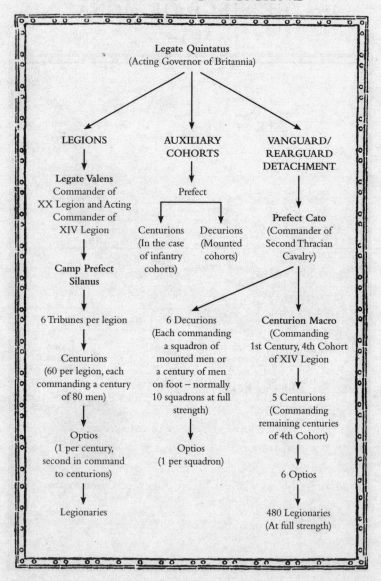

Legate Quintatus
(Acting Governor of Britannia)

LEGIONS

AUXILIARY COHORTS

VANGUARD/ REARGUARD DETACHMENT

Legate Valens
Commander of
XX Legion and Acting
Commander of
XIV Legion

Prefect

Prefect Cato
(Commander of
Second Thracian
Cavalry)

Centurions
(In the case
of infantry
cohorts)

Decurions
(Mounted
cohorts)

Camp Prefect Silanus

6 Tribunes per legion

6 Decurions
(Each commanding
a squadron of
mounted men or
a century of men
on foot – normally
10 squadrons at full
strength)

Centurion Macro
(Commanding
1st Century, 4th Cohort
of XIV Legion

Centurions
(60 per legion, each
commanding a century
of 80 men)

5 Centurions
(Commanding
remaining centuries
of 4th Cohort)

Optios
(1 per century,
second in command
to centurions)

Optios
(1 per squadron)

6 Optios

Legionaries

480 Legionaries
(At full strength)

CAST LIST

At the Fort
Second Thracian Cavalry 'The Blood Crows'
Prefect Cato
Decurions: Miro, Themistocles, Corvinus, Aristophanes,
    Harpex, Plato
Trooper Thraxis
Surgeon Pausinus
Optio Pandarus

Fourth Cohort, XIV Legion
Centurion Macro
Centurions: Crispus, Festinus, Portillus, Lentulus, Macer
Optios: Croton, Diodorus

Eighth Illyrian Cohort Detachment
Centurions: Fortunus, Appilus
Optios: Saphros, Mago
Auxiliary Lomus

The Mona Invasion Column

Legate Quintatus, *Commanding Officer*

Legate Valens, *Commanding XX Legion and Temporary Commander of XIV*

Camp Prefect Silanus

Tribune Livonius

Others

Aulus Didius Gallus, *incoming Governor of a province in turmoil*

Caius Porcinus Glaber, *Gallus's Chief of Staff*

Venistus, *a venal leader of the camp followers of the Eighth Illyrian Cohort*

Julia, *an unfortunate army wife*

Petronius Deanus, *a mercenary northern trader*

Lucius, *son of Prefect Cato and Julia*

CHAPTER ONE

October, AD *52*

'What do you think?' Prefect Cato asked as he stared down the slope towards the fortified settlement sprawling along the floor of the valley. While it was not nearly so formidable as the vast hill forts he had seen in the southern lands of Britannia, the Deceanglian tribesmen had constructed their defences well. The settlement had been built on raised ground close to the river that flowed swiftly through the valley. A deep ditch surrounded a turf rampart topped with a sturdy palisade. There was a fortified gateway at each end of the settlement where sentries kept watch up and down the valley. Cato estimated that there must be several hundred round huts within the defences. There were many animals penned in there as well, together with what looked like a cluster of tents – the covers of the stone-lined grain pits used by the natives.

Lying next to the young officer was Centurion Macro, his lined face crinkling as he squinted into the late-afternoon sunlight flooding the valley, giving a burnished glow to the stubbled fields and the dark-green boughs of the pine trees covering the slopes either side of the settlement. Both men had taken off their helmets and left them with the small patrol waiting on the other side of the ridge. The same men who had reported the unusual activity at the village the day before. With their dull brown cloaks and their cautious approach to the vantage point through the stunted trees covering the hill, Cato and Macro had avoided being seen by the enemy as they took stock of the Deceanglian warriors' preparations.

Macro, a tough veteran, pursed his lips briefly. 'Looks clear enough to me. They've gathered in men from the outlying villages. See that mob by the horse lines? Right by that stock of spears and shields. Ten denarii gets you one; that ain't no hunting party.' He paused and made a quick estimate of the enemy's strength. 'Can't be more than five or six hundred of them. No immediate danger to us.'

Cato nodded. It was true. The fort they had been posted to ten miles to the east was well positioned and garrisoned by the two units under his command: Macro's cohort of legionaries from the Fourteenth, and his own part-mounted auxiliary cohort. The Blood Crows, as they were known, thanks to the design on their banner, had once been a cavalry unit. The recent campaigns in the mountains of the west of the province had caused the loss of many of the army's horses. The training depot at Luntum had been working hard to supply remounts, but there were far too few to satisfy the needs of the army. As a result, half the men of Cato's cohort now served as infantry, and the unit had been posted, along with Macro's men, to one of the outposts tasked with protecting the frontier of Emperor Claudius's new province. A fresh draft of replacement troops had filled out the ranks of both units and brought them nearly up to the strength with which they had started the campaign against the moun-

2

tain tribes. With over four hundred legionaries together with as many auxiliary troops, they were in no danger from the war party gathering in the settlement.

Which raised a question.

'So what are they up to?' Cato exchanged a brief look with his subordinate and guessed that Macro's thoughts were heading in the same direction. 'I'll send word to the Legate. Chances are there'll be similar reports from other outposts. In which case it looks like the Druids are back in business and we're going to have trouble again.'

'Bastards,' Macro hissed. 'Bloody Druids. Don't those wild-haired shits ever know when to give in?'

'It's their land, Macro. These are their people. Would we respond any differently if we were in their boots?'

'If we were in their boots, sir, the legions would never even have got a toehold on this island.'

Cato chuckled at his friend's hubris. 'While I admire your estimation of our fighting qualities, I can't help but grieve at your lack of empathy.'

Macro snorted. 'Any warm feeling I might have had for those hairy barbarians disappeared a long while back, about the time they should have been smart enough to realise that they weren't ever going to give us a beating.'

'They've come close enough at times.'

Macro cocked an eyebrow. 'If you say so, sir.'

'And it's not as if they haven't contested us every step of the way.' Cato sighed. 'It's been nigh on ten years since the army first landed, and we don't feel much closer to securing the province. Of course, it doesn't help when even the natives who are supposed to be on our side are treated little better than animals.'

His companion shot him a weary look. Macro had heard his friend talking like this before and put it down to the younger man's peculiar appetite for the affectations of Greek philosophy, and a corresponding tendency to overthink the situation. It did not seem to have done the Greeks much good, he mused. After all, their land was now a province of Rome, just as the whole of Britannia would become one day. He cleared his throat before he responded.

'Yes, well, they'll get better treatment the moment they stop behaving like animals and accept our ways. But first we have to put the stick about and beat some sense into 'em.' He jabbed his thumb towards the settlement. 'Starting with them Druids. I'm telling you, our job here is going to be a lot less difficult the moment we nail the last of the bastards to a cross and leave him out to dry.'

'Maybe so,' Cato reflected. Macro's hostility to the Druidic cult was well founded. Though the island's tribal kingdoms were thoroughly divided, with half of them having made treaties with Rome before the first legionary had set foot on these shores, they were all steeped in reverence towards the Druids and were susceptible to their appeals to resist the invader. Even now, Cato knew, many of the tribes that had supposedly been subdued still looked to the Druids to continue the struggle. Many of their warriors had slipped across the frontier into these mountains to join the ranks of those still fighting Rome. The situation had been exacerbated by the death of the province's governor. Ostorius had been a seasoned commander when he had been assigned to Britannia. Too seasoned, as it turned out. The strain of fighting the mountain tribes had worn him out, and he had collapsed at an officers' briefing and died less than a month later.

4

It was poor timing. The legions had just won a hard-fought victory over the native warriors. Their commander, Caratacus, had been captured and sent to Rome with his family, and the spirit of his followers had been all but broken. And then the governor had died. At once the Druids seized on this as a sign from their gods that the Romans were cursed and that the tribes must continue the fight now that they had won divine approval. The outposts of the frontier were attacked, supply columns and patrols ambushed and the army had been obliged to fall back towards the more easily defended territory that fringed the lands of the Silurians, Ordovicians and Deceanglians. The lack of clear leadership had undermined the Roman position; the replacement governor would be unlikely to take command before spring. And now this fresh evidence that the tribes were gathering to renew the onslaught.

'I've seen enough,' Cato decided. 'Let's go.'

They crept back towards the treeline. Once they were safely within the shadows, the two men clambered to their feet and adjusted their sword belts and cloaks. Above them the boughs were already shedding their leaves. The foliage was russet and yellow, and the gentle breeze sent the more brittle leaves tumbling through the air. Cato, taller and more thin-framed than his friend, gave a shudder. He did not relish the thought of spending the long months of winter confined to the fort, which some wag on the previous governor's staff had given the name Imperatoris Stultitiam – The Emperor's Folly. It had been one of those quips that had passed into practice, and that was how the fort's name was described on all official correspondence. The winter climate of the island was miserable enough, Cato reflected, but here in the hills and mountains it was relentlessly cold, wet and windy.

Cato longed for the comforts of Italia, with its milder climate. More to the point, that was where his wife was waiting for his return, in the home they had bought in Rome. By now, Julia would have given birth to their first child, and Cato was anxiously awaiting a letter from her to set his mind at rest. It would be months, years maybe, before Britannia was settled enough for him to request permission to return to Rome, so he had already decided that he would ask Julia to travel to the island. The first towns of the new province were rapidly expanding, and although they were primitive affairs, they featured enough comforts to offer a semblance of the civilisation found in the rest of the empire. Besides, he and Julia would be able to see each other more easily, and Cato could savour some of the home life that he had been yearning for the moment he received news of her pregnancy.

Macro led the way up the slope through the trees, boots rustling through the fallen leaves and softly cracking the twigs underfoot. The ground soon evened out as they reached the crest of the hill and started to descend the other side towards the track where the squadron of auxiliary cavalry was waiting for them. With the hill between them and the enemy, the officers felt safe and able to speak in normal tones now that the danger of detection had passed.

'Do you really think those bastards are going to stick it to us before winter comes?' asked Macro.

Cato thought briefly before he nodded. 'More than likely. The Druids will want to strike swiftly while their people are still celebrating the death of Ostorius. They're going to make things difficult for us, but I doubt they will have the strength to drive us out of the mountains. Thank the gods they don't have Caratacus to lead 'em any more.'

'Yes, thank fuck for that,' Macro growled with feeling. 'Bastard had more tricks up his sleeve than a ten-sestertius whore.'

Cato arched an amused eyebrow. 'Colourful.'

Macro spat on the ground. 'And just our luck that we won't get any reward for capturing him, not once but twice. Instead, it's going to be some other lucky bastard who claims the credit.'

Cato could well understand his friend's bitterness. There was no justice in the situation, but he had served long enough in the army to know that a soldier rarely received his due. Not when there was a politician around ready to claim the success of others as his own.

'Wonder how Caratacus is going to be received in Rome when he arrives in chains,' Macro continued. 'Hope they give him the same treatment that Caesar gave that Gaul.'

'Vercingetorix?'

'Him, yes.'

Cato recalled the man who had opposed Julius Caesar a hundred years before. Beaten at Alesia and taken prisoner, he had languished in a dungeon beneath Rome for several years before being dragged out into the streets and strangled as the centrepiece of Caesar's triumph. An unworthy end for a noble enemy, Cato thought. He hoped that Caratacus would be spared such a miserable and humiliating death by Emperor Claudius. He had fought bravely and tirelessly against Rome and deserved the respect of his enemies. Despite what Macro might feel.

'I hope not.'

Macro shot a wry glance over his shoulder. 'Pity for the noble barbarian?'

Cato smiled. 'Something like that.'

'Shit, when are you ever going to learn, lad? There's us, and there's them – the barbarians – standing in the way of Rome and our destiny. If they're smart, then they give way to us. If they don't, then more fool them. There's no room for pity in this world. That's all you need to know in our line of work.'

Cato shrugged. Such an informal exchange between a centurion and his commanding officer might usually be frowned upon, but the two of them had served side by side since Cato had joined the legions a decade earlier. In private company they still conversed with the informality of earlier years, and Cato valued that. Far better to have a comrade who could be relied on to speak his mind than one who would just obey mindlessly.

'Besides,' Macro continued, 'do you think for an instant that they return the favour? Not a bit of it. They hate our guts and would cut our throats in a trice if they could. The only people who believe in noble barbarians are those literary ponces back in Rome turning out their bloody histories. There's no such thing as noble barbarians, just barbarians.'

'I think you might have mined out this rich seam of invective long ago,' Cato responded. 'Why not do me a favour, and save your breath, eh?'

Macro pursed his lips and frowned. 'Please yourself, Prefect.'

The reference to Cato's rank betrayed Macro's hurt at

the slight, and Cato sighed to himself as he followed his friend in silence. There was light ahead through the trees, and a moment later they emerged on to the native track that passed through the forest. They paused, breathing hard, and glanced to both sides, but there was no sign of the soldiers they had brought with them from the fort.

'I don't recognise this spot,' Cato muttered. 'Must have started out further along.'

'Which way?'

He looked up at the crest of the hill and spotted some crags he had seen earlier. 'To the left. Let's go.'

They paced quickly along the track, hemmed in by the trees on either side, the breeze swishing through the branches. A short distance further on, the path turned to follow the line of the slope, and there, fifty paces ahead, stood the patrol. Ten men waiting by their mounts, while one held the officers' horses as well as his own. Their cloaks, leggings and boots and the flanks of their horses were covered with mud. As soon as he spied the officers, Decurion Miro alerted his men and they readied themselves to mount.

'You were right, Decurion,' said Cato as they reached the patrol. 'There's trouble brewing.'

Miro bowed his head in acknowledgement, relieved that his commander agreed with his assessment. 'Your orders, sir?'

'Back to the fort. Then we'll pass on what we've seen to the legate.'

Miro stared at him. 'And what do you reckon Quintatus will do about it, sir?'

'It's not our place to second-guess the legate, Decurion.' Cato pulled himself up on to his saddle and swung his leg over the back of his horse, then gave the order. 'Mount!'

The rest climbed into their saddles with a chorus of grunts, creaking leather and the snorts of their sturdy mounts. Once the men had taken up their reins in their left hands and settled their lances into the saddle rests, Cato waved his hand forward and eased his horse into a trot along the track. It was narrow enough to oblige the Romans to ride in single file for a while before it left the forest and passed over open ground. Then Macro eased his mount forward to draw alongside the prefect.

'We'll need to get the lads ready to march, sir. In case Quintatus gives the order.'

'I'm aware of that. I want you to prepare a full inventory of our supplies. I'll see to any shortfall at headquarters. We're not going to have a repeat of that nonsense earlier this year.'

Macro nodded with feeling. The two units of Cato's command had been tasked with guarding the baggage train, and the army's supply officer had put them at the back of the queue for replacement kit. It was only when Cato had cornered the junior tribune concerned and given him a thorough bollocking that the baggage train escort had finally been given what they needed. If Quintatus was forced into a fresh campaign, then this time it would be essential to ensure that the Blood Crows and Macro's legionaries were properly equipped and supplied for the rigours of mountain fighting.

Cato abruptly threw up his arm and reined in. In the time it took Macro to react, his horse had continued another length before drawing up. The remaining riders followed suit as Cato leaned forward in his saddle and scrutinised an outcrop of rocks looming over the track a short distance ahead.

'What is it, sir?' asked Macro.

'There's movement up there. I saw someone in the rocks.'

Macro stared a moment and puffed his cheeks. 'I can't—'

Before he could finish, a slight figure in a woollen tunic rose up and drew a bow. Macro instinctively reached for the handle of his sword, then paused before letting out a scornful laugh as he saw that it was a scrawny youngster.

'Be on your way! Before I tan your bloody hide!'

The Roman soldiers chuckled nervously, now that the tension had eased. The boy cried out defiantly in his own tongue and released the arrow. The shaft arced towards the horsemen and disappeared into the grass to one side of the track.

'Bloody cheek!' Macro snorted. 'I'll teach the little sod some manners before we take him prisoner.'

He spurred his horse towards the rock, cheered on by some of the auxiliaries. The boy drew another arrow and notched it before raising the bow again and taking aim at the cantering rider.

Cato cupped a hand to his mouth to call out a warning. 'Macro! Look out!'

The second arrow leapt from the bow and Cato saw at once that the youngster had aimed true, or was simply lucky given his moving target. Macro jerked in his saddle. His horse slowed to a trot, then stopped as the centurion leaned forward to inspect his leg.

'Fuck . . . Fucking little bastard has hit me.' His tone was more surprised than pained, and Cato urged his own mount forward. The boy stood above them, his mouth open in surprise at what he had done. Then the spell was broken as he lowered his bow and turned to flee.

'After him!' Decurion Miro bellowed.

Cato reined in beside Macro and saw the dark shaft protruding from the leather breeches covering his friend's thigh. Already blood was pulsing up around the wound and running down his leg to drip on to the track. The centurion shook his head in wonder, his lips twisted into a wry grin as he gritted his teeth. 'He's got me good, the little toerag. Lucky shot.'

Swinging himself down from the saddle, Cato approached to examine the wound. He felt a sick feeling in his gut as he saw that the blood was flowing freely. He was aware of the dark shapes of the riders pounding past as Miro led them after the native boy, and had the presence of mind to stand back and call after the decurion.

'Leave the boy! Decurion! Call your men back!'

The auxiliaries reluctantly abandoned the chase and watched the fugitive nimbly picking his way up the rocks towards the crest of the hill. It would be a fool's errand to pursue him. The boy was shrewd enough to stick to ground that was impassable to horses, and in any case, he would easily outpace the soldiers weighted down by their armour if they pursued him on foot. Cato turned back to his friend.

'We have to stem the bleeding, Macro. It's bad.'

'I can see that for myself, thank you.'

Cato drew a sharp breath. 'You know what I have to do?'

'Just get on with it.'

'All right.' Cato closed his left fist about the shaft and locked his arm. Then with his right he grasped the arrow a short distance further along. He tensed his muscles. 'Ready? On three.'

Macro nodded and looked up.

'One . . .' Cato suddenly snapped the shaft, and his friend roared with pain and glared wildly down from the saddle.

'You cheating bastard, sir!'

Blood welled up from the end of the shaft embedded in Macro's thigh, and Cato hurriedly undid his neckcloth and tucked one end under the centurion's leg before he fed the rest of it around the limb, alternating to each side of the shaft and making the rough dressing as tight as he could. Dark stains appeared through the cloth as he tied it off, and he reached up. 'Give me yours.'

Macro undid the strip of cloth from around his thick neck, and Cato bound it over his own to complete the dressing. Despite the pressure, the wound was still bleeding, and he realised that Macro was losing too much blood, too quickly. He must get him back to the fort as soon as possible so that he could be treated by the garrison's surgeon.

'Miro! I want one of your men either side of the centurion. Keep him steady in his saddle.'

While the men moved into place, Macro shook his head. 'I don't need any bloody nursemaids. I'll make my own way.'

'Shut up, and do as you are told,' Cato snapped as he remounted. He took up his reins and looked up to see the boy some distance above them now. He had stopped to hurl insults down at the Romans, and his piercing voice echoed off the rocks. Soon the alarm would be raised in the settlement and they would be sure to come after the patrol. 'We have to get out of here.'

With a stab of anxiety, he saw that Macro was swaying slightly in his saddle, already light-headed from shock and the loss of blood. Then Cato's anxiety turned to fear. Fear that he might lose his closest friend in the world as a result of this absurd confrontation and the blind chance of the boy's second shot. The irony that Macro should be laid low by a skinny youth when he had bested some of the most formidable enemies of the empire was almost too much for Cato.

'Shit. Shit,' he muttered as he met his friend's wavering gaze. 'Not you. Not now. Not in this place.'

'No fucking way,' Macro growled back. 'Don't you worry about that, my lad.'

Cato nodded and then turned to Decurion Miro. 'Back to the fort! We stop for nothing. Let's go!'

CHAPTER TWO

'Get him on the table,' the surgeon ordered as the auxiliaries entered the treatment room in the small infirmary next to the fort's headquarters block. Macro hung limply between them, an arm draped round each man's shoulder. He was barely conscious and his head lolled, and Cato was shocked to see how white and drained his face looked. Outside, the day was drawing to a close and a trumpet had just sounded the changing of the watch. The daily routine of the garrison continued without regard for the small drama played out as the patrol galloped in through the main gate.

Surgeon Pausinus was one of the rare medical officers who was not Greek or from one of the eastern provinces, where medical expertise was more readily come by. He had been selected from the ranks to train as a wound dresser before advancing to his current position, where he had many years' experience in attending to the wounds, injuries and illnesses of soldiers. The examination table had a thin leather bolster at one end for patients to rest their heads. The men supporting Macro heaved the centurion up on to the hard surface, and Cato stood to one side as Pausinus took charge.

'Take off his harness and armour. Boots, too. Just leave him in his tunic.'

While the auxiliaries did as they were told, Macro muttered curses at them, his eyelids fluttering as he rolled his head slowly from side to side. Meanwhile the surgeon took out his case of instruments and carefully selected a small range of tools, which he set out on a stool set down beside the table. He called for one of his orderlies to fetch linen dressings, vinegar and his herb chest, then opened the shutters of the window on the other side of Macro to admit as much light as possible.

'Out of the way there!' He swept one of the auxiliaries aside. 'Stand back.' He bowed his head towards Cato. 'Not you, of course, sir. Just keep to one side, though, eh?'

Cato nodded and stood where he could see his friend's pale face without hindering the surgeon or his staff.

Once Macro's armour had been removed, Pausinus undid the neckcloth dressings and tossed the blood-stained strips of cloth into a wooden pail below the table. He leaned closer to inspect the stump of the arrow, then straightened up and addressed Macro.

'I'm going to have to cut your breeches open to get at the wound, sir.'

'No . . .' Macro protested feebly. 'Only just worn them in . . .'

'That's too bad.' Pausinus took up a small pair of shears and began to cut the leather up to the wound, then carefully picked his way round the shaft and continued to Macro's hip until the breeches were laid open and could be peeled away from the centurion's thigh. Dried and fresh blood was smeared around the clotted mass where the arrow had pierced the flesh. The surgeon tested the area around the wound with his fingers, and Macro let out a deep groan.

'Hmmm. Nasty. I can't feel the head of the arrow. It's gone in deep.' Pausinus stroked his bristling chin, leaving a crimson smear on his skin.

'What are you going to do?' asked Cato.

'It's straightforward enough, sir. A progressive extraction should do the job.'

Cato sighed and raised an eyebrow. 'Care to explain?'

'While I work, yes, sir. The centurion's still losing blood, so there's no time to waste.' Pausinus turned to the auxiliaries. 'Roll him on to his side and hold him there. When I get started, he can't be allowed to move. Understand? Good! Then let's do it.'

'Let me.' Cato pushed one of the auxiliaries aside and took Macro's shoulders.

Pausinus glanced at him with a surprised expression, then shrugged. 'As you wish. Ready? Now.'

With the surgeon guiding them, they eased Macro on to his side, with the wound uppermost and the shaft facing into the room.

'Hold him down,' Pausinus instructed as he took up a bronze scalpel and sighted the angle of the shaft as it entered the thigh. He took a deep breath and inserted the tip of the instrument into the flesh on the opposite side of Macro's thigh. Bright red blood spilled from the fresh wound and streamed down Macro's skin on to the table. The centurion let out a fresh groan and tried to move. Cato held his friend down while the auxiliary pinned his legs in place. He felt Macro's body trembling in his grip.

'If he's losing blood, then why cut him a fresh wound?'

Without looking up or pausing, the surgeon replied calmly, 'As I said, the missile has penetrated deeply. Furthermore, I can feel that the head is broad. A hunting arrow most like. If I try a regressive extraction and attempt to move it out the way it came in, then it will cause much more damage and loss of blood. So the trick is to make an incision opposite the point of entry and draw the arrow through from that direction.' He glanced up. 'Of course it's harder than it sounds. It's no wonder Celsus was always bitching about it. I don't suppose you've read his work.'

'I've heard the name.'

'Hearing the name and knowing his work is not quite the same thing, sir,' Pausinus said wryly as he continued his incision. 'The *De Medicina* is the standard reference text for army surgeons. Celsus covers most of the ground well enough, but there's no substitute for experience. It's like Hippocrates said: "He who desires to practise surgery must go to war." And thanks to the protracted campaigns we have been fighting in Britannia, I've been getting rather more experience than most in my profession. Certainly more than some.' He nodded towards the orderly. 'So you can rest assured that the centurion is in good hands.'

He withdrew his scalpel and laid the bloodied instrument down on the stool, then reached for a probe. 'Now comes the delicate part.'

Using the fingers of his left hand, he eased the incision apart to reveal the raw red muscle beneath. The blood flowed freely.

'Need to staunch that. Orderly, some vinegar here!'

His assistant leaned over the wound, pulled out the stopper of a small flask and poured liberally, wiping the excess and the blood from around the wound before splashing more directly into the incision. Macro lurched beneath Cato's hands and bellowed: 'Fuck! That . . . hurts . . .'

With a groan, he went limp. Cato's heart froze. 'What's happened?'

'Passed out, that's all. Not surprised, really. He's a tough one, the centurion. Most faint from lack of blood and shock before this. Guess the vinegar finally tipped him over the edge.' Pausinus pulled the flesh further apart and carefully inserted the probe. Clenching his jaw, he worked the instrument around, then nodded. 'Found it. Get the levers on the incision and then hand me the extractor.'

The orderly hesitated, and Pausinus hissed with frustration. 'That one there, with the notch.'

With the required instruments to hand, the surgeon looked at Cato. 'This is where it gets interesting. I think you might have a steadier hand than this fool.' He nodded at the orderly. 'Would you change places, sir? I need to be sure I have someone who can be relied on under pressure.'

Cato swallowed. 'If it helps.'

He eased his hold on Macro and the orderly took over. Pausinus handed Cato the levers: two slender instruments with blunt hooked ends. 'I need you to hold the edges of the incision open so I can get at the arrowhead. Not so wide that you do the centurion more harm, but wide enough that I can see what I am doing. Is that clear?'

'I think so.'

Pausinus scrutinised him for a moment and spoke gently. 'He's not just a comrade, is he? He's more than that. A friend?'

19

'The best,' Cato replied. 'I've known him since I joined the army.'

'I see. Then you must understand this. If we are to do the best for him, then we must not be moved by his suffering. We have to do what is necessary to save him.'

'I understand.'

'Then to work! Get the wound open and keep out of my way as much as you can while I do the rest.' When he saw Cato hesitate, the surgeon nodded at the incision. 'It's not going to hold itself open, sir.'

'All right, damn you.' Cato held the levers out and pressed the hooked ends into the cut flesh, then eased the skin apart to expose the crimson muscle inside. At once Pausinus sluiced the opening with more vinegar.

'Keep your hands still, sir.'

Cato tightened his grip on the levers and tensed his arms while Pausinus edged to one side to let the light from the window fall on the incision. Then he went in with the original probe, teasing the muscles apart as he searched for the head of the arrow again. Knowing roughly where to look from his first incursion, it was the work of a moment.

'There you are, my little friend. Do you see?'

He held apart a section of fibrous muscle and used the extractor to indicate the iron point.

'Very nice,' Cato responded, feeling somewhat sick. 'What does Celsus say we do next?'

Pausinus did not reply at first as he slipped the extractor over the arrowhead, turned the notched end to engage the bottom of the iron head and gave it the gentlest of pulls.

'Damn . . .'

'What is it?'

'As I feared. A hunting arrow. The head's flat and flanged with barbs. I'll do more damage if I try and take it out as it is. Never mind. Just have to use a different tool, eh?' He put the extractor down beside the incision and reached for a delicate set of pincers. As he concentrated on the wound once more, he commanded the orderly to hold the shaft still.

While the man did as he was told, the surgeon reached in with the pincers and pushed aside the damaged muscle tissue to expose the first of the barbs. Clamping the pincers round the sharply angled iron, he nipped it off as close to the centre of the arrowhead as possible.

'There's one.' He pulled the barb out and held it up for Cato to see before tossing it into the bucket under the table. 'Now for the other.'

He repeated the procedure before setting the pincers down and taking up the extractor. 'Now we can finish the job.'

Cato watched with morbid fascination as the surgeon reinserted the bronze instrument, eased it over the flat arrowhead and twisted it to gain purchase.

'Here we go,' Pausinus muttered as he began to draw the arrowhead towards the incision. The iron was coated with blood, which made it slippery, and the extractor lost its grip. The surgeon patiently took hold of the missile again and continued to draw it out until it stood proud of the incision, between the levers in Cato's hands. As soon as he could see enough of the shaft to get his finger and thumb around it, Pausinus lowered his instruments and eased the shaft out of the incision. Another eight inches of the gore-coated wood emerged, and then, with a soft plop, it came free and the

21

surgeon held it up as he straightened his back. 'Very nasty indeed.'

Cato nodded as he examined the wide, flat iron head with its nipped-off barbs. It was easy to see now why it had been necessary to follow the procedure that Pausinus had chosen. Any attempt to pull the arrow out the way it had gone in would have torn Macro's thigh badly, ripping apart muscle and blood vessels.

'Now we need to clean out and close up,' Pausinus announced. Taking some lint from the medicine chest, he placed it in a small brass bowl and then soused it in vinegar. When it had soaked up as much of the liquid as it was going to, he took it out and packed it tightly into the incision, then did the same for the entry wound.

'You can remove the levers now, sir.'

Cato carefully worked the hooks free and put the slender bronze rods down on the table. Meanwhile Pausinus soaked two sponges and held them out for the orderly. 'Put pressure on the wounds until I say.'

'Yes, sir.'

As the orderly took over, the surgeon stood up and rolled his shoulders. 'That went as well as it could. Managed to avoid doing any further damage. Provided the wound does not become mortified, and he rests and lets it heal, he should make a good recovery. He's going to find the leg a little stiff for a few months, but that's to be expected. You don't take a hunting arrow in the thigh and shrug it off. Is he the kind of man who is likely to make a bad bed-patient?'

Cato made a face. 'You can't imagine . . .'

'Well then, you must order him to do as I say, sir. Just because he is an officer doesn't entitle him to jeopardise my hard work. I dare say you will need to issue him with strict instructions to do as he's told until he has recovered.'

'I will see to it.' Cato could imagine how that was going to go down with Macro. Still, orders were orders and his friend would just have to endure it.

'Then I'll arrange a bed for him in the dormitory.' Pausinus turned his attention back to his medicine chest and took out a needle and a length of twisted gut. Once the needle was threaded, he added three closed pins to his prepared materials. 'The entry wound is small enough to suture,' he explained. 'The fibulae are to close up the incision of the exit wound. The beauty of them is that you can pop them in and out if you need to examine the wound. Of course, it hurts like hell, but there's no getting round that. All right, take the sponges off.'

The orderly released the pressure on the wounds and tossed the sponges into the bucket while Pausinus gently extracted the lint. He smiled. 'There! Now that's left things nice and clean. No visible clots. There will be some, there always are, but it will all come out when we drain the pus from the wound over the next few days. It won't look pretty. There'll be some inflammation. That's normal, and a little of it is good. Too much might indicate mortification. If that happens . . .' He sucked his teeth. 'You might want to make an offering to Asclepius on the centurion's behalf.'

'I'll see to it personally.'

'Good. Then let's finish the job.' Pausinus pinched the torn flesh around the entry wound together and poked the point of the needle through Macro's skin. 'You have to go deep enough so that there's no chance of the stitches tearing. I use a twisted sheepgut thread. It's strong enough for the job.' He put in four stitches and then cut the thread and tied it off. Next he turned his attention to the incision and closed it up with the fibulae, before taking one off to make an adjustment and then poking the point through Macro's flesh one last time. He nodded with satisfaction. 'There. Orderly, get a dressing on that.'

Cato looked on as the linen was wrapped round Macro's thigh. 'And now?'

Pausinus crossed the treatment room to the bowl and ewer on a small table in the corner. He washed the blood off his hands as he addressed his commanding officer. 'Now? We have to wait and see if your friend gets better. Aside from the danger of mortification of the wound, he's going to be in a lot of pain. Usually I'd give my patients a few drops of poppy tears. It's easy enough to come by in the eastern provinces, but rare as a boil on Venus's backside here in Britannia. I exhausted the last of my stock months ago. So the centurion will have to settle for mandragora root soaked in heated wine. It'll dull the pain and make him drowsy. If he's sleeping then he can't disturb his wounds too much.'

'How soon will we know if he's going to recover?'

The surgeon finished rinsing his hands and then dried them on a strip of linen. 'By the fifth day, as a rule. By then, the degree of inflammation will tell us all we need to know. If it's bad, then there's likely to be something left in the wound that's causing the problem. In which case I'll have to go back in, clean it out with more vinegar, followed by warm honey in water, and then stitch him up again.'

'I see.' A thought occurred to Cato. 'And if there's no inflammation, then I can take it that Macro will be on the mend.'

'Hardly. If there's no indication of inflammation at all, then that's almost always a bad sign.'

'It is?' Cato could not follow the logic of the surgeon's statement. 'Why's that?'

'It means the flesh is dying. Although if that's the case, I'll be able to tell from the smell coming from the wound. In which case, all I will be able to do is make him as comfortable as possible before he dies.' Pausinus stood over his patient as the orderly turned Macro on to his back. He tapped a finger on the centurion's shin. 'If the wound was lower down the limb, I would be able to cut away the dead flesh, and a small amount of good flesh to be safe, saw through the bone and amputate the leg. His soldiering days would be over, but he would stand a fair chance of surviving that. Against certain death if we didn't cut it off. But this high up it is tricky. The procedure takes longer and there's more loss of blood.' He reflected for a moment and shrugged. 'So let's pray that Asclepius is looking kindly on us and Centurion Macro makes a full recovery.'

Cato was growing a little tired of the surgeon's manner and rounded on him with a cold expression. 'I am making Macro's recovery your personal responsibility. You will see to it that he is given constant attention and that his needs are met. Food, drink and toilet. He is the kind of officer it is extremely difficult to replace, and the army needs him. I will be displeased, to say the very least, if he dies. I can always find a place in the front line for an ex-army surgeon. Do I make myself clear?'

Pausinus met his stare unflinchingly. 'There's no need for threats, sir. I take my responsibilities every bit as seriously as you do. And I don't favour any particular one of my patients.

They all get the best I can manage, regardless of rank. I give you my word on that.'

Cato searched his face for any sign of insincerity, but there was none and he relented. 'Very well. Keep me informed of his progress.'

'Yes, sir.' Pausinus bowed his head.

Cato turned to look down at Macro before he left. His friend's breathing was shallow and more regular than before, and a pulse flickered on his neck. Cato patted him lightly on the shoulder. 'Take care, my friend,' he said softly.

Then he made for the door and left the fort's small hospital block. Outside, the dying light of the day filtered low across the battlements and cast long shadows over the lines of garrison blocks with their wood-shingle roofs. He crossed the main thoroughfare and made for the entrance to headquarters, exchanging a salute with the sentries at the gate. His personal quarters comprised a modest suite of rooms at the end of the main hall. As soon as he reached his office, he slipped his cloak off and called out for his servant. Thraxis, a dour-looking Thracian with cropped dark hair, emerged hurriedly from his sleeping cell.

'Prefect?'

'Help me remove my armour.'

Cato raised his arms and leaned towards Thraxis, working his way out as the servant gathered the folds of the scale vest and pulled them over his head. The layer of padding followed. With a relieved grunt, he stood up and stretched his shoulders. Then he saw the streaks of dried blood on the metal scales and looked down to see more caked on his fingers.

Macro's blood.

It was a moment before he shook off the feeling of dread for his friend. Clearing his throat, he addressed the servant.

'I want meat, bread and wine. And get a fire going in the brazier. You can clean my kit afterwards.'

'Yes, sir. And will Centurion Macro be joining you?'

Cato hesitated. He was too weary to explain. 'Not tonight.'

'Very well, sir.'

The Thracian left him alone. Cato stared dumbly at his hands for a moment before following the example of the surgeon and washing his hands using the bowl and Samian-ware jug of water on the camp table opposite his simple desk. He had to work at the dried blood, using his fingernails to flake it away from his skin. When the last of it had been wiped clear, he gazed down into the stained water and sighed in frustration. What had Macro been thinking when he charged towards the young native? It had been foolhardy, and he had paid a grievous price for his folly. If he died, it would be an ignominious end. But then so many soldiers shared that fate. Far more died due to accidental injuries or sickness than fell in battle. But somehow Cato had never imagined his friend's end coming in any way other than at the head of his cohort. That was the character of the man.

He dried his hands and moved across the room to sit on the stool behind the desk. With Macro bed-ridden for an indeterminate period, his men would need a temporary commander. The obvious choice was Centurion Crispus. A giant of a man, though what he possessed in physical presence, he certainly lacked in good humour. But there was no helping it. Crispus would have to do. Cato resolved to tell him as soon as he had eaten.

First, there was one other matter that could not wait. Taking one of the blank folded slates at the side of the desk, he flipped it open and picked up the brass stylus lying beside it. Thraxis had made a good job of preparing the wax, and the surface was smooth and unmarked. Cato sat still for a moment, staring at the opposite wall, as he composed his recollection of what he had seen at the native settlement, then he bent to his task.

'To Legate Gaius Quintatus, of the Fourteenth Legion, greetings. I respectfully beg to report . . .'

CHAPTER THREE

'How are you feeling?' Cato asked as he pulled up a stool and sat down beside Macro one morning early the following month. The latter was propped up on a bedroll stuffed with heather and straw. His bandaged leg lay flat, and Cato was pleased to see that there were no dark stains on the linen dressing. A few days earlier, Pausinus had reported that Macro's wound was clear of any mortification and a healthy amount of pus had been cleaned away with a further application of vinegar before a fresh dressing had been applied. It only remained for Macro to take the mandragora and wine as required, and rest, and a full recovery was expected. He was more than happy to take the wine, despite finding the flavour of the root extract disagreeable.

'How do I feel?' The centurion sighed deeply. 'Bored out of my fucking mind. This ain't no place for a soldier to be.'

'It is if the soldier in question is recovering from being shot in the thigh by a hunting arrow.' Cato smiled. 'Besides, the army can get by without you for a month or so.'

'You think?' Macro arched a brow. 'I hear that you've got Crispus running my cohort while I'm in here. How's he doing?'

'Well enough. He's cut from the same cloth as you, but lacks your warm and charming manner.'

'Very funny.' Macro scowled before Cato continued.

'Seriously. He's doing a good job. You don't need to worry about your lads. They're not going to the dogs. Crispus is drilling them hard for the coming campaign. That's when he's not sorting provisions and making sure we have enough kit, carts and mules for when we get our marching orders.'

'He's welcome to that part of the job. Never did like the paperwork.'

'Comes with the rank, Centurion Macro. Why do you think they pay you so much more than a common legionary?'

'I'd always assumed it was on account of my warm and charming manner.'

They shared a laugh before Macro's mirth faded and his expression became serious. 'So Quintatus is going to take the army off into the mountains?'

'I think so. Mine wasn't the only report of the tribes gathering their warriors. It looks like the Deceanglians and the Ordovices have made some kind of pact against us. No doubt brokered by the Druids. The legate has instructed the Twentieth and the Fourteenth, and six auxiliary cohorts – including the Blood Crows – to make the necessary preparations.' Cato clicked his tongue. 'Shame you won't be able to join in.'

Macro shuffled up on his bedroll and sat erect. 'Sod that. I'm coming. Just stick me in one of the supply carts until the leg's better. I can still fight if I need to.'

Cato shook his head. 'I've already written the orders. You'll stay here. The legate's sending for some reserve units to take over the frontier forts while he leads the rest against the enemy. Two centuries from the Eighth Illyrian will be sent here when we march out. You're to take command in my absence, as soon as you are back on your feet. Try not to make their lives too difficult, eh?'

Macro sniffed. 'The Eighth Illyrian? From what I've heard, they're a useless shower. Beardless boys, invalids and veterans scraped from other units for a job-lot discharge ceremony as soon as the emperor has signed off. The gods help me . . .'

Cato patted his friend on the shoulder. 'Then you're just the man they need to lick them into shape.'

'I know how to train men well enough. But I can't perform bloody miracles.'

'No one's asking you to perform a miracle, just to do your duty. Besides, it was you who complained of being bored. Soon you'll have plenty to keep you occupied.'

They were interrupted by the sound of footsteps in the corridor outside, and a moment later a breathless auxiliary entered the dormitory and saluted.

'Duty optio sends his compliments, sir. There's a column of riders approaching the fort.'

Cato stood up. 'From which direction?'

'The east, sir. On the track from Viroconium.'

Cato thought briefly. It was likely that they were Roman, coming from the fortress where the bulk of the army was in camp. All the same, it might be a ruse. The enemy had been known to use captured armour. 'Ours or theirs?'

'I couldn't tell, sir. We saw them in the distance, before they disappeared into the mist on the floor of the valley.'

'I see.' Cato scratched his chin. 'And how many of them?'

'I'd say . . . at least thirty, sir.'

'No direct threat, then. All right, return to your post and tell the optio I'll join him directly.' Turning to Macro, he shrugged apologetically. 'I'll be back as soon as I can.'

'Don't worry, sir. I'm not going anywhere, more's the pity.'

Cato followed the auxiliary out of the hospital block and hurried to his quarters to tell Thraxis to bring his armour, weapons and cloak to the eastern gatehouse. Then he strode across the fort, resisting the temptation to break into a trot. He subscribed to the school of thought that it did the men good to see their commanding officer appear calm and unperturbed at all times. As he reached the steps at the foot of the gatehouse tower, he was gratified to hear the optio give the order to turn out the rest of the unit. A sharp note from a brass trumpet rang out across the fort. Three quick blasts, then a pause, before the signal was repeated. The officers roused the men in their barrack blocks with harsh shouts and curses. The doors of the section rooms crashed open as the men hurried outside, where they helped each other into their mail vests before taking up the rest of their kit and hurrying to their assigned stations along the ramparts.

Cato climbed the ladder to the platform above the gate and joined the duty optio and another sentry at the wooden hoardings. They exchanged a salute before Cato turned his gaze to the track leading away from the fort and down into the floor of the valley. It was a cool morning, and the sun was obscured by the overcast, which presented a gloomy prospect to the wild landscape. As the sentry had said, there was a thick mist lying across the low ground, like an ashen tide that surrounded the hillock on which the fort had been constructed. An enemy could easily get within bowshot of the outer ditch without being detected, Cato estimated. He turned to the duty optio from Miro's squadron.

'You did well to order the stand-to.'

The soldier briefly showed his pleasure at the praise. 'We've seen no more of them since I sent for you, sir.'

There was a silence on the tower, against the backdrop of the garrison's boots pounding along the duckboards on the ramparts as they took up their positions. Then, when the last of them was in place, Cato leaned forward on the wooden rail and strained his ears. At once he heard the distant thud of hooves, and a moment later the chinking of bridles and other kit.

'We'll know who they are soon enough,' he said, and instantly cursed himself for making the unnecessary comment. So much for the imperturbable commander, he castigated himself.

The ladder creaked as Thraxis clambered up on to the platform, Cato's kit bundled under one arm. The Thracian was breathing hard as he set it down then helped Cato into his scale armour and settled the sword belt across his shoulder. 'And the cape, sir?'

Cato shook his head, his attention focused on the mist.

'There!' The sentry beside the optio pointed down the track from the gate. The prefect and the optio followed the direction indicated and saw the vaguest shimmer of definition of the riders approaching through the mist. Cato picked out the shape of a Roman standard, and a moment later the leading horsemen rose out of the mist on to the open ground in front of the gate. The tension on the watchtower eased, until Cato saw the plumed helmet and gilded breastplate of the rider a short distance behind the standard.

'It's Legate Quintatus.'

'Shall I call for a full honour guard, sir?' asked the optio.

'Too late to put on a show. Just get the gate open.'

The optio crossed to the rear of the tower and bellowed down to the section of auxiliaries waiting behind the heavy timbers. Cato hurried down, emerging from the gatehouse as the grunting soldiers drew the groaning gates inwards.

'Stand to attention!' he snapped, then stood stiffly to one side as the men took up their shields and spears and formed a line to his left. The thunder of hooves filled the air before the riders reined in a short distance outside the fort and walked their mounts through the gate. A squadron of mounted legionaries from the Fourteenth entered first and moved a short distance down the main thoroughfare, forming a line to one side and edging their horses into dressed ranks. Then came the legate's personal standard, followed by Quintatus himself, face flushed from the effort of his ride on this chilly morning. Quintatus was the most senior of the four legion commanders in Britannia and had taken control of the province following the death of Ostorius. Cato regarded him as a competent enough soldier, but like many men from his social class, he harboured political ambitions. Sometimes at the expense of the soldiers such men commanded.

Cato filled his lungs. 'Present!'

The auxiliaries advanced their spears to the acting governor of Britannia. Quintatus swung a leg over his saddle and slid to the ground. While the standard-bearer reached for the reins, the legate approached Cato with an easy smile.

'Prefect Cato, it's good to see you again. How go things? Any more sign of enemy activity?'

'No, sir, though the other side have been sending out parties to harass our patrols and keep them at bay.'

Quintatus nodded. 'More proof that they're up to something.'

'Yes, sir.'

'And all the more reason why we must strike at them soon. Before they take the initiative. It'll be a fine opportunity for your column to win itself some more battle honours, eh?'

Cato did not respond. There were better reasons for going to war than the prospect of garnering such rewards. Quintatus looked round. 'And where's that fire-eater Centurion Macro? I am certain he will be champing at the bit to get stuck in to the enemy.'

'The centurion is recovering from a wound, sir. He's in the infirmary.'

Quintatus frowned. 'Oh? Nothing serious, I hope.'

'Arrow wound, sir. He is making a good recovery. The surgeon says he will be able to return to light duties by the end of next month.'

'Too bad. He's going to miss the fun.'

'Yes, sir.' Cato gestured towards the headquarters block at the heart of the fort. 'Would you care for some refreshment in my quarters?'

'Indeed. Lead the way. But first, I'd like a quick tour of the fort to inspect your men.'

As they strode up the middle of the thoroughfare, the officer in charge of the escort gave the order for his men to dismount and water their horses, while the signal for the garrison to stand down echoed across the fort. Quintatus passed a professional eye over the troops and the orderly manner in which the fort was maintained.

'How are your men?'

'Sir?'

'Are they in good spirits? They've been at the forefront of the action this year and taken some heavy losses. I know most of them are replacements. Can they be relied on?'

Cato collected his thoughts before he made to reply. 'I have confidence in them, sir. All of them. The veterans are as tough as they come and they set the standard. Centurion Macro and I have been working the new men hard and they're shaping up well.'

'Good.' Quintatus nodded to himself. 'That's what I hoped to hear. You might wonder why I am paying you a visit.'

Cato shot him a quick look. 'It had crossed my mind to ask, sir.'

The legate smiled and then his expression grew serious. 'I've had reports similar to yours from most of the frontier outposts. The enemy are gathering their strength sure enough. I am certain they intend to strike at us before the new governor arrives. So it's my intention to strike first. But I'll tell you the rest when we've some privacy.'

Later, in Cato's quarters, Thraxis left a tray with a glass jar and two silver goblets and bowed his head to the legate before leaving the guest alone with his commanding officer. Cato filled the goblets and handed one to Quintatus before taking his own and sitting on the stool beside his desk, while Quintatus occupied the more comfortable chair. As he sipped the wine, he realised that it must have come from the last of his stock of Falernian, and sighed inwardly at the prospect of the remaining jars of cheap Gaulish wine that were left in his personal stores.

Quintatus raised an eyebrow appreciatively at his goblet before he set it down on the table and turned his gaze to Cato.

'We have a chance to deal the enemy a blow they may not recover from, Cato. If they are foolish enough to mass their warriors and save us the effort of hunting them down, then we should seize the opportunity they are presenting us with. I can't tell you how sick and tired I am of enduring their raids and then rushing after them only for the bastards to give us the slip in these mountains. So it is my intention to re-form the army, drive into the heart of their territory and destroy every last one of them that stands before us. Particularly their Druids. If we threaten the Druids then they will call in all their allies to support them, and save us the job of trying to hunt them down piecemeal.'

'That will mean taking the Druids' lair on Mona, sir.'

'Which is why I have given orders for one of the navy's squadrons to meet us on the coast and support our attack on the island. When we're done, the Deceanglians are going to be a mere memory, and the last traces of the Druids and their sacred groves will be erased from the face of the earth.' He paused to let his words sink in. 'Once the Silurians and the Ordovicians hear about the fate of their northern neighbours, they'll sue for peace. And then, at last, we will have made the province safe and secure.'

Cato moved the cup around gently in his hand. 'With respect, sir. That's what Ostorius tried to do. But far from scaring the enemy into negotiating, it only hardened their resolve to fight us.'

'That was while Caratacus was there to lead them. Now that he is gone, there is no one left to unite the tribes.'

'Except the Druids.'

'Yes, true, but I mean no single figurehead to unite behind. No one with the charisma sufficient to get these barbarians to stop going for each other's throats long enough to take us on. If we make an example of the Deceanglians, perhaps the rest of the tribes on this island are going to realise that the choice before them is submission to the will of Rome, or extermination.'

Cato laughed nervously. 'Extermination? You're not serious, sir?'

Quintatus stared back at him, his expression quite cold. 'Deadly serious, Prefect. Right down to the last infant and animal.'

'But why?'

'Sometimes only the harshest lesson will do the job.'

'And what if it teaches an entirely different lesson, sir? After all, didn't Ostorius attempt what you're advocating? He only succeeded in fuelling their resistance to Rome.'

'He lacked the conviction to see it through. Or perhaps he was just too exhausted. If he had been a younger man, it would have been a different story. As it is, it would appear that I am the one that fate has chosen to continue Ostorius's legacy. Whatever the situation, Prefect Cato, I have made my plans. We may lose the chance to bag ourselves a fortune from selling the captives into the slave trade, but that's too bad. As for the wider perspective, if a sharp dose of ruthlessness convinces the other tribes of the futility of resistance, then we can save many lives in the long run.' He scratched his cheek. 'Even those of the natives. Surely you see the logic of it? An intelligent fellow like you?'

Cato thought for a moment. There was enough reason to back such a plan, but it seemed unduly wasteful to his thinking, and besides, it would be better for future relations between Rome and the population of the new province to try and minimise the latter's suffering and win them over. That said, he was a soldier and had given an oath to obey the emperor and all those the emperor chose to place in positions of authority over him.

'Yes, sir. I understand.'

'Good.'

They each took another contemplative sip from their goblet. Cato's thoughts returned to an earlier question he had not had adequately answered. He cleared his throat. 'Sir, you could have summoned all your column commanders to headquarters to tell them this. Why come here in person? If I may ask?'

Quintatus smiled slowly and raised his goblet in a mock toast. 'Your circumspection does you great credit, young Cato. I say that more in praise than condescension. For a professional soldier, you have a keen grasp of the political realities of the world. Tell me, why do you think I have come here?'

Cato felt his heart quicken. The legate knew about his past, and that of Macro, when they had both been recruited to work as the agents of the emperor's imperial secretary, Narcissus. Quintatus knew this because he had served a similar function for the secretary's arch-rival, an imperial servant named Pallas. The two freedmen had been locked in a struggle for supremacy for years, and with Claudius's strength starting to fade, it was only a matter of time before Pallas propelled his preferred successor, Nero, towards the imperial throne. Even here, on the very edge of the empire, the deadly struggle continued. It had been a deliberate move to send Cato and Macro to a dangerous posting the moment they had returned to the province. A move arranged by Quintatus on the instructions of Pallas. Following Cato's resolution of the situation at the outlying fort of Bruccium, and the part he and Macro had played in finally capturing Caratacus, he had hoped that an unspoken truce had arisen between them and Quintatus.

'I have no idea, sir.'

'Come now. I am disappointed. I suspected that you might have feared I was here to do you ill. Let me put your mind at rest on that account. That is not why I am here. Quite the opposite. I came to see you for a number of reasons. The first was purely military. I wanted to gauge with my own eyes the readiness of your men for the coming campaign. And I am pleased by what I have seen. Both your cohorts are in good shape. Unlike some of the garrisons I have visited over the last few days. The second reason is more to do with you individually, Prefect Cato.' Quintatus set his cup down and folded his hands as he gazed into Cato's eyes. 'We have sometimes been at cross-purposes before now.'

'That's putting it mildly, sir.'

The legate frowned. 'We are all someone's man. You were forced to work for Narcissus and I was persuaded to work for Pallas. We have satisfied the requirements of our puppet masters for the present.'

'I am no man's puppet,' Cato said firmly.

'You think not? Really? Now you do disappoint me. But putting that aside for the moment, I need you to understand my real intentions behind the coming campaign. So hear me out.' Quintatus picked up his goblet and settled back in the chair. 'The situation in Rome is going to change very soon. Emperor Claudius is an old man, and old men have a propensity to drop dead rather suddenly. People are inclined to attribute that to natural causes. Which rather advantages those who seek to ameliorate the mortality process. If you follow me?'

All too well, Cato thought. A few years earlier, he and Macro had been involved in an undercover operation to protect Claudius from would-be assassins operating within the imperial palace. Both they and the emperor had barely survived the experience.

'These days, poison or a blade between the ribs has come to be regarded as natural causes at the palace. It's a pity, but there we have it. While plotters are no doubt already conspiring away to arrange the emperor's early departure, that leaves my man and yours jostling to get their candidates on to the throne once Claudius is dead. At the moment, the odds favour Pallas and Nero, but who knows? Maybe Narcissus can scheme his way into putting Britannicus in his father's place. Certainly Britannicus has the advantage of being the natural son of the emperor. But Nero has his mother, and there are no lengths that bitch Agrippina won't go to in order to get what she wants. Narcissus may yet surprise us all. He's in a corner, and that's when he is most dangerous. You are fortunate that he is on your side.'

Cato stifled a bitter laugh. 'Fortunate? Macro and I had no say in it. We were forced to do his bidding and he put us in the way of danger time and again.'

'Nothing you aren't used to. After all, you are a soldier.'

'Yes, sir. And while I am prepared to sacrifice my life for Rome, I am not prepared to lay down my life for that reptile Narcissus.'

'A fine, laudable principle. But like so many principles, it is utterly divorced from the reality we so frequently find ourselves in, nay? Besides, it is better to have a snake like Narcissus at your side than at your throat. Only a fool would believe otherwise, and you are no fool.' Quintatus raised his cup to Cato, then drained it before setting it down sharply. 'So let me share my thinking with you. There is an opportunity before me. The new governor will not reach Britannia for some months. Time enough for me to strike at our enemy and crush them once and for all. It is my intention to destroy the Deceanglians, and to take the island of Mona and wipe the Druids out. With them off the scene, there will be no one left to co-ordinate resistance between the tribes. I will force these barbarians to submit. The victory will be mine. And since I am due to be recalled to Rome next year, it would be very useful to have a successful campaign behind me. Assuming that Nero succeeds his adoptive father, and Pallas remains the power behind the throne, then my star looks set to rise. Now, like all powerful men, I need followers I can depend on. Capable men, with a good record and underhand skills and experience to match. You are such a man. And so is your friend Macro. I would be honoured to count you amongst my supporters.'

'I'm sure you would.'

Quintatus froze for an instant and then continued in a quiet, menacing tone. 'Prefect, before you adopt that sanctimonious posture, let me remind you of the realities. It is almost certain that Narcissus will be one of the first to be proscribed when Nero comes to power. I know Pallas well, and he will ensure that Narcissus's followers are eliminated along with their master.'

'I am not his follower.'

'You may believe that, but it makes no difference to the way Pallas regards you. To him, you and Macro are merely details. He will not pause to consider the rights and wrongs of it. Your names will go down on his list, and in due course a warrant will be sent to Britannia authorising your arrest and execution. And that will be the end of it. Although not quite. You have a wife, I believe. If you are condemned as a traitor, then your estate will be confiscated. Your wife will be left with nothing. Think on that.'

He waited a moment to let his words sink in before continuing more reasonably. 'However, if you were my men, then I would vouch for you. I would ensure that Pallas knows that you no longer serve Narcissus and that you can be relied on to be loyal to me, and by extension Pallas and Nero. Of course, it would strengthen your cause immeasurably if you went one step further . . .'

Cato understood the implication. 'And feigned loyalty to Narcissus while helping you and Pallas destroy him?'

'Why not? Like you said, the man is a reptile. He has put your life at risk. You owe him nothing.'

'And I owe nothing to Pallas or you either, sir.'

The legate laughed. 'You say that now. In a year, two years, things will be very different, and then you will be

43

grateful for my protection. Not just for you and Macro, but for your family too.'

Cato felt his guts twist with anxiety. 'Are you threatening my family?'

'On the contrary, I am offering to protect them. Sadly, those we love and make sacrifices for tend to become our Achilles' heel. If you want to control a man, then you must first control his fears. I take no pleasure in saying that. As I said, I am just pointing out the truth of the situation. Only you can choose what to do about it.'

'There is no choice,' Cato said quietly, fighting to control his temper. 'Is there?'

Quintatus shook his head gently. 'I am afraid not. If it comes as any comfort to you, my own family are under the scrutiny of Pallas. He came to me once, as I do to you, and made the same offer, and the same threat, and I have been condemned to do his bidding ever since. That was ten years ago. While Pallas was still slithering his way up the greasy pole.'

'But you chose not to carry out his orders to ensure we were eliminated.'

'You think so? I sent you to what I thought would be certain death at Bruccium. Yet you won through, against the odds. For that I admire you. It would be unfortunate to have you eliminated unnecessarily . . . Come now, Cato. You understand the situation. Surely you can see there is no alternative. No painless one, at least.'

'I can see that,' Cato admitted.

'I understand your despondency. But you will get over it. The lack of any real choice will see to that. All that remains is to adapt and survive. After all, isn't that what life teaches us?'

He waited for a reply, but Cato was too angry and bitter to trust himself with any remark. He wanted to refute the argument being put to him. He wanted desperately to stand on principle and defy the will of powerful men who decided the fates of others. He earnestly longed for a world in which honour, honesty and achievement counted for more than guile, avarice and ambition. Yet here was the proof that his longing was mere wishful thinking. Despite all he had accomplished, every battle he had fought in and won, every promotion he had earned, he lived on the whim of men like Narcissus and Pallas. They were not even proper Romans. Merely freedmen who had learned how to play their former master like a cheap flute. Worse still was Cato's awareness of his vulnerability to their machinations thanks to his marriage to Julia. And their child too, in due course, would become an unwitting hostage in the deadly game of political intrigue that those inside the imperial palace played as instinctively as other men drew breath.

He sighed.

'It is clear that you see reason,' Quintatus observed sympathetically. 'That is good. No man should choose to die for lack of reason. I will leave you now. You will need time to consider all that I have said, and accept it. We'll talk again when you are ready. I thank you for the wine.'

He stood up, and Cato followed suit. The informality of a moment earlier vanished and the legate was once again his commanding officer, brusque and demanding.

'Your replacements will reach the fort the day after next. When they arrive, you will march your column out immediately and make for Mediolanum. There you will join the Fourteenth Legion, a vexillation from the Twentieth and the other auxiliary cohorts assigned to the campaign. As I will be in overall command Valens will assume control of the Fourteenth while Camp Prefect Silanus takes charge of the Twentieth. It is my intention to commence the operation in five days' time. We will enter the mountains, burn to the ground every enemy settlement we find, locate and destroy their forces and eliminate every living thing we encounter. Thereafter we shall do the same on Mona. By the time the new governor takes over the province, there will be order. There will be no one left to challenge Rome's supremacy. More to the point, there will be no conquest for Ostorius's replacement to claim credit for. That will belong to me, and those who follow me. Is that understood, Prefect Cato?'

'Yes, sir.'

'Then we have nothing more to say. I shall see you at Mediolanum.'

CHAPTER FOUR

'Hmm, they don't look up to much,' Macro grumbled as he surveyed the small column of men entering the fort. 'As miserable a bunch of miscreants as I have ever seen. Bloody Eighth Illyrian aren't even fit to scrub out the latrines. The gods know what use they'll be if the enemy have a go at us while you're gone.'

He was sitting on a bench outside the headquarters block, his crutch propped against the wall beside him. It was late in the afternoon, and though the sky had been clear all day, the temperature was dropping and both men wore their thick military cloaks. Cato stood in the street that ran across the fort. He shaded his eyes as he made his own first assessment of the garrison's replacements. The Illyrians were an unprepossessing bunch to be sure. They made no pretence of marching in step, and their armour was dull through lack of polish. Some of the men wore their helmets, but most had them hanging from their sides, or from their marching yokes. At the front of the column was a short, broad officer with flabby cheeks veined and tinged with red. Clearly a man who enjoyed being in his cups, thought Cato.

The prefect was in a foul mood. The replacements had been expected around midday, releasing the garrison to join the rest of the army gathering at Mediolanum, two days' march away. The Thracians and the legionaries under his command had already carefully prepared their marching yokes, and the garrison's small baggage train of carts stood in line behind the rampart ready for the mules to be hitched up. In fact, the animals had been placed in harness shortly before noon, ready for a swift departure. When there was no sign of the Illyrians at the appointed hour, nor the two hours that followed, Cato had reluctantly given orders for the mules to be returned to their stables, as well as the horses of his mounted contingent. The men of the garrison had been dismissed too, now that there was no prospect of setting out until the following morning.

Cato paced slowly into the middle of the street to await the auxiliary centurion as the rest of the new arrivals fell out of line and spilled into the open ground between the ramparts and the barracks blocks.

The centurion ambled forward and bowed his head in salute, then gave a gap-toothed grin. 'Fuck me,' he wheezed. 'That was some march, sir. Never thought we'd make it before nightfall.'

'Stand up straight!' Cato snapped. 'And make your report properly, man.'

The centurion's jaw sagged a little before he recovered his wits, grounding his vine cane and drawing back his shoulders. This had the unfortunate effect of pushing out his large stomach, so that Cato was reminded of an egg. The comparison became even more apt as the man's cheeks seemed to fold into his neck, and the whole angled down to merge seamlessly with his rounded shoulders. Yes, Cato thought. An egg. A very fat egg.

The officer drew a deep breath and introduced himself. 'Marcus Fortunus, Fifth Century, Eighth Illyrian Cohort, sir! On detachment. Here are my orders, sir.' He felt inside his side bag and took out a slate. Cato flipped it open and swiftly scanned the comments etched into the wax. The orders followed the standard format, authorising Fortunus to take two centuries to the appointed installation to serve as a temporary garrison until notified of further instructions. They bore the name of the legate's chief of staff and the impression of the legate's ring seal. He snapped the slate shut and returned it to the officer.

'Quintus Licinius Cato, prefect of the Second Thracian Cavalry, and commander of this fort. You're late. We were expecting you around noon.'

'The road wasn't easy, sir, and the camp followers slowed us down.'

'Camp followers?' Cato looked past the man towards the gate. Sure enough, the last of the soldiers had entered, and now came an extended throng of women and children, together with a handful of mule-drawn carts.

'Jupiter give me strength!' Macro spat. 'What the hell is all that?'

Fortunus glanced over his shoulder, not without difficulty. 'Some of the men have families in the vicus at Viroconium. A few of the demobbed veterans are in business with some of my men. No more than a hundred or so in all. The fort has been constructed to accommodate a thousand men, so there'll be plenty of room. Besides, it's good for morale.' He looked curiously at Macro, uncertain if he should defer to him. The latter was in a plain tunic and cloak and had no insignia to indicate his rank.

Macro quickly put an end to his dilemma. 'Centurion Lucius Cornelius Macro, Fourth Cohort, Fourteenth Legion. I'll be in command while the prefect is absent.'

'In command? I was led to believe that I would be . . . sir.'

'Well you're not,' said Cato. 'Centurion Macro is recovering from a wound and is unable to lead his cohort in the coming campaign. He will be remaining here.'

'More's the bloody pity,' Macro added through clenched teeth.

Fortunus shook his head. 'I'm sorry, sir. But my orders are quite specific. I've been appointed to command the fort in your absence. The legate's chief of staff said so.' He patted his bag. 'You saw for yourself.'

Cato gestured towards the dishevelled men of the Illyrian cohort and the last of the civilians trudging in through the gate. 'I am not leaving a forward outpost in the hands of the man who commands that rabble. I have made my decision. If you have any problem with it, take the matter up with the legate himself.'

'But . . . but he's about to set off into the mountains,' Fortunus protested. 'It could be months before he responds.'

'That's not my problem,' Cato snapped. 'Until then, my decision holds. And you will call both me and Centurion Macro "sir" when you address us. Clear?'

'Yes, sir.'

'That's better.' Cato glanced at the new arrivals crowding the gate. 'For now, you can get your men and the camp followers into the stables at the end of the fort.'

'Stables?' Fortunus grimaced. 'Sir, I—'

'My men need the barracks tonight, thanks to your tardiness. And my horses will have the better of the stables. You will occupy what space is left and be thankful I don't order you to camp outside the fort until I lead my men out tomorrow. Now get them out of my sight.' Cato dismissed him.

Fortunus saluted and turned away to join his men as Cato and Macro looked on with grim expressions.

'Now that,' Macro said quietly, 'is the most miserable fucking example of a soldier it has ever been my misfortune to meet.'

Cato cocked an eyebrow and glanced at his friend. 'Really? What about that skinny recruit that joined the Second Legion back in Germania a while back? "A pointless streak of piss" was the phrase, as I recall.'

Macro shrugged. 'Oh, that he was. Completely. But he turned out well enough in the end. The army made a decent soldier of him.'

'I thank you for your faint praise.'

'You don't need me to praise you. Your record since then has done the job well enough.'

Cato experienced a ripple of unease. He never felt comfortable with his achievements, as if they were more the result of blind fortune than his own efforts and therefore he was as undeserving of praise as any man who had simply benefited from good luck. He cleared his throat.

'Now you'll have the chance to lick Fortunus and his men into shape while I am gone. Should keep you busy.'

'That lot?' Macro laughed bitterly. 'Fat chance. In the case of Fortunus, literally. I'll be lucky if the fort is still standing and habitable by the time the campaign is over.'

Some of the garrison had emerged from their barracks to inspect the new arrivals, and looked on with bemused smiles, or hurled good-natured insults at the Illyrians, who replied in kind before Fortunus ordered them to fall in, bellowing loudly – more to impress the senior officers at the fort than to encourage his men, Cato guessed. The auxiliaries shuffled into place, grounded their spears and waited for the last of their comrades to join them from amongst the camp followers.

Macro turned his head and spat into the open drain running past the headquarters block. 'I could train monkeys to drill better than that lot. They're a fucking disgrace.'

'Well, now they're all yours, my friend.'

'Thanks a lot.'

Cato chuckled. 'Just keep 'em out of trouble. And look after my fort. And make sure you rest that leg as much as you can. I want you back on your feet and ready to stick it to the enemy as soon as possible. How is it coming on, by the way?'

Macro patted his thigh above the dressing. 'The scar is healing nicely. But the muscle hurts like buggery and feels like it's pulled in every direction. Still not good enough to put much weight on, and too stiff to walk without looking like a Subura whore after a double shift.' He sighed. 'I've had worse, but nothing quite as humiliating as being picked off by some native kid. Still, he had balls, I'll say that for him.'

'Him and all the other barbarians in these mountains.' Cato's mood soured as his thoughts returned to the coming campaign. It was a bad time of year to commence a large-scale military operation. The army would begin its march with the autumn well advanced, and the frequent rain in these lands would quickly make the ground hard going for the baggage train, not to mention the miserable prospect for the infantry of plodding through the glutinous mud of the native tracks, which would quickly be churned up by the hooves, wheels and nailed boots of the Roman column. The natives would have the advantage of being familiar with the ground, and would no doubt attempt to continue with the harrying tactics that had served them well in earlier campaigns.

However, if the legate's aim to use brute force and ruthlessness to shatter the Deceanglians and the Druids produced the anticipated results, there was a good chance that the army could return to their winter quarters before the short, cold days of the season settled over Britannia. Already the chill and the damp had begun to make Cato's hand ache where he had endured his own arrow wound earlier that year. He rubbed the knotted white scar tissue behind his knuckles and on his palm and felt the familiar tingle that shot down to his fingertips and up his arm as far as his elbow.

Macro saw him wince. 'Hand still troubling you, sir?'

Cato dropped his arms to his sides. 'Just thinking.'

He glanced round to make certain they would not be overheard. The sentry at the entrance to headquarters was the closest other person, and Cato lowered his voice to be safe. 'Have you had a chance to consider what I told you?'

'About Quintatus? Yes, I've thought about it. Can't say I'm happy to throw my lot in with another schemer after all we've been through with Narcissus.'

'Me neither. But I don't think we've got much choice in the matter. It's true what he says. Narcissus's star is waning.

He won't be able to offer us any protection soon. He won't even be able to protect himself.'

'Well I shan't be grieving for him when the snake has to fall on his sword. Shit, I'd be more than happy to lend him my blade to do the job. Or stick it in him if he lacked the guts to see it through.' Macro smiled grimly at the thought of providing the necessary service to the imperial secretary.

'It's not him I'm worried about,' Cato continued. 'It's us. And those who depend on us.'

'You need not worry about Julia. Her father would look after her. Sempronius is popular enough in the Senate to make Pallas think twice before making an enemy of him.'

'I hope so. But I don't think Pallas is the kind of man who would baulk at the thought of making enemies in the Senate. Not while he has the ear of the emperor's wife, and the chance to put Nero on the throne. Much as I despise the idea of becoming followers of Quintatus, it would be the sensible thing to do. For now, at least. If for any reason Pallas falls from favour, then we can cut our ties to the legate.'

Macro sighed deeply. 'We shouldn't have to live like this, Cato. We're soldiers. Not spies. Not assassins. Certainly not servants of some bloody freedman with ideas above his station in life. I am bloody sick of living under the threat of being knocked on the head, right here at the arse-end of the world, about as far away from Rome as you can get, just because I have pissed off some flunkey back in Rome.'

'Believe me, Macro, I share your feeling. But wishes are cheap, and no help to us right now. I don't see that we have any real choice. Not if we don't want to spend every day guarding our backs. We've got enough to worry about dealing with the enemy. Much of Britannia is a province in name only. There's plenty of work for us here.' He paused and ran a hand over his dark curls. 'Time enough to demonstrate that we're more use to the empire alive than dead.'

'Fuck that!' Macro's expression darkened. 'We don't have anything to prove to anyone, Cato. Not us. We've shed our blood time and again for Rome. And sweated our guts out on long marches through hostile lands. Not to mention wading through all the shit of Narcissus's dark little schemes. We've earned the right to be left alone to get on with our lives. We've earned it a thousand times over.'

'Macro—'

The centurion shook his head. 'I won't do it. I'm not going to trade Narcissus for Pallas. I'm not going to be the lackey of a scheming aristocrat like Quintatus. No! Never again. From now on, my only loyalty is going to be to my comrades, and Rome. If you want to continue playing games with the likes of Quintatus and Pallas then that's up to you. But I'll have no part of it, see?'

Cato recognised that his friend was determined in his desire to escape from the lethal world of politics and plotting. This was not the occasion to try and reason with him. There was not enough time, or privacy, in which to talk it through. Besides, he sympathised with the principles behind Macro's position, dangerous though they might be. Neither of them deserved to be treated as the tool of self-regarding men whose only care was the pursuit of power. But such men paid scant regard to the idea of principle, and were unlikely to be impressed by the stand that Macro was taking. Worse, they might even regard it as an act of defiance. One thing that Cato had learned about the likes of Pallas was that they did not tolerate defiance. To be seen to do so would imply weakness. An example had to be provided to all others who might be tempted to similar acts. Macro was playing with fire. In doing so, he was placing not only himself in grave danger, but Cato as well.

As night fell over the fort, the usual routines of posting the first watch and distributing the watchword continued with little regard for the unaccustomed presence of women and children. The shrill cries of the latter as they played in the lanes between the barracks and the other buildings lent the fort the ambience of a small village rather than an outpost of empire on a hostile and dangerous frontier.

At headquarters, Cato was hosting a meal for the officers of the garrison. He had not intended to, but the delay in marching meant remaining in the fort an additional night, and since all preparations had been made, there was little for the officers to do. Thraxis had slaughtered the last of the suckling pigs owned by the prefect, and roasted it with a honey glaze. Macro rubbed his hands in glee as the glistening side of pork was brought out on a large wooden platter and set down on the long table in the main hall of the headquarters block. The meat was accompanied by bread, cheese and the best of the remaining wine. Aside from Macro, Cato had invited Crispus and the centurions from the legionary cohort, as well as the decurions of his own auxiliary cohort.

Cato was not accustomed to entertaining his subordinates, as other men of his rank were wont to do in such outposts. He did not have an inherited fortune to subsidise any more lavish entertainment than what was on offer, and secretly he was anxious that it would give his officers, Macro excepted, reason to regard him with the quiet disdain usually reserved for 'new men', as those climbing Rome's social hierarchy were referred to. Even though the pay of a prefect was of an order of magnitude greater than that of lesser ranks, Cato had family obligations to consider: his home in the capital, with a wife and child to support in a style befitting the equestrian status he had won through his promotion. Before leaving Rome he had arranged for most of his pay to be made over to Julia. What was left, together with the meagre savings he had from his service to date, barely sufficed. Particularly as his pay had been coming through in dribs and drabs since he had arrived in Britannia, and no amount of cajoling had spurred the imperial officials charged with paying the empire's soldiers to bring it up to date.

Consequently, he made do with the same limited issue of clothing as he had done while a centurion, his armour was functional rather than decorative, and while a prefect from an aristocratic background might afford a small retinue of servants and slaves, Cato was served by Thraxis alone. As he looked on the meagre fare spread along the table, he winced and wished he had not decided to entertain his subordinates after all. More than likely they were already regarding him with something like pity, and his heart smouldered with shame even as he tried to affect the calm, easygoing air of a good host.

Fortunus and the other centurion from the Illyrian cohort were the last to arrive, wary of taking their places after the prefect's cold reception that afternoon. Cato gestured to the end of the table.

'Gentlemen, I present Centurion Fortunus of the Eighth Illyrian Cohort.' He turned his attention to the other officer, a man as thin as his comrade was fat. His bald head was fringed with cropped grey hair and he wore a patch over one eye. 'And you are?'

The man bowed his head briefly. 'Centurion Gaius Appilus, sir. Sixth Century.'

'Then sit down, Appilus.' Cato introduced the other officers around the table in turn. 'Centurion Macro, who will command in my absence. Centurion Crispus, temporarily taking over the Fourth Cohort, Fourteenth Legion. The others are Centurions Festinus, Portillus, Lentulus and Macer, and that's Optio Croton, filling in for Macro. On the other side of the table are the Blood Crows. My mounted squadrons, led by Decurions Miro, Themistocles, Corvinus and Aristophanes. Lastly, those in charge of my foot centuries, Harpex and Plato – no relation.'

Fortunus stared at him blankly for a moment. 'No relation to who, sir?'

Cato shrugged. 'Never mind. Tuck in, gentlemen, tuck in! This all needs consuming, or else it will be left to Macro to work his way through what remains of my private stores. I suspect he will be less inclined to share such spoils even with the few officers that will remain after the garrison marches to war.'

'Damn right!' Macro nodded vigorously, then drained his goblet, picked up the wine jug and refilled to the brim.

Around the table, the other officers reached in with their knives to cut themselves meat and heap it on their platters, together with hunks of bread and cheese. They ate, talked and joked in the high spirits of men on the eve of a new venture. Fortunus and Appilus soon joined in the convivial mood, and the former's heavy jowls quivered as he chewed vigorously on his meat, juice dripping from the corner of his mouth. Thraxis stood to one side, keeping an eye on the wine jug and taking it out to the scullery to top it up whenever it was in danger of being emptied. In the same manner he added to the bread and cheese baskets, and threw fuel on the fire that crackled and hissed in the hearth at the side of the hall, the flames adding their glow to the wan flicker of rush torches in the wall brackets. As the evening drew on, the wine flowed and the faces of the officers grew flushed with the warmth of the fire and the effects of the drink. All except Cato's. He tried to appear as if he was sharing the comradely ambience while at the same time shrewdly weighing up the men he commanded.

Portillus, Lentulus and Croton had served under Macro for less than a month, arriving with the replacements from Rutupiae. The first two were freshly promoted to the centurionate, proven men of at least ten years' standing, while Croton was somewhat younger, and had only been an optio following a promising performance against the Brigantes the previous summer. As for the officers of the Thracian cohort, Miro and Themistocles were the only decurions remaining from the time when Cato had taken command of the unit. Miro was competent but lacked imagination and initiative, and occasionally allowed his nervous disposition to get the better of him. He would hold his place in the battle line well enough, but could not be trusted with any independent command. Themistocles was a different proposition. Tough and experienced, he would carry out any order given to him without thought of the consequences. For that reason he could not be trusted to act alone either.

These were the men Cato was tasked with commanding and fighting alongside, and it was vital that he understood their strengths and weaknesses. Now more than ever, given that he would not have Macro with him. His closest friend was irreplaceable. Tough and fearless, and utterly loyal, Macro had over twenty years' experience of the army, along with a finely judged understanding of the men around him and how to train them and make them ready for battle. When the time for war came, few men were his equal. Cato would sorely miss his friend in the months to come.

In any case, Macro's enlistment would soon be at an end. He had given the best years of his life in the service of Rome and would be entitled to retire with the generous bounty that came with an honourable discharge. Most of the centurions who left the army returned to Italia and bought modest farming estates, or set up in business in provincial towns, joining the small circle of influential men who ran local affairs, largely for their own benefit. However, Cato found it hard to imagine Macro willingly settling into either role. They had occasionally discussed life after the army, in those moments soldiers were prone to in order to distract them from the discomforts of the present. Macro played the game as well as any legionary, conjuring up fantasies of endless drinking and whoring, or, as the mood took him, more bucolic notions of a quiet life in the serene landscape of Campania. But such moments soon passed, and it was clear that there would only ever be one true home for Macro: in the ranks of the Roman legions. He was born to it, and likely as not it would be where his life ended, through sickness, injury or death in battle. Natural causes, as he himself wryly commented from time to time.

Cato smiled fondly at his friend's military stoicism, before his thoughts turned to his own fate. Promotion to his present rank had come rapidly due to the number of campaigns he had fought in since joining the army. Without the benefit of an aristocratic background, there was a limit to any further progress he might achieve. He was denied the most senior posts of legate, consul or governor. If he was extremely fortunate, he might secure one of the two positions still entrusted to men of equestrian rank: commander of the Praetorian Guard, or Prefect of Egypt – neither of which any emperor was prepared to entrust to potential rivals. If Nero succeeded the ailing Claudius, then it would be vital to obtain the patronage of Pallas to stand any chance of winning either post. In the short term, that meant offering his loyalty to Quintatus, distasteful as that might be.

Looking around the table, Cato saw that the officers had finished their meal and shoved their platters to one side as they concentrated on their wine. He beckoned to Thraxis and indicated that he wanted him to clear the table.

Thraxis took up his commander's platter and knife first, leaning in as he muttered, 'Sir, we're down to the last amphora of wine. Do you wish me to open it? There will be next to no chance of picking up any more while we're on the march.'

'Maybe so, but I can live without wine, and besides, I'll need a clear head. Which is more than the others will have come the morning. But let them enjoy the moment . . . Yes, bring them wine.'

Thraxis clicked his tongue. 'As you wish, sir.'

Once the table was cleared and the wine jug was replenished, Macro took a set of carved ivory dice from a small box. 'Now for some sport with my lucky dice, eh, boys? A chance for me to clean you out. You won't need much silver where you're going.'

Crispus leaned his elbows on the table and grinned. 'I'm game.'

'Who else?' asked Macro, glancing round. 'How about you, Fortunus?'

The new arrival nodded and set down a surprisingly heavy-looking purse. 'Why not? Always good to supplement my army pay.'

Macro's eyebrows rose. 'I admire your confidence. What about you, sir?'

Cato hesitated. He did not like playing dice on principle. There was no skill, just random luck, no matter what those who loved the game said. It seemed ludicrous to hazard the small fortunes that were routinely gambled by soldiers. It often caused as much bad feeling as enjoyment, and dice games were the cause of frequent fights, and not a few deaths. However, it was a long-established tradition, and any commander who attempted to curb his men's urge to gamble risked causing considerable bad feeling in the ranks. Sometimes, Cato reasoned, it was better to overlook such vices and take part, in order to better understand those around him.

Stifling a sigh, he sent Thraxis to bring him fifty denarii from the strongbox in his quarters, a sum he could barely afford to lose but one that did not appear unduly parsimonious to his guests. He had no wish to be shown up by Centurion Fortunus.

Once everyone's stake money lay on the table, Macro called for a spare beaker for the dice as his companions placed their bets. Cato examined the circles Macro had chalked on the table and placed a coin on number 7, then, steeling himself, added a second. He watched as the others placed their bets, some going for the higher odds, others spreading their bets. Cato noted each man's strategy, and wondered how much it revealed of their personality; whether they were risk-takers, or whether they played safe. He watched curiously as Fortunus placed a coin on 12 and then three more beside Cato's stake. Macro was the last to bet. He sized up the others' positions and then slid five coins on to the circle marked 6.

'All ready?'

He covered the beaker and shook it hard so the dice rattled noisily inside. Then, with a muttered plea to Fortuna, he tossed the dice on to the table. They bounced and settled and the officers leaned forward to inspect the result.

'Six!' Macro shouted with glee. 'Lucky six for Fortune's centurion!'

The others muttered curses, save Croton, who had placed a bet on an even number and smiled broadly. Macro flicked a coin across to him and drew all the others to one side to form the pot, from which he extracted his winnings. Then he looked up eagerly. 'Tough luck, lads. Time to go again.'

While the others reached for fresh coins, Centurion Fortunus reached out a puffy-fingered hand. He picked up the dice and held them up to the light as he inspected them, rolling them in his palm to test their weight and balance. Macro's smiled faded.

'Something wrong, Fortunus?'

'No. Not at all. Just admiring these. A very fine set, if I may say so, sir. Must have cost you. Where did you get them?'

'Syria.'

'Ah, Syria . . .' Fortunus nodded sagely. 'Of course.'

Macro's eyes narrowed. 'Meaning?'

'Just that that would explain their quality, sir.' Fortunus placed the dice back on the table. He waited until the last of the others had placed their bets, then slid a coin on to 6 and sat back on his stool. Cato sensed his suspicion, but thought it misplaced. Macro was not the kind of player who cheated. He preferred the honest excitement of the game over the prospect of winning under a cloud of dishonest guilt.

Cato played for the odds again and bet on 7. Once again the dice rattled and rapped sharply on the table before yielding their result.

'Two! Castor and Pollux!' Macro exclaimed. 'Fuck my luck . . .'

As the game continued, punctuated by expectant silence, uproar and excited exchanges, each man took his turn at throwing the dice for a few rounds. Cato saw that some muttered prayers, some closed their eyes as their lips moved soundlessly, while others were more matter-of-fact and gave a quick shake before casting. None of which seemed to divert the inexorable good fortune of Macro and Fortunus, whose piles of coins grew steadily while the others shrank. At the sound of the trumpet announcing the change of the watch, Cato decided it was time to put an end to proceedings.

'Last round, gentlemen,' he announced. 'We have a long day ahead of us.'

The others nodded blearily and prepared for the final cast of the dice. Looking down, Cato saw that he had eight coins left. With as much good humour as he could muster, he slid them on to the circle marked with a 10. 'Nothing ventured, nothing gained.'

The final bets were placed and then Macro passed him the dice in the beaker. 'The honour is yours, sir.'

Cato took the beaker with a grateful nod and held it up. 'Best of luck to you all.'

He shook it hard, the dice beating a shrill tempo close to his ear. Then, with a flick of his wrist, he threw them on to the table, where they bounced high, then again, and rattled to a stop. There was the briefest of pauses before Fortunus snorted with disgust.

'Ten! Of all the luck . . .' He puffed his cheeks and shook his head. 'Never mind. I've done all right. Well done, sir. A skilful throw.'

Cato was disappointed by the glib flattery. 'There is no skill in this game. You can only play the odds.'

Macro's brow creased. 'Then how do you explain why some men win more than others, sir?'

'That's life, Macro,' Cato replied patiently. 'Just life.'

'If you say so.' Macro counted out some coins and slid the small heap over to Cato. 'I'd say you have come out about even, sir.'

'Like I said. Nothing gained.' He swept the coins into the purse that Thraxis had brought from his chest, and the others likewise gathered up what they had left. 'That concludes the occasion. I thank you all for your company. We've made a fine night of it.'

The officers mumbled their thanks, more or less co-herently, as stools scraped on the flagstone floor and they rose to their feet, making for the door leading out to the small courtyard of the headquarters block. Macro remained seated, gently rubbing the skin around his dressing.

'Giving you some grief?'

Macro sniffed. 'Just itches from time to time, like a bastard.'

'It won't be for much longer.'

Macro looked up with a sober expression. 'Long enough . . . Long enough to have to sit on my arse and watch you lead my cohort out to battle.'

'Not all of the cohort. I've decided to leave you two sections of legionaries, to provide some backbone to the garrison. And ten of the mounted contingent from the Blood Crows. You'll need them for patrolling and dispatches.'

'Fair enough. Thanks . . . Take care, my friend.'

'I'll be fine. It's time I learned how to stand on my own two feet,' Cato replied lightly.

'You've been doing that for many years. You don't need me. The fact is that I'm the one who needs to be in the thick of the action. I can't fucking stand to miss out.'

'There will be other campaigns, Macro.'

'I know.' The veteran was silent for a moment. 'There's something I want you to do for me, sir.'

'Name it.'

Macro replaced his dice in their box and held it out to Cato. 'Take this with you.'

Cato looked puzzled. 'Why? What for?'

'For good luck. I was told they would bring me luck when I bought them. You saw how well I did at the table tonight. They've worked for me. Now they'll do the same for you.'

'Macro, I—'

'Just take them, please. I'd be happier knowing you had them with you.'

Cato hesitated, until he saw the concerned look on Macro's face. He smiled and nodded. 'Thank you. I'll keep them close. You can have them back when I return.'

'Good.' Macro took up his crutch and struggled to his feet. 'I'll see you in the morning, sir. Good night.'

'Good night, Centurion Macro.'

Macro limped off and closed the door behind him, leaving Cato alone in the dying light of the fire and the two rush torches still burning. He stared down at the box in his hand, then closed his fist over it and walked slowly towards his private quarters. Despite his misgivings about the workings of fate, he might just need all the luck he could get in the days to come.

CHAPTER FIVE

'I expect to see that you have worked your usual magic on Fortunus and his mob by the time I return,' said Cato as he took one last look around the fort.

The garrison was formed up along the main thoroughfare that stretched across the fort, passing the arched entrance of the headquarters block. The riders of the mounted squadrons stood by their horses at the head of the column. Each mount was laden with hay netting and bags of oats. Behind them came the colour party with the collected standards of the two units under Cato's command, followed by the legionaries, standing beside their laden marching yokes. At the rear was the small baggage train: fourteen carts carrying spare kit and marching rations, as well as four of the fort's complement of bolt-throwers. The foot soldiers of the Thracian cohort, organised into two centuries, were assigned to protect the vehicles as well as forming the rearguard. It was the least-regarded duty for those on the march, since they had to endure the choking dust kicked up by those ahead of them during the summer, and negotiate the churned mud of winter.

It was the first hour of the day and the sun had not yet

risen above the eastern rampart, though its light bathed the men of the replacement garrison in its rosy glow as they paced along the ramparts and stood watch on the platforms above the four gatehouses. In the shadow of the rampart the air seemed tinged with blue and felt chilly, so that the men were thankful for their thick military cloaks.

Macro leaned his crutch against the wall beside the entrance to headquarters and rubbed his hands together vigorously. 'Don't you worry. You'll hardly recognise the Illyrians. Especially that tub of lard Fortunus. I see him as my personal challenge. He will shed the fat and get fit, or I'll see that he dies in the process.'

'No need to go that far,' Cato responded. 'Just make sure he can actually get into his armour. That will do.'

They shared a quick laugh and then Cato held out his hand. They clasped forearms.

'Take care, sir.'

Cato detected the anxious tone behind his friend's words. 'I'll be fine.'

Macro spoke earnestly. 'Just watch yourself around that bastard Quintatus. Whatever he says, he's still one of them devious bastards out for whatever he can get.'

'I know. I'll be careful.'

'All right . . .' Macro smiled self-consciously and quickly changed the subject. 'And while you're at it, take good care of my lads.'

Cato nodded. 'Don't worry. I'll keep an eye on Crispus and make sure your cohort doesn't come to grief.'

They both glanced towards the head of the legionary column and saw the tall figure of the centurion tapping his vine cane impatiently against his palm.

'They're in good hands,' said Macro. 'Crispus is a fine soldier. Reminds me of myself in younger days.'

'Really? Then he's grown some.'

Macro growled deep in his throat and gently pushed Cato's arm away. 'And fuck you too, sir,' he muttered lightly. 'Get going, and let me get on with sorting these Illyrian bastards out.'

Cato shot him a final smile and turned away to stride towards the head of the column, where Thraxis was holding his horse. As Centurion Crispus became aware of his approach, he quickly grounded his cane and drew a deep breath.

'Column! Form line of march!'

The infantry instantly broke off their muted conversations and took up their yokes, shuffling the sturdy shafts into as comfortable a position as possible on their shoulders. The four squadrons of Thracians took the reins of their mounts and steadied them as Miro glanced round to make sure they were ready for the next order.

'Second Thracian Cavalry! Prepare to mount . . . Mount!'

The riders grasped their saddle horns to lift themselves up and used the momentum to help them swing their legs over the backs of their horses before settling into the saddle and taking up the reins. With the tightly packed hay in nets fastened over the rumps of the horses, together with the bags of oats, it was no easy feat, and it took a moment before the lines were dressed and the cavalry stood ready. Cato was glad that his horse was simply saddled and free of such encumbrances. Thraxis handed him the reins and bent over to make a step with his hands. Once Cato's boot was in place, the sturdy Thracian heaved the prefect up and

Cato landed in his saddle with a modicum of grace. He adjusted his grip on the reins and sat as erect as he could as he looked back down the column and saw that every man was ready and waiting.

He drew a deep breath. 'Open the gates!'

Fortunus snapped an order to the section of Illyrians standing by the gatehouse, and they rushed forward to remove the locking bar and draw the timber gates inwards, releasing a flood of dazzling sunlight that streamed into the fort. Cato was forced to squint as he raised his arm and swept it forward. 'Column! Advance!'

He urged his horse into a walk and felt the familiar swaying motion as his mount clopped forward. Behind him rode Thraxis, carrying the prefect's personal standard, then two of the headquarters clerks, followed by Decurion Miro and the first of the squadrons of Thracian cavalry, beneath their black banner with its depiction of a red crow, hanging limply from the crosspiece in the still morning air. As soon as they had cleared the ditch surrounding the fort, Miro ordered his squadron forward and they cantered past on either side of Cato and took up their place quarter of a mile ahead of the rest of the column, watching for any sign of the enemy.

As the last of the Thracian auxiliaries tramped out of the fort, Macro eased himself up on to his feet and took up his crutch. He picked his way towards the gatehouse as Fortunus shouted the order for the gates to be closed and barred, pausing at the foot of the wooden stairs rising up the rampart to the palisade.

'You!' He addressed the nearest of the Illyrians. 'Help me up here.'

With the soldier supporting him on one side while using the crutch on the other, Macro hopped awkwardly from step to step until he reached the palisade, then clutched the roughly hewn logs as he stared down at the column snaking slowly along the valley. The sun had crested the rim of the hills to the east and the shadows rapidly began to shrink away as the day began. Macro stood and watched for a while longer, catching the twinkle of light on polished metal and squinting slightly as he strained to pick out the red cloak of the prefect close to the head of the column. He was worried for his friend. Over the years, they had become so accustomed to guarding each other's backs, from enemies on all sides, that it felt unnatural to be watching helplessly as Cato marched to war.

No, not helplessly, Macro corrected himself. He had a job to do. Cato had left him in command of the fort and the replacement garrison. That would keep him occupied and give him something useful to do. He smiled to himself at the prospect of what he had in store for Fortunus and his Illyrians. It would be like old times.

The head of the column crested a small hill at the mouth of the valley and began to disappear from view, like a shimmering insect. Given the season, and the recent rain, there was none of the usual dust that was kicked up in the wake of soldiers, horses and carts on the move, and Macro was clearly able to see the last of the men reach the top of the hill and disappear from sight. Then the valley was still, and the quiet landscape stretched out around the fort nestling between the two forested ridges that led into the mountainous land of the Ordovices. Autumn was well advanced, and the branches of many of the trees were almost bare, while the ground beneath lay covered in brown and yellow leaves. Macro sniffed the air. He liked the dank, musty odour at this time of year, and the way the sunlight seemed to bring out the richness of the colours of nature.

He stood erect quite suddenly and frowned with irritation. 'What the fuck am I thinking?' he muttered. 'Poncing around like a bloody poet.'

Taking up his crutch, he turned to look over the fort, and soon spied Fortunus sitting with his optio on stools outside the barrack block his century had been assigned. Macro filled his lungs and bellowed down from the rampart, loudly enough to be heard easily throughout the fort.

'Centurion Fortunus! I want you and your officers at headquarters as soon as the morning watch is changed. Hear me?'

Fortunus struggled to his feet and saluted. Macro nodded curtly and beckoned to the auxiliary to help him back down the steps, his heart warmed by the thought that he would no longer be subject to the fussy care of the surgeon, who had marched off with Cato.

It felt unusual to be sitting the other side of the desk. Fortunus, Appilus and their optios stood facing Macro, together with the senior legionary of the section Cato had left behind. Lucius Diodorus had served over ten years in the Fourteenth, nearly all of that time in Britannia. He had mousy hair, left rather too long and unkempt for Macro's taste, and a puckered white scar on his cheek. Tall and well built, and with a good record, he seemed a sensible choice for the role of drill instructor. The auxiliary optios, by contrast, looked as useless as the two centurions. Saphros was a small, wiry man in his late thirties with a cunning expression, while Mago was heavily built and dull-looking. The kind of man who might have had a brief career in the arena, where his brute strength would have seen him through until he met an opponent with even a grain of guile.

Macro sighed softly. Such was the stuff of which his new command was made. He leaned forward and rested his forearms on the table as he addressed Fortunus. 'Have the men moved into their barracks?'

'Yes, sir. Just about.'

Cato had assigned them to the blocks closest to the stables, where the camp followers had been lodged, but Macro had a different view of arrangements.

'Then herd 'em up to the barracks opposite headquarters. I want them moved there as soon as you are dismissed.'

Fortunus looked puzzled. 'Move them? Again?'

'That's what I said. I want them where I can see 'em. And I don't want them anywhere near that rabble in the stables until they are off duty. Even then, the men will sleep in their barracks. Is that understood?'

'Yes, sir. But is it necessary?'

'Are you questioning my orders, Centurion Fortunus?'

'Of course not, sir.'

'Then you will do as I say. This is an army outpost, not a bloody veterans' colony. I want your men to act like proper soldiers, even if they fall rather short of *being* proper soldiers. That's where Diodorus comes in. I have chosen him to help me knock them into shape.'

Fortunus bridled. 'The Eighth Illyrian are a good unit, sir. We're not raw recruits. You saw the battle honours on our standards.'

'I did. So tell me, how recently were those awarded?'

Fortunus shifted his weight on to the other foot. 'Before my time, sir.'

'I see. Then when were you and your unit last in a fight?'

'Back in Pannonia, sir. A few years before we were ordered to Britannia.'

Macro's brow creased briefly in concentration. 'I don't recall hearing about any war in Pannonia.'

'It was not a war as such. The cohort was ordered to quash an uprising, sir.'

'Oh? Tell me more.'

'There were some villages who refused to pay their taxes. We were sent in to restore order.'

'So you knocked a few heads together, razed the odd building and so on, right?'

Fortunus flushed. 'You could put it that way, sir. But as I recall, the locals were very hostile indeed.'

'I dare say they were. Let me guess. They shouted insults at you and followed up with lobbing a few stones, or turds, and you chased them off.'

Fortunus opened his mouth to protest, then paused, thought a moment and pressed his lips together in a thin line.

Macro nodded. 'Thought so. This is no place for a glorified town watch. We're right on the frontier, facing an enemy who will fight to the last breath. And they're wily buggers too. Somewhat more of a challenge than a bunch of surly taxpayers. The gods only know why some idiot at the imperial palace selected your unit to be sent to Britannia. Though it does explain why you've been kept back with the reserves. But you're here now, and you have to be fit and ready to fight properly. I'll see to that.

75

'First thing you need to know is that I am far from happy that you've arrived with camp followers in tow. In different circumstances I wouldn't have let them inside the fort. But being where we are, that would be tantamount to leaving them to the mercy of the enemy. So I am stuck with them. But that doesn't mean they won't be subject to the same discipline as the garrison. I want you to appoint a leader of the civilians. Someone reliable and preferably trustworthy. He will be responsible for seeing that they abide by the fort's rules and regulations. Do you know any likely candidates?'

Fortunus and Appilus exchanged a look before the latter spoke.

'What about Venistus? Most people look up to him.'

Fortunus nodded. 'He's the best man.'

'Venistus it is, then,' Macro announced. 'You can break the good news to him and tell him to come and see me at once, so I can explain his duties.'

'Yes, sir.'

'Then I want a barrier set up across the fort to keep the civilians in their area. No one is to move to or from the civilian blocks unless they are on duty or have authorisation.'

'Sir, some of the men have families . . .'

'Not according to military regulations they don't. The army does not allow marriage, or families, for rankers. Your men might need reminding of that.'

'That may be true, sir, but it's a long-established custom.'

'Not in my fort it isn't,' Macro responded tersely. 'And if they don't like it, then they're free to make their own way back to Viroconium.' He sat up. 'That's all for now, gentlemen. You're dismissed. Diodorus, stay behind.'

Fortunus and the others saluted, then left the office.

When the door closed behind them, Macro turned his attention to Diodorus.

'What do you think?'

The legionary's expression remained neutral. 'Sir?'

'You've seen the officers and the men of the Illyrian cohort. Thoughts?'

'If I may speak freely, sir?'

'Please do.'

'They're a useless shower. They don't march in step, they don't look after their kit and they don't look after themselves. Some of them are old enough to be my grandad, and others are young enough to be my son. Gods forbid, but if it comes to a fight, the only danger they pose is that the enemy may die laughing at the fucking spectacle presented by Centurion Fortunus and his men. Other than that, they're a fine body of men who do the emperor proud, sir.'

Macro smiled. 'My thoughts, more or less. They're shockers right enough. But now they're your problem, Optio Diodorus.' He saw the brief flicker of confusion in the legionary's eyes before the sestertius dropped. 'That's right, I'm giving you a field promotion. You know the drills. I want you to begin working the Illyrians from tomorrow. Get 'em fit first. Then move on to weapons training. I want Fortunus and his layabouts ready for action as soon as possible.'

'You think we're likely to be attacked, sir?'

'More likely than ever, Diodorus. You can count on it that the enemy will know about the change in the garrison here. They'll be aware that the fort's strength has been reduced. Once the legate opens his campaign, they'll also know that there will be no relief column marching to our

77

aid from Viroconium in the event of an attack. It'll be as good a time as any to try to take the fort.'

The optio nodded. 'I see, sir.'

'Then you'll also see why we have to toughen the Illyrians up as soon as possible. Much as I like training soldiers, I'm not just doing it to keep myself entertained. If it comes to a fight, we need to know that Fortunus and his men can be relied upon. And that goes for the civilians, too. Any man there who is fit enough to train is to join the auxiliaries. Pray that we don't need them. But if the enemy does try to seize the opportunity, then they'll face as many swords as we can find to man the fort's walls.'

'Yes, sir.'

'I'll do what I can to help, but until I can get rid of this bloody crutch, it's up to you to train those bastards. I think you're the right man for the job, Diodorus, but do you?'

The legionary drew himself up to his full height. 'I won't let you down, sir.'

'Glad to hear it. Dismissed!'

They exchanged a salute, and the newly appointed optio turned on his heel and marched out of the room. As Macro listened to his steps echoing through the main hall of the headquarters block, he smiled. This was what proper soldiering was about. Training men for war, and then, if need be, putting that training into practice. It was what he was born to do.

More footsteps approached the office, and one of the handful of clerks Cato had left behind knocked on the door frame and entered. He was carrying an armful of waxed tablets.

'What's that lot?' Macro demanded.

'Report on the damage to the granary, sir. One of the piles collapsed and the rats got into the grain. Ruined ten modii of barley. Then there's the promotion authority for Diodorus, sir. The rest are the strength returns and records for the Illyrians. I assumed you'd want to see them.'

'Of course. On the desk.'

The clerk unloaded his burden and left Macro staring at the pile of tablets. He let out a frustrated hiss. So much for proper soldiering. If Cato had still been here, he would have been dealing with all the paperwork. 'The lucky bastard,' muttered the centurion sourly. Then, for the first time, he saw the small dice box near the edge of the desk, half hidden beneath a waxed slate, and felt his guts lurch. His friend had forgotten to take the lucky dice with him. Macro could not help thinking it was a bad omen. A bad omen indeed.

CHAPTER SIX

'Prefect Cato, greetings!' Legate Quintatus smiled warmly as he looked up from his evening meal. 'Come, sit with me and I'll send for some more food.'

'Thank you, sir, but no. My men have force-marched to get here. They're tired and I need to see that they're assigned tent lines and find some food for them. I just came to report my arrival.'

'Look after the men first, eh? Good for you. I wish there were more officers like you.' The legate chewed quickly and swallowed. Then his expression became formal. 'So why the forced march and the later than expected arrival?'

'We were delayed because our replacements were late in arriving, sir. I did not think it prudent to leave the fort without a garrison.'

'And why were the Illyrians late, I wonder?'

Cato did not feel comfortable informing on a fellow officer, but he had been asked directly, and Fortunus had done nothing to deserve being defended.

'It might have had something to do with the camp followers that came with them.'

Quintatus raised his eyebrows in surprise. 'Camp

followers? Who would authorise that? No, wait! Let me guess. It would be that corrupt dog, the prefect of the Eighth. No doubt he took a decent backhander from the centurion on behalf of the families and traders who supply his men.' He laughed briefly. 'That Placidus is an ambitious fellow. He has the necessary greed and venality to go far in the world. Perhaps I should keep an eye on him.'

'That might be a wise notion, sir, given that he should be furthering the military aims of Rome rather than lining his own purse.'

Quintatus eyed Cato warily. 'Not all of us share the same highly developed sense of morality that you clearly think you possess in such abundance.'

Cato stiffened. 'I merely wish to serve Rome to the best of my ability, sir. And I expect others to do the same.'

'Do you? Why, I wonder? I find it hard to believe that someone with your undoubted intelligence and experience would insist on such a naive sense of duty from those higher up the scale than the common soldiery. The Glory of Rome is an idea that the aristocrats have sold to the plebs since the earliest days of the Republic, in order to justify their self-aggrandisement.'

Cato experienced an instant of cold fury at the other man's cynicism. 'I imagine you are right in some cases, sir. But there are men of honour even in the Senate.'

'Then they're fools, and you're a fool for believing in them.' All trace of good humour had faded from the legate's face. 'I had hoped for better from you, Cato. After all you have done in the service of Narcissus, I had considered you a man after my own heart.'

'I am not sorry that I have disappointed you, sir.'

There was a brief pause as the men stared at each other and the muffled sounds of the army in camp continued heedlessly. At length Quintatus pushed his plate away, his appetite ruined. 'Be careful what you say, and to whom you say it, Cato.'

'I am not afraid of you, sir. Nor Pallas.'

'You should be. Particularly of Pallas. He has a heart darker than Hades, and he is more cunning than a pit filled with snakes. I am a mere shadow of that man, yet I alone present more than enough of a threat to you.'

'I am aware of that, sir,' Cato said bitterly as he recalled the dangerous posting that Quintatus had assigned to him and Macro when they had arrived in Britannia earlier that year.

'Then do I understand that you have decided not to offer your services to me?'

Cato felt a calmness in his mind. He had rehearsed this moment many times during the march from the fort. He breathed deeply before he framed his reply. 'Sir, I respect your offer, and I respect your view of the realities of politics in Rome.'

'But . . . ?'

'But I do not share your ambitions or values. How could I? I was not born into the senatorial class. I have reached equestrian rank and have no expectation of ever becoming a member of the Senate. That naturally curtails any ambitious instinct I may have. But I am no fool, and I know that it would be better to serve you than be your enemy. If only for the sake of my friends and my family. I just wish you to know that I choose to serve you with a heavy heart.'

'I see.' Legate Quintatus smiled thinly. 'And now that you have had your moment on your high horse and told me your low opinion of me and those like me, I assume you believe that that in some way saves your honour?'

'On the contrary, sir. I think it renders me a hypocrite.'

'Hypocrite?' Quintatus shook his head sadly. 'Do not feel so bad about that, Cato. The term loses its pejorative burden when you have no choice in the matter. Trust me, I know. But if you wish to be hard on yourself, that's your affair. Just as long as you serve me, you can pinch your nose against the stench as much as you like.' Quintatus's lips curled into a faint sneer. 'You and that oaf Macro.'

'Centurion Macro may be many things, sir, but he is no oaf.'

'I don't care what he is, just as long as he is on my side. Else he is an enemy.'

Cato felt his stomach give a nervous lurch. 'Sir, Macro is a fine soldier, but he has no political head. It is better to leave him to get on with soldiering and accept my services alone.'

The legate's eyes narrowed shrewdly. 'You told him about my offer?'

'Yes, sir.'

'And he rejected the chance to serve me?'

'In so many words, yes. And he's right, sir. Macro has not got the taste for such a line of work. It is best to leave him out of it.'

'That's for me to decide. The centurion is a formidable man, in his way. As the saying goes, it is better to have such men inside the fort pissing out rather than outside pissing in.'

'Macro is not important to you, sir. He would serve you best if you just left him to fight the enemy.'

'While I admire your efforts to safeguard your friend, we both realise that Macro has knowledge of certain realities inside the imperial household that Pallas cannot afford to permit any wider circulation. You understand what I am talking about?'

Cato knew all too well what his superior was getting at. Two years earlier, while he and Macro were carrying out an undercover operation in the Praetorian Guard, Macro had caught Pallas and the emperor's wife in a compromising embrace. Given the lack of mercy that had been shown to the emperor's previous wife and her lovers, Pallas would not rest easy until Macro was safely contained, or eliminated. Through no fault of his own, he constituted a threat to the imperial freedman, and that was not something the likes of Pallas would tolerate. Cato felt afraid for his friend.

'Macro is not loose-lipped, sir.'

'Except when he is in his cups, I understand.'

'Even then, he has more than enough sense to keep such knowledge to himself. You and Pallas can afford to leave him alone. I give you my word on that. I'll make sure that he says nothing.'

'Your word? How noble of you.' Quintatus sniffed. 'But since you are not noble, such a pledge carries no weight. I'm sorry, Prefect, but you must persuade Macro to join you in serving me, or I will not be able to protect him. I may even be called upon to silence him.'

Cato felt a cold fury seethe in his veins. 'If you cause any harm to come to Macro, then I swear by all the gods that I will avenge him.'

'No you won't, Cato. Not if you value the life of your wife and your son. Lucius, I believe he has been named, in accordance with your wishes.'

'My son?'

Quintatus wiped his hands clean on a strip of cloth and smiled without any genuine warmth. 'I suppose I should really congratulate you.'

'A son?' Cato was bewildered. 'How could you know?'

'I receive regular reports from Pallas. He tells me anything that might be of use for me to know in my dealings with soldiers and aspiring politicians here in Britannia. So, your good news is my good news, insofar as it gives you a new reason to obey me. All the same, you must be very proud.'

Cato felt off balance. He experienced a surge of joy in his heart, together with love for Julia, and then an acute sense of longing to be with her and his infant son. Then the moment was soured by the cold reality that Quintatus had sluiced over him. His child was a new hostage in the secretive games played by the legate and his ilk. One more means by which Cato could be coerced into doing their bidding. He tried to keep control of his raw emotions as he addressed his superior.

'When did this happen, sir?'

Quintatus thought for a moment. 'Nearly three months ago. Your wife named the boy Lucius, no doubt in honour of your close friend Macro, since that is his praenomen.'

Cato reflected on this and nodded. Julia well knew the closeness of their friendship, and that this would please her husband and his comrade in arms. 'A good name. She chose well . . . What other news of my family do you have, sir?' he asked, trying not to sound too much like he was pleading for information.

Quintatus was enjoying the power of being able to grant or withhold knowledge that was like food to a starving man. He paused just long enough for Cato to swallow and take a half-step forward, ready to demand or beg him to speak.

'The mother and child flourish. Pallas has your house under constant surveillance, and you will be pleased to note that your wife has taken no lovers in your absence. Unlike many wives of the senior officers here in Britannia, my own included. There will be a reckoning when I am eventually recalled to Rome. But your wife's virtue is intact, Prefect Cato. Not that Julia would have found that an easy matter in her pregnant state, and even more so now that she has an infant to care for. Lucky you.'

If it was meant to be a sop of comfort, which Cato doubted in any case, the last words fell flat. He felt confident enough of Julia's affections to trust her in his absence. And yet there was a moment's uncomfortable doubt as his imagination played with the notion. After all, his own origins were humble, and the Sempronius family had a long and moderately distinguished tradition. Such aristocrats were notoriously aloof, and though neither Julia nor her father had made Cato feel socially inferior, there was that lingering doubt in his mind about what they really thought of him; the constant needle in the side of all those who had risen above the station they were born into in Rome.

'You will be equally pleased to note that your wife has not received any visitors on Pallas's watch list. She is wise to steer clear of those whose influence comes with certain dangers attached. There are still some who wish Rome to return to the days of the Republic, while others are plotting to further the interests of their preferred candidate to succeed

Claudius. He won't last much longer, not if the empress has anything to do with it. There's not much about poisoning that she doesn't know. Why, she could do for preparing poisons what Apicius did for cuisine.' Quintatus paused to chuckle at his small joke, before he became aware of Cato's stony expression. 'In short, Julia is giving Pallas no cause for concern, and therefore nothing to add to your burden of worry for her safety, as long as you play your part when asked to.'

He let the point settle in Cato's mind before continuing. 'However, her father is a different matter. Senator Sempronius has been observed in the presence of many of the ringleaders of the faction backing Britannicus, and therefore Narcissus, in the question of the succession. Whether he is actively colluding with them is not yet known. But that will not be enough to protect him when Nero becomes emperor. And he will. That is almost certain. When he does, Pallas will clean house to ensure that Nero's reign starts with as few opponents as possible. So, Sempronius will be likely to feature on the list of those proscribed, unless Pallas has good reason to protect him from such a fate.'

'Good reason being my willingness to serve Pallas?'

'Yes,' Quintatus replied directly. 'As long as there is no evidence that Sempronius is directly involved with the other faction. In that case, even your efforts could not save him.'

'I see.' Cato felt helpless. 'Then you leave me with no option but to serve you and Pallas.'

'That's right. I am glad that you see reason. But then, that's why I made the offer, and I am sure that Pallas will approve of my decision. It seems a shame to waste such potential when it could be harnessed.'

'Harnessed. Like a mule.'

'Don't be so bitter, Cato. This could all work out to your benefit in the long term. There will be plenty of rewards for those who serve the new emperor and his faction. Why shouldn't you take your share of the spoils? That wife of yours could be kept in fine style, and your son raised in comfort and security. And you yourself will profit from the arrangement. There are plenty of military and civil posts that could be yours for the taking.'

'And what is the price of those rewards? What is it that you would have me do exactly?'

Quintatus shrugged. 'Nothing immediately. But you may be called on to perform a service. All that matters is that you are ready to do so, without question, if the moment arises.'

'If?'

'All right, then, *when* the moment arises . . . as it is bound to under the new regime. But for now, it is enough for me, and Pallas in turn, to know that you are on our side. There is no need to openly break with Narcissus. Indeed, if he thinks you are still in his service, then so much the better. He might entrust you with information that could be useful to us.'

'I was never in his service. At least, I never made any agreement such as the one you are trying to force on me.'

'My dear Prefect, you are priceless! As if it makes a difference. You worked for Narcissus, willing or no, and now you serve Pallas. Do you really think you have a choice in the matter? The only choice is between accepting that and awaiting the day when you are knifed in the back, or, if you survive your military career, answering the door of your fine house in Rome to a squad of Praetorian Guards. Then, your choice will simply be to die by your own hand or let them do the job for you, before they take your family.'

Cato gritted his teeth. 'There are times when I wish I had remained a centurion, or even an optio, and served out my days in that rank,' he replied quietly.

'Wishes are ten a sestertius. In any case, you richly deserved your promotion. What you didn't account for was the unpalatable truth that the higher you rise, the more you are enslaved to the will of those above you. A sad but vital truth.'

Cato stood still, feeling powerless to move or speak, as if tightly bound and tongueless. There was no escape from the force of the legate's logic. None at all.

'Look here, Cato, you must accept the situation. For now, all that need concern you is leading your men in the coming campaign. I have no doubt that you will add lustre to your fine reputation, and that can only help your prospects. Concentrate on that, eh?'

Cato swallowed. 'Of course, sir,' he replied calmly. 'That goes without saying. I am, and always will be, a soldier.'

'Good. Then you will appreciate the role I have assigned you. Your column will not be tasked with guarding the army's baggage train, like last time. It's time to put your talents to better use. I have decided to place you at the other end of the line of march. Your two cohorts will form the vanguard of the army. You will be my spearhead when we thrust into the heart of these mountains and fall upon the Deceanglian wretches. You will have the honour of making the first strike for Rome.'

'Why me, sir?'

Quintatus wagged a finger at him. 'Not because I wish to endanger you, if that's what you are thinking. No, it's more to do with the reputation that the Blood Crows have earned for themselves since they began serving in these lands. The sight of their banner is enough to strike fear into the enemy. When they see that red crow fluttering in the breeze, they will know that Rome intends to show them no mercy. I want you to make good on that reputation, Prefect Cato. You and your men are going to create a trail of blood and destruction such that when this campaign is over, there won't be a tribe in the whole island that will dare to defy us ever again.'

CHAPTER SEVEN

'The vanguard?' Decurion Miro sighed. 'Why us? Haven't we been in action enough in recent months?'

Centurion Crispus raised an eyebrow. 'You join the army, you do as you're told and that's the end of it. There is no why, just orders.'

Miro opened his mouth to speak, thought better of it and then puffed his cheeks as his shoulders slumped. Watching him, Cato could well understand the decurion's reaction. The previous year the two cohorts had been sent to an outpost deep in the heart of the mountains, and the unit had been in action almost ever since. The enemy had only eased their attacks in the last months to take in the harvest and store their crops for the coming winter. Now that was over, they intended to resume their war against Rome in earnest. Cato had come to understand that Miro was the kind of man who foresaw only the dangers and difficulties in the tasks he was required to carry out. But once in action, his training and instincts took over and served him well. It was no doubt why he had been promoted to decurion in the first place, but also why he had never been entrusted with any further promotion. He was too open about his anxieties, and that kind of sentiment was easily communicated to those he commanded, affecting their confidence and morale.

There was a brief silence in Cato's tent as his subordinates took in the implications of their assigned position in the army's line of advance. For his part, Cato was relieved not to have to trudge at the rear again in the muddy wake of the units marching ahead of him. Moreover, he would not have to contend with the constant need to cajole the baggage train drivers to keep closed up. Of course, there would be different strains to cope with. Those at the front of the column had to have their wits about them in order to avoid ambush. Moreover, they were tasked with scouting ahead to find the best route forward for the rest of the army, following the advice of the traders who Quintatus had questioned regarding the best route to take through the mountains towards the island of Mona. It was also the vanguard's duty to locate the most suitable ground for the construction of a marching camp at the end of the day. It would be demanding work, but it was more engaging than the drudgery of guarding the baggage train.

Cato cleared his throat. He felt tired. The hour was late and the men had only just finished their main meal of the day and retired to their tents for the night. Miro's mounted squadrons had settled their horses and tethered them to the lines, and the musty odour of their sweat and dung carried into the tent. The army would march at dawn, and it was important that Crispus and Miro understood the roles their men would play in the days ahead.

'Apart from being the eyes and ears of the army, Quintatus wants us to be its cutting edge too,' said Cato. 'We're to go in hard whenever and wherever we encounter the enemy.

He wants to cut a swathe of destruction through the lands of the Deceanglians, right up to the island of Mona.'

'But that's the Druids' lair,' Miro interrupted.

Cato quelled his irritation and nodded. 'I am well aware of that, Decurion. That's one of the main reasons why the legate is launching this campaign. If we can break the spirit of the tribesmen, and crush the Druid cult, then who will there be to unite the tribes against us in future? You know what the Celts are like. They're never happier than when they're knocking their heads together. That's always been their weakness. But give them a figurehead to rally behind and they will fight like furies. Now that Caratacus is out of the picture, that leaves the Druids as the only force able to unify the tribes against us. Without them, we'll be able to contain the enemy and finally have the chance to bring peace and order to the new province. The gods know it's taken long enough already. Once we have that, then there can be discharges for the veterans, and some of us will be able to get home on leave.'

Crispus mused. 'Been nearly ten years since I last saw my family, back in Lutetia. I have a woman there, and two daughters. Doubt any of them will recognise me any more.'

Cato felt dread at such a prospect. To be so long from home. Not to see his son grow from an infant into a boy. To have never been known by Lucius, and to be forgotten by Julia. That was worst of all. The thought made him more determined than ever to fully play his part in ending the conflict in Britannia. Every enemy he cut down would bring him one step closer to home, and the embrace of his wife and child.

'But the Druids,' Miro continued. 'You know what

they're like. They're demons in human form. And they have magic. I've heard how they can summon the powers of their gods to strike us down with storms and monsters. And now Quintatus wants to lead us into their most sacred realm, where they will be at their most dangerous. I'm telling you, it's a mistake.'

'Magic? Fuck that.' Crispus sniffed with contempt. 'Hasn't done them much good as far as I can see. Either their gods are sleeping on the job, or they're a bunch of milk-livered pansies not fit to kiss the feet of Jupiter and Mars.'

Miro was not persuaded. 'I've seen what they're capable of. And I've seen the effect they have on their followers. They turn 'em into frenzied beasts.'

Cato had had enough. 'They're men, just like us. They can be just as easily killed. I've done that myself. I can assure you they're no more dangerous than any other barbarian. So I'll have no more of that talk, Decurion. Understand?'

Miro clicked his tongue, then nodded. 'If you say so, sir. I hope you're right.'

Cato ignored the last remark as he turned his attention to more immediate concerns. 'Since we'll be leading the march, there will be no place for baggage in our column. Our carts will travel with the main baggage train. And I don't want our men laden down with yokes. I've managed to get the supplies tribune to allocate us some extra carts for our kit. So we'll march ready for action. That'll please the men.' He smiled, and Crispus responded in kind. The marching yokes were the bane of every infantryman's life on campaign. Laden down with kit and rations, they weighed half as much as the men carrying them, and as a consequence were roundly cursed.

'Just armour, shield and javelin will do for the legionaries,' Cato continued. 'Same for my foot soldiers. The cavalry will leave their feed bags on the same carts, Miro. Along with their kit. We have to be light on our feet, and not so exhausted that we can't put up a good fight, or mount a vigorous pursuit. And we shall want prisoners, when we can take them. I must provide headquarters with good intelligence about the lie of the land ahead of us, and the men we are up against. Given that the legate wants to push forward as far as Mona, we'll need to know precisely what we're facing at every step.'

Cato saw Miro flinch at the name of the Druids' stronghold and felt uneasy that such a man was following him into battle. He'd far sooner have Macro. Someone he could trust with his life. In fairness, Miro had not let him down yet, but neither had he revealed so much fear of his enemy, and Cato wondered how far the sentiment spread through his column, and indeed, the rest of the army.

'One further thing. We will be joined by an officer from army headquarters. Tribune Livonius. He will be mapping the route day by day.'

Crispus frowned briefly, then nodded. 'Livonius. He's a narrow-striper serving with the Twentieth, isn't he?'

'That's right. Do you know anything about him?'

'If it's the same Livonius, then I've heard he's handy in a fight. He led a woodcutting party into the foothills a month ago and they were attacked by a war party of Silurians. Could have ended badly, but the tribune held the lads together and they cut their way free and made it back to the nearest outpost without losing too many men. Sounds to me like he has a cool head. Though why he's been given a job as a cartographer is a puzzle. Men like that should be commanding troops in the line.'

'An accurate map might well be a very valuable commodity, particularly in the mountains,' Cato countered. 'Still, if he's as reliable as you say, then he's a welcome addition to the column. Just as long as he doesn't hold us back. All right, gentlemen, I'd offer you the chance to lose some money at dice, but we have an early start and a long day ahead of us. So unless there's anything more to say?' He glanced at Crispus and Miro, but neither man responded. 'Then I'll bid you good night.'

They rose from their stools and exchanged a salute before leaving the tent. As the flap slid back into place behind them, Cato let out a long sigh and stretched his shoulders until he heard them crack. Almost all the preparations had been made at the fort, and his men were ready to march at dawn. He had some misgivings about Miro, but it was too late to change anything now. To send him back to join Macro would demonstrate to all that he had lost confidence in the decurion. That was the kind of blow to a man's esteem that was hard to overcome. Better to give him the chance to prove himself and gain the confidence that might eventually allow him to get the better of his innate nervousness and caution. After all, Cato reminded himself, he had had to face his own fears earlier in his career. He recalled all too vividly the cold, sinking dread that clenched in his guts during his first combat against the German warriors on the Rhenus frontier. Even now, he still experienced the same moment of fear before a fight, but knew that he must never reveal it to the men who followed him. Even if that meant taking more risks than some of his rank were inclined to do. He must be seen to be courageous and confident, whatever he felt beneath such a hardened veneer.

The tent flaps opened and Thraxis stepped across the threshold. 'Will you be needing anything else, sir?'

'What?'

'Before I turn in? Is there anything you need?'

Cato thought about the one last task he had been putting off, and nodded. 'Some heated wine, and give my cloak a brush. I want the mud off it when we lead the army out of camp tomorrow.'

Thraxis hissed softly to himself, but loudly enough that Cato heard.

'Problem?'

'It's just a little mud, sir. And it'll be in the same state as it is now when we're no more than a mile from the camp.'

'Look, I'm not asking you to comb every fibre out, tread it in urine and rinse it in spring water before drying it in the sun and doing the whole fuller's special. Just get the bloody mud off and hang it with my armour.'

'As you will, sir.' Thraxis crossed to the cape lying bundled on a stool. He picked up the folds of red wool and turned to leave, muttering darkly about the pointlessness of the task.

After he had gone, Cato reached down into his document chest and rummaged until he found a clean sheet of vellum, a pot of ink and a stylus. He laid the sheet on the desk, unstoppered the ink and dipped the nib, taking care to tap the excess off before he poised the stylus over the vellum. Then he wrote neatly, 'To my beloved wide Julia, mother of my beloved son Lucius, greetings.' He cursed, and erased 'wide' with several quick strokes, writing 'wife' above. He was tired and needed to focus his thoughts. This was too important a letter to be composed carelessly. He breathed deeply, then began to write again. He told her that he had heard the news of their son's birth from another officer; he had no doubt Julia had sent a letter relating the same event, only it had not yet arrived. And since the army was about to march, he was taking the chance to write to her expressing his delight at becoming a father and his pride and love for his wife for bearing him a fine son.

That part of the letter was easy to write, and a joy to do so. What came next required much more thought, since his missives to Julia were bound to be scrutinised by an agent of Pallas, or Narcissus, or both, before they were passed into the hands of his wife. He dipped his stylus again and continued, writing that he hoped Julia was well and being careful not to permit too many visitors to their house in case they had an adverse effect on her health. That he trusted her father, the good senator, would look after her affairs while she concentrated on the well-being and raising of Lucius. He paused and read his words back to himself, trying to imagine Julia doing the same and understanding the covert warning he was attempting to convey. Not knowing who would be likely to intercept his letter, it was imperative that he did not name any names, or give any sense of who commanded his loyalties, and yet Julia had to be made aware that she was being watched. She was certainly shrewd enough to guess, and knew about his previous dealings with Narcissus. What she could not know was that Pallas's man had made overtures to her husband, backed up with threats to his family. How to convey that without saying it vexed

Cato's weary mind, and at length he set down his stylus and sat back in his chair.

'Fuck . . .'

A moment later, Thraxis entered and set down a steaming cup. 'Had to get that off Centurion Crispus's slave. I owe him a favour now. If you'd given me some coin earlier, I could have got some from one of the traders in the vicus. But—'

'Thank you. That will be all. Go and get some sleep.'

'Sleep? Still got the cloak to do first.'

'Isn't it done yet?'

Thraxis glared at him. 'It will be done as soon as it can be done, sir.'

'Then don't let me stop you.'

Thraxis muttered something in Thracian as he left the tent, and Cato turned his attention back to the letter, scratching his jaw irritably.

He struggled on by the pale flame of the lamp until the oil began to run out and the flame slowly shrank. He concluded with a brief reaffirmation of his love and then signed his name and read over the letter. It was barely adequate for the purposes he intended – to state that he pined for her and to warn her to stay away from the cross-currents of politics in the capital. Nevertheless, he folded the vellum carefully and then reached for the sealing wax. He dripped it over the fold and pressed his equestrian ring into the swiftly hardening wax, leaving the impression of a mounted soldier hurling a bolt of lightning. Julia had helped him choose the symbol when he had finally been confirmed in his present rank by the emperor and entered the equestrian tier of Roman society. He caressed the seal lightly and left the letter on his desk for Thraxis to take to headquarters in the morning with instructions for the staff remaining at Viroconium to ensure that it was sent to Rome at the first opportunity. He knew that it might take as much as four months at this time of year, and offered a quick prayer to Minerva that Julia would be wise enough to steer clear of political intrigue in the interim.

Sinking down on to his wooden-framed camp bed, Cato shivered in the cold night air. He gratefully pulled up the blanket and sheepskin cover that Thraxis had left out for him, and lay on his back staring up at the dark ceiling of the goatskin tent as a light shower began to patter above. His last thought before he fell asleep was of the expression on his servant's face when he saw the inevitable mud that would result from the rain falling during the night.

He was awake an instant before Thraxis entered the tent, as if by some innate sense of the appropriate time to return to consciousness. It was still dark outside, and the rain was falling in earnest now, making the air chilly and damp as he yawned.

'Your cloak,' Thraxis said as he laid the folded woollen garment on the table. 'Clean, though it might as well have been dragged through the mud instead, given the weather. Do you require food, sir?'

'No time. You can bring me something once we set off.' Cato stood up in his tunic and held out his arms so that Thraxis could fasten on his shoulder padding before helping him to struggle into his scale-armour shirt. The servant carefully fastened the ties that ran down the shield-arm side of the shirt, and then Cato stood still as his sword belt was placed over his head and arranged on his shoulder. Lastly there were his boots and his cape, which he fastened at his shoulder with a brooch.

'How do I look?'

'Like Julius Caesar himself, sir,' Thraxis answered in a weary monotone.

'Just as long as I don't end up like the man.'

'Sir?'

'Never mind. Pack up the kit and have my cart join the main baggage train. I'll see you in camp at the end of the day.'

Thraxis bowed his head. 'Yes, Prefect.'

Cato eased the tent flap aside and looked out over the lines of the Blood Crows and the Fourth Cohort of legionaries. The men were already up, barely visible in the first glimmer of the coming day. Rain drizzled steadily from an overcast sky in a soft hiss as the soldiers took down their tents and carried them to the waiting carts. Cato glanced back over his shoulder.

'And I'll want warm, dry clothes and a fire.'

'Yes, sir. Anything else?'

'Is a sunny countenance too much to ask for?'

Thraxis stared back bleakly.

'Fair enough.' Cato emerged from the tent and made his way over to his horse. One of the Thracians was holding his horse's reins and handed them to Cato before helping him into the saddle. From his elevated position Cato looked out towards the vast sprawl of the fortress of Mediolanum and the surrounding marching camps of the units concentrated there for the campaign. Thousands of men toiled to break camp in the gloom and then form up in their marching columns, hounded into place by the bellows of their centurions and optios. The vanguard was waiting just outside the main gate, and Crispus snapped an order to stand to attention as Cato rode up to join his men. The prefect cast an eye along the ranks of legionaries before he turned to address the centurion loudly enough for all to hear.

'The men are looking hungry for glory, Crispus.'

'Yes, sir! Hounds straining at the leash. That's the men of the Fourth Cohort all right.'

'Then may the gods show mercy to the enemy, because your men surely won't!'

Crispus grinned and drew his sword, punching it into the air as he bellowed the legion's title: '*Gemina! Gemina!*'

His men instantly joined in, giving full throat to their cry, and the other soldiers of the army briefly paused and turned towards the din before continuing to break camp.

Cato smiled at the legionaries, happy to indulge their keen spirits. He gave them a salute and rode on to the head of the column where the Blood Crows sat in their saddles. The two centuries of foot auxiliaries had been assigned to protect the vanguard's baggage train. An officer in a red military cloak was with them, together with a swarthy-looking servant on a horse laden with saddlebags.

'You must be Tribune Livonius,' Cato called out as he trotted up. 'Come to chart the army's passage through the hills and mountains.'

The officer nodded. 'Prefect Cato?'

'That's right.'

'Pleased to meet you, sir.' Livonius smiled. 'I've heard plenty about your exploits and those of the Blood Crows since I joined the legate's staff. It's an honour to serve with you.'

'An honour?' Cato shook his head, immediately suspicious of easy praise. 'My men and I only do our duty and carry out our orders. No more or less than any other soldiers of Rome.'

Livonius pursed his lips with an amused expression. 'If you say so, sir.'

'I do. Now wipe that foolish smile off your face.'

'Yes, sir.' The tribune looked a little crestfallen.

'And who is this?' Cato gestured towards the man at Livonius's side.

'Hieropates, sir. My private secretary and drafter of maps. He's the real brains behind our double act.'

'Is he now?' Cato looked the man over more closely. Hieropates was clearly from the Eastern Empire, and didn't look as if he was enjoying being sent to the far end of the emperor's domain. His dark curly hair was streaked with grey, above a heavily lined face out of which two dark eyes gleamed. His cloak appeared bulky due to the layers of clothing beneath, and his head seemed to hunch into the folds of cloth about his neck, like a bird withdrawing into its nest. 'You have experience of map-making amid such mountains?' Cato gestured towards the grey outlines of the ridges stretching away to the west.

Hieropates bowed his head gracefully. 'Indeed, sir. I and my master Livonius have mapped the eastern frontier from Cappadocia to Nubia, at the command of the Prefect of Syria.'

'A slave, then?'

'Yes, sir.'

'And a bloody good teacher,' Livonius intervened. 'Old Hieropates has taught me all I know about making maps.

And he taught Tribune Plinius before me, on whose recommendation my father bought Hieropates.'

Cato felt a pang of sympathy for the man. He was clearly well educated and might well believe that he deserved to be freed after giving many years of good service to his masters. As it was, he had been passed from one aristocratic family to another to educate the scions of their bloodline. And now here he was in Britannia, far from the warm comforts of the Eastern Empire. Cato smiled faintly at Livonius. 'Then I am pleased that you are assigned to my column. I trust that you and your maps will serve the army well.'

'Indeed, sir,' said Livonius. 'An army needs good maps just as much as it needs regular supplies, fortitude and the blessings of Fortuna. Between Hieropates and myself, we shall detail every step of the route the army takes in bringing the war to the enemy. We shall measure distances and sketch prominent landmarks so that we can shine a light into the darkest valley of the barbarians' mountainous lands.'

'Just as long as you don't hold my column back in any way. We can't afford to stop and wait for you to complete your little sketches and pacing-out of distances. You will need to keep up with us. If you don't, I'll leave you behind. Is that understood?'

The tribune looked chastened and nodded. 'Yes, sir.'

'Very well. You'll ride with the fourth squadron of the Blood Crows. The decurion will remain in command and you will regard yourself as supernumeraries.'

Livonius was clearly struggling to contain his discomfort at being placed under the command of a man several ranks beneath his own, and Cato relented.

'How long have you been in Britannia, Tribune?'

'Nearly three months, sir.'

'Three months . . .' The prefect sighed. It was unlikely that Livonius had much grasp of conditions in Britannia. While Cato appreciated the need for such young men to get some military experience early on in their careers, they tended to serve for too short a time. Most were attached to legions on garrison duty and merely had to adjust to the daily routine of such a life. Livonius had picked the short straw, thrown into a posting where he would need to learn fast just to stay alive. Still, it might be the making of him, if he survived the experience. And Crispus had vouched for him at least. Cato forced himself to smile encouragingly. 'Well then, you'll have something to tell your family when you return to Rome. Observe all that you can, Livonius, and listen to any advice the veterans give you. That's the best way to learn the craft of soldiering.'

'Yes, sir . . . Thank you.'

Cato wheeled his mount around and glanced back down the column. He felt a surge of pride at the sight of the men he was about to lead against their adversaries, the vanguard of the entire army launching itself against the enemy warriors and their Druid allies. He had fought and shed blood alongside these men and knew that they shared his pleasure in the hard-fighting reputation that both units had garnered since he had taken command. It was a pity that Macro was not here to share the moment with him, he reflected briefly.

He raised his arm and drew a deep breath. 'Blood Crows! Fourth Cohort! Prepare to advance!'

The legionaries and auxiliary infantry bent down to lift their shields, while the riders eased their mounts into two columns and adjusted their reins. Cato waited until the last of the men was ready before he turned his horse away from the army's camp and swept his arm down to point along the track leading towards the hills and mountains. A dull overcast made them seem more distant, and already he could see a broad band of darker clouds rolling in from the north, threatening rain.

'Column . . . advance!'

CHAPTER EIGHT

Centurion Macro was sitting on a camp stool on the grass mound beside the modest training area that had been levelled by his legionaries shortly after they had completed the fort itself. Taking advantage of the nearest expanse of flat ground outside the fort, they had removed rocks and clumps of gorse bushes and scythed down the long grass to clear space for the garrison to conduct its training sessions. At one end stood a line of wooden posts, at which Fortunus's men stood in files, each auxiliary waiting to take his turn at hacking the target. The steady clatter of their swords striking the posts filled the air, until Optio Diodorus blew his whistle to signal the changeover. Panting men broke away from the stakes and trotted to the rear of each file before the whistle sounded again and the sword drill resumed.

The other Illyrian century was marching around the training ground, breaking into a trot on each of the longer sides of the rough rectangle. They came puffing past Macro, kit clinking as they struggled to keep up with their commander. Centurion Appilus maintained a steady pace, his crest bobbing as he led his men on. Now and then he dropped to the side, marking time as he shouted threats at those lagging behind their comrades.

'Pick those bloody feet up! Move yourselves! Any man who falls more than a length behind the century is on latrine duty for the next ten days!'

Macro nodded approvingly. Despite his thin frame and the lack of an eye, Appilus was a decent officer who appeared to know his trade, unlike Fortunus, who was at that moment flailing away at one of the stakes, urged on by the optio. When the whistle blew again, the centurion bent forward, gasping for breath, before stumbling to the rear of his file. This was only the second day of training, and Macro was already starting to pick out the more fit and able of the Illyrian auxiliaries. Men who could be depended on if it came to a fight. Of the rest, there were some who merely needed exercise, while others needed to improve their drilling. Only a handful were no-hopers – too old to serve in a front-line capacity. One of those from Appilus's century had already fallen out of formation, slumping to his knees, shield grounded to one side as he struggled to prop himself up with his javelin shaft. At once the centurion shouted at the rest to keep going before doubling back to stand over the hapless straggler.

'On your feet!'

The soldier tried to rise, but fell back and shook his head.

'That was fucking pathetic!' Appilus bellowed, hefting his vine cane as he glared dangerously with his remaining eye. 'On your feet, you fat bastard. I won't tell you again.'

The man on his knees made no effort to obey, and Appilus lashed out with his stick, striking the soldier on the backside. He let out a yelp before scrambling up and staggering after his comrades.

'That's more like it! Keep going! You drop out again and I'll take the bloody hide off you!'

They caught up with the rest of the unit and Appilus increased his pace until he had resumed his position at the head of the column. Macro drummed his fingers on the shaft of the crutch lying across his thighs. The straggler would only be the first of the day. The morning drill was not yet halfway through, and he knew that there would be many more who would fall out of formation before then. It looked like the latrines were going to be kept spotless for the next month or so, he reflected with a wry grin.

He swung the end of the crutch on to the ground and gritted his teeth as he stood. There was the familiar sharp stab of pain as his wounded leg took the load, and he adjusted his balance to favour his other limb. He swore under his breath and waited for the pain to pass. It would be a while yet before he would be able to walk comfortably. Cupping a hand to his mouth, he called over towards the men at the stakes.

'Diodorus! On me!'

The acting optio hurried across to the reviewing mound and stood panting as he saluted his superior.

'Give it a little longer and then swap them round,' Macro ordered. 'Work 'em hard. I want these layabouts to know what real soldiering feels like.'

'Yes, sir.'

'Give them a short break at midday, then get them in full marching gear and take them round the fort until they've covered eight miles. That should sort them out. Anyone who falls out knows what to expect.'

'Latrines, sir?'

'Indeed. While I'm in command of this fort, we'll save shit-shovelling for the layabouts. They'll get sick of the stink soon enough and put their backs into training. See to it.'

'Yes, sir.'

'Right, I'm off. If you need me, I'm at headquarters.'

They exchanged a salute, and Diodorus turned away and hurried back to his charges. Macro took one last look around the training ground, then hobbled towards the track leading up to the fort's main gate. As he approached, he saw that the legionaries charged with keeping watch from the ramparts were watching the auxiliaries with the broad smiles soldiers usually wore for less fortunate companions.

'What the hell are you gawping at?' Macro shouted at them. 'You're supposed to be keeping a lookout for the enemy, not watching those lazy bastards!'

The legionaries immediately returned to their stations and scanned the surrounding landscape intently.

Still wearing a scowl, Macro entered the fort and made his way to headquarters. One of the Blood Crows left behind by Cato was standing guard at the arched entrance and snapped his spear upright as the garrison's commander passed by. With the departure of Cato and the rest of the fort's standing garrison, the building was much quieter, and only two clerks remained at the desks just inside the main hall. Macro addressed the nearer of them.

'I want Optio Pandarus in my office now.'

'Yes, sir.'

Macro was about to head towards the garrison commander's quarters at the end of the hall when the clerk cleared his throat and nodded to one side. Following the direction, Macro saw a civilian sitting on a bench, looking at him expectantly.

'He's asked to see you, sir.'

'Really? Who the hell is he?'

'Venistus, sir. The man assigned to speak for the camp followers.'

Macro gritted his teeth as he considered this uninvited complication to his day. 'What does he bloody well want?'

'I don't know, sir. He said he would only speak to the man in charge.'

'The man in charge, eh?' Macro sniffed. 'This is an army outpost, not an inn on the Appian Way.' He thought briefly about sending the civilian away with orders never to bother him again, but then he relented a fraction. Regardless of how he felt about the presence of the camp followers in the fort, they were here now, and unless he was prepared to order them to return to Viroconium, then he had better get used to the idea. If he sent them away, they would be easy prey for the enemy war bands that ranged through the borderlands between the mountain tribes and the new Roman province. Neither could he afford to send them back with an escort strong enough to guarantee their safety, not without putting the fort at risk. So for now, at least, he was stuck with them. And Venistus. He approached the man with a surly expression.

'All right. What is it?'

Venistus stood up and smiled easily. 'Centurion Macro I believe? We have not yet had the pleasure of making each other's acquaintance.'

'Pleasure does not come into it. Speak your mind and make it quick, Venistus.'

Macro's abruptness barely fazed the civilian, even though he had spent many years in the company of soldiers. His smile did not falter as he bowed his head modestly. 'I apologise for imposing on you, sir, but there are certain arrangements about our accommodation and living conditions that I fear I must bring to your attention.'

'Really? Do tell me.'

'As you know, sir, we were given permission by Legate Quintatus's headquarters to accompany Centurion Fortunus and his men to this posting, and—'

'You got this permission from the legate himself, I take it?'

'Not as such, sir. No. It was authorised by a member of his headquarters staff.'

'Someone with a greasy palm, I'll wager.'

Venistus affected dawning realisation and then shock. 'Sir, are you accusing me of offering a bribe to an imperial official?'

'Do I really have to accuse you?' Macro sniffed. 'We both know it works, so let's not waste time. What do you have to say?'

Venistus's cordial expression disappeared and the hardened features of the market trader came to the fore. 'You've put us in the stables, sir. Treating us no better than animals. Worse. We get the run-off from the barracks up the slope from us. The place stinks. Furthermore, you have confined us to that area and your men refuse to let us move freely about the fort, or indeed to leave the fort at any time. Many of the auxiliaries have families amongst the camp followers, sir. They are not being allowed to see them. This was not the arrangement that pertained back at Viroconium with the rest of the Illyrian cohort.'

'I don't suppose it was. But that might have more to do

with how the prefect of the cohort chose to run things. The Eighth Illyrian is a joke, Venistus. Not fit to take its place in the battle line. Not even fit to be a reserve unit, let alone the garrison of a frontier outpost. That has to change. I will see to it. Those men are going to earn their bloody pay and perform like soldiers of the Roman army. Only then will I cut them some slack and let them enjoy the privileges of real soldiers. And if that means depriving them of their bed rights, then that's just tough on them. Besides, it'll give the tarts from the vicus a chance to rest.'

'But they have to eat, sir. The soldiers are the only customers they have.'

'They will eat. Food, at least. They get the same rations as the men, for now.'

'For now?'

Macro nodded. 'I'll be asking headquarters for an escort to take you and your people back to Viroconium as soon as possible. I dare say that may take a while, given that there'll only be a small garrison there now that the legate has taken the army into the mountains. And perhaps your man on the staff might find a way to scupper my plan. But I want you out. As for the accommodation, count yourself fortunate that I haven't ordered you to set up a vicus outside the fort. At this time of year, shelter from the elements is at something of a premium. The stables may smell, but they are dry and they are safe. You might reflect on that with a bit more gratitude.'

'Of course we are grateful. But what about the men's families? What about our livelihoods?'

Macro sighed with irritation at the demanding tone of the civilian. 'Like I said, this is an army outpost. I set the

113

rules here, and you will abide by them. If any of your people break them, I will have them thrown out of the main gate to fend for themselves. If any of my men try to cross the line into your part of the fort without permission, I'll have them flogged. If you have any objection to these arrangements, then I suggest you have a word with your friend Fortunus. I'm betting the two of you had a cosy little relationship back at Viroconium. If he can't deliver on his side of it now that you're here, then that's your problem. You are free to leave at any time. However, if you choose to stay, then you live under my authority and there is no more to be said on the matter.'

Venistus opened his mouth to remonstrate, but had the wit to still his tongue. Macro glared at him, defying him to protest. The civilian's gaze slipped away and he stared meekly at the floor between them.

'That's better,' said Macro. 'Now you take care of your people and keep them out of my way and out of trouble and we shall get on well enough. Once I have the Illyrians in hand, then perhaps we can arrange for them to have access to the stables once in a while as a reward.'

Venistus looked up hopefully.

'But only if everyone keeps to the rules,' Macro said firmly.

A figure entered the hall and Macro glanced aside to see Optio Pandarus turn towards his quarters and pause as he caught sight of his superior in conversation with the civilian. Macro waved him on. 'I'll join you in a moment.'

'Yes, sir.'

He turned back to Venistus. 'You know where you stand. In future, if you wish to speak with me, then wait until evening watch is sounded. I will not have you interrupt the day-to-day running of the fort, is that understood?'

'Yes, Centurion.'

'Then you may go.'

Venistus bowed his head again and backed away respectfully before turning to leave the hall. Macro watched him depart, gratified that he had put the man in his place, but still frustrated that he had had to deal with the matter at all. It was outside the remit of soldiering as he understood it, and he wondered briefly how Cato might have handled the matter. Perhaps this was precisely the kind of thing that was part and parcel of being a senior officer, he mused. An ability to deal with a range of unexpected and unwanted situations that had little to do with the everyday routines of commanding a line unit. If this was what promotion brought with it, then he wanted none of it, he concluded bitterly.

He let out a deep sigh and turned to limp across the hall to the door leading through to his office and the modest quarters that lay beyond. Pandarus was standing at ease in front of the desk as Macro entered and shuffled round to the chair before slumping down with a grunt. He leaned his crutch against the edge of the table as he addressed the optio.

'It seems you are now the senior cavalry officer in the fort, but don't let it go to your head.'

Pandarus grinned. He was an amiable type, one of the shrinking number of men from the first draft of Thracians who had made up the cohort when it had been formed a few years earlier in a small town on the north shore of the Aegean Sea. The campaigns in Britannia had whittled their ranks down, and the replacements had been drawn mostly from Gaul, from tribes skilled at horse-riding. The recent losses of so many experienced men had helped Pandarus to achieve his recent promotion to optio. When Macro had first encountered the unit, they had resembled wild hill men, wrapped in furs and dark cloaks and wearing their hair long and unkempt. Thanks to the dilution of the original Thracians, the troopers of the cohort now tended to look more like the longer-established auxiliary units. The cloaks and furs remained, but they had braided their hair and favoured long Celtic moustaches instead of beards. As far as the enemy knew, however, this was the same cavalry unit that had terrorised the lands of the Silures, and they dreaded the very sight of the red crow on the black background of the cohort's standard.

'Your ten men are all that I have to do the work of a cohort,' Macro continued. 'We still need to mount patrols of the surrounding area. The difference now is that you're going to have to behave like the prey rather than the hunter. I want you to lead each patrol in person, and take five men with you. The others will stay here in case I need to send a message to Viroconium in a hurry. When you are out in the hills, stay out of sight of the locals. On no account are you to get into any kind of contact with the enemy, no matter how tempting. I cannot afford to lose a single trooper. I just want you to observe and report back. Understood?'

'Yes, sir.' Pandarus nodded and then pursed his lips. 'Are we really expecting trouble, sir? The enemy will have their hands full dealing with Quintatus.'

'You should know how it goes by now, Optio. You've been here long enough. Every time the army pushes forward, it needs to disperse its troops to garrison the territory we've gained. That keeps things under control as long as the enemy

116

does not concentrate its forces so they are strong enough to pick off our outposts. If they do mass their warriors, then we have to pull our forces together to confront them, and that means stripping out every available man from forts like this. Which makes us vulnerable. I hope you're right about the legate, but I'm not taking any risks. If the enemy intends to give us a kicking, then I want to be warned about it in good time.' He looked at the optio frankly. 'You are the eyes and ears of the garrison, Pandarus.'

'You can count on me, sir.'

'I didn't doubt it. Pick the best of your men to ride with you, and make sure they know the score. I don't want heroes, I want information. Starting from tomorrow, you will conduct a daily sweep of the hills to the west. Any settlement you encounter, or any band of hunters or armed men, take down their number and location and report back.'

'Yes, sir.'

'That's all. You're dismissed . . . Wait! One more thing.'

'Sir?

'I'll need a servant.' Macro patted his thigh. 'While I'm getting over this bastard wound. One of yours will do. Who can you spare?'

The optio thought quickly. 'Bortamis, sir. He's the strongest of us, but also the largest, and he'll slow me down. He'll be remaining at the fort.'

'Bortamis, then. You'd better tell him the good news. I'll need him first thing in the morning. He's to bring his kit and use the storeroom of the main hall. You can go.'

They swapped a salute and Pandarus left the office. Macro eased himself back and gently rubbed the dressing above his knee. It itched badly, but the surgeon had told him not to worry it for fear of reopening the wound. So he had to content himself with gentle pressure that only seemed to make it worse.

'Fuck . . .' he growled bitterly as he allowed himself to dwell on his situation. 'Sitting here nursemaiding those soft Illyrian slackers while the army goes off to fight. It ain't right. It ain't right at all.' He cleared his throat and spat into the corner of the room. 'I bet Cato's having a right old time of it.'

CHAPTER NINE

Cato sat hunched in his saddle, trying to take advantage of what little warmth remained in his body. His tunic and cloak were soaked through, and the rain pinged relentlessly off his helmet, all but drowning out the harsh hiss of the downfall around him. Behind him stretched the mounted squadrons of the Blood Crows, and behind them the infantry, men and horses alike drenched by the icy rain and sleet that had beset the army from the first day of the advance. The rough track that they had followed into the hills had become a sucking quagmire the moment the first hundred men had churned it up, and the baggage train required the constant assistance of the escorting troops to keep the wheels of the heavy wagons turning. Instead of the anticipated eighteen miles a day, they had been managing no more than half that since they had set out from Mediolanum, at the price of exhausting the men so that they took far longer than usual to erect a marching camp each night.

Even though the vanguard had been spared most of the physical effort of the advance over such terrible ground, they still had the strain of scouting ahead of the army and ensuring that Quintatus and his men did not march into any ambushes or suffer the harassing raids that had been a favourite tactic in slowing down the advance of Rome's legions. For the first five days, there had been only occasional sightings of the enemy: distant groups of horsemen watching the struggling column from the hilltops. They turned and disappeared the moment Cato sent one of his squadrons forward, and their light ponies and knowledge of the hills and forests meant that they slipped away long before any contact could be made.

But this day the enemy had decided to make a stand. The valley along which the army had been advancing had narrowed into a short stretch of gorge between two rocky crags. A crude barricade of boulders had been constructed across its mouth, and a few hundred warriors stood behind the makeshift defences. The Roman outriders had ridden back to make their report the moment they had encountered the tribesmen, and now Cato raised a hand to shield his eyes from the rain as he tried to discern the details of the enemy position.

'Crispus and his lads should clear them out the way quickly enough,' Decurion Miro commented as he too surveyed the Deceanglian warriors. He turned in his saddle and looked back. 'Ah, here he comes, sir.'

The legionary centurion was trying to stride along the side of the column, but the sodden soil sucked at his heavy boots, already weighed down by mud, and he half walked and half slid as he approached. The rain had soaked the crest of his helmet, and the stiff horsehair looked like old palm fronds, spiky and drooping. He stopped a short distance to one side of the glistening coat of Cato's mount and swallowed in an attempt to control his laboured breathing.

'You sent for me, sir?'

'We've got company.' Cato pointed towards the gorge. Crispus squinted into the gloom until he could make out the obstacles blocking their way, and the silent ranks of the warriors beyond.

'About bloody time. I was wondering when those bastards were going to stand and fight, sir.'

'It's only a delaying action, Centurion. They're merely trying to hold us up and buy time for the main body of their army.'

'Hold us up?' Crispus laughed mirthlessly as he raised one of his boots with a clearly audible sucking sound. 'If we were advancing any slower, we'd be retreating.'

'Then let's waste no time about it. This is a job for infantry. Your cohort will clear the gorge. My auxiliaries will form a reserve. We'll chase them off once you have broken through.'

'Shouldn't take us long, sir.'

Cato turned to Miro. 'Send a man back to the legate to let him know we've made contact with a small enemy force and had to halt. Then get the men off the track to make way for the infantry.'

'Yes, sir.' Miro saluted and turned aside to pass the order on to one of his riders. Then he sat erect in his saddle and cupped a hand to his mouth to ensure that he was heard above the din of the rain. 'Second Thracian Cohort . . . dismount! Form line on the side of the track!'

The weary troopers eased themselves out of their saddles and splashed down in to the mud before leading their horses on to the grassy bank that ran along the ancient footpath. Cato waited a moment longer to inspect the enemy position, but there was no movement there. He knew that they must have lookouts on the hills and have been aware of the Roman presence long before they had come in sight of the gorge. The tribesmen seemed ready to fight it out, and he could not help but feel a fleeting admiration for their stolid courage. They had tested themselves against the men of the legions many times before and been soundly beaten, and yet they had not given in. Still they fought on. Was it courage, Cato wondered, or obstinate stupidity? Or more likely the fanaticism whipped up by the Druids. Now that the Romans were marching against the Deceanglians, they would soon threaten the most sacred groves of the Druid cult on the island of Mona. That would inspire them to fight more determinedly than ever before.

Cato dismounted and handed his reins to Thraxis. 'Tether Hannibal and then bring me my shield.'

His servant shot him a surprised look, the rain running in rivulets down his dark features. But he knew better than to query his superior. 'Yes, sir. Shall I take your cloak?'

Cato nodded, and reached up to unfasten the enamelled pin at his shoulder. It had been a gift from Julia, and he carefully reattached it to his neckcloth where it would be safe. Handing his cloak to Thraxis, he joined Crispus, a few paces ahead of the column. His awareness of the wet and cold faded as his mind focused on the task at hand. The mouth of the gorge was no more than forty paces across, and the enemy's barricade was higher than a man. They would have to scale that to get at the defenders, no easy feat in heavy armour, weighed down by the water that had soaked into the men's clothing.

'It's going to be a messy business,' he said quietly.

Crispus shrugged. 'When isn't it? And this fucking rain isn't going to make matters easy.'

A moment later they were joined by another figure. Livonius eased back the hood of his goatskin cape. It had been well treated with fat to render it waterproof, Cato noted with a touch of envy.

'You're supposed to be at the back of the vanguard, Tribune.'

'I just wanted to see what's holding us up, sir. I heard Miro's man say it was the enemy. First time I've ever had the chance to see any of the mountain tribes up close. Is that them, over there behind the rocks?'

'That's them.'

Livonius squinted at the distant tribesmen before he turned to the other officers. 'What is your plan for dealing with the enemy, sir? A flanking movement?'

'Not today, Tribune. Those crags on either side look pretty sheer to me. It would take us hours to get men up and over. We'd lose the rest of the day. So it's a frontal attack. Crispus and his cohort will soon brush them aside, and then I'll follow up with my lads and make the pursuit. With luck, we'll take a few prisoners.'

'I see.' The tribune was silent for a moment, his hand resting on the ivory handle of his sword. 'I don't suppose I might—'

'You're staying right here,' Cato interrupted him. 'You'll get your chance in due course,' he added gently.

'Sir, with respect, I have already proved myself in the field, and I was sent here to learn how to become a soldier.'

'All in good time. For now, your orders are to draw maps for the army. It's an important job, so we can't afford to let anything happen to you. How is that going, by the way?'

'Not as easily as I had hoped, sir. With this rain, it's been very difficult to investigate the terrain either side of the line of advance. And it's been hard to record accurately the distance marched. There's no way of taking a standard pace in these conditions, so we've marked it up as best as we can calculate it.'

'Can't be helped, Tribune. Consider this an important lesson of soldiering. The first casualty of war is the plan.'

'Ain't that the truth?' Crispus added.

The first century of legionaries came struggling up the track, and Crispus ordered them to deploy a hundred paces forward of the column. The five remaining units followed suit, until the cohort was drawn up in two lines of three centuries. Their officers gave the order to remove their leather shield covers, and the large, decorated curves of the legionary shields gave the mud-streaked soldiers a more uniform appearance. The Thracians formed up behind them in a single line, oval shields and spears at the ready. Cato turned to Thraxis to take his shield and advanced to join the waiting men with Crispus at his side.

'Good luck!' Livonius called after them.

'Pftt!' Crispus sneered. 'Luck has nothing to do with it. It's down to steel, grit and years of back-breaking training. Not that he'll ever have to understand that. Once he's served out his year, he'll be off back to Rome and some cushy number looking after the drains or the markets or some such bollocks.'

Cato was well used to the begrudging tone of centurions towards the young men serving out the military phase of their career ladder, and adopted a mocking tone as he asked,

'Would you want to exchange all the pleasures of soldiering for inspecting the drains of Rome, Centurion?'

'Not fucking likely, sir.'

'Then let's get this over with.'

They parted company as they reached the waiting soldiers, and Crispus went forward to the right of the front line, where the first century of the cohort stood ready. Hoisting his shield and swinging it round towards the enemy, he drew his sword and punched it up towards the lowering clouds. Rain ran down the blade, gleaming dully.

'Fourth Cohort! At the walk! Advance!'

The centuries were drawn up with a frontage of ten men, narrow enough to fit into the mouth of the gorge, with eight files giving plenty of weight to the assault. If all went to form, the second line should not be required to fight, Cato reasoned. The centurion commanding the three remaining centuries waited until the regulation gap had opened up between the two lines before ordering his men to follow on. Cato waited a bit longer, then called out to his Thracians to advance. The grass beneath his boots was drenched, and the soil below soft and yielding, and as the auxiliaries began to follow in the footsteps of the heavy infantry, the ground became churned and slick with mud.

As they approached the enemy, who had been standing still and silent all the while, a great roar tore from the tribesmen's throats, and they raised their weapons and shook them at the oncoming shield wall. The rain provided one blessing at least, thought Cato. It was too wet for archers, and the confined space in which the skirmish would be fought would make it difficult for slingers. A straight fight, then, between the iron discipline of the legions and the fanatical courage of the native warriors. And there was no question who would prevail.

The air filled with the squelching of boots in the mud and the laboured grunts of the tired men struggling to hold their line as they approached the barricade. Over the heads in front of him, Cato could make out some of the faces of the warriors behind the barricade, mouths open as they roared their challenge. There was a sudden blur of motion amid the leaden streaks of rain, and Crispus shouted a warning.

'Shields up!'

The leading ranks of the cohort raised their shields and angled them back to deflect the incoming missiles. Javelins. Cato could see them now, arcing down towards the legionaries. They struck home in an uneven chorus of clatters and thuds. After the din of the first volley died away, one of Crispus's men bellowed, 'You'll get yours, you British cunts!'

'Shut your mouth!' Crispus raged. 'Silence in the bloody ranks!'

The men trudged on, heeding the warning of their centurion, and Cato felt a thrill ripple through his body at being part of the spectacle. There was nothing quite as impressive and terrifying as the sight of these well-trained soldiers advancing in ordered lines beneath their drenched standards without a word escaping their lips. And it seemed that the enemy sensed it too, as their shouts and cries began to die away and their features set in grim expressions, mirroring the faces of their Roman opponents. Another ragged volley of javelins was unleashed, mixed with rocks small enough to hurl from the top of the barricade. On either side the crags loomed up, dark and daunting, and the sound of rain and the shouts of the defenders echoed loudly off the rocks.

'Close up!' Crispus ordered. 'Close up!'

His men were no more than ten paces from the foot of the barricade, and the officer commanding the second line brought it to a halt. Cato held up his arm.

'Blood Crows! Halt!'

The auxiliaries stopped, twenty paces back from the rearmost legionaries. There was a slight rise that allowed Cato a clear view of the mouth of the gorge, and he blinked away the rain that had dripped from the brim of his helmet into his eyes. He could see the first rank of the legionaries starting to clamber up the barricade, shields overhead. The long swords of the natives slashed down at the curved surfaces. Some had axes, and their blows landed with splintering thuds that carried clearly to Cato's ears as he looked on. Most of Crispus's men could barely move under the intensity of the blows raining down at them, but here and there individual legionaries had managed to climb high enough to strike back at the enemy, and the fight raged along the length of the barricade.

'Push on! Push on!' the centurion cried hoarsely, and Cato was reminded of Macro in the man's fearless drive to overcome his foes. 'Keep pushing, lads!'

More legionaries forced their way up to join their comrades duelling desperately in the rain. Swords flickered in savage thrusts and men tried to batter each other with their shields. Some of the natives grabbed at the legionaries' shields and tried to wrench them aside to allow their comrades to strike home. Behind the fighting line, the follow-up ranks of the first three cohorts were densely packed together as they were funnelled into the gorge. For the moment, the attack had stalled as the two sides battled for control of the top of the barricade.

A horn sounded from behind the enemy warriors, a deep braying note that echoed off the crags on either side. At the sound, the enemy cheered again, their voices horribly amplified. A dark shape plunged down from the top of the crag, and the motion caught Cato's eye. He looked up and clearly saw the first of the large rocks as it struck a projection and spun end over end until it smashed down amongst the legionaries packed in front of the barricade. More boulders tumbled down, and Cato saw several men outlined against the grey sky as they picked up fresh rocks and hurled them. Now the legionaries began to look up and realise the danger, but such was the dense press that escape was impossible.

Cato ran forward, pushing his way through the ranks of the second line as he called out hoarsely, 'Back! Fall back!'

The rearmost men in the gorge looked round and began to edge away, easing the pressure on the men ahead of them as more rocks fell, dashing legionaries to the ground, crushing skulls and shattering bones. Ahead of them, Crispus was still urging his men forward, heedless of what was occurring behind him.

'Fall back!' Cato shouted again and again, raging at himself for letting his men walk into this trap. 'Get back!'

Others began to take up his cry, and the legionaries retreated individually towards the second line, thinning out the ranks so that more of their comrades could escape the peril from above.

Cato stood against the flow of men and called out again. 'Centurion Crispus!'

At last the officer sensed something was awry. Thrusting his shield into the face of an enemy warrior, he glanced round quickly and saw for the first time the score of men who had been pulverised by the rocks. He grasped the danger at once and turned to the legionaries still fighting along the barricade.

'Fall back!'

One by one they disengaged and clambered back down to the ground. Away from the danger of the enemy warriors, they still had to run the gauntlet of falling rocks, and Cato saw three more men go down as Crispus waved them away from the barricade. Only when the last of them was far enough away from the cliffs to escape the danger did the centurion back away himself, keeping a wary eye on his enemy. So it was that he missed seeing the rock tumbling through the rain. Cato spotted it too late to shout a warning, and Crispus was driven to his knees by the impact that glanced off the side of his helmet before smashing through his shoulder and chest. He swayed a moment before his shield and sword slid from his grasp and he pitched forward on to his face.

CHAPTER TEN

'The centurion's down!' a voice cried out. 'Let's get the bastards!'

'No!' Cato called back, then blocked the retreat of two men trying to push him aside. 'You and you! With me. Let's go.'

He did not give them a chance to hesitate, thrusting them towards the gorge, then increasing his pace to take the lead as he made for the stricken centurion. Some of the other legionaries were already dragging their injured comrades out of the danger zone, and on the far side of the barricade, the enemy cheered at the spectacle of the retreating Romans.

Their cries were met with a thin chorus from those on top of the crags as they ceased their attack and the last of the rocks thudded on to the ground. All the same, Cato kept his shield up as he rushed forward to Crispus and crouched down beside him. Grunting with effort, he turned the centurion over and saw the misshapen ruin of his shoulder and the deep dent in the side of his helmet. Crispus's face was covered with mud, and Cato wiped it away as best he could.

'I'll cover you,' he told the legionaries. 'You take his arms and get him away from here.'

As soon as they moved him, Crispus let out a gasp and then howled in agony as his head lolled back.

'Keep going!' Cato urged as they dragged the body through the mud towards the safety of the second line of legionaries. There was a shout from the enemy as they caught sight of the officer's crest on Cato's helmet, and three men scrambled over the barricade, jumped down and raced towards him. He drew his sword, raised his shield and placed himself between the enemy and Crispus and the legionaries. Two of the tribesmen were armed with spears, while the third, a short distance ahead of his companions, carried a sword and round shield. Their expressions were wild, eyes glaring and lips drawn back in snarls, as if they were intoxicated. This would be a short, savage contest, Cato realised as he braced his boots in the mud and held his sword ready. The sodden ground, churned up by the nailed boots of the legionaries, slowed the enemy down as they advanced, desperate to claim the head of a Roman officer for a trophy.

Cato held his ground, determined to buy time for Crispus, and gritted his teeth as the swordsman closed in. There was no pause, no sizing up his opponent. The tribesman punched his shield into Cato's and brought his sword round in an arc in a bid to decapitate the Roman. Cato swung his shield out and up just in time to block the edge of the sword, and it glanced over his head. He made to thrust back with his own sword, but his foot slipped and robbed his attack of any power, the blade striking a winding blow on the furs over the man's chest.

Both men recovered their balance at the same instant and made to strike a head blow. The blades clashed sharply and held as each tried to overpower the other. One slip in the mud would be fatal, Cato realised, trying to get as much purchase as possible on the slippery ground. His features twisted into a tight grimace as he matched his strength against that of the enemy, their faces barely a foot apart. Over the man's shoulder he could see the spearmen edging out around their comrade in order to get a clear strike at the side of the Roman officer. There was no time for a man-on-man duel. Cato abruptly angled his sword to let the warrior's blade slide sharply towards his shoulder, trusting to the armour to protect him. As soon as his own sword was free, he raised his right arm and hammered the butt of the handle down on his opponent's head with a sharp crack. At the same moment, the edge of the warrior's sword struck a numbing blow to Cato's shoulder. The tribesman staggered back, blundering into the nearest of the spearmen so that he slipped in the mud and had to thrust his weapon into the ground to steady his balance. The swordsman fell, arms outstretched, knocking his comrade to his knees as he did so.

Cato swung quickly towards the other spearman and tried to advance his shield, but the blow to his shoulder had weakened his arm, and his head remained exposed. The man thrust at his eyes, and he tilted his head to one side and flicked the spear tip aside with the point of his sword. At once the weapon was snatched back ready for another thrust. The initial impact of the blow to his shoulder was fading, but Cato lowered his shield a little further to tempt the warrior to aim high again. The tribesman steadied his grip on the spear shaft and punched forward. Cato was ready for him. Dropping the shield, he snatched at the spear, just behind the leaf-shaped blade, and viciously wrenched the wooden shaft towards him. His opponent held on tightly and lurched forward, losing his balance as he stumbled towards Cato. The prefect's short sword swung up, catching the warrior in the side and penetrating deeply into his vitals. Cato twisted his wrist from side to side and ripped the blade free, then thrust the shaft of the spear back towards its owner, who fell into a sitting position and hunched over his wound with a loud groan.

Cato saw that the remaining spearman was a youth, despite his matted hair and straggling beard. He glanced from the unconscious swordsman to his wounded friend, then lowered his spear and took a cautious step towards the Roman. Brandishing his sword, Cato filled his lungs and bellowed with all the rage he could muster, 'If you don't want to join 'em, then fuck off!'

The vehemence of the words carried ample meaning, and the tribesman recoiled a step, torn between pride and the prospect of fighting the man who had struck down two of his comrades in less time than it took to draw a handful of breaths. He carefully retreated another pace, keeping his spear up and staring hard at Cato.

'That's better,' Cato nodded. 'Now piss off like a good boy, eh?'

The youth retreated further, and Cato kept a keen eye on him as he bent down to retrieve his shield and cautiously edge back towards his own men. When he was sure he was no longer in immediate danger, he turned and trotted after the two legionaries dragging Crispus to safety. The men who had fallen back from the first assault were already re-forming about their standards at the rear of the cohort, while the injured were laid out to one side to wait for the surgeon and his medics to come forward to treat them. As the centurion passed through the ranks of the legionaries, they looked on in shock and anger at their stricken commander.

The two men released their grip on Crispus's arms, and the centurion lay on his back, eyes fluttering as he moaned. Cato set his shield aside and knelt beside him. He saw the blood trickling from the centurion's nose and mingling with the rainwater running over his cheeks.

'Crispus . . . Crispus! Can you hear me?'

The centurion blinked and opened his eyes, staring straight up at Cato. He frowned and then licked his lips as he made to speak. 'Lu . . . luck has nothing . . . to do with it.'

He grimaced, and his eyes rolled up as his body trembled. Cato looked up. 'Surgeon! Over here!'

Pausinus and his bandage dressers were already examining the first victims of the boulders and those who had been wounded on the barricade. The surgeon swiftly tied off a strip of linen and hurried over. He hunkered down opposite Cato and laid his fingers gently on the crushed shoulder.

'His days of soldiering are over, if he lives.' He sensed the trembling and then noticed the dent in the centurion's helmet. 'Help me get this off.'

While Pausinus steadied the helmet in his hands, Cato undid the chin strap and eased the cheek flaps aside. Then the surgeon eased the helmet free, together with the felt skullcap. The latter snagged on something, and Crispus gasped as blood seeped out from under its rim. Before the surgeon could react, the wounded man jerked violently and the cap came free with a large flap of bloodied scalp and a jagged piece of bone to reveal the terrible damage done by the rock that had struck the side of Crispus's head. Blood and brains slooshed out of the cavity opened up by the removal of the skullcap as the centurion writhed and shuddered and then went limp.

Cato looked down at him in horror.

The surgeon packed the felt cap against the wound and eased himself back. 'He's done for. Nothing I can do to save him, sir.'

'Nothing?'

Pausinus picked up Crispus's wrist and felt for a pulse, then let it drop. 'He's dead.'

Cato placed a hand on the centurion's forearm but sensed nothing. No movement at all. He swallowed. 'All right . . . Then see to the others.'

As Pausinus moved away, Cato gave the centurion's forearm a last squeeze. 'Rest easy in the shades, Centurion Crispus,' he muttered. 'You have earned it. Rest well with our fallen comrades.'

He took a calming breath, then rose to his feet and turned back towards the gorge. The enemy warriors were still cheering defiantly. All around Cato, the legionaries glared back. He sensed their bitter, angry mood and their thirst for revenge. The fire of battle burned in their veins, and they were keen to avenge their fallen comrades. That was all very well, he thought, but what could be done? The Deceanglians had chosen a fine position to mount their delaying action. Until the crags were cleared, there could be no further assault on the barricade blocking the gorge. And to reach the men who had broken up the attack would mean a steep climb, all the while exposed to yet more rocks tumbling down on the heads of the Roman soldiers. It would be murderous work.

He reluctantly concluded that there was no alternative but to find another route around the gorge. He went in search of Tribune Livonius and found him watching from the rise, with the mounted contingent of the Blood Crows.

'Good to see you're safe, sir,' Livonius greeted him. 'That was quite a trap the natives set us.'

'Yes, it was,' Cato said. 'You've got your campaign map with you?'

'Yes, sir. Over there.' He gestured to where his servant Hieropates stood by their two mules laden with the mapping tools and the tribune's campaign supplies.

'I want to see it, now.'

Livonius glanced up into the rain. 'But, sir, the ink will run.'

'Not if it's kept out of the wet. Get some of my men to use their shields as a shelter. Do it now.'

'Yes, sir.'

As the tribune hurried away, Cato turned to Miro. 'Decurion, get down to the Fourth Cohort and find out the number of casualties. Tell Centurion Festinus that he's in command. The optio of the First Century can take charge of the unit for the present.'

'Yes, sir . . . Centurion Crispus?'

'He's dead,' Cato responded bluntly. 'Now get on with it.'

Miro saluted and trotted down the gentle slope as Cato made his way to where Livonius was ordering two of the Blood Crows to hold their shields steady overhead. Hieropates, leather tube tucked under his arm, moved into the makeshift shelter and removed a roll of vellum, holding it open for the tribune and Cato as they ducked under the shields. The route of the army had been clearly marked, with estimated distances between camps and notations concerning the lie of the land on either side of the route. Livonius tapped a blank area just beyond the previous night's camp.

'We're roughly here. Of course, we won't have a chance to update it until we make camp.'

Cato shot him an irritated glance. 'Very helpful.'

He closed his eyes a moment as he recalled the day's march. They had spent all of it struggling along the track that passed through the meandering valley. The slopes rose steeply on either side, broken by rocky outcrops. There had been no other obvious routes to take. He thought back to the site of the night before. There had been two further valleys that had led away from the spot where the army had halted. He pointed to the mark and the notes relating to the camp.

'What about the other valleys? Is it possible we can use either of them to work round this position?'

Hieropates shook his head. 'Not unless you want to lose two days, Prefect. I rode a few miles up each as the army was making camp. One turns to the north and bends back almost in the direction of Mediolanum. The other leads south towards Ordovician territory. But the country there was slightly more open.' He tilted his head to one side. 'We could use that to bypass the gorge.'

'Good.' Cado decided. 'If we can get round it, Quintatus can always send a small force back to clear the gorge from the other side and open our lines of communication back to Mediolanum by the most direct route. Of course, it'll mean a delay while the army turns around and takes the southern route tomorrow.'

Livonius clicked his tongue. 'The legate's not going to be happy, sir.'

'I can't help that. Put the map away, Hieropates.'

As the slave carefully rolled it up and returned it to its leather case, Cato turned to take another look at the gorge. The enemy's barricade did not look formidable, nor did the body of warriors behind it. It was the men occupying the impregnable crags who presented the real strength of the position. He hissed in frustration and mentally composed the report he would make to the legate advising him to turn the column around and march back the way they had come. The rank and file would feel bitterly resentful about retracing their steps through the mud. But then soldiers were wont to grumble even when things were going well. It was Quintatus who presented the real challenge. He had wanted to make a quick strike into the heart of enemy territory. Instead, the army had crawled forward at a slow pace, and now would have to turn around. The legate was sure to be furious, but Cato could see no way of forcing the gorge without very heavy casualties.

He was about to give Thraxis the details for a verbal report when there was a commotion a short distance back down the track, and over the heads of the men and beasts of the army who had been held up by the action in the gorge appeared Quintatus's personal standard and that of the Fourteenth Legion.

'It's the legate,' said Livonius. 'Come forward to see for himself, no doubt.'

'Then he's saved me the trouble of finding him.'

They watched as the men on the track, cajoled by their centurions and optios, struggled aside to make way for the army's commander and his senior officers. As soon as he caught sight of Cato, the legate reined in beside him and glared down.

'Why has the column stopped? What are those men doing formed up?'

Cato pointed towards the gorge. 'It's the enemy, sir.'

Quintatus sat up in his saddle and stared briefly at the barricade and the warriors beyond. 'That rabble? Just sweep them aside and get the column moving.'

'We've made an attack already, sir. But they've got men up there on the crags, ready to bombard us with rocks. I lost a centurion and several legionaries. The position's too strong to force without risking further losses. I suggest we fall back and find another way round, sir.'

'What? Are you mad? Are you willing to let a handful of barbarians deflect an entire Roman army? Have you lost your senses? If we retreat from that motley bunch of barbarians, the enemy will ridicule us. Is that what you want, Prefect?'

'Of course not, sir,' Cato replied at once. He accepted that the legate had a point. If the army was forced to turn aside, the Deceanglians would score a moral victory over Rome, and the Druids would make sure that news of it spread rapidly across the island. But if confronting the tribesmen resulted in the loss of many Roman lives, they would be able to boast about the handful of their comrades who had defied a vastly greater force. Either way, the enemy would have cause to celebrate their humiliation of Legate Quintatus and his men.

He thought quickly. 'We could bring forward some of the bolt-throwers and a catapult, sir. Give them a taste of our artillery and I'm sure they'll turn tail and abandon the gorge.'

Quintatus considered the idea and shook his head. 'The artillery is at the back of the baggage train, miles away. We couldn't get it up here before the end of the day. We can't afford to waste time. I want that gorge dealt with at once. That's your job, Prefect Cato. You are in command of the vanguard. Your men are supposed to clear the way ahead for the rest of the army. See to it, at once.'

For a moment Cato was still, but inside his mind was seething with objections to the legate's words. There was no contradicting a direct order, however, and he bowed his head in acknowledgement before turning away and striding back down towards the legionaries, who had re-formed a hundred paces away from the barricade.

'Officers! On me!'

By the time the last of them had joined the small gathering grouped around Cato, he had already formed a plan in his mind. It was simple enough, since there was no alternative, and dangerous for precisely the same reason. He did not like the thought of losing any more of his men. He looked round at his subordinates and noted their grim expressions as the rain streaked down the polished metal of their helmets and dripped on to their shoulders and chests. They were good soldiers and too valuable to be wasted on another futile attempt to rush the barricade, he decided. He cleared his throat and spat to one side.

'The legate wants us to kick the enemy out of the gorge without any more delay. I know that means braving those bastards on top of the crags again, and we're likely to lose many more men before we can get over the barricade and tear into the enemy. Until we can force the barricade, we'll be sitting ducks. Our best bet is to soften 'em up with javelins before forming the leading centuries into testudos as they enter the gorge.'

'Testudos?' Centurion Festinus scratched his nose. 'Begging your pardon, sir, but that's no bloody good. The men's shields aren't going to keep those rocks out. They'll be knocking us down like skittles.'

'Perhaps, but we'll stand a better chance than if we go into the attack with nothing over our heads,' Cato responded. 'But let's do this by the manual. Centurion Festinus, I want you to form the First Century into a skirmish line. The Second is to take all available javelins and feed them forward. Have the men throw them in volleys, and take as much time as you can in expending them.'

'Sir? I thought we were supposed to do this quickly.'

'As quickly as we can, but with as few casualties as possible. That's the way I want it, Centurion. So you take your time with the javelins, and then the same again with forming the testudos and going into the attack. With luck, that should draw the enemy's attention, as well as buying enough time for some of the Blood Crows to scale the crags and deal with the men above the gorge.' Cato turned to the auxiliary officers. 'Harpex, your squadron is going to climb the left side of the valley. Corvinus, your lads are going to the right, with me. Tell your men to leave their spears. They'll need to sling their shields for the climb and use swords when we reach the top. Once you see us there, Festinus, you can begin the attack. By the time the first testudo reaches the barricade, I hope we'll be giving the enemy a taste of their own medicine. See how they like rocks raining down on their bloody heads!'

The others growled with satisfaction at the idea. All except Harpex, who was staring up at the crags. 'Going to be quite a climb, sir. At least two hundred feet.'

'More than that, I think,' Cato replied. 'Be a good chance for them to stop standing around and getting cold in this rain. A little exercise will soon warm them up. All right, gentlemen. We know what we've got to do. Let's make this work and let's do it well. The legate's watching us and the rest of the army is depending on us, and we're not going to let them down. Brief your men and get them into position as soon as you can.'

He exchanged a salute with his officers before they turned to stride back to their units. Then he looked up at the crags again and swallowed nervously. They rose from the valley floor like giant decayed teeth. More like three hundred feet than two, he decided. Every inch of the way the rain would make the going slippery and perilous. And when they reached the top, exhausted by the climb, the enemy would be waiting for them, determined to hold the crags and send their bodies hurtling through the rain down on to the heads of their legionary comrades far below.

Cato felt his guts tighten as he tore his gaze away from the ominous towering masses of rock and strode over towards the auxiliary infantry filing out to each side of the valley. Before the day was out, he would have won the gorge for the army, or his shattered body would be lying with hundreds more of his comrades sprawled across the ground in front of the barricade and the triumphant faces of the enemy beyond.

CHAPTER ELEVEN

'First Century! Halt!' Festinus shouted. The rain had eased to a slight drizzle, and patches of blue sky were starting to appear. Small comfort to the drenched men standing up to their ankles in the churned muddy ground in front of the gorge. The legionaries, formed in a single line, stopped some thirty paces from the barricade, shields to the front as they grasped their javelins in their right hands. The auxiliaries were positioned on the flanks of the line, and from the right, Cato could see that the enemy was watching the fresh Roman advance warily. As the line halted, so their jeering died away as they waited to see what would happen.

'Ready javelins!'

The legionaries adjusted their grip and drew their throwing arms back. At once, a warning was shouted by one of the warriors, and the cry was quickly repeated as they ducked down behind the rim of the barricade. Cato saw something splash into the mud a short distance in front of the legionaries, then again, and realised that the warriors on top of the crags were trying the range with smaller rocks.

Festinus glanced along the line to ensure that every man

of the First Century was ready, then bellowed, 'Loose javelins!'

The dark shafts rippled into the air as the men grunted from the effort of throwing the heavy missiles. The first volley reached the top of the arc, most of them plunging down on the far side of the barricade. A handful fell short, clattering off the boulders and rocks sheltering the enemy. Cato heard the sound of the impacts: the splintering rattle of iron heads striking shields and the dull thud as flesh was pierced. Festinus, according to his orders to slow the pace of the attack, waited several heartbeats before issuing the follow-up order.

'Pass javelins to the front!'

The men of the Second Century handed their comrades fresh weapons from the bundles that each man carried. Once the legionaries were ready, Festinus gave the order to prepare the second volley. Once again, those warriors brave enough to show their faces at the barricade dropped out of sight. Cato turned to Corvinus and the twenty Blood Crows of his squadron and waved them forward.

'Now's our time, lads. Follow me!'

He set off at a trot towards the scree slope stretching up the side of the valley. On the other flank, Harpex had been watching his commander lead his men forward and now did the same with his squadron, making for the base of the crags to the left of the gorge. As they reached the loose stones, Festinus gave the order for the second volley to be loosed, and a moment later another chorus of impacts echoed off the sides of the gorge.

Cato began to climb, testing his grip on the slippery shifting stones as he hurried on as swiftly as he could. Behind him the auxiliaries scrabbled and cursed with laboured breath. As he reached more stable ground at the top of the scree, he paused and looked up at the jumble of rocks and stunted trees that lay ahead of them. It was going to be a difficult climb up the narrow angle between the crags and the rock-strewn side of the valley, he decided, just as Festinus gave the order to loose another volley. Soon the javelins would run out and the legionaries would have to form testudos to make their attack, and run the gauntlet of plummeting rocks. There was no time to waste. Cato pointed up the steep angle. 'This way!'

He was quickly forced to go down on his hands and knees as he struggled up the slope, clutching at rocks and scrabbling for toeholds as he heaved himself up. The weight of his armour and the shield hanging from a strap across his shoulder quickly made exhausting work of it, and the cold and wet of earlier was soon not even a memory as sweat poured from his brow and his heart pounded against his ribs.

The Blood Crows had made it halfway to the top of the crags when Cato heard the order to form testudos.

'Shit . . .' he muttered. Festinus and the leading three centuries of his cohort were about to advance into the gorge, beneath the cliffs from where the enemy would batter them to pieces well before they could reach the barricade and engage the Deceanglian warriors. Cato renewed his efforts, snatching at handholds ahead of him and hauling himself up. Ahead he could see a narrow ledge, and a short distance beyond that what looked like the top of the crags, outlined against the clearing sky. He barely noticed that the rain had finally stopped and that the water on the surface of the rocks was gleaming in the first rays of the sun.

When he reached the ledge, he slumped down on his haunches, gasping for breath. As he waited for the others to join him, he looked down on the foreshortened ranks of the legionaries and saw the last men joining the testudo formations. There was little sense of rush about them, and a moment later Cato saw the legate ride forward and start gesticulating forcefully at Centurion Festinus. The latter saluted and turned to shout an order, and the three centuries began to tramp forward, the formations looking like scaled beetles as they edged into the gorge.

The first ten of Cato's men had joined him on the ledge, red-faced and gasping. There was no time to rest them. 'Come on, lads. One last effort and we're at the top. Then we'll cut those bastards down before they can do any more harm.'

He did not wait for a response but rose to his feet and reached for the next handhold. Thanks to the breadth of the ledge, the others could scale the rocks on either side, and they would reach the top in a wave, rather than singly, he realised with relief. Then there was a cracking noise, and a sudden rush of loose earth, and he turned to see one of his men clinging on desperately with one hand while the rock he had dislodged slid on to the ledge, its momentum carrying it further and over the edge. An instant later there was a sharp cry of alarm, cut off, and then a wild cry as one of the Blood Crows was struck and fell away from the cliff, tumbling thirty feet or so through the air before his head smashed into a boulder and his cries were silenced. But even then, their echoes sounded clearly off the sides of the gorge.

'Keep moving!' Cato called out to his companions as loudly as he dared, fearful that the man's fall had attracted the attention of the enemy above them. The Blood Crows realised the danger well enough and struggled up frantically. Cato saw that he was no more than ten feet from the top and felt the lightness of relief fill his guts. Then a flicker of movement in the corner of his eye drew his attention, and he turned and spotted a fur-clad figure staring down at them, fifty feet away along the crag. The warrior thrust out his arm, at the same time crying out in alarm.

'They're on to us!' one of the auxiliaries called, and the Blood Crows hesitated.

'Keep going!' Cato bellowed, all sense of discretion gone now that they had been spotted. 'Get up! Get up!'

They climbed on desperately as the enemy warrior sprinted across the uneven ground, leaping between the boulders as he drew his sword and charged towards the Romans. He reached the first of the auxiliaries as the Thracian was pulling himself on to the top of the crags. Too late he saw the danger and threw his arm up in an effort to protect himself from the blow. The swordsman's weapon flashed in the sunlight and there was a deep grunt as the heavy blade cut through flesh, shattered bone and all but severed the limb before the edge bit into the auxiliary's shoulder, driving the breath from his body, blood spraying from the stump just below his elbow. Beyond the fallen soldier his comrades were scrambling on to the crags, unslipping their shields and drawing their swords before the enemy warrior could turn on them.

Looking beyond the tribesman, Cato took in the wider scene. There were perhaps twenty more warriors fifty paces away, lining the edge of the crag, heavy rocks in their hands as they prepared to hurl them down on to the approaching legionaries. So far it seemed they had not paid the swordsman's warning cries any attention. But now he cupped a hand to his mouth and shouted to them as loudly as he could. The nearest men turned to look over their shoulders, then, seeing the handful of Romans, abruptly dropped their missiles and began to rush across the rocky terrain to confront the threat to their position. Emboldened by his approaching comrades, the first man buried the point of his sword in the back of his victim's neck before wrenching it free and charging towards the next auxiliary. There were already five men on the crags with Cato, and they braced themselves to deal with the warrior as the prefect glanced back down the side of the cliff to where the rest of his men were still climbing.

'Get up here! Fast as you fucking can!'

Then he turned to join the others as the warrior leapt at them, swinging his sword in a vicious wide arc at the first auxiliary in his path. Despite the strain of the long climb, the man brought his shield up and punched out to deflect the blow, then stepped into his enemy's reach to deliver a brutal thrust of his sword. The tribesman doubled over as the impact drove him off his feet. The point of the blade burst through the fur cloak on his back, having cut through his spine, and his legs buckled, dragging the sword down with him. The auxiliary kicked him to the rocky surface and braced his foot against the man's sternum as he wrenched the bloodied blade free.

'Good work!' Cato slapped the auxiliary on the shoulder, then drew his own sword and readied his shield as his men fell in on either side. Behind him he could hear the grunts and curses of the other Blood Crows as they reached the top and struggled to their feet before joining their comrades facing the enemy. As one of the auxiliaries made to advance across the crags, Cato called out, 'Hold your position! Wait until the others catch up.'

By the time the last of the squadron had reached the top, the first of the enemy had stopped only a spear's length away, expression wild as he weighed up the Thracians, sword in one hand, a small shield barely bigger than a buckler in the other. As his companions began to join him, equally determined-looking, he fixed his gaze on Cato and screamed a war cry, mouth agape, lips stretched back and teeth bared, then charged. Cato just had time to thrust his shield out to absorb the warrior's first blow. It caught the edge of the oval shield, forcing it round in Cato's grip so that his chest was exposed as the man followed up with a savage punch of his own shield. Cato caught it on the guard of his sword, and then pressed on with a weak thrust that delivered no more than a bruising impact to his opponent's chain-mail vest. But it was enough to send the man reeling back a pace before they both recovered their fighting stances and faced off again. Cato was dimly aware of the struggles on either side as his men and the enemy joined the contest for possession of the crags. The scrape and clatter of blades and the crash of blows landed on shields mingled with the grunts and curses of the combatants.

The man facing Cato lowered himself into a crouch, watching intently as he waited for his opponent to make a move. The prefect smiled grimly, recognising that the initiative had passed to him, then stepped forward quickly, leading with his left boot and pushing his shield forward, forcing his enemy to strike out with his sword in order to stand his ground. Cato let his shield absorb the blow before he struck back. Up came the blade, knocking the short sword aside. As the man's arm swung out after the sword, Cato rushed forward into his body. At the last moment, he lowered the brim of his helmet and savagely butted the reinforced brow guard into the warrior's face. The blow was hard and jarred Cato's neck, but the unexpected attack did its job and the man staggered back, dazed. Too dazed to save himself as Cato stabbed his sword up into the tribesman's throat and ripped it free in a welter of blood. The warrior dropped his sword and clasped his hand to his throat as he slumped to his knees, gurgling horribly.

Cato swept past him and looked for another foe. About him the men of both sides were mostly locked in one-to-one duels. Here and there the odds were less even, and some took advantage of the chaos to strike at the enemy's back when they caught a man facing the other way. There was none of the etiquette of the arena: just kill or be killed. Cato caught the gaze of a tall, darkly featured warrior whose hair had been tied back by a leather thong. He carried a long-handled axe in both hands and swung it in an arc as he glared at Cato. His muscled arms strained as the axe flew faster and faster, then he launched himself at the prefect with a loud shout ripping from his lungs.

Cato had seen how much damage such an axe could do, and crouched as he threw his shield up to block the blow. An instant later the top of the shield exploded in a welter of splinters, shattered bronze trim and strips of leather. The impact tore at his grip, but his fist was tightly clenched and he held on. Then the axe head whirled away, and he seized his chance, thrusting his sword into his opponent's thigh, then hacking down at the soft leather and straps of his boot, shattering the bones there. The warrior let out a cry of agony and rage as he staggered backwards. His weapon had lost its momentum and he could only swing it weakly this time, so that Cato's shield easily absorbed the blow. He punched forward, driving the man on to his wounded foot. There was a gasp and a pained groan, and the warrior fell on to his back, the axe slipping from his fingers and clattering to the rocks.

Cato kept his damaged shield and sword up as he glanced round. The Blood Crows were more than holding their own: only three men were down, as against several more of the enemy. Beyond, on the crags on the far side of the gorge, he could see the other group of warriors starting to hurl their first rocks down on the leading testudo. He hissed a curse. Where the hell were Harpex and his men?

He spotted an older, thickset man in a helmet shouting orders and encouragement to his comrades. The enemy leader pushed his way to the front and raised his sword to strike at the auxiliary in front of him. The soldier instinctively raised his shield, and the tribesman grinned ferociously as he grasped the rim with his spare hand and wrenched it aside before striking down with his sword. The heavy blade shattered the Thracian's bronze helmet and smashed through his skull right down to his jaw. The tribesman wrenched the blade free, then kicked the body away, roaring a triumphant battle cry and shaking his bloodied sword high where his followers could see it.

Swallowing his fear, Cato stepped forward and spoke calmly and loudly enough for his men to hear. 'You are nothing but a fat pile of shit, old man, and I am going to cut you down. I am Prefect Quintus Licinius Cato, of the Blood

Crows.' He repeated the name of the cohort again in the fragments of the Silurian dialect he had picked up from the native traders who had come to the fort. He felt a flicker of satisfaction as he saw the man's eyes widen briefly at the name of the unit whose bloody raids deep into enemy territory had earned them a fearsome reputation amongst the mountain tribes to the south.

It took a moment for the tribesman to recover his poise, and he snarled back at Cato, the contempt behind his words clear to the Roman soldiers. His comrades cheered him even as some of them continued exchanging blows with the Thracians. By unspoken consent, a space opened out around the two leaders, and they warily approached to within striking distance and weighed each other up. Cato saw that his foe was past the prime of life but that there was plenty of muscle there, along with the evidence of good living. Blue tattooed patterns swirled down each bare arm, and stretches of white scar tissue spoke of the many battles he had fought.

Cato advanced his shield, looking over the splintered ruin at the top, and raised his sword to chin height, aiming the point directly at the man's face. It was as much a gesture of defiance as a threat, and the veteran warrior's lip curled in disdain as he raised his longsword and gave the shield a hard poke. At once Cato pressed forward, battering at the sword with his shield and trying to get inside the man's reach to stab him with his shorter weapon. But the tribesman was more agile than he appeared and kept his distance, even opening it enough after three paces to turn the attack back on Cato, hacking viciously at the splintered top of the shield so that Cato had little chance to strike back as he struggled to block the attacks. Each blow carved a fresh chunk out of the oval shield, and opened a split that weakened it further. At the same time, the prefect concentrated on working his opponent round so that his back was towards the cliff and he would have nowhere to retreat when Cato made his next rush forward.

The warrior paused to breathe, his chest heaving with exertion as he kept his eyes fixed on Cato and his sword moving slowly from side to side. A sudden break in the clouds bathed the valley in bright sunshine, and the man blinked at the glare. Cato rushed forward, this time alternating between shield and sword as he smashed aside each attempt to block his attacks. His opponent's concentration was so fixed on fending off the blows that he did not realise until the last moment that he had been driven back to the edge of the crags. One of his men shouted a warning and the leader snatched a backward glance, then Cato struck, thrusting forward behind his shield, driving it into the warrior's body and knocking him off balance. As his heel slipped over the edge, the tribesman dropped his sword, snatched at the sides of Cato's shield and pulled with all his might. Cato, caught off guard, felt himself lurch forward, but released his hold on the shield's handle and pushed himself back just in time. The shield fell away and the man toppled back with a desperate cry that was snatched away as he bounced off a protruding rock and cartwheeled to the foot of the cliff in silence, like a child's corn doll.

His followers froze in shock. Before they could recover their resolve, Cato called out to his men. 'Disengage! Now!'

The Blood Crows drew back cautiously, and Cato turned to the enemy and addressed them with authority. 'Drop your weapons! Do it!' He pointed to his own sword and stabbed a finger at the ground. 'Now.'

There were at least ten still standing, and at first none of them moved, although Cato could see that they were unsure and afraid. He sheathed his blade and approached the nearest of them, a youth holding a wavering spear in both hands. He slowly walked round the point and took the shaft away from the boy.

'Sit.'

The native nodded and dropped to the ground swiftly. There was a brief pause before the others did the same, setting their weapons down in front of them. Cato turned to Corvinus. 'Leave five of your men to gather up their weapons and throw them over the cliff before they stand guard on the prisoners. If there's any trouble, they're to send 'em the same way as their leader.'

'Yes, sir.'

Leaving Corvinus to assign the guards, Cato led the others across to the edge of the cliff overlooking the gorge. As they picked their way over the uneven surface, a cry of alarm sounded from the crags opposite, and Cato saw that Harpex and his men had reached the top and were fanning out to form a skirmish line to take on the other party of enemy warriors. There was nothing he could do to help, so he made his way to the edge, where small piles of unused rocks remained. He peered over and saw that the first testudo was breaking up as it reached the barricade, the men starting to climb it to get at the defenders. Several more legionaries had been struck down before Cato's intervention had stopped the bombardment of his men. The second testudo was passing just beneath him, as yet unaware that the crags had been seized by the Blood Crows.

Cato had a clear view of the defenders behind the barricade and saw that there were more of them than he had thought: as many as four hundred warriors, closed up and ready to defend the gorge. In amongst them he picked out some figures in dark robes and cloaks, waving their arms, shouting encouragement at their men and hurling curses at the Romans. Druids, he realised. The enemy would be sure to put up a good fight and hold the line for a while yet.

Then he smiled to himself and turned quickly to the men who had followed him to the cliff's edge. 'Sheathe your swords and down shields!' Once they had done as he had ordered, he pointed to the rocks. 'Let's pay those bastards back in kind. Help yourselves, lads.'

He picked up a rock half the size of a melon and carried it along the crag until he was past the barricade, then heaved it over the edge. He watched it tumble through the air, shrinking to a dot, then saw it glance off a shield and strike the ground. He growled with frustration and turned back to fetch another rock as the Thracians began to throw their missiles down on the enemy, letting out shouts of glee or disappointment as they struck down the natives or missed. Cato's next rock was aimed, as best he could, at the place where the enemy ranks were most tightly packed, and this time he was rewarded with a strike squarely on the top of a warrior's head. The man went down as though he had been hammered into the ground. Some of those around him looked up, their faces white specks surrounded by dark hair. As soon as they saw the auxiliaries far above, they began to point and shout warnings to their comrades. More were crushed under falling rocks, and soon the tribesmen were swirling around as they tried to dodge the bombardment, their attention drawn away from the struggle along the barricade.

Cato saw one of the Druids rush forward, thrusting his fighters towards the attacking legionaries. He had rallied several of the men before he too was struck down, his skull crushed and his body laid out, arms and legs splayed below the bloody ruin that had been his head. The sight of the dead Druid badly unnerved the tribesmen, who began to break ranks and retreat down the gorge to the open ground beyond, where they would be safe from the falling rocks. The panic was infectious, and soon only a handful of defenders remained, desperately fighting an uneven battle along the length of the barricade. Outnumbered and out-fought by soldiers who had been trained and equipped to fight as effectively as any man in the known world, the tribesmen began to give ground, forced away from the barricade as the first of the Romans climbed over and pressed forward.

Turning to his men, Cato called out, 'That's enough, lads! Put those rocks down before you do any mischief to the legionaries.'

Having been delighted at the chance to turn the tables on their enemy, the Thracians reluctantly set the rocks aside and watched as the men of the First Century created a gap in the barricade wide enough for men to stream through and join the fight. The result was no longer in doubt, and a short time later, a native horn blasted three times. At once the remaining fighters broke away from the legionaries and ran back to join their comrades beyond the gorge. One of the surviving Druids pointed towards the side of the valley, and the Deceanglians began to stream up the slope. Seeing their retreat, Cato hurried back to the crags overlooking the Roman column and cupped his hands to his mouth.

'Miro! Decurion Miro!'

The men of the rearguard looked up towards him, and a cheer rose from their throats at the sight of the prefect who had taken the enemy's position. Cato spotted the legate and his staff, and then picked out Miro close to the leading squadron of Thracian horsemen.

'Miro! Mount the men and start the pursuit! Ride 'em down before they can get away.'

If the decurion acknowledged the order, Cato never heard him, but a moment later he was relieved to see Miro vault into his saddle and lead the Blood Crows into the gorge at a trot. They passed through the barricade and fanned out on the far side, their longer cavalry swords drawn, ready to cut down any of the enemy they encountered. Those who had been injured and were slowly making their way to safety were the first to be dispatched without mercy. The rest had started up the slope, and now Cato could readily understand why their leaders had picked such difficult ground over which to make their escape. The inclination of the valley side and the runs of scree made it impossible for mounted men to follow them, and he realised that there would be no effective pursuit of the fleeing tribesmen. It was bitterly frustrating, but he reminded himself that at least the path before the advancing army had been cleared and the column could continue on its way. Or at least it might have done had it been earlier in the day. Looking up at the low angle of the sun, Cato saw that it was a scant few hours before dusk. Quintatus would have to give the order to halt the army soon to allow the men time to construct their marching camp.

The enemy had achieved their goal, Cato mused as he watched them make their escape. It had been a classic delaying action. They had held up the Roman advance for half a day and inflicted a number of casualties. More importantly, they had bought themselves time for whatever plans they had to counter the advance. He felt an icy tingle in the back of his neck at the possibility that the Druids and their Deceanglian allies were plotting something and Quintatus was unwittingly playing into their hands. Then he smiled bitterly at himself. Of course they would try to delay the Romans. This was their land, their home, and for the Druids, Mona was their most sacred soil. They would take every chance to keep the Romans from it. There would be more attempts to delay them long enough for the onset of winter to force Quintatus to withdraw from the mountains. It would be a hard-fought campaign, Cato knew. Contested every step of the way. This afternoon's brutal action was only the first taste of what was to come.

The warmth of the late-afternoon sunlight was causing vapour to rise from the tunics of those around him so that they seemed to be smouldering. As they noticed it, the soldiers began laughing at each other, as men will gladly seize on anything light-spirited after a desperate action against the enemy. Despite his sombre mood, Cato indulged them. Once again the Blood Crows had proved themselves, and they deserved the brief moment of respite.

CHAPTER TWELVE

'Hey, Optio!' one of the men called out. 'Since they're handing out promotions to the rank and file, do you think you could put in a word for me? I'm sick of staring at your horse's arse at the head of the line.'

The other men of the patrol laughed loudly, and Pandarus shifted in his saddle to look back down the narrow track.

'Diomedes, if they ever promote you, then the rest of the rankers will be hard pressed to tell you from the back end of your horse. The army could not afford such confusion.'

The men laughed again, this time at their comrade's expense, and after the briefest of delays, Diomedes joined in, anxious to be seen to take it as well as he dished it out.

It had been a month since Optio Pandarus had been elevated to his new rank, and yet he was still being ribbed by his comrades. And mightily wearing it was becoming too, he mused with a flick of the reins. He was leading the patrol along the forest track that angled up the side of the valley towards a prominent ridge. In the last few days the sky had been mostly clear. But the change in weather had been accompanied by a sharp drop in temperature, and the morning frosts had been bitter indeed. It was close to noon, yet the sun was still low in the sky and gave off little warmth.

The clouds and mists had dissipated, and Pandarus hoped to gain a clear view over the surrounding landscape from the top of the ridge. It would be good to have something of note to report back to the centurion when the patrol returned to the fort at the end of the day – rather than the usual run of fleeing shepherd boys and abandoned villages that had greeted their approach. Occasionally they had seen women and children disappearing into the forests, but there had been no sign of any men. And that was concerning Pandarus and the fort's commander, since it implied only one thing: that the men had gone off to fight somewhere. Perhaps against rival tribes, or, more worrying, they might be gathering to cause grief to the nearest Roman outposts.

Still, he reflected, there had been no sign of any problems yet, and no attempt to make trouble for the garrison at the fort. Which was just as well given the poor state of the Illyrian auxiliaries sent to replace the Blood Crows and the cohort from the Fourteenth Legion. Although they had been drilled hard over recent days, they would only be able to mount a token resistance against a determined enemy attack. Pandarus wondered if they were typical of the reserve formations called forward to garrison the frontier forts stripped of good fighting men to fill out the ranks of the army advancing deep into the mountains. If that was the case, then the first line of defence of the new province was very delicate indeed.

Despite his lowly rank, Pandarus had a sound grasp of the perennial problem afflicting every Roman commander since the invasion of Britannia had begun. Namely that in order to claim new territory, or to meet a threat, it was necessary to concentrate all available forces, but to maintain control over territory it was necessary to disperse forces. Either way, the initiative passed to the enemy, who could harass the frontier defences and then retreat into the mountains at the first sign of a larger Roman force, only to emerge again and continue their harassment once the danger had passed. It was the kind of warfare that the Deceanglians and their allies excelled at, resulting in the long years of attrition as the frontier rippled forward and ebbed back. The tribes' only weakness lay in the occasional desire of their leaders to quench their thirst for glory by meeting the Romans in battle. It had been the undoing of Caratacus, and in time it would be the same for those that succeeded him. At least that was what the Roman high command was depending on, thought Pandarus.

'We should be heading back to the fort,' said Diomedes, breaking into his train of thought. 'At this rate it'll be dark before we do.'

'Scared of the dark, are we?' another rider chuckled. 'Perhaps you joined the wrong cohort, Diomedes. You sound more like one of them Illyrians than a Blood Crow.'

Pandarus looked back over his shoulder and saw Diomedes rein in and drop back alongside his comrade with an angry expression.

'You can fuck right off with that notion, mate. Call me one of those good-for-nothing bastards again and I'll take your bloody head off.'

The man raised a hand and leaned away from Diomedes. 'Easy there! I just said you *sounded* like one of 'em.'

'That's enough!' Pandarus snapped. 'Get moving, Diomedes. We'll turn back to the fort when I say. Not before. Now, all of you, keep your mouths shut and your eyes and ears open. This is the enemy's turf, and it's better that we see them before they see us.'

The men fell silent and the patrol continued up the track. They were passing through a belt of pine trees beneath which dark shadows crowded in on either side, and Pandarus felt a light chill at the base of his neck. He could understand the men's nervous chatter, their need for relief from the wearisome tension that came with every patrol into the enemy's lands. The bitterness of the conflict between Rome and the mountain tribes meant there were few illusions about the fate of any Roman unfortunate enough to be captured. The Celts had a fondness for decorating their huts with the heads of their enemies.

The horses' hooves padded softly over the bed of needles lying over the track. The only other sounds were the faint rustle of the breeze blowing through the tops of the trees close to the ridge, and the cawing of crows wheeling like flecks of soot high above the rocky crest of the mountain. Soon the track widened and passed out of the trees, and Pandarus saw the crest of the ridge no more than a quarter of a mile away. He felt relieved to be back in the open and decided that they would quickly survey the valley on the far side before turning back to the safety of the fort. As they approached the crest, he slowed his mount and halted the patrol. Then he swung his leg over the saddle horn and dropped to the ground. He gently patted his horse's flank to steady the animal.

'Dismount,' he ordered, then held his reins out to Diomedes. 'Keep nice and quiet while I'm gone, eh? Same goes for the rest of you.'

Diomedes bowed his head in mock respect. 'Whatever the optio commands.'

'That's right, Trooper. Don't you forget it.'

Pandarus thought about taking his shield and spear, but dismissed the idea. It was his role to observe, not to get involved in a fight. He patted the sword at his side, out of a sense of superstitious habit, and strode up the short stretch of track to the crest. The wind picked up sharply as it gusted over the ridge, which was bare of anything but rocks and tussocks of grass, and Pandarus shivered as he hunched his neck down into the folds of his cloak. He had grown up in the mountains of Thrace and was well used to the bitter weather that winter brought to such a landscape. Only the most hardy beasts ventured abroad, while the people huddled in their smoky huts and sat out the worst of the snow, ice and wind. It would be no different here in Britannia. Pandarus and the rest of the garrison would spend most of the winter in their barracks, when not on sentry or other duties. He offered a quick prayer to the gods on behalf of the rest of the cohort that Quintatus would crush the Deceanglians and the Druids swiftly and be back behind the ramparts of Viroconium before the first snow fell.

He was breathing more deeply as he reached the crest, and the steam from his breath was torn away in faint shreds as he gazed down into the valley adjacent to the one the patrol had been assigned to explore. The heavily forested hillside dropped away sharply before levelling out far below. At once his eyes were drawn to a large expanse of cleared and cultivated land. In the middle of it lay a modest ditch and palisade enclosing several large huts and small livestock pens. Thin trails of smoke issued from the huts, but there was little sign of movement: just a solitary woman splitting logs. All the same, Pandarus hurried a short distance down the slope so that he would not stand out against the skyline should anyone down in the valley happen to look in his direction. He found a cluster of bare rocks and settled there to shelter from the wind as he continued his observation. At length he spotted a small group of figures, children as far as he could make out, laden with more fuel for the village's fires. But there was no sign of any men.

He raised his hands and blew some hot breath into them before rubbing them together vigorously. There was little to report here. The village posed no threat and might yield a few slaves if Centurion Macro could be persuaded to authorise a raid. As the acting commanding officer of the garrison, Macro stood to gain the lion's share of the value of any captives, and Pandarus would come out of it with a handsome sum to add to his savings. Enough maybe to set aside a decent amount for the funeral club, so that he would have a tombstone worthy of him rather than the usual plain affair, cheaply inscribed, that was all most common soldiers could afford to mark their lives.

The optio watched long enough to conclude that the native village was defended by women and children only, and presented an easy target. He was about to emerge from the rocks and return to his men when he caught sight of movement at the edge of the forest further down the valley. A solitary rider emerged into the open, cloaked and armoured, with feed nets strung behind his saddle. A shield hung across his back and he carried a spear in his right hand. There was no doubting that this was one of their warrior caste. Within moments, another rider emerged from the trees, then more, forming a column that extended out of the forest like the head of a vast snake. At first Pandarus thought it might be a hunting party, returning to the village, but they kept coming, hundreds of them. This was no small band of warriors, he realised with a growing chill tingling at the back of his neck.

The last of the horsemen cleared the forest, and now came the head of a column of infantry, wrapped in furs and carrying an assortment of shields, spears, swords and axes. Some appeared to be wearing armour, helmets and greaves looted from Roman patrols they had ambushed and cut down. Pandarus watched as the enemy column extended along the floor of the valley. There was no mistaking that he was looking at a powerful force marching north towards the line of advance taken by Legate Quintatus. He grasped the significance of the enemy's direction at once, and knew he must return to the fort to make his report without further delay.

He was about to rise to his feet when he heard the snort of a horse close at hand, and froze. At once he reached for the handle of his sword, and drew a sharp breath as he peered cautiously around the boulder that was sheltering him from the wind. A horseman was approaching. A bearded warrior wrapped in furs. His mount was one of the small, stocky breeds favoured by the mountain tribes, and it whinnied as the rider urged it along the slope. Pandarus shifted back into cover, furious with himself for having waited too long before returning to the patrol. He should have anticipated that the enemy would be deploying scouts too, especially if they were concerned to close up on the Roman army unawares.

He considered whether it would be best to try and let the

man pass by and then slip back to the others, then realised that if the enemy scout chose to ride along the crest, he would be sure to spot the waiting auxiliaries and raise the alarm. With their superior knowledge of the terrain and horses better suited to negotiating it, the enemy stood a good chance of running the patrol down. He had no choice. The scout had to be dealt with. And it would be better to take him alive, if possible, to gain intelligence of the enemy's precise intentions.

Pandarus released his grip on the handle of the sword and reached into his side bag for the iron knuckle guard he had bought back in Londinium to give him the edge in the drunken scrimmages that had frequently broken out between off-duty men of rival units. He slipped his fingers into the grip and clenched his fist. The rider was passing the rocks, the soft thump of hooves filling Pandarus's ears. He caught the tang of horse sweat and the more acrid odour of the enemy warrior. The muzzle, head and flank of the animal loomed close by, and he braced his feet, ready to spring forward. His boots ground against the scree, and the horse shimmied as the rider glanced to the side, his jaw dropping in surprise.

Pandarus exploded from behind the boulder and hurled himself at the rider, grabbing him by the arm and wrenching him sideways from his saddle. The warrior just had time to let out a thin cry before the optio smashed his knuckle guard against the side of his head. The blow glanced off at an angle, ripping through the man's scalp. Then they tumbled together on to the slope as the horse bucked and lurched away. Pandarus strained to keep his grip on the warrior's sword arm, slamming his other hand down to steady himself so that he could get purchase with his boots. The tribesman swiftly recovered from his surprise and now lashed out wildly with his spare hand and his feet, kicking at Pandarus's body. Blood flowed freely from the tear in his scalp, and flicked into the optio's face as they fought.

The warrior's free hand came up, fingers stretched out as he clawed at Pandarus's throat. Pain exploded in the optio's neck, and he clamped down with his chin to stop the man throttling him. Swinging his arm back, he bunched his muscles and slammed the knuckle guard into his foe's gut, driving the air from his lungs. Hot breath flushed across his face. For an instant, the grip on his throat slackened, and he jerked back, opening a small gap between their bodies. He struck again, directly at the man's face, and the iron guard tore at his broad nose and crushed the bone beneath. The warrior's eyes widened in agony and rage, and his yellowed teeth bared in a wild snarl as blood coursed from his nostrils. Pandarus drew his fist back and threw all his weight into the next blow, striking directly at the temple. He connected squarely, and the warrior's head snapped to the side, limbs spasming, before his body went limp and slumped into the tussocks of grass on the slope of the hill.

Pandarus crouched over him, fist raised, then saw that his foe was out cold and eased himself back on his heels, breathing hard. Once he had caught his breath, he stood and slipped the bloodied knuckle guard from his trembling hand and returned it to his side bag. The warrior's horse stood a short distance away, eyeing him warily, its ears twitching.

'Easy there, boy.' Pandarus spoke softly, edging slowly towards the beast. He took the reins and stroked the horse's cheek until the animal had calmed sufficiently to be led back to its fallen rider. Then, cutting strips from the man's woven tunic, Pandarus bound his hands and feet, before gagging him and lifting him across the saddle. Satisfied that his prisoner was secure and would not fall off, he took a last glance at the native army snaking across the floor of the valley. He made a quick estimate of their strength and then turned to lead the horse towards the crest of the ridge and his men waiting for him on the far side.

CHAPTER THIRTEEN

'Out of bounds!' Macro shouted from the reviewing mound looking over the drill ground outside the fort. In front of him, an area had been marked out for a Harpastum pitch, with posts at each corner and a shallow chalk-filled ditch marking the halfway line. He had decided to introduce the sport into the training for the Illyrians to toughen them up and get them acting more closely with their comrades. Two sections of eight men were playing at a time, while the rest of the Illyrians and the civilians, who had been given permission to watch, stood on the sidelines and cheered or shouted ribald insults. The officers were included in the games, and Macro grinned openly as Centurion Fortunus picked himself up from the muddy surface and handed the feather-stuffed leather ball over to the opposing side.

Already the other players, in their mud-streaked tunics, were jostling for position around the man holding the ball, and he quickly hurled it towards a comrade who had broken free of the pack and now sprinted for the home side of the centre line, chased down by his opponents. He got within ten paces of the line before being tackled and pitching face first into the churned-up ground and slithering to a halt. At once the other players piled in, desperately struggling to wrestle the ball away.

Macro cupped a hand to his mouth. 'Get stuck in, Fortunus. Get on with it, man!'

The overweight officer hitched up his tunic belt and jogged towards the fray. The two teams fought for possession of the ball, and at length it slipped free and splashed into a puddle at Fortunus's feet. He was slow to react but managed to sweep it up and advance a few paces before he was flattened by one of the opposition. The spectators roared with delight as their commander went down and more men piled in, so covered in mud that it was hard to distinguish which side they were on, despite what was still visible of the red and blue strips of cloth tied around their right arms.

A well-built player with blond hair and beard wrenched the others aside and plunged into the scrimmage, ripping the ball free before making for the halfway line. The other teams threw themselves at him, but he thrust them aside with contemptuous ease, trampling down the last defender. With a triumphant shout he half ran and half slithered the remaining distance to the line marking the home territory and slammed the ball down to the ground before punching both fists into the air and bellowing his war cry. Fortunus and the rest of the team crowded around him to slap him on the back and share his triumph, while the other team looked on in dejection.

'The first section of Fortunus's century wins!' Macro announced. 'The game's over! Next two sections, on the pitch now!'

As the weary, filthy teams left the field and the new contestants took up their positions, Macro called Optio Diodorus over.

'Sir?'

'The big fellow. What's his name?'

Diodorus glanced at the tall figure still grinning as he celebrated with the rest of his section. 'That's Junius Lomus, sir. An excellent man.'

'I can see that. He's got good spirit. Of course, it helps that he's built like a brick shithouse.'

'Yes, sir.'

Macro considered Lomus for a moment. 'Doesn't look to me like he's from Illyrian stock.'

'He's not, sir. He was recruited here in Britannia. His father was a wine trader from Gaul and his mother is from the Cornovii.'

Macro nodded. 'That would explain it.'

Like many long-established auxiliary units, the Illyrian cohort had largely become Illyrian in name only, having accrued replacements from its various postings across the empire. Macro clicked his tongue. 'He's wasted on a second-rate unit like this. I'll see if he's interested in a transfer to the Blood Crows. Lomus is just the type to put the fear of the gods into the enemy. Have him come to see me after the first watch is sounded.'

Diodorus nodded.

Macro waited until the ball was placed to the rear of the team that had won the toss and elected to defend. Then the two sections lined up each side of the halfway line and waited for the signal to begin. The babble from the spectators quickly died away as Macro raised his vine cane. He waited until all was quiet and still, and then slashed the cane down to point towards the playing field. 'Begin!'

At once the attacking team raced forward. The defenders did their best to hold them back by barring the way and roughly shoving them. Inevitably, one of the attackers slipped through, and then both teams turned and rushed towards the ball as the excited spectators shouted their encouragement. The leading attacker grabbed the ball and turned back towards the far end of the pitch, sidestepping the first tackle before he was held by a second man. Then another went low, grabbing his leg and upending him with a vicious lift that sent the ball-carrier splashing into the mud on his back. Another scrimmage started as both sides charged in to fight for possession.

As the crowd cheered, Diodorus leaned towards Macro and pointed towards the nearest of the hills. 'Sir, up there!'

Macro squinted in the direction indicated and saw a small party of riders cantering down towards the fort. He felt a brief moment of anxiety before he picked out their red tunics.

'It's the patrol. They're in a bit of a hurry. Looks like Pandarus has something to report. I'll see to it. You take charge here. It'll be dusk soon. Better make this the last game for today.'

'Yes, sir.'

They exchanged a brief salute before Macro made his way down from the mound and set off towards the nearest gate of the fort. Behind him, a loud cheer went up as a player broke free of the ruck and gained several paces towards his home territory, before being caught and brought down by the other side. Macro glanced back, tempted to watch a little longer, then sighed and continued towards the gate.

Pandarus would make for headquarters as soon as he returned to the fort, since that was where the garrison commander was most likely to be. And if the optio had anything significant to report, it was Macro's duty to hear the news as soon as possible.

'I see you've brought home the catch of the day,' Macro said with a grin a short while later when he emerged from the headquarters building and saw the prisoner firmly in the grasp of Optio Pandarus and one of his men. The enemy warrior's blood had dried, leaving a thick dark crust across much of his face and matting his straggly hair. He glared at his captors and pressed his lips together as if to impress upon the Romans that he would say nothing in answer to their inevitable questions.

Macro indicated the tethering rail to one side of the courtyard. 'Tie him up over there while you make your report.'

The afternoon sun was low in the sky and the fort was bathed in the thin blue gloom of a winter dusk. The air was cold and a breeze moaned lightly over the ramparts and watchtowers. Looking up at the sky, Macro saw a thick band of clouds moving in from the west and wondered if that heralded the icy downpours that were common in Britannia at this time of year, or worse, the first fall of snow. Either would hamper the progress of Quintatus and his army away to the north. And no doubt the Druids would tell their followers that it was a sign that their gods were taking their side against the invader. The thought caused Macro to wonder briefly if there was some plane of existence where the rival deities struggled in parallel to those who worshipped them on a more earthly level. If that was so, he hoped that the gods of Rome had the upper hand. The Roman soldiers needed their help now more than ever.

He waited until Pandarus had carried out the order and posted his comrade to watch over the prisoner. Then, beckoning to the optio to follow him, he limped back into the main hall and eased himself down on a bench while Pandarus stood in front of him.

'So, what's the story? Where did you find our surly guest?'

Pandarus took an instant to gather his thoughts. 'Fifteen miles or so to the west, sir. I had gone ahead of the patrol to observe the lie of the land when I ran into the prisoner.'

'Ran into?' Macro arched an eyebrow. 'How many times?'

'You know what they're like. They take some persuading before they come along meekly.' Pandarus's expression became serious. 'It's what I saw before I took him down that's the reason I got back here as soon as I could, sir.'

'Go on.'

'The enemy's on the march. The man I captured was scouting for a column. Perhaps seven or eight hundred strong. They were heading north, sir.'

'North? Towards Quintatus, then.' Macro paused and rubbed the bristles on his chin. 'Still, not enough of them to pose much of a threat.'

'Assuming that's all there is of them. The track they were following looked pretty well used to me, sir. I doubt they were the only men to pass that way recently.'

Macro considered this and felt a prickle of anxiety at the prospect of a powerful force marching against Cato and his comrades as they advanced on the Druid stronghold of Mona. He took a sharp breath. 'Right. We need to find out exactly what the bastards are up to. Let's have a word with your prisoner.'

'I doubt he'll say much. Nothing we can understand, at least. Unless there's someone amongst the civilians who can speak his tongue.'

'I've got a better idea.' Macro smiled faintly. 'I know just the man we need. Get yourself down to the drill ground. There's a fellow in the Illyrian cohort. Tall, blond-haired and strong as a bull. Lomus. I want him here at once. Tell him that he's just been made acting interrogator.'

'Yes, sir.' Pandarus gave a curt nod and hurried away. Macro leaned forward and carefully rested his elbows on his knees. The enemy was clearly up to something. Though whether that constituted a palpable danger to the Roman army was uncertain. A few hundred more or less of the native warriors made little difference. But what if it was part of a wider plan? He strained his mind to try and divine the enemy's precise intentions, but he could not fathom their thinking and found himself wishing that Cato was here with him.

'The lad would be sure to hit on the answer soon enough,' he muttered to himself. Then, with a hiss of frustration, he rose from the bench and went outside to inspect the captive.

The light was failing and shadows filled the courtyard. One of the auxiliaries was lighting the first of the small braziers that provided a modicum of warmth to the men who would be on sentry duty during the night. Over by the hitching post, the prisoner was squatting, his back to the post, his hands tethered behind him. The man Pandarus had posted to watch over him quickly stood to attention at Macro's approach.

'Diomedes, isn't it?'

'Yes, sir.'

'How is our friend?'

'Apart from stinking the place out and being as cheerful as a tombstone, he's been a real delight, sir.'

Macro shot him a warning glance. 'Better leave the quips to your superiors, soldier. No one in the army likes a smart-arse.'

'Yes, sir.'

Macro stood over the warrior and tucked his thumbs into his belt as he inspected the man more closely. Aside from his injuries, the warrior looked to be in good shape. He wore a tunic, a mailed vest, breeches, and boots cut in a Roman style, no doubt looted from the same victim who had provided the armour vest. The centurion leaned over and took his chin roughly, forcing his head back. The man glared up at him as Macro noted the scars on his cheek and forehead.

'I can see you've been in a fight or two. And from what you're wearing, not all of the fights went badly. So, you're something of a veteran, then. Might even have fought alongside Caratacus in his time.'

At the mention of the defeated enemy leader, the warrior tore himself from Macro's grasp and lowered his head.

'Touchy, aren't we? You can try and play the silent hero if you like, my friend, but trust me, you won't hold out for ever, and you will tell me exactly what I want to know.' Macro prodded the prisoner with the toe of his boot to emphasise the point, and was about to turn away when the native kicked out his bound feet with all the strength he could muster. His boots caught the centurion hard on the shin and he stumbled back, arms flailing, before falling heavily on his backside, jarring his spine.

'Ha!' The prisoner spat and grinned wickedly. Diomedes cuffed him brutally on the side of his head, then hurried over to help his superior to his feet, but Macro scowled at him and thrust aside the soldier's hand, stifling a wince at the pain shooting through his injured leg.

'Very funny. I'd like to see you keep smiling when Lomus gets to work. Meanwhile, you can take this on account.' Without any warning, he balled his hands into tight fists and struck the man hard on both ears in succession, smashing his head from side to side.

The prisoner's eyes rolled up and he let out a deep groan before leaning forward and vomiting into his lap. The sharp stench wafted into Macro's nostrils, and he stepped back, rubbing his lower back. The prisoner heaved again, head hanging low, then coughed and spat before straightening up, easing himself against the tethering post. There was no fear in his eyes, Macro noted, just defiance, and the two men stared at each other until the sound of footsteps interrupted them. Macro turned to see Pandarus and Lomus approaching. The auxiliary's tunic was still streaked with filth, and his beard and hair were matted with mud. Combined with his large, powerful physique, the effect was unintentionally intimidating.

Lomus stood to attention a few paces away and saluted. 'You sent for me, sir.'

'Indeed. I have some work requiring rather specific skills.' Macro limped aside and nodded at the prisoner. 'Our chippy little friend here needs to be taught a lesson, as well as being persuaded to tell us what he knows of the enemy's plans. I want to know exactly where his column was headed and to what purpose. The Blood Crows' interrogator is unavailable, so I'm offering the job to you as you're just the man to put the frighteners on the prisoner. And, I'm told, you have some understanding of native dialects.'

'That's right, sir. My mother taught me.'

'Then it looks like I have chosen well. If you succeed in breaking the prisoner and getting the information I want, the post comes with excused–duties status at pay and a half.' Macro paused to let the terms of the offer sink in. 'Interested?'

Lomus glanced at the prisoner and slowly clenched his right fist, stroking it with the other hand. Then he nodded. 'I'll give it a go, sir.'

'Good man. If you do the job half as well as I hope, there may be a chance for you to become an interrogator on a permanent basis. And a transfer to a better unit, perhaps. The Blood Crows could use a man like you.'

Lomus cocked an appreciative eyebrow and nodded in gratitude.

'You're in charge of the interrogation, Pandarus. Report to me in my quarters when you are done here.'

'Yes, sir.'

'Carry on.' Macro made to move away, but winced as a fiery agony lanced down his wounded leg. He muttered a curse, and watched as Pandarus and Lomus hauled the man to his feet. They stripped him down to his breeches before binding him tightly to the post so that he could not slip down. The defiant expression dimmed as the prisoner looked at each man anxiously, knowing full well what was to come. Lomus stood in front of him, fists clenched and arm muscles bunched, waiting for the command.

'Begin,' said Pandarus.

Lomus threw his first punch, a powerful arcing blow into the prisoner's gut. He followed up with his left, and then, as the warrior gasped for breath, began to work his sides, each fist thudding into the ribs and driving the air from the native's lungs.

Macro nodded with satisfaction, then turned carefully, keeping the weight off his throbbing leg, before proceeding stiffly towards the entrance to the main hall of the head-quarters building.

Back in his quarters, he eased himself down into a chair and stretched out his leg. Though the wound was healing well and the flesh had knitted together, the garrison surgeon had insisted that the dressing should remain in place to support the limb until the stitches were removed. The trouble was, the wound itched like mad, and Macro had to resist the urge to scratch the area furiously. The kick he had received from the prisoner had caused the leg to throb painfully, and as the pain subsided, so the itching increased in intensity.

He reached down and rubbed softly, gritting his teeth at the sharp prickling sensation. Even though he knew he was fortunate that the wound was not going to permanently disable him, as he had seen happen to other soldiers, he still fretted about the length of time it would take him to fully recover. All because some fool of a native had chosen to take a potshot at him and then run for the hills. It took a moment before he recalled that it had been his own idea to go after the boy in the first place. He could quite easily have waited for him to take to his heels, or sent some other man forward in his place, but it was not in Macro's nature to exercise such patience, and he roundly condemned the native boy once again, heaping every curse he could on his young enemy.

Once the pain and irritation had eased, he shifted position to the small desk at one side of the room and began to deal with the routine bureaucracy that was the burden of every garrison commander across the empire. After lighting the lamps suspended from a small stand, he completed the daily entry in the garrison's log, detailing the number of active men, any sick or injured, as well as those absent on other duties, which, given the present posting, rarely needed any notation. In a more peaceful setting there would be frequent authorised absences as men saw to the purchase of food, equipment and horses, or were detached to guard tax collectors, while junior officers were sent to adjudicate disputes in the local population. Then there were those who had been granted a period of leave who might travel to their homes if the unit was raised locally. None of that applied to the garrison of the fort, since any individual who ventured more than a short distance from its ramparts alone was asking for trouble. Next, Macro moved on to the requests from the fort's stores, checking them against the inventory before approving or turning down each submission.

By the time he had finished, it was dark outside. He closed the shutters and called for his orderly to light the fire in the corner of the room and bring him something to eat. Outside in the courtyard he could occasionally hear the sounds of the interrogation: the soft thud of blows landing, and the keening cries and groans of the prisoner, gradually becoming more feeble as his torment continued. The gentle crackle of the flames consuming the kindling and then the split logs drowned out the sound, and Macro ate in peace at his table. He had all but finished his meal of stew and hard bread when there was a knock at the door.

'Come!'

Optio Pandarus strode into the room and stood erect in front of his superior's desk. 'Beg to report, interrogation is completed, sir.'

Macro lowered his spoon and wiped his lips on the back of his hand. 'Well? Did we get anything useful out of the bastard?'

'Yes, sir. It's bad. If he's told us the truth, then Legate Quintatus is leading his army into a trap.'

'A trap?'

'As far as our man knows, the Druids are drawing the column deep into the mountains and on towards the island of Mona itself. That's where they'll turn and make their stand.'

Macro nodded. 'Which is what the legate is pinning his hopes on.'

'Yes, sir. But what he can't know is that the Druids have called on the Silures and the Ordovices to join the Deceanglians. They are marching to sever Quintatus's communications with the rest of the province. They aim to cut him off from his supplies and block his line of retreat until his men starve or he gives the order to surrender.'

'Surrender?' Macro snorted. 'That's bollocks. He'd never dishonour himself, or the army, by doing that.'

'Then he's going to have to cut his way out of the trap and fight every inch of the way back to Mediolanum, sir. The legate's outnumbered by far more than he realises. And the enemy know the ground. If the weather turns and it makes the going even harder, then—'

'Quite,' Macro concluded tersely. 'He needs to be warned at once.'

'But how are we going to get a message through to him, sir? If the prisoner's right, the enemy have already cut him off.'

'That's as may be, Optio. But we have to get through all the same. And the only men we have who might succeed are you and the other men of the Blood Crows still here in the fort.'

Pandarus's eyebrows rose. 'But there's only my section, sir.'

'You won't be alone. I'm coming with you.'

'You? Sir, with respect, you're not in a fit state to—'

'I know damn well what state I am in!' Macro snapped. 'I'll be fine in the saddle. We'll be leaving at first light. Go and get your men ready!'

CHAPTER FOURTEEN

The wind was biting, and Cato had to squint as he climbed the steep slope towards the top of the mountain. The Blood Crows had gone as high as they could on horseback before the prefect had given the order to dismount and taken one of the squadrons on with him. The men had slung their shields over their backs and used their spears to help support them as they ascended. It had been cold enough at the top of the pass where they had left the others, but as they climbed, the wind moaned around them and strong gusts roared in their ears, while raindrops stung their exposed skin like fiery needles.

'Fuck this,' gasped Thraxis, a short distance behind his commander. 'The gods only know why the emperor would want to add this wasteland to the empire. Better to leave it to the barbarians. This is no place for civilised men.'

Cato pulled his neckerchief down to reply. 'You know the saying well enough, Thraxis. We're here because we're here.'

The Thracian sighed. 'Well I wish we weren't, sir.'

Cato slipped the thick cloth back over his mouth and nose and paused a moment to catch his breath before continuing. His military cloak whipped around him and he felt his helmet shift on his head as the wind caught the plume. He twitched it straight and set himself to climb one step at a time. According to the merchant who had offered his services to Legate Quintatus, the Deceanglian capital was no more than five miles distant, and would be clearly visible from the top of the mountain. Looking up, Cato doubted it. The sky was leaden, and darker patches of cloud were scudding overhead, threatening more rain on top of the freezing squalls. Nevertheless, it was his duty as commander of the army's vanguard to scout ahead of the main column and take every opportunity to report the lie of the land, as well as any sightings of the enemy.

There had been precious few of the latter since the incident at the gorge several days earlier. Aside from small parties of riders keeping watch on the Roman advance, the tribesmen and their Druid leaders had refused to give battle or attempt any further delaying actions. Even so, there had been plenty of reminders of their presence: tracks blocked by fallen trees; piles of rocks dislodged from cliffs and crags either side of choke points; reports of harassing raids on the army's thinly guarded lines of communication. With more men, Quintatus might have been able to establish a chain of well-garrisoned forts to cover the supply route back to Mediolanum. As it was, there were scant few outposts or cavalry patrols, and they were prone to sudden attacks. These were more of a nuisance than a genuine threat, and Cato could not help wondering why the enemy was not making greater efforts to strike at the perennial weak spot of a campaigning army.

A sudden cry interrupted his thoughts, and he stopped

and looked back down the slope. One of his men had tumbled off the path and was lying prone beside a large rock that had broken his fall. Two of his comrades were hurrying to his side as Cato turned to Thraxis.

'Keep the men moving. I'll catch you up.'

Thraxis climbed on as Cato made his way back to the fallen man. He exchanged a brief nod with Livonius as the tribune and his secretary toiled up the hill behind the auxiliaries.

'What's happened?' he asked as he drew up, breathing heavily.

One of the Blood Crows glanced round. 'It's Borminus, sir. Don't look good.'

'Let me see.'

They made space for the prefect, and Cato squatted beside the auxiliary. He had already been turned on to his back, and his eyes were fluttering as his mouth opened and closed, struggling for breath. The rest of his body lay inert. Reaching down, Cato's cold fingers fumbled for the ties under the soldier's chin, and he undid the leather thongs and eased the helmet off as gently as he could. Borminus's head lolled back loosely and his lips worked feverishly as if he was gasping for breath, but there was no telltale trail of steam from his mouth.

'What's wrong with him?' one of his comrades asked anxiously.

The stricken soldier's eyes rolled up as his jaw jerked and then fell slack. Cato hesitated, then leaned forward and turned his ear to the man's lips, but there was no sound of breath audible above the wind whining over the small cluster of men, nor any feeling of warmth. He eased himself back up and felt for a pulse on the man's neck, but there was nothing.

'He's gone.'

'Gone? How, sir? He just tripped and fell. He can't be dead.'

'Well the bugger ain't faking it to get off duties,' the other auxiliary chipped in.

Cato glanced towards the rock and saw that part of it protruded like the edge of a broad axe. He eased the body on to its side and examined the man. Just above the line of the neckcloth he saw a livid bruise on the skin. He clicked his tongue.

'Broken neck. Must have struck the rock there. There's nothing that could have been done to save him. Nothing.'

The three of them were still for a moment, buffeted by the wind, before the first man spoke again. 'Poor bloody sod . . . What a way to go. Borminus was a good man. One of the best.'

There was a pause before his comrade added, 'Maybe, but he farted in his sleep and cheated at dice, not to mention messing with another man's wife.'

Cato looked at him and puffed his cheeks. 'That's not much of a eulogy.'

The man shrugged. 'That's how he was, sir.'

'Fair enough.' Cato rose, turning his back into the shrill wind. 'You two get him back to his horse, then stay with the rest of the column.'

'Yes, sir,' the soldiers chorused, before one of them muttered, 'Great, thanks, Borminus.'

Cato left them to it and set off after the rest of the squadron, increasing his pace to get past them and resume his place at the head of the winding column. Thraxis had almost reached the summit and was bent over as he struggled to remain on his feet. The rain had strengthened from the slight drizzle that had plagued them since they had begun to climb and now lashed the bedraggled line of men panting under the burden of their armour, shields and spears. Only the effort of the climb was providing them with any semblance of warmth, and Cato could feel the numbness in his fingers as he grasped for purchase on the slippery rocks.

Finally, his limbs trembling from the cold and his exertions, he reached the top of the mountain, stooping into the icy wind that howled across the summit. He rested his hands on his knees and breathed deeply as the other men slowly joined him and stood with their backs to the wind, their shields giving them some shelter from the driving rain. One of them stumbled and his legs gave way beneath him. As he tried to rise, he staggered and swayed.

Thraxis shook his head. 'Bastard's drunk!'

'What in Hades is this?' Cato shouted angrily as he approached the auxiliary. He was about to berate the soldier when he realised it was the terrible cold, not drink, that had numbed the man's mind and body. He held the soldier steady and shook him until some spark of life glinted in the man's eyes. 'Concentrate! Keep your body moving. Stamp your feet and work your hands together. Understand?'

The auxiliary nodded dumbly.

'I can't hear you!' Cato shouted. 'Do you understand me, Trooper?'

'Yes . . . Yes, sir.'

'Then do as you are ordered.'

The auxiliary began to march on the spot and rested his

spear against his shoulder as he rubbed his hands together.

'Keep it going,' Cato ordered and turned to the rest of the men. 'You too! Unless you want to freeze to death.'

He moved away and carefully made his way across the uneven plateau of rocks and tussocks of grass. On the far side, he could see down the slope, but a skein of grey mist and rain obscured the view a few hundred feet away. Cato swore under his breath. There was no way of verifying the merchant's intelligence in these conditions. He might wait for the gale to pass, but the men had already suffered enough, and he had no wish to lose another of them to a careless tumble down the side of the mountain.

Thraxis came across to join him, teeth chattering as he addressed his superior. 'Sir, with respect, we're going to die up here soon. Some of the lads are in a bad way.'

'I know that. But just a little longer.' Cato glanced up at the sky and thought he discerned a lighter patch of cloud amongst those rolling over the mountains. 'Look there. The worst of it will pass soon.'

Thraxis squinted as he attempted to pick out the area Cato had indicated. 'Can't see anything.'

'Get back to the others. Keep the men moving. It'll help them stay warm.'

'Warm?' Thraxis arched an eyebrow. 'You really think so, sir?'

'That's enough. Get back to the others and ask Tribune Livonius and his servant to join me. Go.'

As Thraxis trudged away, grumbling, Cato turned his attention back to the terrain at the foot of the mountain. There was definitely more light in the sky, he decided. Sure enough, he began to pick out shapes in the mizzle: the pointed caps of pine trees, and outcrops of rock. The wind and rain began to die down a little as the sky lightened. All the time Cato could make out more detail. Then, at last, far below, beside a meandering river, he saw the vague outline of a rampart stretching around hundreds of huts. A handful of tiny flickers of light indicated the presence of fires. But it was too far away to make out any other signs of life.

From the size of the native settlement it appeared that the merchant's information was accurate. If so, then Legate Quintatus could crush the Deceanglians and destroy their capital. After which, it only remained to reach the coast, meet up with the naval forces, and descend on the Druids' stronghold to eradicate them once and for all. Without their influence, the native tribes of Britannia would be rudderless and unable to offer a united resistance to Rome. Then, at last, the new province might know peace. Not only would the conflict with Rome be concluded, but there would be none of the inter-tribal warfare that had plagued the island since long before the first Roman had ever set foot here.

The crunch of footsteps drew Cato's attention away and he turned to see Livonius and Hieropates approaching. Both were shivering, but Cato ignored their discomfort. If he and his men had to cope with the cold and rain then so could the young aristocrat. It would do him good to suffer a little, Cato mused before concentrating his mind again.

'Down there.' He indicated the camp. 'Get it all down on a slate and you can copy it up later.'

While the tribune oversaw the drafting of the plan of the landscape around the settlement as best as he could in the poor conditions and fading light, Cato made a quick estimate of the number of huts and the layout of the place. As soon as Hieropates had closed his slate tablet, the three returned to the rest of the men, huddled together and shivering. Cato could sense their resentment at having been ordered up the mountain, but with this being the very heart of the enemy's territory, only a fool would venture too far in front of the main column without an escort. He pointed back down the slope.

'Let's get out of here.'

'You are certain that it is the enemy capital?' asked Quintatus. 'And that it is inhabited?'

'I saw some fires, sir. Tribune Livonius is updating the map. We managed to get a reasonable view of the area around the enemy settlement before the light began to fade.' Cato stood in his dripping cape before the legate. The heavy leather of the headquarters tent swelled and shrank in the strong breeze blowing over the marching camp, as rain drummed steadily overhead, leaking through the stitched joints. A slave was busy setting up another post over the legate's camp bed to stop water pooling in a slack fold above. Cato cleared his throat and continued. 'And it matches the description given by your source.'

'Good. Then we have them where we want them at last. Assuming they are prepared to defend their homes, at least. I am tired of chasing shadows. Let's hope they've discovered some backbone and that this is not another of their wretched ruses. I shouldn't be surprised if they make another run for it the moment they know we are near.' Quintatus looked thoughtful for a moment. 'Though I am not going to give them a chance . . .'

The legate turned to the slave. 'Find Petronius Deanus and send him to me. I want the camp prefect too.'

The slave bowed and hurried out of the tent.

'Cato, you can take a seat and give me some more details of the enemy position while we're waiting.'

Before he sat, Cato undid the clasp of his cloak and lowered the sodden garment to the ground. His armour and tunic were equally drenched, and the leather vest on to which the scales had been stitched felt twice as heavy as normal. He tried to ignore his discomfort as he collected his thoughts and began.

'The settlement is on slightly raised ground to the side of the river, sir. The land around the ramparts has been cleared for some distance for farming. There are a few huts and pens but nothing else. Perhaps half a mile away is a thick band of forest. Then there are hills rising up on either side of the valley, thickly forested, including the pass we will have to take to enter the valley . . . That's as much as I can recall, sir.'

Quintatus nodded. 'You've done well, Prefect.' He looked at Cato as if noticing his drenched appearance for the first time. 'You must be cold, and hungry, I'll warrant.'

'Yes, sir.'

The partition flap rustled aside as the slave returned and announced, 'Petronius Deanus, master. A clerk has gone for Titus Silanus.'

As he finished speaking, a skinny, grey-haired man entered the tent. He wore an ochre tunic patterned in the chequered Celtic style of the northern tribes, together with brown leggings and sandals. His hair was long, but tied back with a thick leather thong that crossed his high forehead. His shrewd eyes quickly sized Cato up before he bowed to the legate.

'Sir, at your pleasure. How can Petronius, purveyor of the empire's finest luxuries, serve you this evening?'

Quintatus regarded him with a weary expression. 'Finest luxuries within the bounds of this backwards province, you mean.'

'Today I serve my customers in Britannia, but in future my wares will adorn the finest homes in Rome, by the grace of Jupiter, best and greatest.'

'Well, you don't lack ambition. But enough of that. This is Prefect Cato, commander of the army's vanguard. He has checked on the intelligence you provided me with. It seems that the Deceanglian capital is where you said it would be.'

Petronius affected a hurt look. 'You doubted me, sir? A deal is a deal. Whether I am selling goods or information, I never go back on my word.'

The legate understood the trader's point quickly enough. 'I will see that you are paid, as we agreed.'

Petronius bowed low. 'I thank you, sir. It has been a pleasure to do business with you.'

'Our business is not yet complete.'

The trader looked up sharply. 'Sir?'

'Our business will not be over until the campaign is complete. Thanks to you, I know where the enemy is. Now I need to know some more detail. Numbers, condition and so on.'

'But how am I supposed to provide such information, sir?'

Quintatus smiled thinly. 'How do you think? You are familiar with the natives in these mountains. You trade with them. I dare say you even count a few amongst them as friends.'

'Sir, if that were the case, why would I be here, serving Rome?'

'Because Rome pays better. And now Rome requires you to go into the Deceanglian settlement and find out what I need to know about the enemy.'

Petronius shook his head. 'Sadly, sir, our deal here is concluded and I have business elsewhere in the province. If I may just collect my fee, I shall be on my way.'

'Not until you have done all I ask of you. You will be paid, in full, as soon as we have defeated the enemy. Only then will I release you from your service to me. Is that clear?'

The merchant's jaw sagged, then he swallowed and stood as tall as he could before the legate. 'We had a deal. You promised me silver if I told you where to find the enemy. We shook on it. It was my understanding that Roman senators are men who honour their word, sir.'

Cato saw the blood drain from the legate's face. Quintatus took a step forward and glared at the merchant. 'You dare to question my honour? You, a man who deals with the enemies of Rome? A man who would sell out his customers for a handful of denarii? I dare say that if those miserable barbarians could have scraped together enough coin, you would be in their settlement now telling them everything you know about this army. Don't even pretend to claim the moral high ground, you worm.'

'Sir—'

'Silence! You will do as I command. Tomorrow, shortly after dawn, you will drive your cart into the enemy capital and go about your business. You will pay close attention to their defences and the number of fighting men they have. Once you have noted all that, you will bid them a cheerful farewell and return to report to me. After the enemy is defeated, and only then, you will be free to go. Bear in mind, Petronius, that if you turn traitor on me, or try to abscond, I shall have you declared an outlaw throughout the province, and the rest of the empire. If you are caught, you will be nailed to a cross and left to rot.' Quintatus paused and permitted a brief silence. 'Are we clear?'

Petronius licked his lips. 'Yes, sir . . . But if I may?'

Quintatus cocked an eyebrow and drew an impatient breath. 'What is it?'

'It seems that I have misunderstood the terms of our original arrangement. For which I apologise most humbly. However, in light of the perilous nature of what you now ask of me, I feel that a . . . bonus would be justified. In recognition of my loyal and useful service to Rome, may I suggest that I am appointed as your agent in the sale of the captives resulting from the enemy's defeat?'

Quintatus was still for a moment. 'At ten per cent.'

'Sir, I feel it reasonable to suggest a figure more commensurate with my valuable contribution to the defeat of our enemy. Say, twenty-five per cent.'

The legate snorted. 'Not even Crassus would have been so audacious as to make such a demand! You overstep yourself, Petronius.'

'Twenty per cent, then, sir.'

'Fifteen, and I'll overlook your presumption.'

'Seventeen.'

'Fifteen. And that is the end of the matter.'

The merchant made to speak, but thought better of it just in time and nodded in agreement.

'Good. Then I expect to hear your report tomorrow evening. Leave us.'

The merchant bowed low and backed out through the tent flaps. Cato could not help a degree of sympathy for the man. Although it was true that he had traded freely with tribes who were sworn enemies of Rome, and no doubt profited handsomely, circumstances had changed. The natives were on a war footing and were likely to be suspicious of any visitor, no matter how familiar. Still, if Petronius Deanus was smart, he would establish his good faith by offering the enemy some intelligence regarding the Roman army bearing down on them.

Cato's thoughts were interrupted by a new arrival. Silanus, the camp prefect, saluted the legate and stood, feet apart and hands clasped behind his back, straight as the shaft of the legions' standards he had fought under for most of his life.

'Sir, you sent for me.'

'I did. Summon all senior officers to headquarters at once. You may inform them that we shall be attacking the Deceanglian capital at dawn tomorrow.'

CHAPTER FIFTEEN

Cato was standing beside his horse on a low mound no more than half a mile from the settlement. It would be at least an hour before the first glimmer of dawn crept along the horizon, but all around he could hear the movement of men and horses. The army had begun the advance from the marching camp at dusk, with each unit following its appointed guide into position so that by daybreak the enemy capital would be surrounded, with little hope of escape for the inhabitants. It was never an easy thing for an army to manoeuvre at night, and even though the preparations had been thorough, Cato's column had bumped into one of the cohorts of the Twentieth Legion that in turn had been held up. As a result, the Blood Crows and the Fourth Cohort had reached their start line for the dawn attack far later than he had intended, and there would be little chance for the men to rest before they went into action.

It had been a freezing night, but the march had kept the troops warm. The bitter cold had also frozen the ground, and men and horses no longer had to negotiate the quagmire that had hindered their advance into the mountains so far. Mist had pooled in the dips and folds of the valley, and Cato was pleased that it would help to conceal his men as they made their final approach to the main gate of the enemy settlement. The legate had given the vanguard the honour of leading the attack. It was their task to take the main gate and open the way for the follow-up cohorts of the Fourteenth Legion. If the enemy was alert and reacted swiftly, then Cato and his men would suffer heavy casualties. He had therefore made his mind up to launch the assault as quickly and ruthlessly as possible. While the legionaries charged over the open ground towards the bridge crossing the outer ditch, the Blood Crows would race ahead of them with the ladders to scale the ramparts either side of the gatehouse. A small party of legionaries would bring up the rear, carrying the ram to smash through the stout timbers of the gate. As soon as the breach was made, two cohorts of the Fourteenth would burst from cover and storm the settlement. The rest of the army would have the job of rounding up the natives as they fled from their capital. As Petronius Deanus had not returned, there was no knowing precisely how many warriors they faced. Cato's expression soured as he recalled the smarmy merchant. No doubt he had made a run for it rather than risk his skin by entering the enemy's lair. He could not escape the legate's wrath for ever, though, and woe betide him when he was eventually apprehended by the Roman authorities.

If good fortune was on the side of Rome, then the king of the Deceanglians and some of the chiefs of the allied tribes would be killed or captured, and the effective resistance would be at an end in the region. After which it only remained to cross the narrow channel that separated Mona from the mainland and wipe out the Druid cult, then mop up the remnants of the Silurians and Ordovicians, and the west of the province would be secure. Legate Quintatus would win a notable victory, add lustre to his family name and advance his career in Rome. At the palace, the emperor would take the credit for overseeing the triumph of his forces over their barbarian foes and issue a large donative to the army as a reward. No doubt the lion's share of that would be paid to the Praetorian Guard, whose loyalty Claudius prized far above that of troops fighting at the fringes of the empire. The Praetorians, after all, had already demonstrated that they were not above eliminating an emperor and then forcing his successor on the Senate and people of Rome. These realities were not lost on any person with even a passing familiarity with the political world, and Cato could not help regretting the cynicism such awareness fostered. The same went for the triumph the emperor was sure to proclaim, with the craven support of his lackeys in the Senate. An elaborate procession would wind its way along the main thoroughfares of Rome, passing through the Forum and beneath the tiered magnificence of the imperial palace before culminating at the Temple of Jupiter, where the displays of captured enemy weapons would be dedicated. The centrepiece of the procession would be the emperor, standing tall in an ornate chariot, while the captive leaders would follow in chains to await their fate. If Claudius was feeling magnanimous, he would pardon them as a token of the mercy that Rome often bestowed on the defeated. Otherwise they would be strangled before the roaring mob, who would be primed with free handouts of coin, bread and wine.

There would be more immediate rewards for the men of

Quintatus's army, especially those of the vanguard. As was the custom, the first man to scale the enemy's ramparts would be decorated and promoted. The same applied to the first soldier into the breach: one of the legionaries manning the ram would end the day an optio, just one step away from becoming a centurion. A fresh battle honour would be added to the standards of both units, and Cato's stock would rise within military circles. His name would be on the list of those considered for command of the more prestigious units of auxiliary troops.

As he waited in the bitter-cold darkness, Cato allowed himself a moment of private reverie as he contemplated such a pinnacle to his career. He would be an influential and wealthy man, with a fine house in the capital and perhaps a substantial villa in Campania, on the shores of the bay that stretched out beneath the looming mass of Mount Vesuvius. There could be no more tranquil and comfortable place to retire and live out the remainder of his days with Julia and their family. He felt a surge of affection and longing in his heart, and for a moment wished that he could be far from these grim mountains and their barbaric inhabitants. Far from the hardships and dangers of army life. He imagined himself sitting beside a gently crackling fire, playing with their son, with more children perhaps, while Julia looked on with the same loving smile that had won his heart.

'Sir.'

The image faded in an instant as Cato turned towards a barely visible figure who had approached from the mound. He could just make out the transverse helmet crest against the greater darkness beyond, and recognised the voice.

'Festinus. Are the men ready?'

'All but the lads with the ram, sir. But the optio's sent word that they're close. They'll be in place in good time.'

'Very well. And how are the men's spirits?'

The centurion chuckled. 'You know the lads well enough, sir. They're grumbling like short-changed whores about the cold and the delay, but they're raring to get stuck in. Especially as there's rewards and promotions to be had. No need to worry on their account. It's the poor bloody sods over there I'd feel sorry for.'

Both men glanced towards the settlement. Behind the gatehouse and the rampart, rosy hues bloomed from several locations as small fires burned within. Figures were visible along the line of defences, outlined by the loom of the flames, but they showed no sign of alarm as they kept watch over the darkened landscape.

'Do you really think it'll go as easily as the legate believes it will, sir?'

Cato recalled the briefing they had attended the previous morning when Quintatus had outlined his plan. His staff had appeared to cover every contingency, and yet . . .

'Have you ever known a plan that did?'

They shared a brief laugh before Cato softly cleared his throat and spat. 'Just as long as we play our part, Festinus. That's all that need concern us. As long as the Blood Crows can get up on the rampart before the enemy have sufficient men in place, then your legionaries should be able to breach the gate without too much difficulty. There will be some losses, but let's do what we can to keep them small. Best to go in hard, make as much noise as we can and put the shits up those native bastards.'

'I'll do my best, sir.'

There was a brief silence before Festinus blew into his hands and rubbed them together. 'It's a crying shame that Macro isn't here with us. If anyone could do the job well, it's him.'

Cato felt moved to agree. His old friend would be in his element in such an assault, and his example would inspire his men to fight like furies. But Macro was far to the rear, watching over the lacklustre garrison of the fort as he recuperated from his wound. The burden fell on Festinus, and Cato did not want the centurion hampered by comparison with the man he privately considered to be the best soldier he had ever known.

'You can tell him all about it when the campaign is over and we return to the fort. But until then, you are in command of the cohort, Festinus. The men will look to you. So will I. And I know you will do your duty, and do it well.'

'Yes, sir. Of course.'

Cato turned to his horse and unhitched a small wine skin from the rear saddle horn. He offered it to Festinus. 'Here. It's a little brew that Thraxis has prepared to help keep the cold out. Wine and a few spices.'

Festinus nodded his thanks and raised the wine skin carefully. He took the spout in his lips and squeezed gently a few times before handing it back to Cato. 'Ahhh! Good stuff—' Abruptly he coughed and gasped. 'A few spices . . . What the fuck did he use, sir? Pepper?'

'Amongst other ingredients.' Cato took a few quick sips, swallowing cautiously as he knew what to expect. The liquid felt fiery as it slipped down his throat into his stomach and gave him a cheery warmth inside. 'Helps keep the cold out at least . . . Better rejoin your men. I want them primed and

201

ready to run for the gate the instant the signal is given. The gods be with you, Festinus.'

'And with you, sir.'

They exchanged a dimly visible salute and the centurion strode off into the darkness, leaving Cato alone with his horse. Hannibal had lowered his head and was grazing lightly on the frost-fringed blades of grass with a contented champing, oblivious to the concerns of his master and the other men waiting quietly in the night. Cato took up the reins and led the animal down into the hollow behind the mound. The air suddenly felt colder, and damp, and the gathering mist made it seem as if he had plunged under water. He instinctively snatched a quick breath before he took control over his senses again.

Handing his reins to a trooper, Cato went to find Decurion Miro. He was standing with the other decurions of the Blood Crows, who were talking in subdued voices. Cato paused to overhear the exchange.

'Mark my words,' Miro was saying. 'This ain't going to end well. We're supposed to charge over open ground to the walls, weighed down with ladders and grappling hooks? No chance of using our shields, and fair targets for any barbarian bastard on the ramparts with a good eye.'

'You fret too much,' replied another voice, which Cato recognised as belonging to Corvinus. 'That bunch of hairy-arsed barbarian scum are going to run the instant they realise the game is up. Just like they did back at the gorge.'

'That wasn't because they were afraid . . . Listen, Corvinus. No offence or anything, but you've only been in Britannia a few months. What the fuck do you know about the enemy? When you've faced 'em in battle as often as I have, then tell me about it, eh? As it is, I ain't happy about the prefect volunteering us for this. He's a bloody glory-chaser.'

Cato resumed his progress and one of the other decurions quickly coughed and spoke up. 'Commanding officer present!'

The decurions turned towards Cato and stood to attention.

'At ease. And keep your voices down. We're trying to launch a surprise attack, we're not on the drill ground.'

'Sorry, sir.'

Cato looked round at his subordinates. Already he thought he could make out more detail in their faces. The dawn was not so far off. 'All set?'

'Yes, sir,' Miro answered. 'Me and the lads are ready for anything.'

Cato suppressed a smile. 'Delighted to hear it. I'll expect to see you at the head of the charge when the time comes. Show Corvinus here how the Blood Crows go at the enemy, eh?'

There was a brief hesitation before Miro cleared his throat. 'Yes, sir. Of course. You can rely on me. All the way, sir.'

'Just as far as the heart of the enemy camp will suffice for now, Miro. That'll win us more than enough glory.'

Cato let the decurion suffer his embarrassment for a moment longer before he glanced up at the sky and tried to discern if there really was a faint band of lighter sky along the horizon or whether he was imagining it. No, he was certain. Dawn would be breaking soon.

'Better rejoin your squadrons, gentlemen. Get them into

the saddle and ready for the signal. When it's sounded, you know what to do. Let's teach those barbarians a lesson they'll never get the chance to learn from.'

There was a pause before Miro responded uncertainly, 'Sir?'

'Never mind. Just do your job and I'll see you all inside the ramparts. Miro, I will join you and your men for the attack.'

'Yes, sir.'

The small group separated, the decurions striding away towards their squadrons and Cato seeking out Hannibal before leading his mount to the standard of Miro's troopers. Around him in the mist he could just make out the outlines of men and horses and hear the muffled thumps of hooves and the jingle of bits and equipment. Miro stood beside his horse and called out as loudly as he dared, 'First Squadron . . . prepare to mount.'

At the instruction, the men reached their hands up to their saddle horns and braced their feet.

'First squadron . . . mount.'

There was a series of grunts as the men drew themselves up and on to the saddles before swinging their right legs over and sitting up straight and steadying their horses.

'Form a line on me.'

The standard-bearer moved alongside the decurion, and the rest of the men took up position to his side, stretching away into the mist. Their shields hung across their backs but their spears had been left in camp, as they would be encumbered by their scaling equipment. Several had ladders, some twelve feet in height, tucked under their sword arms. Cato edged Hannibal into place beside Miro, and then all was still along the line, save for the occasional snorts of the horses, the flicker of tails and the twitching of their dagger-like ears.

The darkness began to recede from the horizon and a thin smear of pale light edged into the sky, the details of the surrounding landscape gradually emerging from the gloom. Cato could see the rest of the cohort and the dismounted men behind them, shields grounded, spear shafts resting on shoulders as they worked their hands together to keep their fingers from going numb. Some stamped their feet, and warm breath flickered briefly, like grey feathers, and vanished. Twisting in his saddle, he saw Festinus at the head of his cohort, heavily armoured men standing in silent formations beside their large rectangular shields. He felt his heart begin to beat quicker as his ears strained, waiting for the first strident note that would sound the attack. Despite the cold, his palms felt clammy and his throat was parched. There was no sound of life from the enemy settlement, but it was hard to tell above the tiny ripple of noises along the Roman line and the steady thud of blood pulsing through his skull. He felt an urge to edge his mount forward to the edge of the dip in which the vanguard was concealed, just to be certain that nothing was amiss. But he forced himself to resist. It was too late now. The plan was made, and the signal would be given at any moment. All that remained was to brace himself to charge, and hurl himself on the enemy.

CHAPTER SIXTEEN

Even though he was expecting the signal, the distant blast of the bucinas of the army's headquarters detachment caused Cato to lurch slightly in his saddle. At once, the nearest men looked to him in anticipation. He snatched a deep breath as he thrust his arm up and called out, 'Vanguard! Forwards!'

He kicked his heels in, and Hannibal lurched forward, breaking into a canter up the rise and out of the thin skein of mist on to the open ground facing the enemy's ramparts less than half a mile away. To his left came Miro and his squadron, and then the rest of the Blood Crows, horses' hooves drumming across the white-frosted grass. Some of the men shouted their war cries, in defiance of their orders to keep silent, and Cato trusted that their officers would take them to task for that later on. This was no wild charge, laden down as they were with ladders and coils of rope and grappling irons, but every man knew that the speed of the attack was the surest guarantee of incurring as few casualties as possible.

Cato leaned forward and urged his mount on, his eyes fixed on the enemy lookouts, waiting for them to sound the

206

alarm, inaudible as it would be above the din of hooves pounding over the iron-hard ground. But his ears did pick out the sound of more Roman trumpets as the headquarters signal was repeated by the other units of the army surrounding the Deceanglian capital. This too was part of the plan, to confuse the enemy about the direction of the attack and hopefully give Cato and his men a chance to carry out their task before the enemy could oppose them in strength. He glanced quickly over his shoulder and saw the first of the legionaries emerge from the misty hollow and strike out towards the gatehouse at a steady trot. The tension of waiting had gone. They were committed now. Victory and glory awaited them, or defeat and death. But all thought of the outcome was shredded by the sheer exhilaration of the attack, and Cato's lips tightened into a fierce grin as he raced forward.

The enemy lookouts on the ramparts and gatehouse stood their ground implacably, but if the alarm had been raised, their comrades were slow to react, Cato thought, as he rapidly closed the distance to the outer ditch. As he approached, he reined in to allow the rest of his men to catch up. The first riders stopped at the edge of the ditch and dropped from their mounts, leaving one man in five to hold the reins for his comrades. Carrying their ladders and grapples, the men half ran, half slid down the steep outer slope, leaving furrows in the frosted grass. Cato remained in the saddle and rode along the rampart towards the bridge leading over the ditch to the gatehouse. Above him in the thin dawn light he could make out the dark figures of two native warriors. Turning in his saddle, he saw that the auxiliaries on foot were closing up. Some distance behind them trotted the legionaries, a rippling wave of shields and polished helmets. At the rear came the men carrying the ram.

Slipping down from the saddle, Cato steered clear of the bridge, where he would present a clear target for the enemy, and instead scrambled down into the ditch, narrowly avoiding one of the sharpened stakes set at an angle designed to impale a careless attacker. The reverse slope was steeper and presented more of a challenge for the Blood Crows, and they had to use their hands to help them gain the narrow strip immediately below the timber posts of the rampart. An auxiliary was setting one of the ladders up close by, and Cato nudged him aside.

'I'll go first!'

He placed a boot on the first rung and thrust himself up, climbing as quickly as he could. His heart was beating wildly, and any moment he expected to see one of the enemy warriors look over the rampart, or appear directly above to thrust the ladder away. There was not much space to angle the ladder securely, and he was forced to lean into it as he ascended. As he came within a sword's length of the top, he reached for the handle of his weapon and drew it before he continued. Tensing his muscles, he took the last two rungs in a rush, swinging his boot up and over the palisade and heaving his body on to the walkway, where he landed in a crouch, sword raised, ready to fight.

Nothing moved. Above the pounding of blood in his ears, the only other sounds were the grunts of his men scaling the walls and the rumble of nailed boots on frozen soil as the legionaries surged towards the gatehouse. He glanced round swiftly, but he was alone on the walkway, until one of the

Blood Crows joined him a short distance away. Then more men heaved themselves over the top of the palisade. Still there was no reaction from the enemy. Cato could see the head of one of the men on the gatehouse against the grey of the dawn sky, unmoving. Grasping his sword firmly, he strode the short distance to the steps leading to the tower and rushed up them, sword raised. Bursting out into the confined space, he made ready to strike at the first enemy he saw. Only there was none. Just crude facsimiles of men fashioned from wicker and clothed in rags. Their spears were shafts of wood propped up against them.

He stared at them in shock. Eventually he rose from his crouched position and crossed to the nearest of the dummies. He examined it warily, as if it might yet be some kind of trap, then prodded it hard with his sword. It collapsed on to the worn wooden boards, its 'spear' clattering beside it. Cato stared down and muttered softly, 'Fuck me . . .'

Sheathing his sword, he hurried to the rear of the tower and gazed out over the mass of conical thatched roofs. Coils of woodsmoke still rose from several locations amid the huts, but there was no other sign of life. Nor was there any fighting along the parapet on either side. A number of his men were standing there looking about nonplussed. Further along, one of the auxiliaries sprang forward and kicked over another of the dummies, hacking at the wicker in bitter frustration. The steps leading down to the walkway creaked as Decurion Miro entered the tower, still holding his sword ready. The two officers exchanged a look before Cato sighed.

'We've been had. The enemy are long gone. They left a handful behind who made up these dummies, set a few fires and retreated several hours ago. Probably as soon as it got dark.'

'Then where are they, sir?'

Cato rubbed his eyes. 'Who knows? They could be hiding up in the mountains, or dispersing to other settlements. More likely they have fallen back to Mona and think they'll be safe once they have put some sea between them and us.'

Miro looked out over the village. 'What if they're still here? What if this is some kind of trap?'

Cato looked at him and clicked his tongue. 'And exactly what kind of trap would that be? To let your enemy walk through your defences? Take it from me, Decurion. They've gone.'

A shouted order from outside the gate interrupted the exchange. Cato was striding across the tower when there was a loud crash and the structure shook under his feet.

'Miro, on me!' He trotted down the steps to the open space behind the gate. 'Give me a hand with the locking bar.'

Before they could lift it out of the brackets, the gate shook again as the ram struck the other side. Dust trickled down from the seams in the wood above, and Cato blinked it away, then looked across to Miro and nodded. Bracing their feet, they heaved the bar out and dropped it a short distance behind the gate, just as the optio in charge of the party carrying the ram gave the timing for the next strike.

'One . . . two . . . three!'

Without the bar, the gates parted at once and the point of the ram smashed them aside as the legionaries stumbled forward with surprised expressions.

'Nice try, lads,' Miro sniffed. 'But the Blood Crows beat you to it.'

Cato had no desire to indulge any banter and strode out past the ram, calling Centurion Festinus over.

'The enemy's pulled a fast one and abandoned the place.'

'What?'

'They've gone. But just in case they've left anyone behind, I want your men to search every hut. If you find any stragglers, you bring them to me unharmed.'

'Yes, sir.'

Cato hurried back through the gatehouse. 'Miro! Send a rider to report to the legate. He's to say the enemy has abandoned their capital. At once.'

Miro saluted and returned to where his men were gathering at the foot of the rampart, casting suspicious glances towards the nearest huts. Cato knew their anxiety would turn to frustration and anger soon enough. The enemy had evaded them once again and denied them the booty they had been expecting, as well as the chance to win recognition for breaking into the fortification.

As the man Miro had chosen hurried out to find his mount, Cato gave orders for the Blood Crows to join the search, all except one squadron, which was tasked with securing the gate until more forces arrived. He joined Miro's men as they unslung their shields and advanced cautiously up the main thoroughfare leading towards the heart of the settlement. They searched the huts along the route as they advanced, but there was no sign of life, just whatever goods the tribesmen had abandoned in their haste to escape from the Romans. There were not even any animals remaining, these having been driven away with the inhabitants. Cato soon discovered what had happened to their grain supply, as he shifted the ash from the fringes of the smouldering remains of a fire. There would be little of use for the Romans to pick over, and he could not help but admire an enemy who would destroy their possessions rather than allow them to fall into the hands of the foe.

The way ahead curved in the direction of a large hut that dominated the heart of the settlement. Cato guessed it must be the hall of the tribe's ruler. There, if anywhere, they would find anything of value that had been left behind by the enemy. As the Romans turned the corner, the street opened out into a large clear space before the entrance to the compound in which stood the royal hall. There was the remains of another fire – a large pile of ash, thin trails of smoke rising from several sources. A few baskets lay abandoned on the ground.

Cato halted the squadron and ordered the men to search the surrounding huts, then beckoned to Miro and made for the entrance to the royal compound, a wooden arch topped with a display of weathered skulls. A low palisade enclosed the hall and a handful of huts. It was not on the scale of the buildings that Cato had seen in the tribes of the south of Britannia, and the skulls, along with the squalor of the place, spoke of the barbaric nature of the Deceanglian tribe. They paused outside the entrance to the hall, and Cato glanced at Miro.

'You look over the rest of the compound.'

'Yes, sir.' Miro swallowed, clearly anxious about his surroundings. Cato thought about offering him some reassurance, but decided not to. Miro had to master his fear by himself. It came with the rank.

He left the decurion on the threshold and entered the hall. Even though the door was wide open, there was a residual warmth within, and the air was heavy with the stink of sweat, roast meat and woodsmoke. There was a large hearth in the centre of the hall, beneath an opening in the roof, surrounded by long tables and benches. Abandoned platters and drinking horns littered the tables, and it was clear that the enemy had left in a hurry. Towards the rear of the hall was a large wooden chair decorated with swirled patterns carved into every surface. A pile of furs served as a cushion. In front of the throne were two open chests. As Cato approached, he could see that they contained Samian-ware pottery. He took a bowl out of the straw packing and held it up to examine the decorated surface. It was the kind favoured by those who traded with the natives, who had a fondness for its fine appearance and paid well for it, even though it was mass-produced back in Gaul.

'Sir!'

Cato looked up at the cry from outside.

'Sir! Come quick!'

He quickly replaced the bowl and hurried out of the hall. Miro called out again, from behind the building, and Cato ran round to join him, anxiety pricking the base of his neck. Miro was standing a short distance from a cart, his face ashen, his sword arm hanging limply. As Cato strode over to join him, he saw the cause of the decurion's shock. A naked body was bound to the rear of the cart, his arms tightly stretched along the vehicle's sides. A pile of organs and intestines lay in a pool of dried blood at his feet. His stomach had been cut open and the flaps pegged back to reveal the gory cavity. His head was rolled back, eyes shut, mouth gaping where his severed penis had been forced into it, the flesh bruised and cut but still recognisable.

'Petronius Deanus,' Cato said softly. 'Poor bastard.'

Miro swallowed. 'Why did they do this to him? Fucking animals . . .'

Cato tore his gaze away from the corpse and looked further along the side of the cart. 'A warning to us. No, not a warning. A challenge. Look.'

He pointed out a short phrase, crudely written in blood on the side of the cart beneath Petronius's right hand. There was dried blood on his finger, and an icy chill tumbled down Cato's spine as he realised that the merchant had been forced to write the message in his own blood before he had been disembowelled. The words were large enough to make out without stepping any closer.

He cleared his throat and read them aloud as steadily as he could.

'Romans, we await you at Mona. There, you will all die . . .'

CHAPTER SEVENTEEN

Macro tried hard not to reveal his misgivings as he glanced at the officer doing the rounds at his side in the half-light of dawn. Centurion Fortunus had been informed that he was taking command of the fort shortly before, and had reacted precisely as Macro had feared he would. Life had been too easy in the Illyrian cohort for too long, and most of the men and officers had grown used to garrison duty in the comfort of a settled province. Even after being transferred to the army in Britannia, they had served as part of the reserve and had yet to face battle against the island's warlike natives. That particular experience might be closer than they wished, Macro reflected ruefully. The fort was on the frontier, and enemy warriors lurked in the surrounding hills and mountains. It was possible that the natives might have concentrated their forces against the main Roman column. Equally, it was possible that they might have much wider ambitions that included an offensive against the frontier forts and outposts. If they attacked Fortunus and his men, Macro had serious doubts that the Illyrians would prevail. Even though his efforts to toughen them up had gone some way to improving their fitness and fighting skills, they were far from ready to lead into battle. More worrying still was the fact that command of the fort would be entrusted to Fortunus, as the senior remaining officer.

Macro paused at the foot of the steps leading up to the gatehouse tower and leaned on his vine cane to take the weight off his wounded leg. He could still walk no more than a mile before the pain became acute and the joint grew stiff. He waited a moment and breathed out calmly before he addressed Fortunus.

'Get another locking beam fitted to each gate. If there's trouble, that'll help keep the bastards out. And while you're at it, have the blacksmith turn out as many caltrops as possible and sow them in the grass around the walls. That'll put a stop to any attempt to rush the fort and take it by surprise. I've yet to meet the man who has impaled his foot on a caltrop and not screamed his guts out.' Macro smiled fondly as he recalled the effect the vicious iron spikes had had on the Parthians he and Cato had once faced in the eastern deserts of the empire.

'Do you really think there will be trouble, sir?'

Macro sighed. 'Who knows? The point is that we have to be ready to face it at any moment. That's what soldiers do, Fortunus. Professional soldiers, at any rate. You take the emperor's coin and now it's time for you to earn your pay.'

'Yes, sir. I understand.' Fortunus hesitated and glanced at Macro anxiously.

'But? Spit it out, man.'

'It . . . it's you I'm concerned about, sir.'

Macro cocked an eyebrow. 'Really?'

'Yes, sir. You've not recovered from your wound. Better

that you remain here and send another officer in your place to warn the legate.'

Macro felt an instinctive disdain for the transparency of the other man's suggestion. He had little time for officers who did not step up to take the burden of responsibility that came with their rank, not to mention their enhanced pay. He was damned if he would let Fortunus hide behind him and lead his men from the rear. Still, it would do little good to berate the man out here in the open, in earshot of those who would be left in his charge. He bit back on his irritation and shifted his weight slightly so that he stood erect before the other man.

'It is vital that the legate is informed of the enemy's plans, and I am the best man to lead the effort to make sure the warning gets through. That is why I must go and why you must assume command.'

Fortunus stared at him bleakly and then cast his eyes down. 'Sir, I am not sure if I am the best man for the job. It might be better if you chose another.'

Macro's brow creased in an angry frown and he thrust a finger into Fortunus's well-padded gut. 'Shut your mouth. There's no choice in the matter. I am ordering you to take command, and you will fucking well take command. Is that understood? You are a bloody centurion. Act like one. These men will be looking to you. Depending on you. And you will do your duty and lead them as well as they deserve. Their lives depend on it. So does yours, Fortunus. We're all in this together. The difference is that officers must lead by example. You will set the example, give the order, and if need be, die at the head of your men.'

Fortunus winced and Macro paused, disappointed by the

man's lack of moral fibre. It would serve little purpose to fuel his anxiety. Fortunus needed a more subtle approach. Encouragement, perhaps. Macro softened his tone.

'Look here, it's no accident that you were promoted to the centurionate. Whoever decided to hand you the job must have had their reasons. I've been a soldier long enough to know that such men lead from the front and are the last to leave the fight when in retreat. You're supposed to be a fire-eater, Fortunus. It's your job to frighten your men just as much as you frighten the enemy. Maybe you've forgotten that and you need to find it in yourself again. But you will. You have to.' He paused and made himself smile. 'Of course, you'll have to do a few more laps around the drill ground before you are fit enough to outpace your lads!'

Fortunus's eyes narrowed. 'Are you saying I'm fat, sir?'

'Well, I'm not saying you're thin.'

They stared at each other for an instant before the auxiliary officer's face creased into a smile. Macro joined him and they both laughed.

'Right then, the job's yours. Look after my fort, Centurion.'

'Yes, sir. I'll do my best.'

'I expect nothing less. And if you need a word of advice, then sound out Diomedes. He's a good man, and he'll make a fine centurion one of these days. You could do worse than listen to what he has to say.'

'I'll bear that in mind, sir.'

'Good.' Macro clapped him on the shoulder and turned to climb the steps to the tower, gritting his teeth each time he had to flex his wounded limb. He was sweating slightly as they reached the top and moved over to the crenellations overlooking the fort. He leaned on the rail and pointed to the three other gatehouses. 'I know the quartermaster doesn't like having our artillery set up during the winter months, and the cold and damp does the kit no good, but get a bolt-thrower mounted on each tower. If there's one thing I've learned about the natives it's that they have a mortal terror of our bolt-throwers and catapults. Especially when we use fire bolts. You should see them, Fortunus. Like fire from the heavens flashing into their ranks and bursting into flame and sparks. Nothing quite like it. So use them at the first sight of the enemy. If they get past those and over the ditch to the rampart, then it's down to cold steel, brute strength, courage and good training. It's the last that gives us the edge over the enemy, so keep the men drilling and push them to the limit. It's when a man thinks he has reached the point of exhaustion that he finds that last reserve that will give him the confidence to face anything.'

'Yes, sir.'

Macro looked the centurion in the eye and held out his hand. They clasped forearms and Macro nodded his satisfaction. 'You'll do fine, Fortunus. Trust me.'

'Thank you, sir. I won't let you down.'

'If you do, I'll have your bollocks for breakfast.'

Fortunus chuckled, his jowls trembling with mirth. Then the laugh faded. 'If we are attacked, do I take it that will mean the legate has been defeated?'

Macro thought a moment and shrugged. 'Whether Quintatus has been defeated or is victorious makes no difference. You hold the fort until it falls, a relief column arrives or the enemy gives up and buggers off back into the mountains. That's all that need concern you.'

'Yes, sir. I understand.'

Macro caught sight of Optio Pandarus leading his section of mounted men towards the gate and straightened up. 'Time for me to go. As of this moment, you are the garrison commander. The fort is in your hands, Centurion.'

Fortunus cleared his throat. 'Yes, sir.'

They made their way down from the tower and emerged just as Pandarus and the others drew up. Macro ran his eyes over the Blood Crows and their latest recruit, the giant Lomus. The latter was leading a second mount and brought it forward to Macro. Like the other horses, it was laden with feed bags and the minimum kit that Macro would need for the ride to track down Legate Quintatus. He stood beside the horse, holding the reins and his vine cane in one hand, the other resting on the saddle horn. Instinctively he made to thrust himself up into the saddle, but his wounded leg refused to answer the call and he did not even leave the ground. Swearing under his breath, and embarrassed by the need to call for assistance he gritted his teeth and growled at Lomus.

'A hand up, here!'

The auxiliary released his own reins and cupped his hands for Macro's good foot. As if he was lifting a child rather than a grown man weighed down by armour, he swept Macro up and on to his mount. The centurion grunted his thanks and settled himself in place, adjusting his cloak so that it fell across his saddle roll.

'Open the gates.'

The section of Illyrians on gatehouse duty hurried to remove the locking bar and ease the gates open, allowing the dawn light to flood in at an angle. Macro tapped his heels in and urged his horse forward. Pandarus ordered the others to mount, and they trotted out behind the centurion. A moment later the gates thudded back into place and the bar thumped into its brackets. Macro turned briefly in his saddle and saw the bulk of Fortunus on the tower. The new commander of the fort half raised a hand in farewell, and Macro nodded before facing forward and striking out for Mediolanum along a narrow trail that wound up into the hills to the north of the fort, heading for the line of march taken by Legate Quintatus and his army. Macro winced. With difficulty he had adjusted to taking the strain on his good leg and did his best to ignore any pain in the other. Soon the discomfort faded from his mind as he fixed his thoughts on finding the legate and saving his comrades, and Cato, before they fell into the trap being set by their enemy.

For two days they drove their mounts on as hard as they dared, alternating between a steady trot and walking, as the ground permitted. There was too much urgency to advance with caution, and Macro put his trust in a good sword and fierce determination should they run into any armed natives. They passed several villages nestled in valleys, skirting round them without provoking the natives into any attempt to pursue them, and his heart grew heavier as he realised that this could only be because the enemy was gathering every available warrior to hurl against the Roman column when they decided to close the trap. For all he knew, that might already have happened, and the crows and ravens were even now picking over the stiff, cold corpses of the Roman army, their sharp beaks plucking at torn flesh. If that was the case, then he and his small party were riding to their deaths, but the thought did not daunt him. If there was the slightest chance of saving Cato and the others, he was content to put his life at risk, and he drove his men on and fought back against the throbbing agony in his leg. He was gratified to see that although the scar tissue flushed red at times, there was no sign that the hard riding was holding back his recovery.

Each night they camped in whatever shelter they could find, not daring to light a fire for fear of attracting unwelcome attention. They chewed on strips of dried meat and hard bread, washed down with spring water, before doing their best to find warmth, huddled in their thick cloaks as sleep came fitfully.

The morning of the third day, the discomfort of the cold, clammy air of the mountains was made worse by the gathering of dark clouds. By noon it was raining heavily, and the gloom was such that it might have been the thin light of dawn or dusk. Macro, not wishing to run into the enemy, sent Lomus a short distance ahead, then hunched down into his saddle and stared ahead over the straggling mane of his horse as he swayed gently from side to side. As far as he could estimate, they had covered sixty miles, and should strike across the route taken by Quintatus at any moment. There would be no mistaking the passage of such a large body of men. The ground would have been churned up by nailed boots, hooves and the wheels of heavy carts, leaving a wide scar etched across the landscape. They would only have to follow that to catch up with the column, or encounter one of the outposts constructed in its wake to protect the line of communication back to the fortified supply depot at Mediolanum.

He had almost ridden into Lomus before he realised it,

and reined in sharply as the auxiliary saluted and thrust an arm back the way he had come.

'Sir, we've found it. The track's just over there.'

Macro felt a surge of warm relief in his heart. 'Let's see.'

They rode on and stopped at the edge of the broad swathe of mud in which myriad puddles shimmered dully in the falling rain. Macro looked in both directions along the line the army had taken, but saw no sign of life. He gestured to the men to follow him, and turned his mount to the left to follow the route, keeping clear of the glutinous strip of mud that would suck down the horses' hooves. There was no knowing how far ahead of them the army lay, but at least they would be able to find them easily enough now, he reflected contentedly. When they did, and he had reported to the legate, there would be hot food, warming fires and shelter from this pestilential rain.

Late in the afternoon, the rain eased off into a fine mizzle and they passed the outline of a vast marching camp, levelled as far as possible, in accordance with Roman practice, to deny the enemy any potential field fortifications. The ground where the remains of the camp lay was flat and close to a river winding through the valley. Beyond, the route climbed a gentle ridge, and Macro's party urged their weary mounts to make one last effort before they stopped and made camp for the night. There was a forest of tall pine trees running off the ridge towards the steep side of a hill, and Macro decided that would be a good place to halt. He was bone weary and his leg ached abominably, and the prospect of sleeping on a mattress of pine branches, partly sheltered from the elements, seemed like luxury.

Lomus was riding out ahead once again as they reached

the crest of the ridge, and Macro was about to order him to make for the treeline when the auxiliary abruptly reined in and craned his neck. An instant later he turned and waved frantically.

'Up here, sir! Quick!'

Macro spurred his tired mount up alongside Lomus and stared down the far slope into the shallow vale below. Half a mile ahead lay a small wagon convoy, perhaps five of the large four-wheeled vehicles drawn by oxen that were used to move supplies. There was also one small covered cart halfway down the line. Around them, the remains of the convoy's escort, a half-century of auxiliaries, Macro estimated, were fighting for their lives against a contingent of native warriors, perhaps sixty or seventy strong, hacking and slashing at the hated Roman invaders.

The rest of Macro's men reached the ridge and fanned out on either side of the centurion.

'What should we do, sir?' asked Pandarus.

'Do?' Macro's lips stretched into a smile as he reached up to check his helmet strap was secure. His first thought was the need to complete his mission and warn Quintatus of the trap he was marching into. And then there was the enemy in front of him and comrades in peril. Macro and his men might be enough to turn the tide, he calculated. He drew his sword and held the blade against his thigh, where there was little danger of it causing harm to his comrades. 'What do we do? We get stuck into those bastards. But first, you there!'

He pointed to one of his men. 'You stay here out of the fight. If it goes badly for us, you find a way to get through and warn the legate. Clear?'

'Yes, sir.'

'Good. The rest of you – on me!'

He kicked in his heels, and his horse snorted before it plunged down the slope towards the beleaguered supply convoy.

CHAPTER EIGHTEEN

Macro and his detachment of Blood Crows kept well clear of the quagmire marking the line of march taken by Legate Quintatus and his army. Instead they thundered down the grassy slope, swords drawn, drenched capes rippling behind them. The pain in Macro's leg was like fire as the limb lurched against the side of his horse, but he pushed it aside as he got caught up in the excitement and exhilaration of imminent action. Pandarus and some of the others were drawing ahead, and Macro snatched a breath to call out to them.

'Hold the line! Damn you, hold the line!'

He understood the urge to get into the fight, but as an officer he had long since learned the need to keep his men together to strike as one, rather than fritter away the impact of a good charge piecemeal. At his command, Pandarus and the others obediently slowed their pace to let the rest catch up, and they continued in a line abreast. Macro's shout had also alerted the enemy, however, and the nearest had already called a warning to their comrades. Most were still closely engaged with the men of the escort and fought on heedlessly, but a handful, perhaps twenty in all, turned towards the riders and clustered around the end of the rearmost wagon, shields raised and spears and swords readied. Macro saw the driver splayed back across his bench, arms outstretched, while a smaller figure, a boy, lay slumped at his side. Beads of rain sprayed into Macro's face, and he had to blink them away as he approached the enemy warriors. In the last fifty paces the tribesmen braced themselves, and the Romans raised their swords and held their shields close to cover as much of their left side as possible.

'Blood Crows! Charge!' bellowed Macro, and pressed his snorting mount into a final dash, steering the horse to pass to the right of the wagon. He fixed his attention on a trio of natives by the rear wheel. None of them had armour, two carried wicker shields and there was only one sword between them, the others hefting axes. Poorly equipped as they were, Macro could see the fearless gleam in their eyes as they held their ground and snarled their defiance at him. At the last moment, he twitched his reins and his horse swerved abruptly towards the wagon, crushing the men against the wheel. Smashing his shield out, he caught one man square in the face with the iron boss, cracking his jaw and splitting his lips. Then he swivelled as far as his saddle allowed and plunged his sword down, driving the point into the native's shoulder. The horse instinctively lurched away, driving on past the wheel and leaving the men behind. Macro knew that there was no time to come about and finish them off. What mattered was the impact of the wild charge.

Keep going. Knock them down. Strike hard and keep striking. Break their will!

The Blood Crows were getting stuck in on either side of the wagon, hacking and thrusting with their spears and punching out with their shields as they roared their savage battle cry over and over.

Another opponent stepped out in front of Macro. A tall, broad man with a solid kite shield and a heavy spear, the kind used to hunt boar. His long hair was plastered to his scalp and glistened with rain, and he shook a strand from his eye and braced his feet wide as the Roman officer bore down on him. Macro moved to repeat the manoeuvre that had knocked the first three natives aside, but this foe was far more skilled than his companions and quickly dodged round to keep himself on Macro's sword-arm side. He pounced forward and raised his shield to block the Roman's desperate blow, and then made to strike with his spear. Snatching his blade back, Macro swept it out at an angle, just catching the tip of the spear and parrying it aside. He spurred his horse forward, pulling sharply on the reins and turning in to the warrior. The blow was only glancing and the man was able to back away and recover his balance as Macro came on, thrusting his shield into his foe's with a series of clatters and striking out with his sword. But the warrior was too quick on his feet and knocked the blade aside, or shifted easily from his opponent's path, and Macro gritted his teeth in angry frustration.

Abruptly the warrior leapt back, creating a gap between himself and Macro's horse, and then thrust his spear at the beast, tearing a gash in its matted flank. A shrill whinny cut through the air, and the horse reared up and lashed out with its hooves, knocking the warrior's shield aside before sending the native flying violently backwards into the mud and puddles with a great splash. He had the presence of mind to grasp the shaft of his hunting spear tightly, and as Macro loomed over him and leaned forward to strike him on the ground, he thrust the weapon up with both hands to block the blows.

'Just die, you bastard!' Macro snarled in frustration. He struck again, and at the last moment changed the angle of the blow so that the edge of the blade cut diagonally across the knuckles of the man's right hand, biting through flesh and crushing and shattering bones. Two severed fingers leapt from the spear shaft, and the others hung nervelessly from the mangled hand before the tip of the spear dropped into the mud. With only his left hand in action, the warrior roared with rage and tried to adjust his grip so he could still strike back. But Macro had already won the contest and now leaned forward as far as he could to drive the point of his sword into his opponent's neck, tearing open the blood vessels so that the warrior slumped back, blood gushing from the wound.

Sitting back in his saddle, Macro raised his sword and quickly looked round. Most of the enemy around the wagon had been cut down. A handful were fleeing across the open ground towards the nearest trees. A short distance ahead of the wagon, Lomus had ridden straight into another party of tribesmen and was sweeping his cavalry sword in vicious arcs that scattered the enemy and laid open those who were too slow to escape his reach. The fight was still in the balance further along the supply convoy, with the lead vehicle already in the hands of the Deceanglian warriors, who were too busy looting the contents to pay much attention to the arrival of the Roman horsemen.

Macro's attention was drawn to the melee around the small cart in the middle of the column. Ten or so of the escort had gathered about their optio, who held the standard in one hand while fighting off the enemy with his sword in the other. Standing at his side was a slender figure in a gleaming black cuirass decorated with swirling silver motifs. The ribbon tied over the cuirass signified his rank – a senior tribune – and Macro briefly wondered how he had become attached to a small supply convoy. The tribune and his men were hemmed in and fought shoulder to shoulder in a tight formation about the cart as their foes hacked at their oval shields with axes and swords.

Macro's mouth was dry, and he had to clear his throat before he called out to the rest of his men, 'Follow me! Follow me!'

He waited just long enough to see that the others were responding to the order before slapping the flat of his blade against his horse's rump and steering the beast towards the struggle around the cart. The rest of the surviving auxiliaries were fighting back to back or individually as the Blood Crows dashed by, slashing at any foe who came within reach of their swords. Then they were in amongst the men surrounding the cart, horses pushing into the throng as blades clashed with shrill rings and sparks flew brightly in the gloom. Macro held his shield close to his side, covering his leg as much as possible while cutting and thrusting at any target that presented itself. The sudden appearance of the reinforcements had unnerved the tribesmen, and they tried to back away from the ferocious men looming over them on horseback.

'That's it, lads!' the tribune cried. 'The bastards are breaking! Kill 'em!'

The men from the escort surged forward, slamming their

shields into the enemy and punching their short swords out with fresh vigour now that the tables had been turned. A handful of the enemy backed away and ran, and their example quickly spread to their comrades, who retreated after them. Macro saw Lomus urge his horse forward to pursue the warriors streaming away, and shouted after him.

'Lomus! Leave 'em. Optio!'

'Sir?' Pandarus reined in and turned to his superior.

'Take the men and drive the rest of the natives off. But that's all. No pursuit beyond a hundred paces from the wagons. I don't want them blundering into any trap. Understood?'

'Yes, sir!'

Pandarus called his men to form on him and trotted towards the three wagons at the front of the convoy, cutting down any tribesmen who tried to stand their ground. Meanwhile Macro turned to the tribune and exchanged a quick salute.

The tribune offered a relieved smile as he stepped forward. 'And to whom do I owe my thanks for the timely intervention?'

'Centurion Lucius Cornelius Macro, First Century, Fourth Cohort of the Fourteenth, sir.'

'Well met, Centurion. I am Tribune Caius Porcinus Glaber. Not attached to any legion, as it happens. Not yet, at least. And who are those men with you? They do not look like any legionaries I have ever encountered. Unless the Fourteenth has decided to go native.'

Macro chuckled. 'They're Blood Crows, sir. That's to say, Second Thracian Cavalry, but known to most as the Blood Crows.'

The tribune arched an eyebrow. 'Sounds like they've earned themselves something of a fierce reputation.'

'Ask the enemy, sir. There's not a barbarian in these mountains that has not heard of the Blood Crows, and who doesn't fear them.'

'I see.' The tribune scrutinised him closely before he continued. 'And what is a legionary centurion doing in command of a handful of auxiliary cavalrymen? If you hadn't ridden to our rescue, I might think you were deserters. I'd be grateful if you'd explain yourself, Centurion Macro.'

'I have important intelligence for Legate Quintatus, sir. These men are from the garrison of the fort I command.'

The tribune looked round to see the last of the enemy disappearing into the trees, and nodded with approval. 'Then I congratulate you on the quality of your men. The Blood Crows are a credit to you.'

'The cohort is commanded by Prefect Cato, sir. I was left in command of the fort after a wound stopped me marching with him.' Macro touched his leg gently.

'Prefect Cato . . .' Glaber's brow creased into a frown.

'We'd better get the convoy moving again, sir. Where is the commander of the escort?'

'Over there. Poor bastard.' The tribune gestured towards a corpse face down in the mud a short distance away. His crest had been trodden into the ground and was barely visible.

Macro turned his gaze towards the optio, still standing with the standard at the side of the cart. 'Then that makes *you* the new escort commander. Gather your men, see to the wounded and get the wagons ready to move. We need to find an outpost or a patrol before that lot get their balls back and have another crack. Carry on.'

The optio planted the standard firmly in the ground beside the cart before he strode away to round up the survivors of the escort.

'Do you really think they'll come back?' asked Glaber.

Macro puffed his cheeks. 'I hope not. But with the Druids stirring the shit up, the locals have something of a fanatical edge to them, and they're hard to predict. Best we don't stick around and see what happens, eh?'

'Fair enough.' Glaber chuckled.

Macro glanced up and down the supply convoy and noted that several of the mules had been injured and were braying in agony as they struggled in their traces. A handful had been killed outright and had collapsed on to the muddy track. The wagon drivers and their assistants had also suffered losses in the attack, and the dazed survivors were quickly set to work by the optio to remove the stricken animals from their harness.

'We're going to have to abandon at least one of the wagons,' Macro decided. 'And some of the supplies. Of course, we could use a couple of the mules hitched to your cart, sir.'

Glaber stiffened slightly. 'I think not. As you said, we're in a hurry. Best to just crack on and not waste time moving my kit to one of the wagons. You'll need all the space for whatever supplies you can carry from the wagon you leave.'

Macro saw that he would not gain much headway against the tribune and changed tack. 'Mind my asking why you were here with the convoy, sir? I know that the Fourteenth and the Twentieth already have senior tribunes, so you ain't a replacement.'

Glaber was quiet for a moment before he responded.

'Fair enough question, and as I have already put you on the spot, I suppose I owe you an answer. Very well. I am the chief of staff to the new governor of Britannia, Aulus Didius Gallus. I have been sent to inform Legate Quintatus that the governor will reach the province to take up his post before the end of the year. I'm supposed to be liaising with the legate to discuss the handover. However, I had not expected to have to track him down in the depths of these bloody mountains.'

'Gallus?' Macro had heard the name. 'Wasn't he governor in Sicily a few years back?'

'That's right.'

'Nice quiet spot, I believe. He's going to find it quite different here.'

Glaber's brow creased into a frown. 'He has since been decorated by the emperor following a successful campaign in Bosporus, and after that he campaigned against a brigand army in the mountains of North Africa. I think you will find that he is well placed to take command here in Britannia. The barbarians in these climes are hardly going to present much of a challenge.'

'No?' Macro could not help a weary smile. 'They've been keeping our legions at full stretch for the best part of ten years now, sir. And this little tussle you just had is hardly an isolated event. I hope the new governor doesn't think he's going to breeze in and sort it all out in a few short years.'

'Gallus knows what he's doing, Centurion. And I suspect that he is not going to be too impressed by one of his legates rushing headlong through these mountains to grab some glory for himself while he can.'

Macro quickly reappraised his impression of the tribune.

Glaber was no one's fool and had guessed the real motive behind Quintatus's decision to launch this campaign. Still, the centurion had learned enough from Cato to be aware of the need to discuss his superiors in as tactful a manner as he could manage. 'Legate Quintatus is a good enough commander, sir. He saw an opportunity to crush the Druids while the enemy appeared weak and divided, and he took it. But he's advancing into a trap, sir. That's what I've come to warn him about.'

He briefly filled the tribune in on the details that had been beaten out of the prisoner back at the fort. Glaber listened intently.

'Then there's no time to waste. I would suggest that you and your men ride ahead and reach the army as soon as you can, but I dare say this route is being closely watched by the enemy and you'd stand a better chance of getting through if you remained with the convoy.'

'I agree, sir.'

'Then we'd better get moving as soon as the wagons are ready. I'll need a driver for my cart. The previous post-holder thought he'd run for it the moment the enemy pitched up. He was the first man to be cut down.' Glaber looked up at the leaden sky. 'I'd say we're due some rain before night falls.'

'Yes, sir.'

'Frankly, I'd rather be sitting in my study, in front of the fire, back in Rome.'

'I can imagine.'

They exchanged rueful smiles before Glaber wagged a finger. 'I remember now. You did say Prefect Cato, didn't you?'

'Yes, sir.'

'Quintus Licinius Cato, the chap that married the daughter of Senator Sempronius a year or so ago? Julia, wasn't it?'

'That's right.'

'Do you know Prefect Cato?'

'Yes, sir. He is a fine officer, and a good man. I'm proud to call him a friend.'

The tribune sucked in a breath and his expression changed, becoming more solemn. 'Then I have some bad news for you, and the prefect, I'm afraid . . .'

'Bad news?' Macro felt a prickle of anxiety ripple across his scalp. He dared not even guess at the nature of the tidings carried by the tribune.

'My father is a close friend of Senator Sempronius. I heard it from him shortly before I left Rome. It seems that Julia gave birth to a child a while back. It was not an easy delivery by all accounts, and left her weak. She never fully recovered and finally succumbed to a summer chill. Damn shame. At least young Lucius was thriving though. Or was when I left Rome. Always thought Julia was a bright, pretty thing. Bit of a shock to old man Sempronius.' He paused and continued in a more melancholy tone. 'So I suppose I shall have to pass the news on to her husband. Poor fellow.'

'She's dead?'

'Yes. I'm sorry.'

Macro swallowed and shook his head in utter sorrow. 'Cato . . . my poor lad.'

The optio came striding up to them with one of his men and saluted, oblivious to the strained air between his two superiors as he addressed Tribune Glaber. The other man took up the traces of the mules attached to the cart and stood ready to lead the animals on.

'The wounded have been put in one of the wagons, sir. The dead have been placed on the one we're leaving behind, together with the supplies we couldn't carry. The rest of the convoy is formed up and ready to move.'

'Yes. Yes, of course. We had better get going. Centurion?'

Macro shook himself out of his stupor and stiffened his spine as he composed his features and stared at the tribune. 'I'm ready, sir.'

'Good. I want you and your men to scout ahead of the convoy. No heroics. You see anything, you report back at once and don't get stuck in. Clear?'

'Yes, sir.'

'Right, then let's get moving, gentlemen.'

Macro saluted and turned to mount his horse. As he adjusted his position, he looked round. Already a thin wisp of smoke was rising from the cart where several bodies in red tunics had been arranged on top of the sacks of grain and jars of olive oil packed on the bed of the wagon. Mule feed blazed at the tail of the vehicle, and, fanned by the breeze, the bright flames licked at the flammable material above. It was a dramatic and poignant sight, but Macro's mind was elsewhere. He was recalling the last time he had seen Cato and Julia together, just before leaving Rome. Their mutual affection had been clear to see and had touched even Macro's hardened heart.

Now Julia was dead.

And Macro dreaded the reaction of his friend when the news reached him.

CHAPTER NINETEEN

'Where's the rest of the bloody fleet?' Quintatus fumed at Cato as he surveyed the bay below the headland. In the choppy grey water a trireme and four smaller, more slender biremes lay at anchor off the thin strip of sand that ran along the shore. The beach, such as it was, was too small and the surf too shallow to beach the vessels safely, and so they rocked, masts swaying, some fifty paces from the shore. A small fort was under construction on the opposite head-land, the workforce of marines and sailors being screened by pickets from the Blood Crows. There was no sign of the rest of the warships that had been expected to meet the army on the coast, nor of the shallow-bottomed transports that were needed to ferry the troops across the channel separating the mainland from the island of Mona.

Behind the legate stood his staff officers and the mounted contingent of his bodyguard. The party had ridden ahead of the main column in response to Cato's report that he had located the first elements of the fleet. Some five miles to the rear, the army was trudging along a coastal track and should reach the bay in good time to construct a marching camp before nightfall. The advance had slowed after they had reached the Deceanglian capital and moved on, leaving a smouldering ruin in their wake. The enemy had harried the column all the way, launching swift attacks the instant it began to string out, and fleeing to cover when the Romans formed up to repulse them. Reports had come in that the follow-up supply convoys were also being attacked. Quintatus had been obliged to keep his army in close formation, slowing its pace, and had detached one of his cavalry cohorts to patrol his lines of communication and attempt to fend off attacks on the convoys.

All of which was gravely concerning to Cato. The legate's original plan for the campaign had been a swift strike through the heart of the mountains to destroy the Deceanglians before laying waste the Druid stronghold of Mona and then returning to base before the winter set in. But the season was now well advanced, and even though it had not rained for five days, the temperature had dropped to below freezing overnight, so that the water froze in the men's canteens, and frost had to be swept from their goatskin tents before they were struck down. Any advantage to be gained from easier passage over the hard ground had been offset by the need to slow the advance in the face of the enemy's harassing attacks. That morning had seen the first fall of snow, a brief flurry descending from heavy clouds before the wind had swept them away to leave a thin patina of white nestling on the boughs of trees and the rock and grass of the higher ground. There would be more, Cato knew, and should it be heavy, then the army would struggle to retreat from the mountains, let alone continue to advance deeper into enemy territory. All hinged on a rapid descent on Mona, a decisive victory, and an untroubled return to winter quarters. None of which seemed likely, especially given the misfortune that had struck the fleet as it had made its way up the coast to join the army.

Cato's forward patrols had found the handful of ships in the bay the afternoon before and spoken with the shaken trierarchs in command before setting them to work constructing the fort. He had sent a message back to the legate with the briefest details, which had resulted in this encounter on the headland to make his full report.

'As you know, sir, the fleet was hit by a storm three days ago and scattered. The survivors in the bay say that they witnessed some ships founder before they lost sight of the others and made the best speed they could to find the nearest shelter once they had rounded Mona. I have sent a patrol further along the coast to search for any sign of the rest of the fleet. They will return and report at dusk.'

'Well, they had better find some more ships for me. We need them, and the transports, if we are going to take Mona.'

'Yes, sir.'

It was an obvious point, and Cato realised that it had only been proffered out of anxiety. He could see that the legate's expression was strained, and for an instant he felt a flicker of sympathy for his commander. This campaign was supposed to deal a knockout blow to the native tribes' willingness to continue their ultimately futile resistance to Rome. It was intended to bring peace, and with that the acclaim that would have been bestowed on Quintatus. Instead the campaign had been beset by misfortune and was now in danger of becoming undone thanks to the onset of winter and the enemy's stubborn refusal to meet the legions in battle. Then the moment of sympathy passed as Cato reflected that the legate might have allowed his ambitions to overreach his reason. A common failing in the political class of Rome, and a particular hazard when such ambition put at risk the lives of the men who served in the Roman army.

'In the meantime,' Quintatus continued, 'how far are we from the channel?'

'Less than a day's march, sir. Nine, maybe ten miles along the coast from the bay.'

'Good. Then we will make camp on the far headland.' The legate turned to look for Titus Silanus. 'I want a double ditch around the ramparts, since we are close to the enemy.'

The camp prefect nodded. 'Yes, sir.'

'Then I'll leave you to get on with it while I ride ahead with the vanguard to see Mona myself. It'll be quite something to come face to face with the Druid lair.' He lifted his voice so that the surrounding officers would hear him. 'Gentlemen, when our mission here is complete, you will be dining out for the rest of your lives on tales of how you defeated the Druids!'

Some smiled at the prospect but most merely nodded dutifully, too cold and tired to make much effort to please their commander. Quintatus turned back to Cato. 'Let's go, then.'

For many days now, the most that the men of the Blood Crows had seen of the enemy was the distant clusters of horsemen who had tracked the Roman advance, never coming close enough to engage Cato's outriders, always slipping away the moment the auxiliary cavalry drew un-comfortably close. Wary of having his men fall into a trap, Cato had issued standing orders that there would be no attempt to pursue, and so the two sides had kept watch on each other from afar as the column penetrated ever deeper into the mountains.

Now, as they crested the ridge that overlooked the channel separating Mona from the mainland, they caught sight of the enemy army for the first time since the campaign had begun. In the fading light no more than half a mile away, ranged along the shore of the channel, lay hundreds of shelters, and the smoke from fires swirled over the roofs of thatch and moss. The camp was protected on its landward side by a crude turf rampart and a shallow ditch that would not have passed muster in the poorest of auxiliary cohorts. Scores of wide-beamed boats were beached on the shore and three more were ferrying men across the channel, quarter of a mile wide at the narrowest point, Cato calculated. The tide was coming in, but had not yet submerged rows of sharpened stakes extending from a point on the far shore, revealing the presence of a possible route across to Mona at low tide. On the far side he could make out a further line of defences running along the shore and many more huts clustered on the sloping ground beyond. On both sides of the channel thousands of figures were visible.

'We've got them!' Quintatus made a fist. 'We've finally got the bastards where we want them. Once we force them back on to the island, there'll be no escape. They'll be caught in a trap like the rats they are.'

The flat blast of a horn sounded from below, and a moment later the alarm was taken up by others and the noise swelled like a defiant challenge. At once the enemy warriors streamed through their shelters to line the ramparts, while those who had been foraging for firewood outside raced back to the gateways. Cato was impressed by the speed at which the Deceanglians had reacted. Moreover, they were well organised. Small parties of men formed up a short distance to the rear of the rampart to act as reserves, while mounted men raced out in front of the defences to form a picket line to investigate the intruders.

'Sloppy watch–keeping,' Quintatus mused. 'We were almost on them before the alarm was raised. It is astonishing how long these savages have been able to defy us, given their dismal attempts at soldiering. Well, now they're going to be taught a lesson they'll not live to profit from.'

Cato made a quick estimate of the enemy's strength, on both shores. 'Several thousand, but no more than ten thousand, at the most, I'd say, sir. And many of them will be tribal levies. We have the edge in quality of men and equipment.'

'Indeed. Nothing can keep victory from us now.'

'I hope not, sir,' Cato replied as he scrutinised the enemy positions. A boat was setting out from the island, with several figures in dark robes clustered in the bow observing the Romans in turn.

'I say!' One of the junior tribunes pointed. 'Are those fellows in black Druids? I had dearly wished to see some in the flesh.'

The more experienced officers gave him pitying glances before turning their attention back to the scene below. As the Druids reached the shore, they dispersed along the length of the rampart, save one, who mounted a black horse and galloped out of the nearest gate towards a small cluster of horsemen beneath a long-tailed standard that writhed, serpent-like, in the strengthening breeze. Another signal blared out, and hundreds of riders began to concentrate around the standard.

'I think it's time we returned to the camp, sir,' Cato suggested. 'It looks like the locals are starting to resent our intrusion.'

The horsemen immediately around the serpent standard surged forward, and the rest followed, coming on at a fast pace directly towards the legate, his officers and the Blood Crows who were escorting them.

'Fair point, Prefect. Let's go.'

Quintatus took a last look at the enemy army and then pulled on his reins and turned his horse back down the narrow track leading along the coast towards the Roman marching camp. It was not long before a rider came up from the rear of the cavalry cohort to announce that the enemy were pursuing them. Cato looked back and saw that they had reached the ridge and were already streaming down the near side, half a mile behind the Blood Crows. He gave the order to increase the pace to a canter to keep some distance between them and the natives. There was no need to go any faster. Their pursuers had already ridden at full pelt up to the ridge and their mounts would soon be blown.

As they pounded along over the hard ground, he felt a brief sting on his face and blinked as something caught in his eye. Then he realised that snow was falling; small scattered flakes swirling through the wind that was blowing from the sea to their left. The leaden swell rolled in and spray exploded over the rocky shoreline, and it occurred to Cato that what was left of the fleet would be struggling to gain the safety of the bay where the first ships to arrive were anchored. The flurry did not last long, and as the clouds began to part, angled rays of golden sunlight spilled across the sea, illuminating the western faces of the hills and mountains and casting long shadows behind them. But it would not last, Cato realised, as he looked over his shoulder and saw a thick band of cloud swelling up. Beneath, the sea was blotted out by a grey veil of more snow as it swept in over Mona, heading for the mainland. The blizzard would strike soon.

The track crested a low rise, close to the sea. Cato looked back and was relieved to see that the enemy had called off the pursuit and reined in some distance behind the Blood Crows, sitting in their saddles as they shook their spears defiantly. Pausing to detach one squadron to keep an eye on the tribesmen, Cato ordered the column to slow to a walk as the legate and his staff led the way back to the camp, just beyond the headland.

Decurion Miro abruptly halted his mount and looked out to sea, then thrust out his hand. 'Sir! Look there!'

Cato edged his horse over to the side of the track and stopped beside the decurion. Miro's cry had been picked up by the legate and his staff, and they too halted, their gaze following the direction indicated.

'What is it?' Cato demanded.

'A warship, sir. There!'

The heaving grey of the winter sea, flecked with whitecaps and brief sheets of spray, made it hard to pick out much detail. Then, two miles or so out at sea, Cato discerned the outline of an oared vessel as its sharp prow rose on the crest of a swell before plunging into a trough.

'There's more of them!' one of the tribunes called. Straining his eyes Cato saw that there were indeed other vessels out there, running before the wind towards the coast. As they drew closer, he counted six warships, biremes, and several of the smaller, unwieldy, wide-beamed transports.

Some had closely reefed sails while others were proceeding under jury rigs and oars as they strove to reach the safety of the bay before darkness fell. It would be a close thing, Cato decided. And the coming of night was not the only danger. Some miles behind the ships, the sky was almost black beneath the heavy pall of storm clouds racing across the grey swell of the sea. The Romans watched from their saddles a moment longer before Quintatus voiced what most of the others were already fearing.

'They're not going to make it.'

One of the junior tribunes turned towards him. 'They're not so far away, sir.'

'Quiet, you fool. Can't you see? The storm will be on them before they reach the bay. They haven't got a chance.'

'Poor devils,' Cato muttered to himself. He could see that the legate was right, and watched the crews desperately drive their vessels on as the sea began to broil around them. White-capped waves rose and fell, and clouds of spray burst across their decks.

The full wrath of the storm struck home as the leading ships were no more than half a mile from the comparative safety of the bay. Even though the earlier arrivals were in the shelter of the headland, their commanders had laid out additional stern anchors to secure them in the rough waters, and the ships fetched up with sharp jerks against their cables as they were battered by the waves. But the men anxiously watching for any signs of the anchors dragging were in far less danger than their comrades battling the storm raging across the open sea a short distance away.

A collective gasp amongst the officers drew Cato's attention back to the other ships just in time to see one of the transports struck side on by a large wave. She lurched drunkenly, men tumbling down the canted deck, before rolling over completely. For a moment there was no sign of the transport, or the men she had carried, as if the sea had swallowed them whole. Then the keel and the bottom of the hull broke the surface, glistening like the back of some large creature. Cato could just make out a handful of figures splashing in the sea nearby. One of them found the stern strake and climbed on to the hull, where he lay at full stretch, desperately holding on for his life as the icy waters burst over him. There was no hope of rescue by the other ships, whose crews were fighting for their own lives.

The wind and rain suddenly blasted over the headland, driving stinging sleet into the faces of the horsemen watching the disaster unfold. Cato's cloak whipped about him, and his horse turned away from the wind and needed a firm hand to force it back into position.

'Prefect Cato!'

He turned to see Quintatus beckoning to him, head hunched down into the folds of sodden cloth covering his shoulders. 'Sir?'

'There's nothing we can do here. I'm returning to camp. You and your men are to stay and keep watch for the enemy. If there's no further sign of them by nightfall, then post one of your squadrons on picket duty. The rest can return to camp.'

'Yes, sir.' Cato saluted.

The legate urged his mount forward and trotted back on to the track leading towards the camp being constructed above the shore. His officers followed, icy sleet sweeping over them in the rising wind.

Beside Cato, Decurion Miro snorted bitterly. 'Well thank you, Legate Quintatus. Just go and warm yourself by a fire while the rest of us freeze our arses off, why don't you?'

'That's quite enough,' Cato cut in. He looked round and saw a small copse a few hundred paces away. 'Get the rest of the men over there and into what shelter you can find.'

Miro saluted and turned to give the order to the column of men huddled into their cloaks. As they moved off, Cato spared a glance for the men still on picket duty, keeping watch in the direction of Mona. There was at least an hour of daylight left that they would have to endure. But their suffering was as nothing compared to the fate of the crews on the ships making for the bay. The first of the warships was passing the rocks below the end of the headland, a line of dark jagged shapes amid the swirl of waves and bursts of spray. The trierarch wisely held his course for another quarter of a mile before steering into the bay. From his elevated position Cato could see the ranks of men at the oars straining to drive the ship on, and could imagine their dread and terror at being at the mercy of Neptune's wrath. One by one the other warships and the first of the transports edged past the rocks and made for shelter.

But they were not safe yet. Cato felt his heart clench as he saw a transport's mast snap and plunge over the side, the reefed sail acting as a drag that slewed the ship's bow round to point towards the headland. At once the crew set to work, hacking desperately at the rigging to free the sail as the waves carried them in towards the rocks. Their work was hampered by the sea crashing over them and sweeping across the deck, and Cato could clearly see that they were doomed. Even if they cut themselves free, they would then have to rely on the long sweep oars, which were designed to manoeuvre such vessels over short distances. It would not be enough to keep them away from the rocks.

The last strand was cut and the broken mast and sail abruptly plunged into the sea and were swept past the stern of the transport. The oars, two on either side, were slid out and the first clumsy strokes heaved the ponderous ship round parallel to the line of rocks, a scant hundred paces away. Then, out of the storm, a huge wave rolled in, the steely grey mass lifting the ship and swinging the bows back towards the coast before dumping it much closer in so that it was obscured by the cloud of spray that burst over the rocks as the wave struck the shore. The crew strained at the oars, forcing the vessel back on its original course and driving it forwards through the tempest. Cato felt a surge of hope that they might be saved after all. Then another monstrous wave rolled in from the sleet-streaked gloom, gathering up the ship and carrying it high on its shoulders before it broke on the rocks.

As the water swirled away, Cato saw that the transport was wedged at an angle on top of the glistening black rocks, its back broken, the keel shattered on impact. There were still men on the deck, clinging on, doomed to live a little longer yet before the waves pounded the ship to pieces, and them along with it. Cato watched in horror, his stomach knotted with pity at their fate. Then he looked again at the rocks, the distance from them to the pebbled beach off which the three warships lay at anchor, and reached a decision.

Snatching at his reins, he spurred his horse into a gallop and caught up with Miro and the Blood Crows as they plodded through the sleet towards the trees.

'Halt!'

The men stopped in their tracks. Cato reined in hard as he reached the waiting decurion, the blood pounding in his ears as he caught his breath and began.

'Your squadron is to come with me. The rest can wait in those trees. Tell Aristophanes to take over and keep an eye on the enemy before you come after me.'

Miro frowned. 'What exactly are you intending to do, sir?'

Cato quickly explained about the transport and the peril faced by its crew. 'They can still be saved.'

'Sounds like they're already dead men, sir.'

Cato frowned. 'Not while there's still a chance. Not while we can do something. You have your orders, Decurion. Move!'

Leaving Miro to organise his men, Cato turned and spurred his horse down the slope towards the storm-lashed shore. In all probability the decurion was right. But he'd be damned if he would abandon any man to such a terrible fate while there was still the slimmest chance of saving him.

CHAPTER TWENTY

The violence of the storm was even more apparent when Cato reached the beach curving around the bay. The roar of the surf and the rattle of pebbles filled his ears as he reined in his horse and dropped from the saddle. To his left, the cliff beneath the headland shielded him from the worst of the wind, and here in its lee the sleet had already turned into snow. Large flakes spun through the air and melted almost as soon as they landed on the stones. Ahead, the line of the cliff ended where the rocks began; great boulders that lay as if the end of the cliff had been pulverised by the fist of Jupiter himself. The line of rocks continued into the sea for another two hundred paces or so, to where the transport was being pounded by the great waves rising from the depths of the ocean. The stern was taking the brunt of the storm, being steadily broken up. The bow section was protected from the impact of the waves at present but would feel their full force before long. Several men were huddled on the sloping deck, and another stood over the bows waving desperately to those on the shore, no doubt imploring them to attempt a rescue.

But their comrades were looking on helplessly, scores of

sailors on the decks of the anchored vessels, and more watching from the beach. Cato approached one of the naval officers overseeing the construction of a shelter at the top of the beach, beyond the line of tenders lying along the shingle. The trierarch was shouting orders above the noise of the surf to make his men return to their work.

'Why aren't you doing something?' Cato demanded.

'What business is it of yours?' The trierarch turned to address Cato, saw his rank and knuckled his brow in salute. 'Sorry, sir.'

'Why aren't you rescuing those men?'

'There's nothing that can be done to save them, sir. Not without putting more lives at stake. It'd be suicide to attempt to get them off that wreck. Besides, it'll be swept away soon enough, and them too. It's too bad, sir. But we can't help them.'

Cato stared hard towards the rocks and saw a fresh wave break over the doomed ship, briefly obscuring it in spray, before the sea surged back and exposed the remaining timbers of the ruined stern section. The man who had been beckoning to those on the shore slowly eased himself down on to the deck beside his comrades and hugged his knees with a resigned air. Quickly calculating the distance between the rocks and the nearest of the anchored warships, Cato rounded on the trierarch.

'I am not going to stand by and let men die,' he said fiercely. 'I want one of your tenders and four good men on the oars. Strong swimmers all.'

The trierarch clicked his tongue. 'Sir, I really don't think—'

'I don't give a shit for what you think! Just carry out my orders. At once!'

He did not give the man a chance to respond and strode back to his mount just as Miro and his men drew up. Hurriedly unfastening the straps of his helmet, he placed it on the shingle. His cold fingers removed his cloak and sword belt and then he turned to Miro. 'Give me a hand with the armour!' The decurion slid from his saddle and helped with the fastenings before Cato slipped the scale vest off and dropped it beside the rest of his kit. He stood in his boots, breeches and tunic, too tense to tremble in the biting cold. Beyond Miro he saw the trierarch directing several of his men to drag one of the small boats belonging to the warships down towards the roaring surf.

He cleared his throat to make sure that it did not betray his nerves. 'We're going to try two approaches to the wreck. I want you and your squadron to take a rope and make your way along the rocks. Get as close as you can without risk to life, and throw a line to those men. Meanwhile I'll try to get to them from the boat there.'

Miro looked along the line of rocks stretching from the headland, and his eyes widened anxiously as he watched the waves exploding over them.

'Decurion!' Cato grasped him by the harness. 'We are not letting those men die. Clear?'

Miro blinked rapidly and then nodded. 'Yes . . . Yes, sir!'

'Good man. Now, let's get to it.' Cato gave him an encouraging punch on the shoulder before striding down towards the sea, where the four sailors chosen by the trierarch were setting up their oars, their comrades doing their best to hold the small boat steady in the creamy surf. The water felt icy as it closed round Cato's legs, and it was up to his waist as he reached the side of the boat and heaved himself aboard.

He took his place in the stern and pointed to the bireme anchored nearest to the rocks. 'Get us over to that ship!'

The sailors braced their feet, and with one of them calling the time, they bent to their work and rowed free of the breaking waves into deeper water. As they drew alongside the warship pitching roughly in the surging water of the bay, Cato cupped a hand to his mouth and called up to the crewmen watching the drama on the rocks.

'I need a rope here! You!' He pointed at the nearest sailor. 'Get one end tied around the foot of the mast. Then pass me the rest. And a couple of spare coils while you're at it. Move!'

The men at the oars kept the small craft in position while two coils were tossed down from the deck of the warship, followed by the length that had been fastened around the mast. Cato tugged it sharply to satisfy himself that it was secure before he gave the order to make for the lee of the rocks. At the foot of the headland he could see the figures of Miro and his men, roped together, carefully picking their way in the gathering gloom. At the sight of the prefect, Miro increased their pace, slipping and stumbling over the glistening rocks and clutching for handholds as spray began to burst over them. The sailors on the stricken transport rose to their feet as the boat headed towards them trailing the rope attached to the anchored bireme. Some beckoned frantically while the others looked on clutching the side rail. The stern of the vessel had all but disappeared, pounded to pieces by the waves. Only the stern strake and a few ribs remained amid the shattered timbers.

As the boat approached, Cato had a brief moment in which to think, and was horrified by the peril in which he had placed himself. He hated being in the water at the best of times and was a poor swimmer. Now he was in imminent danger of being pitched into the icy depths of a wild sea. Yet there was nothing he could do about it. He was committed to this reckless attempt to save the sailors and must see it through. No more than twenty paces ahead, through the swirl of snowflakes, he saw the gleaming mass of a rock break the surface as the trough of a wave passed over it and the surrounding water eddied violently.

'Easy oars!' he shouted. 'Hold us here.'

The sailors ceased rowing and made minor strokes to hold the boat in place as Cato stared at the rocks, the wreck and the sea and swiftly considered how to proceed. The remains of the transport were more than forty paces away. Even if they got as close to the rocks as they dared, they would still be too far from the wreck to have any hope of throwing a rope to the men waiting in the bow section of the vessel. He turned his attention to the rocks stretching back towards the headland. Though the waves were crashing over them, there was an unbroken line leading almost up to the wreck before an open patch of water separated them from the jagged rocks on which the transport was caught. If Miro could reach the gap, a man with a good arm could heave a line to the sailors, Cato calculated.

Bracing himself with one hand clasping the wooden bench, he half rose and waved a hand to attract the decurion's attention. Miro was still over a hundred paces away, and Cato could see that he and his men were making painfully slow progress. Too slow. Night was coming, and there was no hope of saving the men in the dark. As Miro looked his way, Cato waved frantically with his spare hand and then pointed towards the gap in the rocks. The decurion hesitated, then nodded and continued picking his way forward, pausing only to brace himself against the deluge of seawater boiling over the rocks as the waves struck home on the seaward side of the natural breakwater.

'That's it,' Cato said to himself as he sat down heavily on the bench. 'Keep going, man!'

As the roped men continued making their way towards the gap, Cato saw beyond them the loom of a large wave rolling in. A moment later it smashed into the rocks, inundating Miro and his auxiliaries. One was too slow in bracing himself for the impact and tumbled down towards the water with a shrill cry that carried even to Cato's ears, almost dragging down his companions on either side. Miro turned back at the sound. In the brief respite between waves, the man was hauled back on to the rocks and lay a moment catching his breath. Cato breathed a quick sigh of relief and then craned his head forward as Miro edged back towards his men.

'What are you doing? Get moving.'

But instead, Cato saw the line of men begin to turn back towards the headland, and he felt the blood rise in his veins as he ground his teeth in anger. He restrained himself from making any comment. The situation was too serious for that now. Miro could be dealt with later. Then he noticed that the sailors in the boat were looking at him anxiously as they worked their oars enough to hold the boat in place. He cleared his throat.

'Right then, it's down to us. Get me close to that gap in the rocks.'

None of the men responded at first, and Cato saw the

fear in their eyes. He regarded them squarely. 'Those are your comrades over there. Would you leave them to the storm? Would they leave you if you were in their place?'

'It's madness to try to save them, sir,' said the man at the bow oar.

Cato felt tempted to snap back and tell him to shut his mouth, but he bit back on his anger and continued gently. 'I won't ask you to sacrifice your lives. Just get me close enough to do what I can. That's all.'

The sailor nodded and called the time for the others, and the boat surged towards the wrecked transport. Cato peeled off his drenched tunic, took up one of the coils of rope in the bottom of the boat and looped it over his shoulder. 'If I make it, I'll heave the end of this back to you. You'll need to tie it to the ship's cable. Clear?'

'Aye, sir.'

'One final thing. If I fail, don't try and save me.'

The man smiled grimly. 'Is that an order, sir?'

Cato forced himself to smile, then untied his bootstraps and kicked off the heavy military sandals, shivering in the biting cold as he crouched in only his loincloth, summoning up his courage. He thought briefly of Julia, and their child, who might soon be widow and orphan, and pushed them from his mind. Then, without hesitation, he leapt from the boat and plunged into the rough sea.

The first sensation was the terrible cold of the water that briefly closed over him, as if a giant fist was clenched around his body. Then his head burst free and the roar and hiss of the sea filled his ears. At once he struck out for the rocks beneath the hull of the transport. They seemed close, but he was fighting the swirling currents and knew that he must reach them swiftly. There was not much daylight left, and the agonising cold of the sea would soon sap his strength.

He made for a low step in the rock and had almost reached it when a fresh wave broke over the transport's bows. The surf carried him back a short way before it ebbed, drawing him closer. Taking advantage of the current, he kicked out with all his strength and groped for a handhold as he reached the rock. The sea rose up underneath him and he allowed himself to move with it, then grasped the hard surface tightly and clambered out of the water, drawing himself several feet higher before he paused to take stock. He was crouching on a flat-topped rock, above the waves. The hull curved up a short distance away, and Cato looked down on the foredeck, where the sailors had been watching his progress with anxious expressions. Now there was a spark of hope in their faces, but they had not been saved yet.

Trembling violently in the biting wind and snow, he uncoiled the rope and stood, feet braced and arm drawn back as he beckoned to the men in the boat to draw closer to him. They worked hard at the oars, and when they were within twenty feet of the rock beneath him, the sailor closest to the bow shipped his oar and turned to take the rope. Cato hurled the loose loops out and they snaked through the air, splashing just short of the boat.

He gritted his teeth and snatched the rope back, hurriedly looping it, and adding another length, then threw again. Fortune was with him. The swell lifted the boat closer and the rope fell across the bows. Instantly it began to slide back and the sailor snatched at it, missed, then tried again. This time his fingers closed tightly, and he pulled it in and fastened it to the rope trailing back through the sea to the warship before looking up at Cato and nodding.

Turning back to the transport, Cato hefted the remaining coils of rope and looked over the rocks between him and the open sea. Another huge wave loomed, sending frothing sheets of water surging up the shattered deck and swirling round the rocks beneath. Then the sea receded and he clambered down from his perch and scurried over the glistening mass of rock and thick growths of seaweed, stopping directly under the bows.

'Take the rope!' he shouted at the faces looking down at him. He swung his arm and threw the loops up. Hands snatched at them and pulled the cable in, then Cato quickly worked his way round the hull until he found a gap in the shattered timbers and climbed on to what was left of the deck, gasping for breath as his frozen body trembled uncontrollably. He staggered towards the others just as a fresh wave struck, sweeping him off his feet and tumbling him across the deck. He tried to grab hold of something to prevent himself being drawn back by the sea, then, just as he felt the first stab of despair, a hand closed tightly around his forearm, bringing him to a stop, and then more hands drew him up and out of the water and he saw the faces of the sailors staring down at him. The nearest was grinning through a dark, glistening beard.

'Mate, you have got balls of solid iron! Here, let me.' The sailor hauled Cato up on to his feet and steadied him as the others slapped him on the back. Beyond them, Cato saw that the rope had been securely tied around the bow post and was taut as it angled down towards the sea where the boat bobbed. Now that it was fastened to both the warship and what was left of the transport, the small craft was held steady in the swell. Then he noticed two more boats approaching, drawing towards the cable and pulling themselves along it. He glanced round at the sailors and counted nine of them.

'We have to get off here as soon as possible. One at a time, down the rope, into the boat.'

The burly sailor who had kept him from being washed away pointed to the nearest of his companions. 'Sallus, you go first. Porcinus, you next, once he has reached the boat.'

The small group of men gathered by the bow post while Sallus swung himself out. He hung downwards, legs locked on to the rope as he used his arms to draw himself out over the rocks, then the sea, towards the boat that had carried Cato out from the shore. By the time he had reached the craft, the other boats were alongside and he was manhandled into the nearest of them as the second man began his descent.

'Look out!'

Cato's head snapped round in time to see a cloud of spray above his head. He gripped the side rail as he was engulfed by the icy torrent. The man on the rope gave a brief cry, and when the spray cleared, there was no sign of him, just the rope trembling as water dripped from its length.

'Poor bastard,' the burly sailor muttered before he slapped the next man on the shoulder. 'You're up. Get moving!'

As they watched the man swing himself on to the rope and make his way down to the waiting boats, he turned to Cato. 'The name's Talbo. If we survive this, I'll buy you the best jar of wine I can find, my friend.'

He thrust his hand out and Cato clasped his forearm. 'Good. We'll need a drink after this. I'm Cato.'

'You're from the *Medusa*?' Talbo gestured towards the nearest warship. He continued before Cato could respond. 'I hope your skipper writes you up for a medal for this. You bloody deserve it, my friend.'

Cato bowed his head slightly. 'Thanks, but let's not count our chickens just yet, eh? Fortuna likes to play her games to the very end.'

Their exchange was interrupted by a lurch in the deck beneath them and a grating crunch, and they looked back to see a section of the deck collapse no more than ten feet away.

'Not long now,' said Cato.

The sailors calmly took their turn and the first boat turned back to the shore with those it had rescued. At last only Talbo and Cato remained.

'After you.' The sailor gestured towards the rope.

Cato shook his head. 'You're a big man. You'll need more time. You first. Go.'

'Calling me fat? Ah, shit, I was just getting to like you.'

Talbo heaved himself over the side and started to shimmy away, leaving Cato alone on the foredeck. Another wave struck, and the wreck shifted again, more noticeably this time, and a section of the deck split open. His judgement of the sailor was correct, and Cato had to restrain himself from shouting encouragement to the man to move faster. He was shivering violently now and the feeling had gone from his toes. He rubbed his hands together hard and clapped them to try and keep them from locking up.

At last Talbo reached the side of the boat, and the sailors hauled him in. At once Cato clambered over the rail, grasped the rope, swung his legs over it and pulled himself hand over

261

hand along it. Each time the sea washed over what was left of the wreck, the rope jerked and he swayed over the rocks and then the surging foam of the sea. Dropping his head and glancing back, he saw that he was close to the boat and the sailors were urging him on with desperate gestures. At first he did not grasp their anxiety, then he looked up and saw that the last section of the bow was swaying from side to side. Suddenly the bow post gave a lurch and toppled, the rope slackened and he plunged down into the sea.

Once again he was violently seized by its icy grip, and this time he held his breath and clung to the rope rather than try to reach the surface. If he released it, he knew he might not have the strength to swim to safety. As he hung on, he felt a tug, and his body moved through the icy depths. Just as his lungs were starting to burn, he broke the surface a short distance from the boat, and then hands grasped him and pulled him over the side and dumped him unceremoniously into the well of the craft.

'Cast us loose!' Talbo roared. 'Before the fucking wreck takes us down with it! Don't untie it, you fool! Cut it! Out of my way.'

Cato looked up in a daze and saw the sailor against the failing light of day sawing at the rope with his knife. The hemp parted strand by strand and then the severed end flickered and was gone. Talbo sheathed his knife and gave the order to head for the shore. Then he picked up Cato's sodden tunic and laid it over him as he lay shaking in the water slopping about the bottom of the boat.

'Rest easy, Cato. Your job's done, mate.'

Talbo patted him on the shoulder and then called the time for the men on the oars as the little craft rose and fell on the rough sea, lurching away from the danger of the rocks and making for safety. Cato felt a terrible weariness seep through his body and was tempted to close his eyes and drift off. But he feared that call to sleep. What if he never woke? Instead he propped himself up against the stern bench and hugged his knees as he shivered, teeth chattering.

At last his ears filled with the crash of waves on shingle and the boat lurched as it grounded, lifted again and then thudded home more solidly. The sailors shipped their oars and jumped over the side to draw the craft up the beach. Talbo leaned back in, offering a hand. Cato took it willingly and allowed himself to be helped out on to the pebbles. Dusk was gathering along the shore and the gloom was made worse by the snow, which was falling heavily now.

'My boots,' he said weakly, and the sailor reached in and handed them to him.

'There you go, mate. I'll see what I can do about a cloak for you, and some wine, food and a warm fire. Then I'll get you back to your ship.'

As Cato nodded dumbly, the sound of footsteps racing over the shingle reached his ears.

'Sir! Sir! Prefect Cato!'

He glanced up and saw Miro and several of his men rushing forward with excited and relieved expressions. One had already removed his cloak and now pressed it around Cato's shoulders as Talbo looked on with raised eyebrows.

'Prefect Cato? Well, I . . . I . . . Fuck me.' Talbo laughed. 'I thought you was a sailor. One of us. Never thought I'd have my life saved by a landsman. An officer at that.'

'It takes all kinds, Talbo.' Cato smiled thinly.

They clasped arms again and grinned with the delight and

relief of men who had faced grave peril together and lived through it.

'And as for that wine? Make it Falernian, and bring it to my tent. I'll hold you to it.'

'Aye, sir. That I will. On my word.'

There was a pause, and both men instinctively looked back towards the rocks. There was no longer any sign of the transport. The storm had destroyed it completely and swallowed the remains. Out in the white-capped waters of the bay, the battered survivors of the fleet were dropping anchor or being beached by their exhausted crews amid the wind and snow that was starting to settle on the surrounding landscape. Winter had finally arrived in earnest, Cato reflected grimly, and he wondered if their troubles were only just beginning.

CHAPTER TWENTY-ONE

Cato winced as the headquarters trumpets blared into the morning air and a moment later the first battery of bolt-throwers went into action. The usual crack of the throwing arms springing forward was reduced to a softer snap by the layer of snow that had blanketed the landscape during the night. Three inches or so, and it had drifted in front of the enemy palisade and against their shelters beyond. Puffs of white exploded where the iron-headed bolts smashed into the palisade timbers encrusted with frost and snow. At once the enemy warriors who had been lining the defences, shouting insults at the Romans, ducked out of sight. After the last of the bolts struck home there was a brief pause before the dark dots of their faces reappeared along the defences. The jeering began to start again, prematurely, as the second battery unleashed its missiles, concentrating on the same stretch of defences at the centre of the enemy line. As Cato watched, one of the defenders, bolder than his comrades, stood tall, waving his fists. An instant later a bolt struck him squarely in the chest and he was hurled back out of sight.

'First blood to us,' chuckled Legate Valens of the

Fourteenth Legion as he stood at Cato's side. 'Those savages never seem to learn what modern weapons can do. Won't be long before we knock their defences to pieces.'

Cato nodded. Over a hundred bolt-throwers and catapults had accompanied the army, and between them they would be more than enough to breach the enemy's defences, as well as causing them heavy losses. However, the advantage would only lie with the Romans with respect to the defences on this side of the channel. The artillery would lack the range to attack the Druids' defences lining the shore of Mona. He turned to gaze along the coast to where the four surviving warships were leading what was left of the transports towards the northern entrance of the channel between the mainland and Mona. The warships had a handful of artillery pieces with which to support the landing on the island, but Cato doubted they would be enough to turn the tide of battle. The assault troops would have to struggle ashore through the icy shallows before attacking the fortifications protecting the narrowest stretch of the channel. He could see that the rest of the shoreline facing the mainland was protected by lesser earthworks and lines of sharpened stakes. The only other option was the narrow, muddy causeway that was briefly explored at low tide. Even that was protected by a thick belt of sharpened stakes. It was going to be a bloody business.

Legate Quintatus and his senior officers were watching proceedings from a small hillock a short distance behind the men of the Fourteenth, who were still moving into position in preparation for the attack that would go in once a number of practicable breaches had been torn through the enemy's palisade. On the flanks of the legion stood the four auxiliary cohorts chosen to support the assault, two of which were missile units comprised of archers and slingers from the Balearic islands. The Blood Crows were positioned on the right flank. Their horses were still in camp; the entire unit would be fighting on foot, together with the legionary cohort to which they had been attached since the beginning of the year. Such was the fear that the Blood Crows struck into enemy hearts that Quintatus had decided to have them join the assault.

Although there was no wind and the sea was calm, the leaden sky threatened more snow, and many of the Roman soldiers had chosen to wear their cloaks into action, knowing that they might have to wait a while before the order to advance was given. Those in the cohorts that had already formed up on the slope leading down to the enemy's defences were stamping their feet and rubbing their hands in an attempt to stave off the cold. Their comrades in the Twentieth Legion and the remaining auxiliary cohorts were being held in reserve in the marching camp sprawling across the crest of the hill that overlooked the narrowest point of the channel. They still had the comfort of the fires burning inside the ramparts of the camp as they stood ready in case they were called on to fight.

It had been two days since the storm had passed, the following morning revealing the extent of the damage wreaked on the hapless fleet that had been sent to join Quintatus and his column. The shore had been strewn with wreckage and corpses for miles either side of the bay, and fully two thirds of the vessels and their crews had been lost. The bodies had been gathered up and cremated on pyres constructed from the shattered timbers of the ships before the army made its final advance to the hill overlooking the enemy's positions either side of the channel. In that time Cato had recovered from the effects of the cold and exhaustion caused by his rescue of the sailors. They at least had been saved from the savage storm, and that was some small comfort to the prefect. Now he turned his attention to the pending assault and the wider situation as he continued the conversation he had been having with Legate Valens.

'We'll deal with their position on this side of the channel easily enough, sir, but getting across the water and taking the island itself is going to be a much tougher proposition. Either we try crossing at low tide through those obstacles, or we go straight across the water. Not easy given how few transports made it through the storm.'

Both men glanced at the vessels edging into the mouth of the channel, keeping as close to the mainland as they dared in case the enemy attempted anything with the scores of small craft they had beached along the shore of the island. Besides the warships, there were eight transports, each capable of carrying no more than fifty men.

'With only four hundred in each wave, it's going to be difficult,' Cato commented. 'The first men across are going to have the fight of their lives.'

'It won't be easy,' Valens conceded. 'But I'd bet on the boys in the Fourteenth against that screaming mob of barbarians any day. They just have to get ashore and hold on long enough for the follow-up troops. Once we've numbers on the ground, nothing can stop us. We'll crush those Druids like eggs. That'll knock the stuffing out of any other tribes thinking of taking a pop at us, eh?'

Cato made himself smile reassuringly. 'Yes, I imagine so.'

Valens had a point. Without the Druids to unite the tribes against Rome, the standard policy of divide and rule would work its usual magic. That was what made it possible for the tiny city state that Rome had once been to hold sway over a vast expanse of the known world. And it would be no different here in Britannia. The entire population would be held down by three or four legions and several cohort units, with the aid of those native rulers whose loyalty had been bought with Roman silver. That would be the price of peace for the natives of Britannia.

As they had been talking, the ballista crews had been given permission to fire at will, and as each loaded at its own speed, the distinct volleys that had opened the barrage blurred into a continuous, rhythmless series of cracks. The enemy, who had been using the initial intervals to show their defiance, now hunkered down behind their palisade to ride it out, ready to spring forward again the moment the Romans ceased shooting. The concentrated impact of the heavy bolts was already shattering the timbers of the palisade, and there was a cry of triumph from the watching soldiers when a section of the rampart fell into the outer ditch, carrying away some of the earth from beneath it.

'Officers to your units!' Quintatus called out from his station a short distance in front of his command post. The camp prefect repeated the order with a loud bellow to ensure that it was heard by all, and then the commanders of the units about to go into action moved off to join their men. Cato strode part of the way with Valens and noted the man's irrepressible confidence as he greeted his subordinates and took his place close to the standard-bearers on the right of the line.

'Good fortune go with you, sir,' said Cato as he bowed his head briefly.

'And with you, Prefect Cato!' Valens nodded. 'Stick it to 'em, Blood Crows!'

The legate turned to give a final address to his senior centurions, the time-honoured tradition of commanders before a battle. Cato had sometimes favoured the men under his command with similar treatment, but he doubted its necessity now. They would fight come what may, and a few hackneyed boasts and appeals to duty would not be likely to boost their chances of winning a battle. Better, he thought, to show them a calm professionalism and let them trust to their training and experience. So he affected a diffident manner as he approached the colour party of the Blood Crows and undid the clasp fastening his cloak, handing the garment to Thraxis before taking the shield held out for him by his servant.

Out of habit, he hefted the shield and tested its weight, then rolled his shoulders to loosen them before he nodded to Thraxis.

'All ready . . .' He paused and fixed his servant with a brief appraising look. He had made a decision about the Thracian's future earlier that morning, and it seemed an appropriate moment to break the news. 'You can leave the cloak with the dressing party and then take your place beside the standard-bearer, as his second.'

Thraxis could not help showing his surprise. 'Sir?'

'You've served me well. Though not always with good humour, eh?' Cato chuckled as he remembered the many occasions when Thraxis had seen to his needs like a man nursing a perpetual hangover. He was rewarded with a fresh scowl, but the expression swiftly disappeared as Thraxis smiled at his good fortune. To be the second to the standard-bearer made him responsible for the man's safety in battle, and if the standard-bearer was killed or badly wounded, it would fall to Thraxis to take the Blood Crows' standard and keep it raised high. The post came with a pay increase to one and a half times his previous rate, as well as being excused-duties status. There would be no more of the drudgery of cleaning latrines, fetching firewood and cleaning his superior's kit. It would also mean that Thraxis was well placed to rise to the rank of optio, and after that decurion. As his mind raced through the opportunities extended to him, he paused and looked at Cato.

'Who will replace me as your servant, sir?'

'I'll trust you to find the right man for the job once we return to Mediolanum. There's no hurry. All I ask is that you make sure he has a sunnier disposition than the current post-holder.'

'That crack ain't funny, sir.'

'I know. That's why I'm replacing you.'

Thraxis grinned and nodded appreciatively. 'Thank you, sir. I'm very grateful.'

'No need for that. It's clear enough to me that you have the potential to make a decent junior officer. Congratulations.'

Thraxis hurried off with Cato's cloak and left it with the auxiliaries who were busy preparing their dressings and splints in readiness for the flow of casualties when the attack went in. He returned a moment later with his own shield and took his place alongside the standard-bearer. Around them the Blood Crows stood formed up in their squadrons with their decurions posted on the right flank, puffs of steam swirling from the men's lips each time they exhaled into the bitterly cold morning air. The snow on the ground muffled the sounds of voices and the chink of loose equipment and lent an unnatural quiet to the scene. On Cato's orders they had left their spears in camp. The close-quarters fighting that lay ahead favoured the use of swords.

Cato watched the fall of the shot from the ballista batteries and noted with satisfaction that they were tearing numerous gaps in the centre of the palisade. His attention passed along the enemy's defences to the small redoubt at the end, directly opposite the Blood Crows. That fortification was as yet untouched, but the first of the biremes was already dropping anchor within range of it, and a second anchor was dropped from the stern in order to provide a secure platform, side on to the action. Cato could see the crews of the deck-mounted bolt-throwers loading their weapons and turning them to bear on the redoubt. This was the objective assigned to the Blood Crows. If it was taken, then the cohort would be able to charge on the enemy's flank and roll up their line. The bireme was late in reaching its station and adding its weight to the bombardment, and Cato let out a long, frustrated breath.

As the last clanks of the loading windlasses died away, the trierarch in command of the warship raised his arm to call his ballista crews to attention, then thrust it forward. The dark shafts of the heavy bolts arced across the water and smashed into the defences, unleashing a shower of splinters. The crews fired a few more volleys before the headquarters trumpets sounded and the batteries ceased shooting. As if to try and make amends for their tardiness, the sailors released a few extra shots before standing down.

A hush fell across the snowy battlefield as the Romans stood waiting for the order to attack. Along the defences, the first faces appeared as the enemy warily returned to their positions and prepared to make their stand.

'Fourteenth Legion!' A voice bellowed from the heavily armoured ranks to the left of the Blood Crows. 'Prepare to advance!'

The men raised their shields and held them at an angle across their bodies.

'Advance!'

The front ranks of each cohort moved forward, and those following rippled after their comrades, pacing out across the virginal white snow in front of the natives' fortifications. The order to advance was repeated in the flanking missile cohorts, and the archers and slingers surged ahead of the legionaries, ready to harass any of the enemy who made easy targets of themselves. Cato steadied himself and drew a deep breath before he too called out into the crisp air.

'Blood Crows, make ready . . . Advance!'

He stepped out, and his men followed suit on either side as the black standard with its red crow stirred above the formation. The snow crunched softly under his boots as he descended the gentle slope towards the outer ditch and the round earthwork of the redoubt. Two hundred paces ahead he saw the enemy warriors waiting to receive them. The usual mix of tribesmen with armour and those without, waving spears, swords and axes. The few bowmen amongst them were hurriedly stringing their weapons, plucking arrows from their quivers and notching them as they waited for the Romans to march into range.

A century from the cohort of archers trotted ahead of the Blood Crows, pausing to loose arrows as they approached the ditch. The defenders began to shoot back, and the slender shafts arced to and fro against the grey sky. The advantage lay with the enemy, who were able to duck into cover, while their Roman opponents were in the open and had to rely on quick reactions and deft footwork to avoid being struck down. Some were not so lucky, and Cato saw one of the auxiliaries lurch as an arrow caught him in the shoulder. Slinging his bow, the man tried to work the arrow free as he fell back, passing the Blood Crows and making for the field dressing station.

A faint *phut* reached Cato's ears, and he saw a shaft quiver momentarily in the snow not ten feet ahead of him. He raised his shield to cover his chin and continued forward without breaking his pace. Another arrow whirred close by and he had to force himself not to flinch in case the men on either side of him noticed. The archers had stopped a short distance ahead and now began to move aside to fall back between the squadrons of the Blood Crows as they marched towards the outer slope of the ditch. The shafts and feathered flights of the enemy's arrows sprouted from the snow like slender flowers. Cato was briefly struck by the comparison and smiled, until he caught sight of an archer on the palisade directly ahead, lining up his shot. As their eyes met, the man drew back his right arm and cocked his head. Cato just had time to lift his shield before the man released his arrow, and then he felt the impact as the iron head smashed through the leather and strips of glued wood, splintering just a few inches from his face. More arrows and slingshot zipped through the air as the defenders desperately tried to shoot down as many attackers as they could before the Romans closed the gap and engaged them hand to hand.

A cry close by caused Cato to glance round. He saw one of his men stagger to a halt and lower his shield as he reached up to grasp the shaft that protruded from his shattered cheekbone. A moment later he was struck again, this time by a slingshot that caught him squarely on the front of his helmet, jerking his head back violently and knocking him senseless. He collapsed into the snow and lay still as his comrades advanced relentlessly around and over him.

Cato risked a quick glimpse over the rim of his shield and saw that they were almost on top of the ditch. He slowed his pace as he began to descend the outer slope. The ditch was no more than ten feet deep and the bottom was strewn with sharpened stakes set into the ground at an angle. The obstacles would have presented a danger to a headlong attack, but the measured advance of well-trained Roman soldiers meant that the attackers had time to push the stakes aside and continue to the inner slope before clambering up the far side. Cato led the way, making for a point where the navy's ballista had smashed several timbers to splintered remnants. As he began to scramble up the inner slope, having to thrust his hands into the snow to gain purchase on the frozen ground beneath, he saw the enemy lining the palisade above. Many had hair stiff with limewash and bore swirling tattoos on their faces. Their lips curled back and their mouths were wide agape as they screamed insults and curses at the Romans. Some were hurling rocks down from the palisade, crashing on to the oval shields of the Blood Crows, or glancing off helmets and armour. A few unlucky men were struck on exposed limbs or dazed by sudden blows to the head. They fell back and slid down into the ditch, stunned.

On hands and knees Cato crawled up the slope, keeping his shield raised and wincing each time it was struck by a rock. At the foot of the palisade he crouched by the timber posts and quickly took stock of the situation. On both sides his men were swarming around the defences of the redoubt, crowding those points where the bireme's brief barrage had battered the timbers. He saw that the palisade was fastened with intertwined lengths of rope that helped to hold the posts in place. At once he drew his sword, thrust it into a gap between two of the posts and began sawing. As the strands parted, he was joined by the standard-bearer and Thraxis, who took out his own blade and, following his prefect's example, began to cut at the rope higher up. Other men did the same around the redoubt, while the enemy continued to hurl missiles down at them, desperate to drive them away.

The rope parted and Cato sheathed his blade so that he could work the strands free of the posts on either side. Then he called forward two of his men, big, burly soldiers who reached up to where the ballista bolts had shattered the timbers. Groping for handholds, they strained and pulled at the posts while Cato thrust his sword back through the gap and tried to help work them loose. Soil began to trickle out, and then one of the posts gave a little lurch and shifted at an angle to the others.

'It's working!' Cato shouted. 'Keep at it.'

With Thraxis helping, the post moved again and then began to lean out. A final effort by the two auxiliaries brought it out of the ground, leaving a modest pile of soil behind. As the post slid down into the ditch, the Romans began work on those either side of the gap, and these began to move more easily. Then a shadow loomed above Cato and he glanced up to see a native leaning over the palisade, a long hunting spear in his hands, drawn back and ready to strike at them. As the broad leaf-shaped point stabbed down, Cato thrust his shield up and blocked the blow, deflecting the point back into the nearest timbers. At once he dropped his sword and grasped the spear shaft, wrenching it away from its owner with all his might. He gained a few feet before the warrior took hold again, and for a brief moment each strained to wrestle the weapon from the other. Then Cato swung the shaft out at an angle and thrust it back. The butt caught his opponent under the chin, snapping his jaw up and his head back, and he tumbled out of sight.

'Nice one, sir!' Thraxis laughed.

A second post began to shift and then broke free of the soil and snow, leaving a gap just wide enough for a man to squeeze through. Cato held his shield out and passed it between the posts on either side as he used his spare hand to clamber up the unstable slope of earth on to the rampart. He was on his knees when he reached the top and snatched out his sword as he was instantly spotted by the nearest enemy warriors. A large man in a fur cloak swung round to face him, raising his battleaxe over his head as he let out a roar and plunged towards the Roman officer. Cato just had time to brace his feet as the warrior swung his axe down.

Glimpsing the glint of the sharpened head of the weapon, he angled his shield to deflect the blow, but the impact was sudden and violent, the axe crashing against the iron boss, jolting his hand badly. The axe head skittered off the shield and the edge bit into the compressed snow and ice atop the rampart in a spray of white and dark soil. Powering off his back foot, Cato punched out with his shield and felt it connect solidly with the axeman, who stumbled back a pace as he struggled to retain his footing on the icy surface. Tearing his sword from its scabbard, Cato opened out his shield enough to permit a quick thrust, and the point stabbed home into the fur cloak belted around the enemy warrior. He felt the hide give way, and the blade plunged on into the man's flesh. He twisted it one way, then the other, and wrenched it free as his opponent staggered back with an angry bellow and raised his axe to strike again.

This time Cato backed away quickly, out of reach, and glanced over his shoulder to see Thraxis emerging from the gap in the palisade. Beyond him, two warriors armed with kite shields and swords were rushing forward, eager to cut him down before he could gain the top of the rampart. Cato swung round, away from the wounded axeman, and charged past Thraxis, twisting his shield round so that it would present a broad target to his enemies. Neither side dared to stop too suddenly on the icy surface, and they came together in a loud clatter of shields and clash of blades before tumbling on to the rampart in a tangle of limbs. Cato landed heavily, and the impact drove the air from his lungs in a violent gasp. He lay half on top of one of the warriors, while the other sprawled across his legs. He had lost his shield, and although his sword was still in his hand, the first of his enemies was lying on it and he could not shift it. Instead he clenched his left hand and struck the man hard on the jaw, again and again, until the warrior managed to raise his arms to protect himself. The other warrior shook his head, and Cato, aware of a sharp pain in his knee, realised that the joint and the man's head must have connected during the fall. As he regained his senses, the warrior roared at Cato and reached for the sword lying beside him.

There was nothing Cato could do to stop him retrieving his weapon, and he punched the closer man hard again before trying to wrench his trapped sword hand free. 'Get off me, you barbarian bastard!' He made one last effort, and the warrior rolled slightly on to his side, moving just enough for the Roman to rip his blade away.

Instantly he propped himself up, at the same time as the second warrior was starting to swing his sword round in an arc. At the last moment, Cato managed to sweep his short sword in between himself and the Celtic blade. There was a ringing clash and sparks flew before the longer blade forced Cato's weapon aside and he felt the flat of the sword strike the crest of his helmet and glance overhead. He hacked at the warrior's exposed forearm and struck a large silver torc, which stopped any injury but caused the man's fingers to spasm and release his sword. Cato raised his own blade and drove the point deep into his enemy's throat before ripping it to the side in a rush of pulsing blood. The warrior slumped back on to the rampart, trying to clamp both hands over the mortal wound.

Cato drew a deep breath of relief and quickly pulled himself free, retrieving his shield and standing up just in time to see Thraxis hack at the axeman's arm, cutting skin and breaking bone so that the man cried out. He tried to draw his axe back for another blow, but howled with agony as the broken limb refused to bear the weight of the war axe. Thraxis followed up with a thrust of his shield and knocked the man to the ground at the edge of the rampart, where he rolled down the snowy bank.

Both Thraxis and Cato paused, hearts racing, eyes and ears alert for trouble, but none of the enemy threatened them as the Blood Crows' standard-bearer climbed in through the breach, followed by the two large auxiliaries who had pulled the posts down. Below them, more men were crowding the gap, anxious to feed through into the fight. Looking around the redoubt, Cato could see that two more parties of his men had found their way on to the ramparts and were struggling to defend their footholds while others climbed up to join them. The interior of the redoubt was perhaps fifty paces across, and from where he stood, Cato could see the formidable line of stakes studding the flank leading down into the channel. In the other direction stretched the rampart that covered the narrow channel between the mainland and the Druids' island.

Several hundred men were defending the rampart, and so far there was no sign that they had conceded any of the breaches that had been opened up by the legions' ballista batteries. Given the greater weight of their armour, it was not surprising that the men of the Fourteenth were taking longer than the Blood Crows to get into action, Cato realised.

A chorus of battle cries drew his attention back to his immediate surroundings, and he saw a party of enemy warriors surging along the rampart towards him and the handful of men around the Blood Crows' standard.

'Steady, lads,' he said as calmly as he could. 'They're all mouth and no heart. Let's show 'em why they are right to fear the Blood Crows!'

Thraxis and the others presented their shields and swords and braced their feet as they stood shoulder to shoulder, ready to hold their ground. Behind them the standard-bearer grounded the staff and held his sword ready. Cato took his place beside Thraxis, on the edge of the rampart, and gritted his teeth as he faced the enemy. They were already spilling out on to the reverse slope of the rampart, ready to envelop the small knot of Romans around the narrow breach. Those atop the rampart were moving fastest, and a moment later they crashed, shield to shield, into Thraxis and his two comrades. At once the auxiliaries thrust forward, using their nailed boots to advantage on the icy ground as they pressed the natives back against their companions following them up. Then they stabbed into the packed ranks before them, pushing their swords home, working the blades inside their enemies before tearing them free. The first of the warriors slumped to his knees and was ruthlessly thrust aside, sent sprawling down the inner slope by one of his companions anxious to throw himself into the fight.

More of the enemy were moving along the slope to get at the Romans, and Cato angled his shield down as he struck at the first of them, a pockmarked man whose face was rimmed with a thick beard and straggling hair. He carried a wicker shield and a hunting spear and he lithely sidestepped Cato's thrust before covering his cloaked body and stabbing the broad-bladed spearhead at the Roman. Cato used his shield to deflect the blow down, and gasped as he felt the edge of the blade gash his calf just above the ankle. Raising his boot, he stamped down on the head of the spear and made a cut towards the man's exposed hand. The edge of the sword missed and struck the spear shaft instead, splitting it and rendering the weapon useless. With a cry of bitter outrage, his enemy cast the spear aside and snatched an axe from his belt. Even though it was small, the head still looked formidable as the warrior climbed closer and swung it hard at Cato's shield. It split the wood above the lower trim, and the native wrenched it out and struck again and again, a series of savage blows, hacking away at the shield that Cato had to keep presenting in order to protect his feet and shins.

More of the enemy were advancing along the slope, and the standard-bearer was forced to step in, sword raised towards a short but broad-shouldered youth wearing a Gallic helmet and a mail vest under his embroidered cloak. Clearly one of the local nobles, Cato decided as he blocked another blow from the axe that was relentlessly hacking the bottom of his shield to pieces. As his opponent began to swing his arm back for another strike, Cato thrust his arm up and battered the jagged edge of the shield against the man's jaw, gouging the flesh beneath his beard so that drops of blood spattered down on to the snow at his feet. Before the warrior could recover from the surprise, the Roman struck him again, knocking him back so he tumbled down the slope into the snowdrift at the bottom.

A cry to his side drew Cato's attention, and he turned to see the standard-bearer standing with his mouth agape as he looked down to where the nobleman had stabbed him deep in the groin. The Briton's lips split in a cruel smile of triumph as he worked the blade around and then tore it free with a rush of blood that sprayed down the standard-bearer's breeches. The auxiliary trembled violently, his fingers losing their grip on his sword handle and the shaft of the Blood Crows' standard. It rippled in the cold air as it fell towards the enemy nobleman, who dropped his shield and caught the staff with a cry of jubilation, then scurried back down the slope with the standard held aloft, waving it from side to side.

It had all happened before Cato could react, and now several more of the enemy had moved along the slope between him and the nobleman. With a sick feeling of shame, he cried out in anguish, 'The standard! Save the standard!'

CHAPTER TWENTY-TWO

Thraxis glanced round, his expression aghast as he saw the standard-bearer crumple on to the rampart. 'The bastards have taken the standard!'

For a brief moment the fighting inside the redoubt slackened as the men of both sides took in what had happened, then the natives let out shouts of triumph and defiance while the Romans looked on in bitter shame. Four more men had climbed up behind Cato, and he turned to Thraxis and the man nearest him. 'You two, with me. The rest, hold this position.'

He edged a few paces along the rampart to allow the others to take up positions on each side of him. 'Let's teach that cocky bastard a lesson. No one snatches our standard and lives long enough to celebrate it. When I give the order, we go straight for it and keep going. We stop for nothing until we have it back. Then it's your job to keep it, Thraxis. Are you ready for that?'

Thraxis rolled his head to loosen his neck and growled. 'Yes, sir. I'm sorry . . . I should never have let it happen.'

'Later. Now it's time to redeem ourselves. Ready?'

'Yes, sir.'

'Aye,' added the other auxiliary, before spitting to the side. 'Let's take the fucking bastards apart, sir.'

Cato nodded, then took a deep breath as he adjusted his grip on his sword and held it firmly. 'Let's go!'

He started down the slope, hurrying but being careful not to slip in the snow. The others followed, just behind his shoulders, and the small wedge drove into the loose cluster of enemy warriors below. Cato increased his pace at the last moment, smashing the first man to one side, then lashed out with the guard of his sword, striking another enemy in the face and knocking him away. Thraxis, on his left, punched his shield into two more men and sent them tumbling down the slope, while the Blood Crow to his right slashed out with his blade, slicing open a warrior's tattooed arm, cutting into the bone. The three Romans increased their pace, charging to the bottom of the slope and bursting through the last men straight at the noble, who was looking up at the standard with glee. His gaze dropped as he heard a warning cry and his eyes narrowed at the three Romans charging towards him. With a defiant snarl he punched the spike at the bottom of the staff into the ground and stepped in front of it, arms held apart in a show of contemptuous defiance for his enemies. Four more of his men, giants in chain vests and Celtic helmets, holding their ornately decorated round shields, came running across from the far side of the redoubt. These were either noblemen like their companion or his bodyguards, Cato decided.

'Take care of them!' he ordered. 'This one is mine.'

Even as he spoke, he could not help a mental wince at the braggadocio of his tone, and realised that it was the sort of thing Macro might have said in such a situation. He could not help a brief laugh. Was this what it meant to be a veteran soldier, comfortable in his own skin and feeling that being on a battlefield and risking life and limb was a natural state of being? The native nobleman was frowning at him, as if irritated by Cato's humour. He arrogantly beckoned the Roman officer closer and raised his sword as he stood tall and puffed out his chest.

'All right then, my friend,' Cato responded softly. 'Let's see what you are made of.'

A clash of blades distracted him and he glanced aside as Thraxis and the other auxiliary began their duel with the nobleman's heavily armed companions. They were outnumbered two to one and would only be able to give Cato a limited chance of retrieving the Blood Crows' standard. He tapped his sword against the side of his shield and strode forward to meet the warrior's challenge.

The young nobleman's expression intensified, his dark eyes like gleaming beads as he began to swing his blade in a circle to build up momentum. Suddenly he leapt forward and unleashed his sword, slashing it diagonally down at the crown of Cato's helmet. Only the swiftest of reactions saved Cato as he threw up his left arm and took the blow squarely on the top of his shield. The impact jarred his arm and shoulder and drove the shield back to crash against the crosspiece on the brow of his helmet, and his jaws snapped together so that he bit into his tongue.

The pain was instant and acute and he tasted the iron tang of blood in his mouth. But there was no respite as the sword came swishing in again, battering the shield and forcing Cato to give ground. A crack opened up in the lower part of the shield and extended as the third blow landed, and Cato knew that it would not endure more than a handful of impacts before it fell apart. Without it he would be armed only with his short sword, with half the reach of his opponent, and in such a contest it was unlikely that he would survive long.

His reaction was instinctive and took him by surprise almost as much as it did his opponent. As soon as the next blow landed, he launched himself forward, throwing his full weight behind the damaged shield. He'd intended to knock the man down, but the nobleman's reflexes were as sharp as Cato's, and he swung aside and avoided most of the force of the impact. Cato glanced past him, and released the useless shield as he ran on a few more paces to the standard, turning beside it to face the nobleman, who came on, fully aware that the advantage had swung to him. Cato drew his sword back high behind his shoulder, as if to make a wild cut, then swung it forward and released his grip. The blade spun end over end towards his startled opponent, who took it hard on his left shoulder. It struck edge on and deflected up and over the man before falling soundlessly into the snow and ice a few feet behind him.

'Ha!' The nobleman smiled grimly. He shook his head and came on, sword held out ready to strike down the defenceless Roman officer.

There was only one chance for Cato now. He plucked the Blood Crows' standard from the snow and held it in both hands, lowering the point towards his foe as if it was a spear, with the fall of dark cloth hanging down from the cross-piece. He feinted, but the other man just laughed and casually swatted the head of the standard aside with his sword and strode forward to finish Cato off. Quickly stepping back, Cato swung the end of the standard. The weighted folds of cloth fell across the warrior's face, obscuring his vision, and he stopped dead, raising his spare hand to brush the cloth away. Pulling the staff back, Cato let it drop so that the head was between his opponent's legs, then twisted it round so that the cross-piece was behind the man's ankle. He yanked the shaft back viciously, and as the man's leg came flying up, he lost his balance and fell, both arms flailing. He landed heavily, the breath driven from his lungs with a deep grunt. Cato stepped over him, and their eyes met as the nobleman struggled to bring his sword up and round to protect himself.

'Drop it!' Cato raised the spike at the end of the standard and pointed it at the man's chest. There was a beat when he thought his opponent would surrender, but then the nobleman's eyes narrowed and he made to swing his sword at Cato's flank. Gritting his teeth, Cato bunched his arm muscles and drove the spike into the opening below the man's chin, then pressed down hard, feeling the iron point tear through flesh and grind between bones before it burst out of his body, through the mail vest and into the ground.

The nobleman's head snapped back and his jaws opened wide in a gasp, flecks of blood spraying out on his breath. His sword arm went limp and the blade slapped into the snow at his side as Cato worked the standard round in a crude circle to do as much damage to his opponent as he could. Then he braced a foot on the man's mailed chest and pulled the base of the standard out, dark and slick with blood that steamed in the cold air. The young nobleman writhed weakly as he bled out, feet working in the snow, head rolling from side to side. He muttered quietly to himself, and the Roman briefly wondered if it might be a prayer, or some final words to a loved one.

Cato retrieved his sword and looked round to make sure he was in no immediate danger. Close by, Thraxis was standing over a stricken enemy, while the other Blood Crow was staggering back, nursing a wound to his thigh. Blood was flowing freely down his leg and spattering the white ground beneath. The three warriors who had come to the aid of the man Cato had felled now backed away, aghast at the mortal wounding of their leader. Their shocked reaction was swiftly shared by many of the other defenders, who fell back in a moment of doubt.

A cheer rose from some of the auxiliaries on the rampart as they saw that Cato had recaptured the standard, and their comrades added their voices. At once Cato grasped that a decisive point had been reached and raised the standard high over his head, calling to his men, 'Blood Crows! Blood Crows! On to victory!'

The auxiliaries charged forward, hurling themselves on their shaken enemy. All the time, more of their comrades were climbing through the gaps in the palisade to add their weight to the fight. The companions of the dying nobleman quickly recovered, however, and fell back to try and rally their followers, who had abandoned half the fortification to the Romans. They still had the advantage in numbers and might yet hold the position, despite their wavering spirits. Cato knew that he had to keep the initiative.

'Thraxis, over here!'

The Thracian trotted across. 'Sir?'

'Give me your shield and take the standard. Quickly, man!'

The auxiliary did as he was ordered, and a moment later he stood beside his prefect, a grim look of satisfaction on his features as he glanced up at the standard that had been entrusted to him. Cato took a firm grip on the handle of the shield and made ready to advance towards the enemy, who were re-forming their ranks on the far side of the redoubt. His throat felt hot and dry, despite the cold, and he had to clear it before he called out again.

'Blood Crows! Rally to the standard!'

Those who were not engaged hurried across to form up on either side of Cato, and others joined them as they entered the fortification. As soon as twenty or so men had assembled, Cato swung towards the enemy and paced forward. 'Follow me.'

The Blood Crows advanced, shields to the front and sword arms bent as they made ready to strike. On the rampart, their comrades continued to battle with the defenders there, but Cato knew that the fight for the redoubt would be won or lost here in the centre of the earthwork. No more than fifteen paces away, the enemy was facing up to receive them, a dense mass of wild-haired warriors, many sporting swirling tattoos on their faces and arms as their features fixed into expressions of defiance and hatred. There was fear there too, Cato noted, and he found an echo of that sentiment in his own heart as he did every time he went into battle. It was that instinctual desire to turn and run for safety that he had long since forced himself to master.

One of the enemy noblemen raised his sword and let out a roar before swinging the blade down, pointing it directly at Cato and launching himself into a charge. His comrades reacted a moment later and followed him, two paces behind.

Cato did not react to the challenge but continued at a steady pace so that his men would enter the fight together. He almost smiled at the impulsive nature of these warriors and how it so often played into the Romans' hands, as he aimed to demonstrate in the next few heartbeats.

The man leading the charge thrust his shield forward and swung his sword in a high arc to smash it down on Cato's helmet and split his skull open. Cato dropped to his knee and punched his shield up to take the blow. An instant later, he lurched back under the impact of first the sword and then the warrior's shield. As soon as the latter made contact, he swung his own sword slightly out and round before angling the point up, feeling the steel bite deeply into his opponent's thigh. He twisted and withdrew the blade as the man staggered to a halt with an enraged bellow. Then, rising, he shoved his shield hard and pressed close to the man as he stabbed again, this time into his shoulder, tearing through muscles and opening up a terrible wound that at once started to bleed profusely. Another shove sent the man staggering back across the snow, and he fell against his followers before slumping to the ground. Those closest to him slowed and stopped in their tracks.

'Blood Crows! Charge!' Cato screamed the order, and with a savage cry his men burst into motion and hurled their weight behind their shields as they crashed into the wavering ranks of the tribesmen. The Thracian auxiliaries had won a reputation for their ferocity in action and now added bloody lustre to their fame as they carved their way into the dense mass of natives before them. They pressed hard, working their swords in quick savage blows, and crimson drops and splashes streaked and smeared the packed snow and ice underfoot. The viciousness of the counter-charge and the loss of their second leader quickly took its toll on the natives, and any hope they had of saving the redoubt gave way to a fight to save their skins as they began to back away, desperately warding off the Blood Crows' swords.

Long years of training came into their own as Cato battered his way forward with his shield, pausing to strike and recover and advance again. He could see over the heads of the tribesmen immediately in front of him that some of those at the rear had turned to run and were clambering over the palisade to flee into the space behind the main line of fortifications, where the Fourteenth Legion was battling to break through.

'Keep going!' Thraxis yelled from behind Cato's shoulder. 'Carve them up, lads!'

Though they still outnumbered the Blood Crows who had made it inside the defences, most of the enemy were only levies – farmers and hunters with little training in the art of war – and now they were paying a high price for choosing to fight the invader. Scores had already been cut down and lay bleeding on the freezing ground. Some were finished off by the auxiliaries, the rest ignored as the slaughter continued, the Blood Crows leaving enemy bodies strewn in their wake.

Cato had just knocked a man cold with the guard of his sword when he next looked up and saw that they were close to the base of the rampart. The slope above was filled by tribesmen desperately attempting to escape the bloodshed. A few had cast aside their weapons and dropped to their knees, begging to be spared, but in the heat of battle there was little mercy. Cato saw a thin older man crying out as he implored an auxiliary to let him live. The response was swift and fatal. The Thracian split the man's skull with the edge of his blade, the crack of bone clearly audible to Cato's ears as blood and brains leapt into the air. The sight and sound brought back some semblance of cold reason in his mind, and he stopped in his tracks.

'Blood Crows! Hold fast! Let 'em go!'

One by one his men halted and stood panting, swords and shields bloodied, glaring after the fleeing enemy. Not even the most stalwart of the warriors had any fight left in them, and all climbed over the palisade and dropped out of sight. As the last of them disappeared, Cato lowered Thraxis's battered shield and looked round the interior of the redoubt, his chest heaving from his exertions as he exhaled puffs of breath into the cold morning air. Bodies, many still moving, lay all about, and to his grim satisfaction, he saw that very few of them were his men. He caught sight of Decurion Miro entering through one of the narrow breaches and called him over.

'Detail ten of your squadron to get the wounded out of here and back to the dressing station.' He turned to the small gate at the rear of the redoubt, its locking beam still securely in place. 'I want the rest of the men formed up over there at once. Get to it.'

'Yes, sir.' Miro saluted and trotted away to carry out his orders. Cato watched him briefly, wondering why it had taken the decurion until now to enter the fortification when he should have been at the head of his men as they attacked. Then he climbed up on to the rampart and cautiously looked over the palisade and down the length of the enemy's defences.

A ferocious battle was raging along the line of fortifications. It was at its fiercest in the breach that had been opened halfway along, where a dense mass of enemy warriors was managing to hold off the legionaries. In the immediate foreground, Cato saw the natives who had abandoned the fort streaming down towards the shore, where a line of small shallow-bottomed craft had been beached. A handful of men struggled in vain to hold them off as they began to drag the nearest boats out into the channel. A short distance beyond, Cato noticed a small party of cloaked figures on horseback, together with a man in the dark robes of a Druid. They had seen the men fleeing from the redoubt, and already the Druid was giving hurried orders. There was no time to waste in pressing home the opportunity that had been won by the swift fall of the flanking fortification.

Cato turned back and saw that most of his cohort had formed up just below him, the rest still climbing up through the breaches. The first of the casualties, the walking wounded, had to stand to one side as their comrades hurried to join the men gathering for the next action. Scrambling down, Cato pointed towards the gate and called across to Miro, 'Get that open!'

As the decurion took a section forward to deal with the locking bar, Cato turned to address his men. 'We've done well so far, lads. Already enough to warrant another medal for the standard.' He pointed to the gilded discs attached to the staff that Thraxis was holding. 'But let's seal the deal with the kind of charge that only the Blood Crows can deliver. Outside, there're thousands of those Celt bastards waiting, but they're a little distracted by the Fourteenth Legion at the moment. Legate Valens's boys are making hard work of it, and it's up to us to help 'em out.'

'Bloody legionaries!' a voice cried out from the ranks. 'You want the job done properly, you call on the Blood Crows!'

The men cheered lustily before Cato could identify the miscreant, and he went along with their hubris and grinned. 'Quite so! Now is our moment. When I give the order, I want the cohort to double out of the gate and form a line across the enemy's flank. When we go in, we go in hard and fast. Miro's squadron will clear the rampart and the rest of us will sweep the ground behind. You hold the line and you stop for nothing. Clear?'

The excited men shouted their assent and punched their swords into the air. Their blood was up and Cato knew he could depend on them to finish the job that Quintatus had assigned the cohort. He turned to the gate and hefted his shield before he noticed that blood had run down the blade of his sword and on to the handle. He paused to bend down and wipe it off on the hem of a dead man's tunic, then straightened up, ready to do his duty.

'Blood Crows, advance, at the trot.'

He picked up his feet and broke into a light jog, his scabbard and dagger sheath jostling at either side. The rumble of his men's boots on the frozen ground sounded at his back, together with their laboured breathing and the clatter of kit against shields.

'Miro, your section leads the way, then once we're in the open, get over to the rampart as fast as you can.'

'Yes, sir.'

With Miro and his men taking their place at the front of the column, the auxiliaries poured out of the redoubt and round the curve of the ditch until the shoreline opened up in front of them. Keen to ensure that the sight of thousands of enemy warriors did not unsettle them, Cato urged his men on with as calm a demeanour as he could muster. To his right he saw several boats heading clumsily across the channel, manned by those who had fled. No doubt they would be given a cold reception by their comrades watching from the island. That was too bad. They should have put up a better fight. Now those tribesmen still defending the beach would pay the price for their lack of nerve.

He chose a point fifty paces from the redoubt, close to the water, and halted and extended his arm towards the rampart.

'Form line!'

The decurions took up their positions for their squadrons to assume the required formation, while Miro and his men continued across the snowy ground towards the place where the long defence earthwork joined the redoubt. Only a handful of the enemy stood in their immediate path, as most had been drawn into the fight raging around the centre of the line. Miro led his men up the slope and then formed them into a tight column, ready to unleash them along the line of the rampart when Cato's order came.

As the last of the men fell in, Cato turned to gauge the ground ahead of them. The strip of land between the rampart and the water was narrow, no more than forty paces deep at its widest. The cohort, still some three hundred strong, would be able to bring its weight to bear at the start of the attack, but he had no illusions about how far they would go in rolling up the enemy flank before they ran out of impetus or encountered sufficient resistance to halt them in their tracks. The best he could hope for was to shake the tribesmen badly enough that the alarm spread through their ranks as far as the breach being fiercely contested by Valens's legionaries. If the Fourteenth broke through in numbers, then the struggle was as good as over, on this side of the channel at least.

He faced front and raised his sword.

'Blood Crows, forward!'

They set out across the churned snow and shingle, a thin line of oval shields, glinting swords and grim faces, the standard rippling gently above them. Thraxis held it high, where it would be clearly visible to the enemy, so that they would know who it was that was bearing down on them. The party of riders Cato had seen shortly before had dispersed, with several riding along the line to warn of the flank attack. The Druid and a few others remained, trying to rally and cajole the men who had fled from the fort, as well as hurriedly ordering those on the palisade to turn and face the new challenge. But already Miro and his squadron were forcing their way steadily along the rampart, cutting down or thrusting back those who stood in their way, without losing any momentum as they kept up with the rest of the Blood Crows.

They approached the first of the boats drawn up on the shore, and Cato noticed a streak of blood on the ground beside the hull, and more blood staining the bows. As they passed by, he saw a youth, no more than fifteen years old, slumped inside the boat, his arm almost severed at the shoulder. Their eyes met briefly and then Cato marched on. A hundred paces ahead, the Druid and his companions had succeeded in gathering two or three hundred of their followers and were hurriedly jostling them into a makeshift battle line.

'Keep going!' Cato urged his men. Glancing to his left, he saw that a large group of warriors had turned to confront Miro's party, enough of them to stall the Blood Crows' progress along the line of the rampart. His original intention to keep the cohort together was not going to be possible. All that remained was to keep driving on for as long as they could.

They had halved the distance to the waiting tribesmen when Thraxis shouted a warning. 'Incoming!'

Cato glimpsed the blur of arrows rising from the enemy ranks, and raised his shield and angled it to protect his head as he shouted the order. 'Shields up!'

Along the line, the Blood Crows followed suit as the first volley flitted down from the grey sky. Arrowheads rattled loudly off the shields. Some struck home more directly, splintering the wood and lodging in place. There were other impacts, louder, and Cato realised that they were also being targeted with slingshot, often a greater danger than arrows due to the force of the impact. Sure enough, there was a cry from nearby, and he turned to see one of his men stumble, his shin shattered by the crushing impact. The soldier tried to cover his body with his shield as his comrades left him behind.

Cato had to steel himself to maintain a steady pace and not slow down in the face of the steady barrage of missiles, nor increase his speed in an attempt to cover the distance more quickly and make contact with the enemy, at the risk of losing the cohesion of his battle line. So they endured several more casualties before they closed on the tribesmen.

At the last instant Cato risked a glance over his shield and saw the fierce expressions of most of the men facing him, and beyond them the Druid screaming encouragement to his followers and no doubt hurling curses at the Romans. Then the two lines came together in an uneven thud of shields and bodies, accompanied by the scrape and ringing clash of blades.

For a moment the opposing sides were pressed together, but then the superior equipment of the auxiliaries shifted the balance of the struggle as they began to cut down their more lightly armoured enemies, many of whom had little more than wicker shields and padded cloaks to protect them. Cato drew a deep breath and shouted, 'Push and step! One!'

On the count, he punched his shield forward and then stepped in behind it before thrusting with his sword. The other Blood Crows had followed suit, pressing the enemy back, and with Cato calling the time, and the decurions relaying the order, the cohort gained ground, passing over the fallen, who were finished off mercilessly to prevent them from attempting to fight on where they lay.

Splashing sounded close by and Cato saw three men edging out into the water to try and get round the end of the Roman line. He called over his shoulder to the nearest men in the second rank. 'You two. Cover the flank!'

The pair rushed past into the shallows, surging calf-deep through the icy water as they moved to counter the enemy, and Cato continued calling the advance. At the next push he felt his shield lurch to one side and glanced down to see fingers clamped round the left side, attempting to wrench it aside. As the shield moved, exposing some of Cato's body, he saw a spear head thrusting at his midriff. Only a frantic last-moment jerk of his sword arm deflected the blow. He tried to regain control of his shield but could not break his opponent's grip. He lunged forward and sank his teeth into the fingers just below the knuckle, biting hard. He felt the skin give way, and blood coursed over his lips and on to his tongue. The man gave a sharp cry and instantly released his grip, and Cato quickly covered his body again and slammed the shield forward, driving it hard into the face and body of the tribesman he had just bitten. A vicious, tearing stab with the point of his sword put the man out of action, and he fell clutching the rent in his guts, through which blood and intestines began to spill.

Already Cato could see men breaking from the rear of the enemy line, backing away with frightened expressions, some turning and making for the nearest boats. The Druid and the other mounted men attempted to block their path and drive them back into the fight with angry shouts and blows from the flats of their swords. But most of the tribesmen managed to dodge past and run for their lives. Then panic rippled through the ranks and suddenly the entire line was crumbling, flowing away from the Blood Crows, until the last of them broke contact, backed off and turned away to escape.

The auxiliaries, exhausted and bloodied, halted and let out a gasped victory cry, shouting insults at the backs of their fleeing enemy. The Druid and the other riders gave up their fruitless attempt to stem the tide of their followers and glared at the Blood Crows. Then Cato saw the Druid gather in his reins and raise his sword as he turned his mount towards the standard. Before he could charge, one of his companions steered his horse in front of him, blocking his path, and angrily gestured at him to turn aside. After a final bitter stare at his enemy, the Druid gritted his teeth, swung his horse around and spurred it away from the Roman line, making for the greatest concentration of warriors further along the shore.

The men who were fleeing were already running past groups of their comrades who were still formed up, and the latter at once began to waver, then follow their example, as the enemy's left flank continued to collapse.

'Onwards!' Cato swung his sword after the enemy. 'Keep at 'em!'

Tired as they were, his men had the taste of victory in their mouths and were keen to feed their appetite. They needed no further encouragement as the line resumed its advance. Up on the rampart, the example of their comrades had broken the will of the men confronting Miro, and they too retreated. While some of the tribesmen strove to escape to the safety of the far end of the defences, those with more wits about them made for the boats, dragging them into the water and piling aboard, to be joined by yet more of their comrades in a desperate bid for self-preservation. A routing enemy was only ever a briefly delighting prospect, Cato decided. Very quickly the sense of gleeful triumph gave way to a feeling of disgust at the naked selfishness of men willing to trample over their comrades to save their own skins.

The rising panic spreading down the enemy line had reached those fighting to keep the Fourteenth Legion out of the main breach, and they too began to give way, until the shore seemed alive with tribesmen hurrying to evade the closing trap. A short distance further on, the shoreline ran closer in towards the rampart, and Cato halted the Blood Crows at the narrowest point and re-formed his remaining men into three ranks in close formation. With their shields overlapping, the front line presented an impenetrable obstacle to the enemy, and all that remained was for Legate Valens and his men to seal the victory. Already those warriors still fighting in the breach were being pushed back by the weight of numbers before them, and then Cato glimpsed the dull glint of an eagle standard as the helmets of the legionaries surged into view and they began to fight their way into the open breach behind the defences.

Miro came striding up to Cato, a look of naked elation on his face. 'We've done it, sir! By the gods, we've done it!'

'Not just us.' Cato pointed with his sword to the legionaries pouring through the breach, and others climbing on to the rampart as the enemy gave way. All resistance seemed to have collapsed, and the shallows of the channel were filled with men splashing through the freezing water to try and fight their way on to the boats to make good their escape to Mona. Hundreds of others were climbing over the palisade at the far end of the line of earthworks and fleeing along the shore then inland for the safety of the snow-laden pine forests.

'It's a fine victory, sir.' Miro beamed deliriously. 'We've crushed the bastards. Completely crushed them.'

'Yes, we have,' the prefect agreed in a measured tone. 'Fine work to be sure. Bloody fine work. But it's only half the job.'

He turned to survey the even more formidable defences along the shore of Mona, and the silent ranks of warriors and Druids who had been watching the struggle on the mainland.

It stood to reason that they would not run like their comrades. There would be nowhere to run to. Their choice was simple. They must hold Mona, or die. He felt a feather-light touch of something cold on the back of his hand and looked down to see a snowflake melting against his skin. More flakes drifted down as he looked at the sky, now a dark grey. Within moments they gave way to a steady fall, settling over the shore and the bodies scattered along its length. Cato cleared his throat and spat.

'This was the easy bit. Taking Mona is going to be a far more difficult prospect. Mark my words . . .'

CHAPTER TWENTY-THREE

The heavy snow of the previous day had made it hard going for Macro and the small convoy he was leading through the mountains to Legate Quintatus and his army. After his party had joined the survivors of the enemy ambush, Macro had driven them on as speedily as possible. The wagons, and Tribune Glaber's raeda carriage, were kept closed up while the auxiliary infantry escort marched alongside them, screening the flanks. Macro had divided his mounted party, tasking Pandarus to scout ahead with three men while Lomus brought up the rear, hanging back a quarter of a mile to keep watch down the track in case the enemy decided to follow them. Macro's horse was hitched to the rear of the raeda, and the centurion sat on the bench beside Glaber, who held the traces since the tribune had lost his driver during the skirmish. Glaber's personal chests had been piled behind the driver's bench to make way for three of the wounded, who were forced to endure the constant jolting of the light carriage as well as the pain from their injuries. Distant figures were sighted from time to time, but it was impossible to divine if they were the enemy, or merely the inhabitants of the mountains warily giving the Romans a wide berth. Not that it made much difference, Macro reflected. In these lands, everyone seemed to be an enemy of Rome.

The snow had started no more than an hour after they had left the site of the ambush, a few light flurries at first, and then a continual fall of soft downy flakes that quickly began to settle and blanket the landscape in a winter mantle of white. Soon the track was covered and they had to follow their instincts where it was not possible to discern the route that led through the valleys. As night fell, the snow stopped and Macro gave the order to halt when they reached an abandoned farmstead. Anything of value had been carried off when the natives had fled, or had been looted by the Roman soldiers passing by. At least the structure had been spared and offered the small party shelter for the night. Sentries were posted and a fire was lit in the hearth of the largest hut, and the men huddled round it to get warm and cook their rations.

Tribune Glaber had been content to allow Macro to take command and made no secret of the fact that his was a purely political appointment. He was keen to serve the minimum amount of time that he could in the army before resuming his career in Rome the moment the new governor gave him permission to quit Britannia. As they sat in the glow of the fire, Macro had gently pressed him for any more details about Julia, but all Glaber could tell him was that the illness had come on suddenly and she had lived a few more days before dying at her father's house in Rome, in the same bed in which she had been born. At least her child, Lucius, had survived, Macro mused. According to Glaber, the infant boy was thriving in the care of a wet-nurse purchased before

Julia had fallen ill. Macro hoped that that at least might offer some comfort to his closest friend when Cato heard the dreadful tidings.

They were not troubled during the night and continued on their way at first light, pausing only to clear the worst of the drifts that had accumulated on the track. As the men toiled to shovel the snow to one side, Macro felt a growing sense of unease at the change in the weather. Legate Quintatus had taken a risk launching a campaign so late in the year. He had gambled on a quick knockout blow to the enemy with a view to returning to Mediolanum before winter set in. The snow had come earlier than expected, and if it remained for any length of time, then it would severely hamper the ability of the army to negotiate the mountains of the Deceanglian tribe. He glanced round at the cloud-shrouded peaks and pulled his cloak tighter about him as he spoke to Glaber.

'The new governor, Gallus. Any idea what his plans are for the province?'

Glaber paused to cup his mittened hands and blow warm breath into them before he responded. 'That's his business, Centurion. However, there was a certain amount of gossip doing the rounds in Rome before I set off, and the word is that the palace is starting to get anxious about the situation here. Best part of ten years in and Britannia is still a drain on the imperial purse. There have been considerable losses in manpower, and no immediate prospect of the province turning a profit. Frankly, it's all starting to make the original decision to invade look like a mistake. But the emperor has built his reputation on the conquest of the island and has too much invested in it to let Britannia go.'

Macro nodded. 'We've lost a lot of fine men to get this far, sir. It would be a bloody shame if it was all for nothing. Quintatus thought it could be resolved with one more push. One final effort to wipe out the Druid cult for ever. He could be right about that.'

'He might be. Quintatus may not be my patron, but I cannot help hoping that he has already done as you say. With the Druids off the scene, maybe the will of the tribes of these mountains will be broken and your mission to warn him will be rendered moot.' The tribune stamped his boots on the foot board and took up the traces again. 'Be that as it may, when Claudius is gone, it will be a different matter entirely.'

Macro looked at him sidelong. 'How so?'

'Depends who becomes the new emperor. If it's Britannicus, then I dare say the current policy will continue. We'll keep piling men and treasure into the island until we have killed off every tribe that resists us and bought off all the rest. That, or Britannicus is going to have to find himself a completely new cognomen.'

They shared a brief smile before Glaber continued. 'On the other hand, if we get Nero as emperor – and that's what the smart money is saying – then he has nothing to lose in terms of withdrawing from Britannia. He'd be free to say that he never accepted the need to invade in the first place, and that it was all a very costly exercise in self-promotion by his predecessor. Which is a fair enough argument to make. Anyway, Nero could give the order to pull out without losing any face. Which is why I think Gallus would be wise to bide his time rather than trying to complete the conquest of the entire island. If I were him, I would definitely wait until I knew who had succeeded to the purple before I risked losing any more men.'

Macro thought about this for a moment before he puffed his cheeks impatiently. 'If the natives got wind of the fact that the new governor was sitting on his hands, they could make life very difficult for us.'

'Quite!' Glaber laughed. 'It's going to be a tricky situation all round, until Claudius drops off the twig. I guess that is always going to be the way while we have a drawn-out succession. Much easier when emperors do the rest of us a favour and disappear from the scene quickly and unexpectedly rather than wait for natural causes. Though these days an assassin's knife in the back is natural causes for those who would be emperor.'

Macro was not amused. He had long since decided that he hated and despised the endless conspiracies swirling around the imperial household. Moreover, he was growing resentful over the way in which soldiers on the frontiers of the empire, like himself and Cato, were regarded as no more than playing pieces to be moved by those vying for power in Rome. A reckless expenditure of life might yet win the throne for Britannicus, while a craven retreat from Britannia might benefit his rival, Nero. Either way, soldiers would die.

The way was clear ahead. The men hurriedly bundled their shovels on to the back of one of the wagons and the small convoy rumbled on over the snowy ground. An hour later they were climbing a gentle gradient when the young tribune's keen eyes caught sight of a faint smudge of haze in the distance. He alerted Macro, and shortly afterwards the veteran was able to make it out as well.

'Looks like smoke from campfires, sir.'

'Then let's hope it's our lads, not theirs, eh?'

They reached the top of the slope and the ground began to even out. As they struggled round a large formation of rocks, there, quarter of a mile ahead, lay a fortified outpost blanketed in snow. It had been constructed to guard the pass linking the two valleys and, thanks to its position, was subject to the worst of the weather. Macro spared a brief moment of sympathy for the small garrison before his gaze extended to the valley beyond, which opened out on to the coast and the grey expanse of the sea. To the left, behind a line of hills, the smoke from the large camp was far more evident; a dark stain against the overcast.

'Not far now, then,' said Glaber. 'Be glad to find some proper shelter, not to mention safety in numbers.'

Macro glanced round at the snowy landscape but could see no sign of movement, no sign of the enemy. 'We should be safe to leave the wagons and escort now.'

They halted outside the outpost and the two officers climbed down from the raeda as Macro called in the horsemen riding ahead and behind the wagons. The outpost commander, a swarthy optio from a cohort of Dacian auxiliaries, emerged to greet them and the three exchanged a salute.

'What news of the campaign?' asked Macro, nodding towards the smoke from the camp. 'I take it that's Quintatus and the army.'

'Yes, sir. The legate's been having a crack at getting across to the Druids' island. Started well enough – they shifted the lot on the near shore. But it's been tough going since then from all reports.' The optio gestured towards the wagons. 'Supplies? Food supplies?'

'That's right.'

'About time, sir. It's the first supply convoy I've seen in days. My men are getting hungry. We're down to the last few bags of barley and hard tack. Any chance you could spare some?'

'Ain't down to me, lad. That's the purview of the army's quartermaster. Best you send a request to him.'

'I have. Two days ago, and had nothing back.'

Macro saw the concern in the man's expression. 'I'll mention it when I reach headquarters. Best I can do.'

'Thank you, sir.'

The muffled sound of horses' hooves interrupted the exchange as Lomus and his men joined the convoy. Macro took a horse for himself and another for the tribune, and left orders for the men remaining with the convoy to continue to the camp. Then he led the party down into the valley towards the distant sea. As they approached the coastal strip, they saw the outline of an abandoned camp close to one of the headlands overlooking a sheltered bay. Another outpost lay in one corner of the camp, and they exchanged a brief greeting with a sentry before continuing along the coast. As they rode over the final ridge, the panorama of the struggle to take Mona lay spread out before them.

To their immediate front sprawled the army's camp, large enough to accommodate the two legions, their attached auxiliary cohorts and the draught animals and vehicles of the baggage train. Scores of fires burned brightly, those still in camp huddling round them to warm themselves. Horses and mules stood in their roped enclosures, nuzzling aside the snow as they searched for the stunted tufts of grass beneath. A quarter of a mile from the camp lay the Roman battle lines: artillery batteries deployed on ground levelled by engineers, covering the channel over which the army must pass, and laying down a steady bombardment at long-range of the enemy positions directly across the water. Their efforts were aided by the three warships anchored in the channel, their bolt-throwers trained on the fortifications along the shore of Mona. The tide was out, and a thin sliver of exposed mud snaked across from the mainland to the island. It was no more than ten feet wide and had been thickly sown with sharpened stakes to render it impassable, though it was clear that the Romans had made some attempt to clear the obstacles.

Not without cost. Macro could see scores of corpses, some impaled on the stakes. Around the bodies lay abandoned kit – helmets, shields, swords and javelins – much of which was already half submerged in the mud. On the near side of the channel stood two cohorts of legionaries, each century formed up four abreast. More legionaries stood further back, ready to reinforce their comrades.

As Macro watched, a signal sounded from below and the trumpet call was echoed by others. The century nearest to the causeway began to advance. At the same time, the artillery batteries peppered the earthworks on the shore directly opposite. The defenders there remained hidden from sight, but further along, their comrades lined the defences to watch the attack, quite unperturbed.

'By the gods, they're plucky fellows,' said Glaber.

Macro guessed that they had become accustomed to the Roman assaults and knew that they were safe as long as the missiles rained down on the defences immediately in front of the low-tide crossing point.

311

As the legionaries moved out on to the causeway, their pace suddenly slowed and the following ranks began to bunch up. The centurion and optio struggled alongside to cajole their men back into formation, and the century continued advancing across the narrow strip of mud. Macro could well imagine the effort it would take a heavily armed legionary to make any progress across such a quagmire. They encountered the first of the remaining stakes close to the mainland, and pairs of men peeled off to deal with each obstacle, using their swords to work the bases of the stakes free before tossing them aside.

'I need to find the legate.' Macro lifted his reins.

'Me too,' said Glaber. 'If I'm not mistaken, he should be over there. Behind the rightmost battery. Do you see?'

Macro squinted and a moment later picked out the party of riders in scarlet cloaks. He nodded. 'Let's go, sir.'

They descended the slope, passing between forage parties and the cavalry pickets assigned to protect them, and skirted the outer ditch of the vast marching camp. They were still afforded a view of the legionaries wading out across the mud. As the men approached the as yet undisturbed thickets of stakes, a Roman trumpet signalled the artillery to cease shooting. The last of the bolts arced across the channel and plunged harmlessly into the turf and log rampart. There was the briefest of pauses before a war horn sounded and the enemy rose from behind their battered defences, unleashing their own barrage of missiles against the approaching legionaries. Arrows, slingshot and light javelins rattled down on the heavy curved surfaces of the legionary shields. Occasionally a missile found its way past the wall of shields and injured one of the men, who was then forced to drop

312

out of formation and do his best to return to the friendly shore. Some were too badly injured to turn back, and instead did their best to take cover behind their shields as they waited for help.

The centurion gave an order to his men, and they paused to form a testudo before plodding slowly towards the defences, where the men inside the formations began to work on clearing the stakes away as best they could as the missiles clattered around them, splintering shields, glancing off armour and striking down any of their comrades who were unfortunate enough to be on the receiving end of those weapons that found their way through a gap in the shields.

Macro turned his gaze aside and looked towards the army's camp, knowing that Cato was most likely in there somewhere. He felt a sickening dread at the prospect of breaking the news about Julia's death, and made himself resolve to do that the moment he had warned Legate Quintatus about the enemy's scheme to trap the Roman army.

He dismissed the men who had ridden all the way from the fort with him and sent them to find the Blood Crows' tent lines in the camp. Then, together with Tribune Glaber, he turned the corner of the fort and rode down the side in the direction of the artillery battery. A screen of legionaries surrounded the legate and his headquarters party, and as the two men approached, an optio stepped into their path and raised his hand.

'Halt and state your business, sir!'

Macro reined in a short distance away. 'Centurion Lucius Cornelius Macro, Fourth Cohort, Fourteenth Legion. I have to see Legate Quintatus at once.'

The optio leaned to one side. 'And who is the other officer?'

Glaber trotted up alongside Macro and looked down at the man. 'Senior Tribune Gaius Porcinus Glaber, envoy of Governor Aulus Didius Gallus. I also need to speak to the legate.' He paused and bowed his head towards Macro. 'Though I'd say the centurion's case is more pressing. Let us pass.'

The optio stood his ground. 'Sorry, sir. Standing orders. No one is to interrupt the legate while he is conducting the battle. Not without the say-so of his camp prefect, Silanus.'

'It's vital that I speak to him,' Macro growled. 'Now get out of my way!'

As the centurion clicked his tongue and urged his mount forward, the optio quickly gestured to the men of his section and they hurried forward to block him, their javelin tips lowered.

'This is bloody absurd!' Macro thundered. 'When I'm done speaking with the legate, I'm going to have your balls for breakfast.'

'That's enough of this nonsense!' Glaber intervened sharply. 'Optio, send one of your men for the camp prefect at once. Tell him, in my name, that we demand to see the legate. I want permission to pass, or Silanus himself down here at once. Move!'

The optio stepped back a pace, flustered, then turned and shouted an order to one of his men. The legionary left his shield and javelin in the charge of one of his mates and ran off towards the group of horsemen a hundred yards away on a rise that overlooked the battlefield. Macro turned to the tribune and nodded his thanks.

Out on the causeway, the leading century had stalled. Covered in clinging mud and still being battered by missiles, the testudo was starting to fall apart. A long string of casualties was struggling back to the mainland, nursing their injuries as they backed away behind their shields. Some helped their less able comrades, while a handful just lay in the mud, too weak to move. Another signal sounded and a fresh century started forward as the first began to fall back, losing more casualties on the way. They edged aside into the shallows as the new formation struggled past and moved closer to the obstacles they were tasked with clearing, immediately coming under the same deluge of missiles that their predecessors had endured. They stopped and hurriedly formed a testudo before proceeding.

'The lads are getting a hammering today,' Macro said quietly.

Glaber had also been following proceedings and clicked his tongue. 'It does seem to be a profligate waste of men for such limited results. They can't have removed more than ten of those stakes. With what's left, you would need to work through more than a few legions to clear the passage at this rate, I should think.'

They watched a little longer, until the legionary who had gone to find Silanus returned and breathlessly reported to his optio. The latter turned to his squad and barked an order. 'Let them pass!'

The soldiers stepped aside and Macro and Glaber spurred their mounts on, cantering up to the small cluster of officers and the headquarters staff gathered about Legate Quintatus.

At the sound of their approach, Quintatus turned his attention away from the battlefield and glared at Macro and Glaber as they dismounted. He cleared his throat.

'This had better be important, gentlemen . . .'

CHAPTER TWENTY-FOUR

'A trap, you say?' Quintatus frowned. He had listened to Macro's report without interruption as they stood a short distance apart from the other officers, at the legate's insistence. 'Perhaps you are mistaken.'

'I don't think so, sir. We interrogated the prisoner very thoroughly. I would place good money on him telling us the truth. And then there's the strong force we saw marching north, towards your line of communication with Mediolanum.'

'You may have overestimated their strength, Centurion.'

'No, sir. The leader of the patrol who spotted the enemy is a good man. A reliable soldier. I trust his judgement.'

'Patrol? Then you didn't see the enemy with your own eyes?'

'No, sir,' Macro admitted. 'The presence of the enemy was reported to me by Optio Pandarus. He had gone forward to observe a village and saw the enemy column. He had estimated their strength when he encountered and captured one of their scouts. He took the man prisoner and returned to the fort to make his report. I grasped the significance of his sighting and had one of my best men interrogate the prisoner for the full story.'

'Just a moment, Centurion. Your optio was the only witness to the sighting of the column?'

'Yes, sir. But that's not the point.'

'Oh, I think it is. The man was probably tired and may have misjudged the size of the enemy force for any number of reasons.'

'But what about the prisoner's story, sir? There were witnesses enough to that.'

'And how many of you speak the prisoner's tongue?'

Macro was starting to get a sinking feeling about the legate's cross-examination of his account and had to compose himself as he continued. 'I used an auxiliary from the Eighth Illyrian to translate for us, sir. He has some mastery over the local dialects.'

'An auxiliary. I see . . .'

'I saw no reason to doubt that he was doing his job as accurately as possible, sir.'

Quintatus sniffed. 'I'm sure. That's just one reason why you are a centurion and not a legate. Has it occurred to you that your prisoner might well have been spinning you a story? I can think of nothing the enemy would like better than for you to believe a pack of lies and come racing up here to warn me that the natives are setting a trap for me, and then for me to retreat out of these accursed mountains just as I am on the point of achieving a final victory over the Druid scum and their followers.' He paused briefly. 'Can you not see that, Centurion?'

Macro clamped his lips together and seethed in silence as he reflected that one of the main reasons why he was a centurion and Quintatus was a legate was because the latter had been born with a fucking silver spoon in his mouth. He wished that the infant Quintatus had bloody well choked on it and saved them all a lot of trouble. All the same, he went over the details of what he had reported, step by step, and concluded that if the legate was right in his suspicions, then the enemy had to be very devious indeed. Not only that, but they would have been depending on a chain of coincidences to bring their plan to fruition. It was hard to believe that he had been gulled by them, but equally his story seemed to cut little ice with Quintatus.

'I do not doubt that your interrogator was thorough,' the legate continued, 'but add it all up, Macro. One man, your optio, sees some enemy soldiers, and one of them just happens to fall into his lap. When he gets the prisoner back to the fort so that he can be questioned, there is only one man who is able to translate both the questions and the answers the prisoner gives. It hardly sounds very reliable. And then your prisoner could simply have been lying to mislead us. Isn't that possible?'

'It's possible, sir.'

'Then isn't it also possible that the very last thing the enemy would want is for me to continue the campaign while we are on the very cusp of a great victory?'

'I suppose so.' Macro glanced towards the crossing point, which was fast disappearing as the tide began to come in. Already the second century had abandoned their work of removing the obstacles and were backing away from the enemy-held shore. They picked up their wounded as they clambered through the mud, and left their dead to the rising sea as the last of the enemy's missiles began to fall short. The crossing point was still thick with obstacles and the enemy would almost certainly do their best to set up more stakes under cover of darkness. To Macro's experienced eye it looked as if the legate was very far from being on the cusp of a great victory. It was much more likely that he was on the cusp of a great defeat, unless he took the warning seriously and acted to remove the army from the enemy's trap.

'Then why, in the name of Jupiter, best and greatest, didn't you make the connection between the information that was fed to you and the wider strategic situation? You have been played by the Druids, and played handsomely, I might add.' Quintatus softened his tone. 'There's no shame in admitting it, Macro. The Druids are devious fellows and you have to pay them due credit for orchestrating the whole thing in order to force me to break off and retreat. They knew they would never be able to stop us fighting our way to the shores of their sacred island. They knew that they would never be able to hold the island against us. So they confected this plan to try and divert us from our goal. Surely you can see that?'

Macro briefly considered the legate's argument and had to admit to himself that it made some sense. As he did so, he felt a flush of shame that he could have been manipulated by the enemy into sabotaging the Roman campaign. But then he checked himself. The legate might be right, but there was an equal possibility that the prisoner had revealed the truth about the enemy's intention to set a trap for the Roman army. He had to stand firm on that possibility, not for reasons of pride, but out of concern for the safety of his comrades.

'Sir, I hope you are right. All the same, I think it would be prudent to consider the possibility that our prisoner's information is accurate.'

Quintatus eyed him coldly. 'What would you have me do? Halt the attack on Mona while we send patrols to find this enemy army of yours? Look around you, Centurion. Winter is here. This snow is but a precursor of worse weather to come. We have a brief opportunity in which to crush the Druids and return to winter quarters before the mountain tracks become completely impassable. I will not give up the chance of eradicating the single greatest obstacle to establishing peace in Britannia. Now, I have wasted enough time on this matter. You may remain in camp for the night, but you are to return to your fort at first light and resume command.'

'But sir, my place is here, with my lads in the Fourth Cohort.'

'Your place is where I say it is,' Quintatus concluded, then looked over Macro's shoulder. 'And now tell me, who the hell is that?'

Macro glanced over his shoulder. 'Tribune Gaius Porcinus Glaber, sir. Sent from Rome. I came across him on the way to find you.'

'Tribune Glaber, over here!'

Glaber hurried across and saluted, but did not get a chance to formally introduce himself.

'Centurion Macro tells me that you have been sent from Rome.'

'Yes, sir.'

'Why?'

Glaber was momentarily taken aback by the legate's directness. 'I have been sent on the orders of the emperor to inform you that the new governor of the province has been appointed and will be arriving in Britannia shortly. I am to liaise with you and your staff to arrange the handover.'

'New governor?' Quintatus looked shocked. 'Already? That can't be possible . . . Damn the man, why so soon? Who is he?'

'Aulus Didius Gallus, sir.'

'I know of him. Why Didius Gallus? The man has never stepped outside of the Mediterranean. He has no experience of fighting the Celts, or of a climate like this. A poor choice, made by meddling politicians to settle some debt or curry favour, no doubt. I am perfectly capable of governing the province until spring.'

'I wouldn't know anything about the timing of it, sir,' Glaber responded flatly. 'I am just the messenger.'

Quintatus sniffed. 'You are Gallus's man. And you will have to wait until my work is completed here before we can begin to consider the process of handing over power.'

'My orders are to begin making preparations for the arrival of the new governor immediately. Gallus requires that you provide a full inventory of military and civil personnel, their disposition and functions.'

'He requires that, does he?'

'That, and a number of other requests, sir. The full documentation is in my travel chest, and I am ready to begin working with your staff at your earliest convenience.'

Quintatus laughed. 'Does this look like a convenient moment to entertain any such bureaucratic exercise, Tribune Glaber? I am fighting a war. I will deal with your queries when I am good and ready. In the meantime you are welcome to enjoy the hospitality of my camp. Unless you would prefer to return to Londinium to await the arrival of your master?'

'Having witnessed the hazards of these mountains, I

prefer to remain with the army, sir.'

'Very well, but be so good as to stay out of my way. Understand?'

'Yes, sir.'

The legate turned back to Macro. 'You see? There's even more reason to move to crush those Druid bastards as quickly as possible. Now, I have an army to command. You two are dismissed.'

He did not wait for a response, but turned and strode back towards his command post, crunching across the snow. Glaber waited until he was out of earshot before he let out a low whistle.

'Touchy character, our legate. Is he always like this?'

'Only when someone is after his job, I should imagine, sir.'

Glaber turned to him with an amused expression. 'No doubt you think this is all about politics and the endless round of backstabbing that passes for after-dinner entertainment in polite circles.'

'I, er . . .' Macro shifted uncomfortably on to his bad leg, winced at the discomfort and shifted back to his good one.

'Well you'd be right. That's exactly what it is all about. My man is on his way up and Quintatus has yet to make his mark. It's too bad for him that the credit for his efforts will probably be pinched by Gallus, but that's the way it goes. I can well understand his mood.'

'That's all very well for you and your class, sir, but for the rest of us it's a bit of a sore point when we're concerned with doing our duty and fighting for Rome and our comrades. When your arse is in the grass and you're knee deep in blood and the only thing between you and the barbarians like that lot over there is your shield and sword, then it's a little disappointing to know that your betters just see you as a piece in their game. You know what I mean?'

They stared at each other for a moment before Glaber nodded. 'Fair point, Centurion. I will try to remember that.'

'Thank you, sir.'

Glaber cleared his throat. 'Since I am surplus to require-ments, I think I might find myself a nice fire to warm me up back at the camp. What about you?'

Macro took a deep breath. 'I need to find Prefect Cato and report to him. Whatever the legate may think, I'm not convinced that the enemy have played me for a fool. Cato will have a view on it. He usually does.' He smiled fondly. 'That's what he's good at.'

'It seems you admire your superior.'

Macro stiffened. 'He's a bloody fine officer, sir. One of the best in the army, and anyone who knows him would say the same.'

'I'll take your word for it. It'll be interesting to make his acquaintance.'

Macro was still for a moment, caught up in the anxiety about the burden of what he must reveal to his friend when he found him. He coughed and looked at Glaber. 'Sir, would you do me a favour?'

Glaber's brow rose slightly in surprise. 'A favour? What is it?'

'What you told me, about his wife. Would you care to come with me to break the news to the prefect? He will want details. It would be better coming from someone who knows more about it than me.'

Glaber eyed him shrewdly. 'You can't face telling him?'

Macro's expression was fixed for an instant before he shook his head slowly. 'It's a hard thing for a man to inform his friend that his wife has died. Cato loved her dearly, sir. She was a good woman. Well, you know that for yourself.'

'You knew her as well, then?'

'I was there when they met in Palmyra.'

'Ah yes . . . That fracas with the Parthians a few years back. I heard about it. I had no idea Julia was caught up in that business. I dare say she kept her wits about her. She was always a tough character as a child, I recall.'

'That she did.' Macro smiled sadly. 'As brave as any soldier. They were a fine match . . . I'd give anything not be the one who breaks his heart.'

Glaber pursed his lips before he replied. 'I'll come with you.'

They returned to their horses, remounted and rode back to the camp's main gate. Macro spared a last look towards the crossing and saw that the tide now covered the muddy route across to the island and only the tips of the stakes appeared above the water. Out to sea, the sky had cleared, and a thin blue hue seeped across the snow-covered landscape. On the near bank, the casualties from the last attack were having their wounds dressed, while the rest of their comrades were scraping the mud from their kit. Their lethargic demeanour spoke eloquently of the poor state of their morale, and from the far side of the channel came the sound of the enemy's jeering. That stuck in Macro's throat in the way that all such reverses chafed the sensibilities of soldiers who had suffered a setback. The trick of it was to turn the sentiment into a cold determination to win through and prove yourself better than the enemy. The alternative was to sink into despair and watch, dull-eyed, as any prospect of victory faded and it all became a matter of grinding endurance.

They entered the camp and asked the duty centurion for directions to the tent lines of the Blood Crows. The auxiliary unit had been assigned an area alongside the other mounted units, down the slope from the legionary tent lines, close to the drainage run-off and the latrines. What little warmth the day had brought had turned the surface of the snow to slush in places, but the temperature was dropping rapidly in the gathering dusk and the men were building up the campfires with the proceeds of the day's foraging.

Macro soon spotted the standard of the Blood Crows rising above the large tent that served as the cohort's field headquarters. Rather than feeling pleasure at the prospect of seeing his closest friend again, he felt his heart contract into the pit of his stomach, and a dreadful weariness settled over him. Beside him, the young tribune pointed to the standard.

'Is that Cato's lot? Have to say, I like the standard. Very dramatic. No wonder the natives quail before you, eh?'

Glaber's tone was forced, and Macro realised that the tribune too was apprehensive. He wished Glaber would just keep quiet and accept the dreadful nature of the task that lay ahead. There was no place for levity in the situation. None at all.

They walked their mounts over to the standard and dismounted before handing the reins to one of the headquarters sentries.

'Is the prefect here?' asked Macro.

'Yes, sir.'

'Very well. See that the horses are watered and fed.'

The sentry nodded and led the beasts away as Macro hesitated outside the threshold to the headquarters tent. Through the narrow gap in the oiled goatskin flaps he saw two clerks sitting at a trestle table, one rubbing furiously as he worked the marks out of a waxed tablet. His colleague was lighting some lamps on a stand with a taper. Smoke trailed upwards to a vent at the top of the tent from a brazier just out of Macro's field of vision.

'Are you ready for this?' Glaber asked gently.

'No. How could I be?' Macro sighed heavily, then ducked through the flaps into the tent. The clerks looked up and Macro turned in the direction of the screened section set aside for the cohort's commander. He could hear Cato's voice, in quiet conversation with someone, and sensed his friend's exhaustion from his tone. He paced over to the gap in the leather screen and saw Cato bending over his campaign desk, Decurion Miro standing to one side.

'You'll have to tell Pausinus I need every man,' said Cato as he tapped a finger on a tablet. 'Every man who can still get in the saddle is to be declared fit for duty. We're below half-strength as it is.'

'Yes, sir.'

The leather rustled lightly as Glaber pushed through and joined Macro. Cato looked up, and there was the slightest of pauses before he straightened up with a broad smile. 'Macro! What in the name of the gods are you doing here? You're supposed to be at the fort.' His smile faded as he noted Macro's leaden expression. 'What's happened? An attack? Is the fort taken?'

'Nothing like that, sir.'

'Thank Fortuna. And who is this?'

'Tribune Glaber. I plucked his arse out of the fire when I came across him and some others who had been ambushed.'

'We had the situation under control,' Glaber protested.

'Anyway,' Macro continued, 'I had urgent intelligence I felt obliged to pass on to Legate Quintatus. At least I thought it was urgent.'

'Tell me.'

Macro explained as briefly as he could, not omitting any detail of the legate's dismissal of his report. Cato listened with an intense expression, nodding at salient points. As soon as Macro concluded, he sucked his teeth. 'I think you were right to warn him. Quintatus is grasping at straws. All he cares about is putting an end to the Druids. If the enemy are trying to cut across our communications, then we're going to be in a sticky position. I'll send patrols out to investigate at first light. The Blood Crows are not required for anything at present, so there's no need to put it through headquarters. If asked I'll say they're on an exercise.' He winked at Macro, and when he saw no reaction, he narrowed his eyes a fraction.

'What's wrong, Macro? There's something you're not telling me.'

'Yes, lad,' Macro said softly. 'There is.'

He cleared his throat to speak, but the words would not come.

Macro swallowed anxiously and gestured to Glaber. 'Please, sir, if you'd wait outside, in case the prefect wants to speak to you later . . .'

Glaber glanced at both men, then nodded. 'Of course. Let me know if there's anything I can do.'

Once he had gone, Macro approached Cato and indicated the chair by the campaign desk. 'Sit down, lad.'

'What is this?' Cato demanded, but he did as he was told, even as Macro remained on his feet. 'What is going on, Macro? Speak up.'

'All right then . . . After the lads and I pitched into the fight to help Glaber, I asked him where he had come from. He told me he'd been sent from Rome. He said his family knew Senator Sempronius, and Julia. It was shortly before Glaber left that he heard the news.'

'News?'

'About your wife.'

The atmosphere in the tent seemed to turn icy around Cato as he leaned forward and stared intently at his friend. 'Go on.'

'Lad, I have to tell you something bad. The worst of all things. Julia is dead.'

Cato said nothing and sat quite still.

'Julia is dead,' Macro repeated, to break the unbearable silence. 'I'm so sorry.'

'I received a letter from her less than a month ago. She can't be . . . How? How did she die?'

'Glaber says she caught a chill. He says she was weak from the birth of your child. Lucius still lives, though. The gods have spared you that loss at least.'

'Yes. I suppose.' Cato sat back and ran a hand through his dark curls. 'She's dead?'

'Yes.'

Abruptly Cato rose to his feet and crossed quickly to the gap, addressing the tribune waiting outside. 'Is this true, Glaber? What exactly do you know about it?'

'It's true, sir. I know very little more than what Centurion Macro has already said. I was told by my father, after he had come back from rendering his condolences to Senator Sempronius. It was all over very quickly. By my father's account, she did not suffer too badly and passed away while she slept. A great pity. She was always well liked by all who knew her. I . . . I . . .' The tribune dried up uncomfortably.

'Yes.' Cato turned away. 'That will be all, thank you, Tribune Glaber. Please find yourself some shelter and get some rest.'

'Of course, sir. Is there anything else?'

'No. Nothing. Go, please.'

Glaber bowed his head respectfully. 'If I am needed, I will be at army headquarters.' He turned away and hurried outside, and Macro heard the snort of a horse as the tribune mounted and wheeled the mount around to trot up the thoroughfare towards the heart of the camp.

Cato walked slowly back to his chair and slumped into it, still too numb to react. At length he looked up at Macro. 'Dead?'

'I am afraid so, sir. Here, you're trembling. Let me get your cloak.' Macro picked it up from where it lay over a chest, splattered with mud and a little damp. He arranged the folds about Cato and then rested a hand on his friend's shoulder. 'I cannot tell you how it grieves me, lad. The gods should never have taken her at such a young age.'

Cato swallowed and looked up at him. 'Please give me a moment to myself.'

Macro saw the rawness in the prefect's eyes and nodded. 'I'll be outside, then. If you need me.'

'Yes, thank you.'

Macro waited a moment to see if there was anything else, and then backed out quietly and joined the clerks in the main part of the tent. He took a last look and saw the prefect lean forward and press his face into his hands, his fingers clenched like claws into his hairline. There was a soft groan, and Cato's shoulders convulsed.

Then Macro pulled the leather section dividers together and closed the gap to afford his closest friend in the world a little privacy to grieve for his lost love.

CHAPTER TWENTY-FIVE

'Here we go again.' Macro leaned on the parapet of the camp's corner tower and looked down towards the crossing. It was late the following morning, and there had been a further fall of snow during the night. The camp, the artillery platforms, the earthworks on both sides of the river and the decks of the warships and transports lay under a gleaming blanket of white. Down by the water's edge, the legionaries were formed up again, waiting for the order to advance across the mud to continue removing the obstacles blocking the route. Overhead whirred the bolts unleashed by the Roman artillery – the 'morning hate', as the common soldiers referred to the barrage of missiles raining down on the enemy positions. Not that it seemed to have any particular effect on the natives, Macro mused, watching the small puffs of dirt and splinters as the missiles struck the defences. The Deceanglians and their Druid leaders were keeping well under cover, waiting for the bombardment to cease before they took their turn against the legionaries attempting to remove the stakes from the crossing. Macro could see that they had used the cover of darkness to replace many of those obstacles removed the previous day.

'Looks like it's going to snow again,' said Glaber as he stood beside Macro, watching proceedings.

Macro glanced up, then round at the band of dark clouds gathering over the mountains. 'Just to add to our woes.'

Both officers turned their attention back to the tidal crossing point and watched quietly for a while before the tribune commented, 'I find it hard to believe there isn't an alternative way of going about this.'

'Oh, there are a few alternatives all right, sir,' Macro responded. 'But since the storm destroyed almost all the transports and most of the fleet, an assault directly across the channel is off the menu. As is any question of making a landing elsewhere along the coast of Mona to get round their defences. I dare say the Druids have stockpiled plenty of supplies and we'd go hungry long before we could starve them out. If you want my opinion, the best thing the legate can do now is give up and withdraw to Mediolanum and have another crack at Mona in the spring, when he's had a chance to replace the ships that were lost. But we know he won't be doing that, thanks to the imminent arrival of the new governor. So that's why he'll stick with this approach, blunt as it is.'

'Blunt is the word.'

They both looked down towards the raised and flattened ground of the artillery battery, where Quintatus was survey-ing the enemy positions stolidly while his officers clustered round a freshly lit brazier in which flames crackled fiercely and bright sparks flew a short distance into the air before dying away against the grey of the distant landscape of Mona. The legate waited until the tide had ebbed sufficiently to uncover enough ground for the leading century to advance on an eight–man front, then turned and gave an order. The headquarters trumpeters raised their brass instruments, puffed their cheeks and sounded the advance.

Just as had happened the previous day, the leading century tramped across the snow and down on to the stretch of mud leading towards Mona. And just as before, they were pelted with arrows and slingshot as they approached the stakes.

'Good morning.'

Macro turned to see Cato climbing into the tower. His friend looked drawn and exhausted. Even so, he forced a bleak smile on to his lips as he approached Macro and Glaber.

'Good morning, sir.' Macro greeted him evenly, unsure of the tone he should adopt. He had lived with death for so long that it had become almost part of everyday life and there had been comrades he had grieved for, but nothing seemed to have prepared him for the pain he felt for his best friend's loss. If there had been any way he could have traded his life for Julia's, he would have freely done so. There was a haunted expression in Cato's eyes that cut him to the quick, and he looked away towards the channel and cleared his throat as he struggled to find something to say.

'The legate's going straight at it again.'

Cato nodded. 'Third day running, and we're still not likely to gain the far shore for another three days, at least. It's too slow.'

Glaber glanced at him. 'Too slow for what, exactly?'

'Those wagons you brought in yesterday were the first to reach the army for two days. With this snow, I expect the planned supply convoys are being held up. For that reason, or something more worrying.'

'Such as?'

Cato hesitated before he replied. 'What if Macro's information is right? What if the reason we are not being supplied is because the enemy have cut us off? Either way, we're going to be on half-rations before we ever get on to the island, and then we'll have to fight our way across Mona step by step. Who knows how long that will take?'

Glaber considered this briefly. 'Are you saying the army is in danger?'

Cato gave a short, dry laugh. 'Tribune, the army is always in danger. The trick of it is to make sure that you are ready to respond to any potential peril that fate throws in your path. As the saying goes: proper planning and preparation prevent piss-poor performance. Our problem is that the legate's original plan has been scuppered by the storm. That's why we're stuck with trying to force a passage across the causeway. Nor are we adequately provisioned to prepare for a siege. So on current form, I'd say that leaves us with the prospect of piss-poor performance. At the very least. My greater worry is that we're in danger of being caught out on a limb, and Quintatus is refusing to accept that.'

'Do you really think the enemy is planning to trap us here?'

'We'll know soon enough. I sent those patrols out, like I said. Before dawn so that they didn't attract too much attention. If the enemy are lurking close by, we'll find them.'

Macro regarded him with concern. The last he had seen of Cato before finding a billet with the Fourteenth Legion the previous night was his friend breaking down in tears. Now it seemed that Cato had permitted himself only a scant few hours of sorrow before taking up his duties again. It was doubtful that he had slept, and more than likely that he had not eaten, neither of which was advisable if there was a day's soldiering to be done.

'You should get some rest, sir, while you wait for the patrols to come back. I'll wake you myself if there's any news.'

A slight frown creased Cato's brow. 'Certainly not. There's no need for that. I don't need any rest, thank you, Centurion Macro.'

Macro was about to reply, wounded by the cutting formality. But then he thought better of it. Cato might be his friend, almost a brother or son to him, but he was also a senior officer and had forcefully reminded him of the fact in a way that brooked no informality. He swallowed before he replied tersely, 'Yes, sir.'

There was an awkward silence as they all regarded the action taking place towards the shore of Mona. A screen of legionaries was doing its best to block the enemy missiles as their colleagues wrestled with the obstacles driven into the seabed. As the three men watched, one of the soldiers was struck down by an arrow piercing his neck. He stumbled back and then fell to his knees in the mud as blood coursed over his shoulder and down his arm. He swayed a moment, dizzy from loss of blood, and then folded on to his side and lay in the mud, writhing fitfully. The leading century's optio detailed two men to help him, and they dragged the wounded legionary back to the safety of the dressing station on the near shore before rejoining their comrades.

A voice called out from below. 'Where's Prefect Cato?'

'Up there, sir. In the tower.'

Moments later, boots sounded on the floor below, the

ladder creaked and Decurion Miro climbed on to the platform to join the others. He hurried across to Cato and saluted.

'Sir, beg to report, but we've had word from one of the patrols. They've sighted an enemy force not far from the camp.'

The other officers exchanged anxious looks before Cato responded. 'How far from the camp?'

'No more than five miles away, to the east, right across our supply route. In the vale, there, sir.' Miro indicated the gap between two hills not far from the camp.

'What's their strength?'

'The optio reported seeing thousands of them, sir.'

Cato turned to Macro and raised an eyebrow. 'It seems your information was right.'

'Not that you doubted me, of course.'

'Have I ever?' He turned back to Miro. 'Where is the optio now?'

'Still with his patrol, sir. He's keeping tabs on the enemy. He sent one of his men back with the information. He's waiting below. Shall I send him on to headquarters, sir?'

Cato considered for a moment. 'I'll go with him. You have the rest of the cohort called to arms and formed up outside the camp. Dismissed.'

As Miro hurried away, Cato turned to Macro and Glaber. 'Will you join me? I'd appreciate someone witnessing this.'

Macro was surprised. 'Why? What difference can it make?'

'No, he's right,' said Glaber. 'If we get out of this, Quintatus may well cast about for a scapegoat. You think ahead, sir. That's a good quality.'

'It's a survival strategy. I've enough experience of the senior ranks to know how this works. Let's go. You going to be able to keep up, Macro?'

The latter grinned. 'Just try and stop me, sir.'

They descended the tower and emerged in its shadow, where a trooper stood to attention as he saw them.

'Phalko, isn't it?' said Cato.

'Yes, sir.'

'Follow us, Phalko.'

They marched out of the gate, across the boarded ditch and made for the headquarters party close to the main artillery battery. Macro walked stiffly, pushing himself to keep up and grimacing with the effort of fighting the shooting pain in his leg. They were passed through the outer cordon and approached Quintatus and his staff officers as they watched the latest attempt to breach the lines of defence blocking the tidal crossing to Mona. Cato brushed aside the camp prefect and made his way towards the legate, turning to address Phalko at his side.

'Just repeat what the optio told you to say. And if Quintatus asks you any questions, make sure you give him as much detail as you can recall, particularly on the number of the enemy. Clear?'

'Yes, sir.'

Quintatus noticed their approach out of the corner of his eye and half turned towards Cato. 'Prefect Cato, what is it?'

Cato did not hesitate before replying. 'We've been set a trap, sir. Centurion Macro's information is correct. One of my patrols just reported that they have sighted the enemy.'

'One of your patrols? What patrols? I never gave any such order.'

'The men were sent out on my authority, sir.'

'Your authority?' Quintatus's nostrils flared. 'And unless something has happened that has escaped my notice, have you replaced me as commander of this army, Prefect Cato?'

'No, sir.'

'Then how is it that you decide to order your men to go looking for the enemy without clearing it with headquarters first?'

Cato knew better than to enter into such an altercation. Besides, there was no time for it. He spoke forcefully, and loud enough for many of the staff officers to hear. 'Sir, we can deal with the breach of protocol later. The important issue is that the enemy are close at hand and the army is in danger. This man,' he indicated Phalko, 'has ridden from the patrol. Tell the legate what you saw, Trooper.'

Phalko stood stiffly as he made his report. 'We'd ridden perhaps five miles from the camp, sir. We were in this valley and it got a bit misty, like. That's when the optio orders us up a hill to get an overview of the surrounding terrain. We climbed above the mist but still couldn't see much, apart from the tops of hills. The sun broke through the clouds for a bit and the mist began to thin out down in the valley. And that's when we saw 'em, sir. The enemy. Coming out of the mist. A cavalry screen first, then the head of the main column. They was still a few miles off, so the optio says we should wait until we can get a better idea of their strength before we turn back to report. But they kept coming, sir. By the thousand. That's when the optio sends me back to raise the alarm.'

Quintatus looked doubtful as he considered the man's report. 'How many men exactly?'

The trooper hesitated. 'The optio told me to say at least ten thousand, sir.'

'And what did you think?'

'I ain't good at numbers, sir. But I'd say there's at least as many of the bastards as we've got. Maybe more.'

'Sounds just like Centurion Macro said, sir,' said Cato. 'In which case, there is every reason to accept the rest of the intelligence he brought you.'

The legate took a deep breath and gritted his teeth as he considered the situation. Then he let out an explosive sigh and turned to his staff officers. 'Silanus! Call off the attack. Post a cohort to guard our side of the tidal crossing. Then I want five cohorts of the Fourteenth, together with Iberian archers, up to cover the mouth of that valley. At the double. We could do with some cavalry as well.'

Silanus bowed his head as Cato cleared his throat. 'I've given orders for the Blood Crows to prepare for action, sir.'

Quintatus stared hard at him. 'It seems you are a step ahead of me, Prefect.'

Cato kept quiet.

'Very well, send your men ahead to cover the lads of the Fourteenth. But you stay here. I'll need to hold a full briefing for all unit commanders, once I've considered our options.'

'What about the artillery, sir?' asked Silanus. 'Shall I have the carts brought up and the bolt-throwers broken down?'

'No. If the Druids see that, they'll know for sure we plan a retreat. Besides, if they try to break out from Mona, then we can cut 'em down the moment they venture out of their earthworks.' Quintatus took one last, longing look at the far shore and turned away. 'All senior officers to headquarters at once!'

★ ★ ★

By the time Cato joined the others in the largest of the headquarters tents, the rest of the patrols had returned with news of more sightings of the enemy. Small mounted bands for the most part, scouting ahead and along the flanks of the main force. The patrols were sent to join the rest of the force sent to block the mouth of the valley. Fortunately, it was narrow, and steep rocky slopes and crags looming up on either side restricted the frontage. The legionaries had carried some field fortifications with them, and baskets of iron caltrops to swiftly scatter before their lines to break up any charges by the rapidly approaching native army. Despite the continued presence of the artillery batteries and the troops along the shore of the mainland, the Druids and their followers had already guessed the significance of the cancellation of the attack and the movement of men towards the mountains. The sound of cheering carried across the waters of the channel, and clusters of figures lined the high ground behind the defences as they looked for the first sign of their allies' arrival to close the trap on the Roman army.

The mood in the tent was grim, and the only warmth came from a brazier at one end. Constant footfall and the heat of bodies had melted the snow and ice and rendered the ground muddy and slick, and the officers waited for the legate to appear from his private quarters, where he had been conferring with the camp prefect and his closest staff officers. Cato crossed to the tent flap and ducked his head outside. The scattered breaks in the cloud that had flitted across the sea and mountains at noon had given way to an uninterrupted overcast that was the colour of grimy linen. More snow was on the way, then, he mused. It would hinder the enemy as much as the Roman army, but the critical difference was that the legionaries and auxiliaries were a long way from their base and their supply line had been severed, whereas the enemy were on their own soil and could draw on the supplies of grain and meat that had been stockpiled by the natives of these mountains.

'So what do you think?'

Cato turned to see Glaber standing at his shoulder. 'I think it's going to snow again.'

The tribune flashed a smile. 'Very funny. I mean what do you think he'll do?'

Cato let the flap slip back into place. 'We'll know soon enough.'

'You're very reticent about offering an opinion all of a sudden.'

'The legate has as much information as he needs. The decision is his, not mine. I'm not going to second-guess him. Especially not in front of the man who represents his incoming superior.'

Glaber stroked the stubble on his chin. 'You don't have to worry about me. I'm not a spy, and I'm not gathering information to dish the dirt on anyone. I'm just an officer like everyone else in this tent, and I'm in the same predicament. I'm just curious to hear your professional opinion on our situation. That's all.'

'My professional opinion is that the legate is in command and will take the course of action he decides is most prudent. It is my further opinion that officers below the rank of legate should avoid being embroiled in politics as far as they possibly can, if they know what's good for them.' Cato paused, then added, 'Speaking from personal experience.'

'Oh?' Glaber cocked his head to one side. 'Care to elaborate?'

'No.' Cato stepped round the tribune. 'Excuse me.'

He made his way back over to Macro, stifling a yawn. His eyes ached and the thick atmosphere inside the tent was making him feel tired and a little nauseous. Macro folded his thick arms and ground his teeth.

'By the time he's finished conferring with his cronies, it'll be bloody Saturnalia at this rate.'

Before Cato could reply, Silanus appeared through the flaps leading to the legate's private tent and stood to one side as he announced, 'Commanding officer present!'

At once all conversation ceased and the officers stood to attention as Quintatus entered, followed by a handful of tribunes and Legate Valens. Quintatus waited until everyone was still and then nodded to the camp prefect.

'At ease!'

Allowing a brief pause to gather his officers' attention, Quintatus began his briefing. 'As you know, a large enemy force has appeared to our rear. No doubt that's why none of our supply convoys have reached us in the past few days. And that'll mean we have to manage the supplies we have in camp very carefully. But the immediate danger is that we are caught between the new force and the enemy opposing us on Mona. At the moment we've blocked their advance at the mouth of the valley. But we can be sure they will find a way round during the night, or tomorrow morning. At the same time, we can reckon on the Druids and their friends pulling up their obstacles in preparation for attacking us from Mona.

'Given the new situation, we have little time to decide

on the best course of action. We could try to throw our full weight across the channel and take the island. Then we could easily hold the enemy's main force off for as long as we needed.' He smiled. 'It would be pleasing to see them put up with what our lads have endured the last few days. The trouble is, any attempt to force a crossing would be costly, and if the Druids attempt a scorched-earth policy, then we'd be bottled up on Mona without anything to eat over the winter. Not an appealing prospect, gentlemen. So I've decided, very reluctantly, to withdraw to Mediolanum.'

The officers stirred a little uneasily, and Cato could well understand why. The army had suffered hundreds of casualties to get to this point, and just when it seemed that the Druids were about to be eliminated once and for all, they would escape destruction.

'I have no choice,' Quintatus continued. 'And believe me, I know that I will have to face the consequences when word of this reaches Rome. But that can't be helped. If we tried to take the island we would most likely fail and be crushed between the two enemy forces. If Mona cannot be taken, then it is my duty to try and save the army.' The legate stepped aside and gestured to one of his tribunes. 'Livonius, the map, if you please.'

The tribune and his scribe, Hieropates, brought forward a wooden frame upon which hung the map they had been drafting each day since the army had begun the campaign. When it was in place, Livonius stood to one side as the legate continued his briefing, indicating the most recent additions to the map.

'That's where we are, gentlemen. Over a hundred miles from Mediolanum by the route we took. Now that the enemy has chosen to deny that to us, we face a choice. Our first option is that we attempt to batter our way through them and retrace our steps. Man for man we are better soldiers than they are, but we can expect heavy losses. They outnumber us – substantially once their garrison on Mona tips the scales. If, and more likely when, that happens, they'll be able to attack us from the front and rear at the same time. Not a happy prospect. Even if we do break through their main army, we'll have to fight every inch of the way along the route back to Mediolanum, with this snow only making matters worse. We'll struggle with the baggage train, that's for certain.'

He paused to let his words sink in and then indicated the coastline. 'The alternative, which I prefer, is to take this route, towards the fortress at Deva. Not so direct as far as returning to Mediolanum is concerned, but easier going for our wagons. It presents one clear danger, namely that if the enemy hit us from the front, flank and rear, then we'll have our backs to the shore, and if we are forced to fight a major engagement and lose, we'll be driven into the sea. In that case, the entire army will be lost.'

Cato knew that the loss of the army would have far-reaching consequences. The destruction of the best part of two legions and their attached auxiliary units would greatly enhance the authority of the Druids and inspire every Celtic warrior who hated Rome to rise up in revolt. There would be too few soldiers left in Britannia to put them down and the stark possibility that the new governor would land on the island with no province left to rule.

'The trick of it,' Quintatus continued, 'is to keep moving as fast as we can along the coast. If we can hold off their army for long enough to get our men on the move, the enemy will not be able to block our line of march and will be forced to follow us, even if their two forces combine. They'll be snapping at our heels, to be sure, and the rearguard will have its work cut out, but we'll be able to cover our retreat until we're clear of the mountains in seven or eight days' time. As long as we keep the column closed up and maintain the pace, we should be able to withdraw without too much difficulty. Any comments or questions?'

There was a brief pause as the officers reflected on what they had been told. Then Legate Valens raised a hand and Quintatus nodded at him.

'Whichever route we choose, sir, the men and horses will need feeding. We haven't been resupplied for some days already. How well provisioned is the army at the moment?'

'The camp prefect can tell you the answer to that.'

Silanus cleared his throat and glanced round the tent. 'We have two days' full rations left for the men and three days' feed for horses and mules.'

There was some anxious muttering amongst the officers before Quintatus called for silence and addressed them steadily. 'That is why I have given orders that the men are to go on half-rations as of this moment. You will inform your quartermasters accordingly. There will be some units that carry more than three days' stock of barley and meat. They will report their excess to Silanus. The same applies to those units with less than two days' rations. What we have will be shared fairly. That goes for the officers too. Each one of us must accept the same as the men. Any private stocks of food and wine will be surrendered to headquarters. If anyone is caught hoarding, I will treat it the same way I would treat theft – the individual concerned will be beaten by his comrades and denied food or shelter until we reach Mediolanum.'

Given the situation, and the arrival of bitterly cold winter weather, such a punishment was as good as a death sentence, and every man in the tent knew it. There was silence, except for the low moan of the rising wind outside.

'Very well, I think we can all appreciate the need to move as swiftly as possible. The army will start leaving the camp as soon as darkness falls. Our wounded will be transferred to the surviving warships and transports to make their way along the coast ahead of us. At least they will be spared the discomfort and danger of the march. The artillery will be broken down under cover of darkness and loaded on to their carts. The camp will be abandoned. We can't afford to waste time demolishing it. We'll leave a few of our dead set up on the rampart to look like we're still here. It won't fool the enemy for long, but it may buy us a few hours at least. The force blocking the mouth of the valley will be relieved at dusk by the remaining cohorts from the Fourteenth, and Prefect Cato's Thracians and the archers can remain in place. They will light campfires and arrange more of our dead around them before pulling back to join the column on the march. With a bit of luck we will be several miles away before the enemy are aware that we have gone. After that, gentlemen, the race is on.'

Cato quietly sucked in a breath. Some race, he reflected. The army, hungry and cold, would have to march through ice and snow without let-up. Those too slow to keep their place in the line of march would lag behind and be at the mercy of the Druids and their allies. The only prize offered in this race was survival, at a terrible cost in suffering and danger. The price of losing would be that every man standing there in the tent, every man in the camp beyond, would die. For himself he cared little. What did life mean to him now that Julia was no longer there? He felt an awful abyss filled with grief opening up before him and forced himself to step back. He had to be strong, for the sake of his men, for Macro, and for his son. Until the campaign was over. Only then could he afford the luxury of grief.

CHAPTER TWENTY-SIX

Dawn was still some hours away when Cato reported to Legate Valens, who was warming himself by the embers of a campfire to the rear of the cohorts deployed to hold the mouth of the valley. With him were the commander of the archers and the centurions of the five cohorts tasked with holding the enemy off. The sky had been clear for most of the night, and a half-moon hung low above the horizon, adding its glow to the tiny glint of the stars. The enemy had tried to force their way through late in the afternoon, and again at dusk. Each time the attack had been broken up by volleys of javelins and arrows, and the caltrops and hastily erected field fortifications set up by the legionaries. After the second attempt, the natives had sent large parties of men up the sides of the valley to try and outflank the defenders. The Romans had countered the move, with the two sides struggling through deep snowdrifts to get at each other, dark figures flailing with sword, spear and shield against the white backdrop. At length, the fighting ceased as each side pulled back for the night and foraged for whatever wood was available to light fires, so that they could eat and stay as warm as possible during the bitterly cold night.

Cato and the Blood Crows had been positioned to the rear, ready to cover any retreat in the event that the infantry were forced back from the mouth of the valley. But they had not been needed, and once night had fallen, Cato gave orders for each squadron in turn to feed their mounts and remove their saddles to rest the horses' backs and minimise the risk of saddle sores. Thanks to the ambient light of the moon and stars and the dull gleam of the snow, there was no opportunity to attempt any surprise movements, and a wary calm settled over the serene beauty of the mountainous landscape.

Then, in the depths of the night, the stars began to blink out, a dim veil of cloud appeared across the face of the moon and a light dusting of snow crystals began to fall. That was when Valens decided to call in his officers and make ready to carry out the most difficult part of his orders.

'You sent for me, sir?'

'Ah, Prefect Cato, then we're all present. Come and stand by the fire.' Valens gestured to a space amongst the men crowding the warm glow from the dull golden gleam wavering over the embers of the campfire.

Cato spotted Macro and nodded a greeting as he stepped into place beside him. He gestured towards his friend's leg. 'How has it been?'

Macro had resumed command of the Fourth Cohort and had marched at its head when they had relieved the men already guarding the valley as night had fallen.

'Still a bit stiff, but I'll manage.'

'No surprises there. You always do. Tough as a horse, you are.'

'An old horse, maybe. But I'm not ready for the knacker's yard. Not by a long shot.'

'Delighted to hear it.' Cato smiled for a moment and then lowered his voice. 'I have a mount set aside for you, in case you need it.'

Macro pursed his lips. 'Thank you. Let's hope I won't, eh?'

As they were speaking, Valens looked searchingly towards the scatter of distant fires spread across the valley floor over a mile away that marked the position of the enemy's army. Then he returned his attention to his officers.

'It's time to begin the withdrawal. Prefect Parminius and his archers will go first. Then the first of the legionary cohorts, allowing for a quarter of a mile between units. The Fourth Cohort will be the last of the infantry to leave, once they have carried out their final task.'

Macro could not help a glance towards the carts laden with corpses that stood a short distance away. He was not looking forward to that. But even in death his fallen comrades might yet be of help to those that lived, and he steeled himself for the job at hand.

'The final element of Quintatus's plan is that the Blood Crows will remain here to keep the illusion going that we are defending the line in force. Prefect Cato, you and your men will pull out only when the enemy rumble our little deception. Not before. I want you to buy us as much time as possible to rejoin the main column.'

Cato nodded firmly. 'You can depend on the Blood Crows, sir.'

'I dare say that was why the legate chose you to command the rearguard, Cato. The same reason why you were given the vanguard during the advance. First into the fight, and last out. You're earning quite a reputation, eh?'

'Maybe, sir. But the trick of it will be living long enough to enjoy having a reputation in the first place.'

The comment drew some welcome laughter from the other officers, and the tension over their difficult duty eased a fraction. Then Cato sensed a blur of motion pass his eye and felt something brush his cheek. Glancing up, he saw the swirling veil of snowflakes settling over the mountains. The others were looking at it too, and there was a brief silence before Valens coughed.

'You have your orders, gentlemen. Prefect Parminius, begin pulling your men out the moment it is safe to do so. Keep your heads, keep your men quiet, and may Fortuna march at your sides. Dismissed!'

The snowfall increased and began to blot out the surrounding terrain, and the light from the enemy's fires diminished into faint blooms of red. As soon as he was sure that the withdrawal could not be observed, Valens gave the order to the archers, and Parminius led his men down towards the coastal route being pursued by the rest of the army. When they were almost out of sight, the First Cohort of the legion followed, the men wrapped up in their cloaks as they hoisted their yokes on to their shoulders and trudged off quietly through the steady sweep of snow layering the rocks, trees and ground. The legate mounted his horse and rode off with the last of the detachment, leaving the rearguard of the Fourth Cohort and the Blood Crows behind.

As the dim figures of the legionaries dissolved into the gloom, Cato turned to Macro with a grim expression. 'Time to get started.'

'Can't say I'm terribly keen on this,' said Macro. 'It's not the kind of send-off the poor lads expected when they joined up.'

'They're dead, Macro. They won't be aware of any indignity. Besides, if it were me, and I knew that I could still help my mates, then it would please me.'

Macro eyed him doubtfully. 'I suppose.'

'Besides, it fooled us when the enemy did something similar earlier in the campaign. To work, then. I'll get the Thracians forward and let the other side know we're still here. The Fourth can start work on moving the bodies. No time to waste, Macro. The sooner it's done, the better. It could stop snowing, and the last thing we want is the enemy to see what we're up to.'

'Yes, sir.' Macro nodded and turned away to gather his men for the job. Half remained under arms, standing to along the thin line of defences facing the valley. The others approached the wagons and began to unload the corpses. The bodies were taken over to the campfires and posed around them, propped up seated or standing as if they were taking advantage of the warmth of the fires. Once they were in position, Macro ordered that the fires be built up so that they would burn until long after the living Romans had left the scene. When the snow did stop, the enemy would see the bodies huddled around the fires clearly enough, and would no doubt wait until dawn, when the field defences would be visible, before preparing to attack. By which time the Romans would have stolen several miles' march on them. More importantly, they would not be caught between the Druids on Mona and their allies debouching from the mountains.

Cato led his men forward, stopping a short distance from

where the ground had been sown with caltrops. The fresh snow had covered the telltale indents where the iron spikes had been placed, and now the unblemished expanse of white neatly concealed the danger lurking beneath, waiting to cripple any man or horse unfortunate enough to step on one of the vicious devices.

'Miro!'

'Yes, sir?'

Cato hurriedly considered how to position the hundred mounted men he still had under his command. 'I want a squadron posted on each flank, with two to patrol the ground between and the last one held in reserve. Don't go beyond this point, and make sure none of the lads gets it into his head to go tearing after any enemy pickets that venture too close. We can't afford to get drawn into a fight.'

'Yes, sir.'

As Cato waited for his orders to be carried out, he watched for the enemy. Occasionally he caught a distant glimpse of a figure as one of their lookouts edged closer to observe the Romans, but they would always draw back out of sight. At length he was satisfied that the enemy was unlikely to mount any attacks, and he moved back to find Macro. He found him overseeing the placing of the last bodies around a fire. It was not an easy task. Some corpses had stiffened in postures that lent themselves to being set up hunched beside a fire. Others had not, and had to be propped in standing positions or laid down on the ground, their capes swaddled about them as if to preserve their body heat. It was an eerie sight. Their faces, some mutilated by their wounds, were lit by the flames, their jaws slack and their eyes blank and unseeing. In life they would have sat round just such a fire sharing wineskins, jokes and comradeship. Now their still, silent bodies seemed to mock the idea of the vibrant existence they had once shared in the army. All their memories, experiences and ambitions – gone.

Macro draped a cloak over the shoulders of the last corpse and stood up to examine his handiwork. Then he patted the head gently and turned away with a sad expression, catching sight of Cato.

'It's done, sir. They're all in position.'

'Good job, Macro.'

'Can't say I am happy about it, even if I understand why it has to be done. These lads deserve a proper funeral.'

'They'll be properly honoured when we reach Deva. I swear it.'

Macro chuckled. 'You mean *if* we reach Deva?'

Cato cocked his head. 'What's this, Macro? Are you losing heart so soon? You haven't even started to lay into the enemy. Must be a sign of your years.'

Macro frowned. 'On that subject, with the deepest of respect, sir, I would kindly ask you to just fuck off out of it.'

Cato laughed. 'That's better! There's been too much doom and gloom of late . . .'

Then his expression changed and he clenched his mouth shut tightly for an instant before he regained control over the grief that threatened once again to overwhelm him. He knew that he could not afford to give in to his private tragedy. Not now, when the lives of his men depended upon him concentrating all his efforts on doing his duty. There would be time to dwell on Julia's death later. And if he did not survive the challenges of the coming days, then so much the better. He would be spared the awful anguish of losing his beautiful wife and they would be reunited in the shades that followed this life. He did his best to thrust all thoughts of Julia aside as he drew a long, deep breath and his expression became serious.

'You must get your men out of here, Centurion.'

'What about the wagons, sir?'

Cato looked round and saw the vehicles, snow drifting up against the wheels. The mule teams stood in their traces, heads down, as flakes settled lightly on their hides before immediately starting to melt.

'Leave them behind. They'll only slow us down.'

'And the mules?'

That was a different matter. Mules were valuable and could not be allowed to fall into enemy hands. In other circumstances Cato would have ordered Macro to kill them all, but they might be of use to the army. 'Unharness them and take 'em with you. They can carry kit, or casualties. And if the time comes, they are always useful as meals on the hoof.'

'Yes, sir.' Macro made a face. 'Not my first choice of meat.'

'With what may lie ahead, I doubt it will be the worst thing we eat. You'd better get going, Macro. And be certain to take that horse I assigned to you.'

They clasped forearms and Macro spoke. 'Don't take any unnecessary risks, you hear?'

'We'll be fine. The mounts are fresh and we'll be able to keep ahead of the enemy. Just make sure you're ready to turn and support us when we rejoin the column.'

'I'll see to it. Good luck, sir.'

Macro released his grip and they exchanged a salute

before he turned away and called the order for his cohort to form up. The legionaries waded calf-deep through the snow to take their places, and when all were ready, Macro gave the order to advance. Cato watched as his friend climbed into the saddle of his mount and trotted to the front of the cohort to lead his men away through the flakes drifting down from the night sky. Soon they were gone, leaving the Roman lines to Cato, his men and the dead. The latter were like sculptures, thought Cato, as he watched the snow building up against them and settling on their heads, where there was no longer any warmth to melt it. They would be covered by dawn if the snow continued. Ill-defined hummocks in the winter landscape, waiting to be discovered by the enemy.

Cato pushed the morbid image aside and made his way forward to the centre of the line, where Miro and the reserve squadron stood with the Blood Crows' standard. The men were walking up and down to keep their feet from freezing, and cupping and blowing into their hands. Their mounts stood, heads down, as a slight breeze picked up from the direction of the mountains and blew down the valley.

Cato exchanged a nod with Miro before the latter spoke. 'How long are we staying here, sir?'

'Long enough to give Valens and the others time to reach the main column. Till dawn at any rate.'

As he spoke, Cato realised that he had lost all sense of time, thanks to his mind being dulled by exhaustion. At that point he would have given a year's pay just to be sitting by a fire in the warmth of a barrack block in Viroconium, sipping heated wine. Or better still, back in Rome, with

Julia at her father's house. The sharp stab of agony that came with the unbidden image drove away his weariness at once, and he cleared his throat.

'Better make sure the horses are fed. They'll need their strength later. Pass the word to the other squadrons.'

Miro bowed his head and spoke to his men before climbing into the saddle to carry out his orders. Cato was relieved when he left, as he had become weary of the decurion's constant fretting. He began to pace up and down in front of the standard to keep his limbs from growing numb. The snow was already seven or eight inches deep, and he kicked it up until he had worn a narrow track as he strode to and fro, thirty steps at a time. At length Miro returned and they stood waiting as snow began to sweep in at an angle on the strengthening wind, until it became a blizzard, swishing past Cato's ears.

It was an hour or so later, as best he could estimate, when a rider came in from the right flank, snow bursting from the ground as his mount's hooves kicked it up.

'Beg to report, enemy's on the move, sir!'

'What are they up to?' Cato snapped. 'Exactly.'

The rider swallowed and drew a breath. 'We sighted a party of infantry moving to outflank us. Decurion Themistocles says he will shadow them until he receives further orders.'

Cato nodded to himself. It was time, then. The natives were clearly keen to clear the mouth of the pass as soon as possible, so that their army could move against the Romans at first light.

'Tell the decurion to wait for the trumpet signal. The moment he hears it, he is to fall back to the campfires. Go!'

The rider pulled on his reins, swung his horse round and galloped back through the snow. Cato turned to Miro and the others. 'Mount up!'

The men needed no encouragement to climb into their saddles, and the squadron swiftly made ready. As they waited, spears in hand, Cato stared directly ahead, squinting into the gloom. At last he saw them, a line of figures advancing across the snow. At the same time, he heard muffled shouts from his left and he turned to the trumpeter.

'Give the signal!'

The trumpeter raised his brass horn, pressed his lips to the mouthpiece and blew. A thin, uncertain note issued from the flared end, and Cato realised that the cold must have chapped the man's lips.

'Spit, for Jupiter's sake! Spit, man!'

The trumpeter turned his head aside and hawked up a gobbet before turning back to his instrument. This time he puffed his cheeks and blew, and the note was sharp and penetrating. He repeated it three times before resting, then gave the signal again. As he did so, the enemy warriors in front of the squadron halted, unsure of what lay ahead of them. Then a voice bellowed, angrily, and they came on again, apparently heedless of the caltrops that had surprised them the previous day.

'Blood Crows!' Cato called out. 'Fall back!'

The Thracians wheeled about and trotted towards the glow of the fires, which still burned faintly through the gloom. A short distance further on, Cato glimpsed more horsemen to his right, and for an instant wondered if they might be the enemy, but then he saw the squadron pennant and breathed a sigh of relief. He halted Miro and his men close to what was left of the fire where he had last seen Macro. The blaze had died down and only small flames flickered in the wind amid the embers and ash. Around the fireplace, the bodies were almost covered in snow. Cato waited anxiously for the first squadron to reach them, then two more came in: those assigned to patrol the front. Then the left flank. Only Themistocles and his squadron remained out in the blizzard.

Corvinus approached Cato with an anxious expression as he reined in alongside. 'They're moving round the left flank, sir. We saw 'em just after I heard the signal.'

'They're trying to force both ends of the line. Makes sense,' Cato replied. Then he heard shouts to his right, and the unmistakable clash of steel. All the men with him instantly turned towards the sound, and it took a beat before Cato recovered his wits and shouted the order to form a line to the right. The Blood Crows hurriedly fanned out, hefting their shields up to cover their bodies and adjusting the grip on their spears. The sounds drew louder, and then Cato saw the first of the flank squadron's riders tearing through the snow towards them. He rode ahead of the line to intercept the man and saw that he had been wounded in the leg, blood dripping from his boot, black in the night.

'What's happened?' Cato demanded. 'I ordered Themistocles to stay clear of any fight.'

'The decurion's dead,' the man responded, breathing hard as his horse snorted. 'We kept 'em in sight and then they hit us from three sides. Lost several men before we even knew what had happened.' He glanced back over his shoulder in alarm. More riders were emerging from the gloom, and Cato ordered them to form up behind Thraxis.

He turned back to the wounded man. 'How many of them?'

'I— I don't know, sir. A hundred. Maybe more.'

'Right, get to the rear!'

Cato returned to his position in the centre of the line and waited until it seemed that the last of the riders had rejoined the cohort, then he craned his neck forward and squinted until he saw the enemy, scattered figures on foot charging forward wildly. If they reached the fires, the ruse would be spotted at once. If they could be checked violently now, and driven off, then it might delay any pursuit until after first light. He drew his sword and swept it forward.

'Blood Crows! Advance!'

He urged his horse into a walk and then at once increased the pace to a trot, then a canter. The distance between the riders and the oncoming natives decreased rapidly. At the very last moment, no more than thirty feet from the nearest of the enemy, Cato bellowed the order to charge, and the Blood Crows roared an inchoate war cry as they spurred their mounts on and lowered the tips of their spears. Snowflakes pattered into Cato's face and he had to blink them from his eyes as he braced himself in the saddle and held his sword out high and to the side ready to strike. The natives had been triumphantly pursuing a broken enemy but were now on the receiving end, and their cheers died in their throats as the Blood Crows charged at them. Cato saw several men in a loose cluster directly ahead of him and steered straight at them.

The natives scattered, hurling themselves aside into the snow. One, slower than his companions, went down directly beneath the horse, his cry cut off as the weight of the beast crushed his chest. Cato slashed his sword at the last man in his path, and the blade cut into his back and shoulder and drove the native down on to his knees. Then he wheeled round and turned on those who had avoided his charge. Two men kept low and ran crouching from his path. The last braced himself as he wielded an axe. Cato swerved to take the blow on his shield and then twisted in his saddle to make a cut at the man's head. His opponent had swift reactions and blocked with his shield in turn, then backed off. His attention fixed on the Roman officer, he never saw the Thracian coming up behind him, spear lowered, and he lurched forward, off his feet, as the bloodied point burst out of his throat.

Cato saw that the charge had completely crushed the enemy, who were now streaming back in the direction they had come, some abandoning their weapons as they sought to escape the Blood Crows. Thraxis and the trumpeter were close by, and Cato turned to them.

'Sound the recall!'

The shrill note rose above the wind and the scattered sounds of combat, and the officers bellowed to their men to return to their standards. Some took more persuading than others until threatened with punishment. But soon the last of the enemy had disappeared, save those who had been cut down in the charge, and the Blood Crows re-formed into their squadrons. Themistocles and several of his men were missing, and Cato took personal command of the survivors. When the men were all in place, he turned his mount towards the coast and waved them forward.

Already he could see further into the distance and make out more detail, and he realised that dawn was not far off.

He glanced back towards the fires and the still forms of the dead and prayed to Fortuna that the enemy would take some time to recover following the charge, and would be held up further by the sight of the Roman soldiers still in place. Long enough for the Blood Crows to steal a sufficient advance before they were cut off by the enemy making the crossing from Mona.

As the sky brightened, so the snow began to abate, until only light flakes, like dust, were carried on the breeze. Cato and his men hunched their heads down into the folds of their hooded cloaks. To their left loomed the vast outline of the army's camp, sprawling over the uneven ground. There, too, fires had been lit, stoked up and left to burn, their smoke rising at an angle, giving the appearance that the Romans were still there. Along the palisade and in the towers stood the distant figures of more of the army's dead. The effect was quite convincing, Cato thought, and it should fool the enemy for a while yet.

He led his men in the direction of the sea, grey and ruffled with streaks of spray as it rolled in and dashed itself against the rocky coast in a dull rhythmic roar. They happened upon the route taken by the rest of the army almost by accident. Snow had covered the tracks of thousands of boots, hooves and wagon wheels, but the uneven surface was just visible, and Cato was able to follow it easily enough as he turned the column and increased the pace of the Blood Crows to a steady trot. The snow kicked up by the hooves was like a swirling cloud along the ground, and the absence of the usual drumming thunder of horsemen on the move added to the sense of unreality that Cato was experiencing. Despite the grave danger faced by him and his comrades, and the soul–numbing cold, his thoughts inevitably returned to Julia.

That she could be dead still seemed impossible. She had been blessed with a divine spark of vivacity that had struck him from the very first. Self-assured, she had taken on every challenge they had faced together with all the courage and endurance of a seasoned veteran. From the siege at Palmyra, the shipwreck off Crete and her subsequent capture and humiliation at the hands of Ajax and his rebel slaves. For a moment, as he sat swaying gently in his saddle, Cato recalled her face. The slightly squared jaw, small nose, grey eyes and dark eyebrows that occasionally rose archly when she was gently mocking him. And then the dark hair sweeping out from her widow's peak to flow down to her shoulders. He realised how much he missed her, physically just as much as he did emotionally. She was slim, with breasts that he could easily cup, and a flat stomach that gave way to the soft dark tuft of her pubic hair – the sight of which always sparked a fire in his loins. The gentle curves of her buttocks were smooth and flawless. Her legs had been short in proportion to her back, another small deviation from the ideal, one of many, that had defined her perfection to Cato. His heart ached unbearably at the knowledge that she breathed no more. That he would never feel her warmth beside him ever again. She was like the others, those who had been left to the enemy, dead and cold. But where they would be abandoned to the forces of steady corruption, at least Julia would have been spared that when her body was cremated. The brief thought of her beauty being reduced to withered skin stretched over bone and shrunken muscle and organs made Cato feel sick.

He opened his eyes with a start and was furious to see that he had wandered a few paces off the faint path left in the snow. A twitch of his reins brought his mount back on course and he told himself firmly that he must accept the fact of Julia's death. He knew that she would want him to live on and try to be happy. But Cato knew, as surely as the sun rose with the dawn, that he would forever look back to the time he had shared with Julia, and the present and all prospect of the future would be haunted by her memory. Every spring day, every budding flower, the jade gleam of young leaves and the heady scent of new life would never refresh his soul as they once did. For him, it would be a perpetual winter of the soul, all life shrunk beneath a mantle as white as bone, cold as ice and swept over by a wind filled with the sighs of every lost joy now denied him. And nothing would ever change that.

'Sir!'

Cato started, and blinked hard. Miro was alongside him, craning his neck as he pointed ahead. A mile away he could make out the end of the Roman column stretched out across the winter landscape. Wagons were interspersed with units of infantry, some of whom toiled at the wheels to budge forward vehicles that had become stuck or were struggling with a steep incline. The cavalry formed an extended picket line to the landward side of the route, while the coast guarded the other flank. More riders were just visible in the distance, scouting the way ahead. Cato strained his eyes to look beyond them, to the east, the direction that held out the prospect of the army's salvation. And yet in his heart, he felt that he was already dead and merely looking over the thousands of men who would soon share that fate in reality.

'Keep them going,' he said to Miro, and steered his mount off the track then turned to look back the way they had come. The cohort had kicked up a clear trail through the snow, and until there was another fall, it would be easy to follow, like a finger pointed directly at the retreating Roman army. The enemy would find it soon enough. And then they would hurl themselves into a savage pursuit of their prey, determined to run them to ground and tear them to pieces.

CHAPTER TWENTY-SEVEN

There was little sign of the enemy for the first two days, even though their scouts had established contact with the Romans as early as dusk on the first day of the retreat. The native horsemen were first seen in the distance, over two miles to the rear of the column. Having found the Roman army, they galloped forward and were only driven off when Cato and the Blood Crows turned to confront them. No attempt to engage the Romans was made, and the enemy were content to ride up into the hills on the flank and survey them as they kept pace. That was not a hard task for the native warriors due to the army's difficulties in negotiating the snowdrifts that blocked the way. Each time the wagons had to be halted while the men took up their trenching tools and cleared a path. There was additional trouble once the passage of feet and wheels packed down the snow and compressed it into sheets of ice that made the going difficult for those following on. The only cheering thought for Cato was that the Druids and their followers would be enduring the same conditions, though they would not be burdened by carts and wagons as the Roman army were.

Legate Quintatus drove the men on as far as he could before giving the order to halt for the night. Due to the head start that the Romans had gained, he did not judge it possible for the natives to catch up for at least another day. And so no camp-in-the-face-of-the-enemy was constructed, the soldiers merely setting out a perimeter of field defences using the spiked lengths of wood that slotted together to make barricades. Come the dawn, these were easily broken down and carried on the back of carts or loaded on to mules. As soon as the tents were erected, those off duty scrambled inside to shelter from the wind and cold as best they could and chew disconsolately on their meagre rations.

The men of the rearguard were not so fortunate. Quintatus had given orders for the Blood Crows to stand watch, and Cato's men were able to rest for only half the night. Once again, Macro's cohort was assigned to Cato's small command, and was to provide the backbone of any stand that had to be made in order to hold the enemy at bay. But at least the legionaries were spared the rigours of mounting a picket on a freezing winter's night. As the watch changed, Cato rode forward with a small escort, warily picking his way back down the track for a few miles. If the enemy scouts were keeping an eye on the Roman column, they made no attempt to stand their ground and challenge the small party. And then, from the crest of a hill, Cato caught sight of the enemy's campfires, some eight or so miles behind the Roman column. Less than a day's march, and much closer than he had anticipated, given the earlier ruse to delay the natives.

The Romans broke camp and marched on at first light. For the first time in days, the sun rose into a clear sky.

However, it shed little warmth over the winter landscape, and the mountains and hills cast long shadows across the snow. The rations had been halved the day before, and the first pangs of hunger made themselves felt by the end of the second day. Exhausted by the long hours of marching, the men had worked up a ferocious appetite, which had to be satisfied by the mean allocation of barley and dried meat.

During the afternoon, the enemy horsemen tracking the army had grown significantly in number, and as the column halted, just before dusk, Cato's scouts reported that a large force of native infantry was no more than four miles away and closing. Just before the last light faded, they appeared along the skyline, silhouetted against the glow of the red sunset. They remained there in silence for a while before falling back out of sight. This time Quintatus had given orders to surround the camp with a ditch and rampart, and the men laboured into the night, struggling to break up the frozen ground, before their commander was satisfied.

Thin clouds were scudding across a starry sky as the tired officers shuffled into the headquarters tent at the first change of watch. Cato and Macro had made a final round of the pickets posted outside the camp and were the last to arrive. As they stood with the other officers, Legate Quintatus cleared his throat and coughed, then took a long look over the faces of his subordinates before he began the evening briefing.

'Gentlemen, the situation has become somewhat more serious now that the enemy are upon us. We can assume that they will attempt to engage us on the morrow. Tempting as it is to turn about and give 'em some stick, that would only delay us and play into their hands. They will have guessed that we are short of rations and the longer they can keep us in these mountains, the weaker we become and so easier to defeat. We must keep moving. That in itself is going to become an increasing challenge thanks to the weather and the reduction to quarter-rations, effective tomorrow.'

Macro gave a low groan at the words, as did a number of the other officers. But the legate ignored them as he continued. 'There is no choice in the matter. Quarter-rations will give us two more days. After that, we march on empty stomachs, until we are resupplied. Which is being arranged. I sent Tribune Glaber and a squadron of Dacian horses ahead of the column yesterday. He has orders to organise a supply convoy at Deva and bring it to us along the coastal route. At best it will take four days before we encounter them, which means our men will go hungry for two days.'

'Hungry?' Macro muttered. 'They'll starve, more like. In this cold, it will hit the men all the harder.'

'Yes,' Cato agreed.

'There has to be something else we can do.'

'There is.' Cato stepped forward and raised a hand. 'Sir, if I may?'

'What is it, Prefect?'

'We won't last long in this weather without finding something for the men to eat. It's time we slaughtered some of the mules. Enough to give us meat for a few days. Perhaps even enough to see us through until we reach Glaber and his convoy.'

'And which mules did you have in mind? The gods know we have few enough of them.'

'We slaughter the animals drawing the artillery train.'

'To feed the men who will have to step into their traces to replace them?'

Cato shook his head. 'Not what I was going to suggest, sir. I say we leave the artillery behind.'

Quintatus's eyebrows rose. 'Abandon our bolt-throwers and catapults to the enemy? Are you mad? Rome would never forgive me.'

'With respect, sir. Rome might be even less forgiving if we attempted to save the artillery at the expense of the entire column.'

It was a bold assertion, and the other officers could not hide their surprised expressions as they glanced from Cato to their commander to see how the latter would react. Quintatus shared their consternation, but Cato continued before he could respond. 'We don't let the enemy capture our weapons. We burn the lot . . . but only after we give them one last taste of what it feels like to be on the receiving end.'

Quintatus regarded him thoughtfully, torn between admonishing his subordinate and listening to his plan. In the end, the legate sucked his teeth and nodded. 'Let's hear it.'

The natives came rushing up to the brow of the hill as the last cohort of the Twentieth Legion was marching out of the camp, just behind the baggage train. The ramparts had been hastily shovelled into the ditch to deny the enemy any shelter, and the outline of the fort was preserved in the dark stain of turned earth against the white of the surrounding winter landscape.

Only the rearguard remained to defy the enemy, drawn

up in a thin line across the route taken by the column the evening before. Cato had reversed the usual deployment by placing his mounted Thracians in the centre and the auxiliary infantry and Macro's legionaries on either flank. The cavalry were in close order, with the narrowest of gaps between each rider. This served to screen the line of bolt-throwers just to their rear. Snow had been heaped in front of the stands to help conceal them from the enemy, and dry feed and pails of pitch were packed about the base of each weapon, ready to be set alight. The legionary crews stood by with wicker baskets containing the last of the army's supply of bolts. Four braziers glowed some ten paces behind the line, and thin wisps of smoke eddied a short distance into the sharp dawn air before the light breeze dispersed them. All along the line the men breathed faint puffs of steam, while plumes jetted from the nostrils of the horses.

'Noisy bastards, aren't they?' Macro opined as he settled his helmet on to his padded skullcap and fastened the ties securely under his chin.

On the ridge, the Druids were pacing along the front of the native horde, arms raised, working their followers up into a battle frenzy. Cato had witnessed it many times before, but even so, he felt a shiver trace its way down his spine at the terrifying din rising from the dense ranks of the enemy. He swallowed and did his best not to seem perturbed in front of Macro and the other men.

'I hope our little surprise puts a dent in their hubris.'

'Dent? Fuck that. I want it to tear a bloody great hole through their hubris, and their hearts whilst we're at it.'

Cato could not help a wry smile. Nothing ever seemed to disturb his friend's equanimity in the face of imminent battle. Then his expression hardened as he considered Macro's hot-headedness when his blood was up. 'Keep in mind that this is just a delaying action. The point of the exercise is to give them a hiding and make them pause for thought while we pull back in good order.'

'That will rather depend on the enemy, sir. They might want to get stuck in all the same, despite our plans. That's one thing life in the army teaches you early on: the other side doesn't always play along with the plan.'

'Yes, well thank you for that pearl of wisdom.'

'No need to get shirty with me, sir. Just saying. Besides, once they see the bolt-throwers going up in smoke, they might feel emboldened to go for us again.'

'They might,' Cato conceded. 'That's why my lads have been issued with caltrops.'

He gestured towards one of the nearest of the Thracians, who had a thick leather bag hanging from his saddle. 'They'll sow those across the ground behind the bolt-throwers after we fall back. If the natives recover their nerve enough to come after us, they'll soon have a new reason to think twice about it.'

Macro pursed his lips and looked at his friend admiringly. 'Seems you have thought of everything.'

'Hardly. But I do try to cover the possibilities as far as I can. It helps to keep me alive.'

'Which is always a good thing . . .'

'Quite.'

The Druids had finished working up their followers, and war horns brayed from the top of the hill. A moment later, the warriors launched themselves down the slope towards the thin line of Romans waiting for them. The air filled with the sound of their war cries, invocations to their gods and the insults they screamed at those who had the temerity to invade their mountainous lands. Cato looked along the line and noted with satisfaction that the men under his command showed no reaction, but stood their ground and watched in silence. Such silence could be just as intimidating as the raucous din of a Celtic rush, speaking eloquently as it did of hard discipline and ruthless training.

'I'll see you afterwards, sir.'

'Look forward to it.'

They exchanged a salute before Macro strode back to his position at the right flank of his cohort, hiding the discomfort in his leg as best he could. Cato heaved himself up into the saddle, not without some difficulty given his tiredness and the weight of his scale vest and equipment. Once settled, he adjusted his grip on the reins and eased his mount to the centre of the line, taking up position behind the concealed bolt-throwers. He nodded to the centurion in command of the battery, and the latter cupped a hand to his mouth.

'Bolt-thrower crews . . . load!'

The legionaries who had been standing ready by the windlasses now threw their weight into cranking back the torsion arms with a steady clacking of the ratchets, the rhythm slowing as the strain increased, then stopping as the cords, tense as lengths of iron, were held in place by the trigger mechanism. Finally, shafts were plucked from the ammunition baskets and carefully placed in the channel running down the length of the beam that passed between the thick twisted cords that powered the throwing arms. The telltale noise of the ratchets was lost amid the din of the charging warriors, and Cato could see no slowing or hesitation in those careering down the slope towards him, half a mile away.

As they approached, the first flakes of the day began to fall, drifting down from a dark sky. So much the better, thought Cato. The snow would help to reduce visibility so that there was less chance of the ruse being exposed and the charge halted before it entered the range of the Roman weapons. Timing was everything. If Cato gave the order too soon, the Blood Crows would reveal the ambush prematurely and the Druids might have time to call off all but the most headstrong warriors. If he gave the order too late, the bolt-thrower crews might only get off a few shots before the charge crashed home and shattered the Roman line. He waited as long as he dared and then barked the order.

'Blood Crows! To the rear!'

Alternate riders walked their horses forward a length to allow space for their comrades to turn, before turning themselves and filing back between the bolt-throwers to form up and wait for fresh orders. Now that their target was clearly in view, the artillery crews hurriedly made last-minute adjustments to elevation pegs and aim, and then stood back as the team leaders stepped up ready to pull on the trigger pins. Now, at last, the enemy divined the nature of the threat that faced them. The men in the forefront of the charge slowed their pace, and there were pockets of confusion as those following on ploughed blindly into their backs. Cato raised his hand and shouted a fresh order.

'Artillery! Prepare to shoot!'

The men eyed him tensely, and Cato was pleased that the firm discipline ensured that no man beat him to the trigger and unleashed a bolt prematurely.

'Release!'

The legionaries wrenched the trigger levers back, and the throwing arms snapped forward and cracked against the densely stuffed leather buffers. The bolts leapt from their grooves, spinning viciously as they darted towards the enemy in a shallow arc and disappeared into their ranks. The impact of the first volley inspired awe and horror in Cato. There were nearly fifty serviceable bolt-throwers in the line. The rest – those needing repair – had already been broken and burned in camp. The volley descended like a fine veil on the enemy, and then it was as if the natives had run full pelt into an invisible wall. Scores were skewered and hurled back into the mass, and in places it was as if some great beast had ploughed a path through their ranks, striking men down and aside without mercy. The wild war cries died in their throats and the charge stumbled to a halt, those at the rear continuing to surge forward and adding to the confusion.

Cato looked on with grim-faced satisfaction before he turned to the centurion in command of the battery and called out, 'Shoot at will!'

The crews worked as swiftly as possible and the air was filled with the clatter of ratchets and the sharp *thwack* of the throwing arms striking the buffers. A near-constant hail of bolts slashed down into the tightly packed mass of enemy warriors halted on the slope, while around them the snow was spattered with crimson, bright as poppies, thought Cato. Already, little heaps of bodies, some still writhing, lined the enemy's front, and more fell all the time, torn down by the Roman artillery. A Druid ran forward a few paces and turned to cajole his followers, waving his arms frantically and thrusting a spear in the direction of the Roman line. An instant later he was caught squarely in the back and hurled several feet before collapsing in front of the tribesmen. A groan rose from their lips and spread through the throng, and then Cato saw men peeling away, falling back up the slope. Uncertainly at first, but then breaking into a run as they got further from their comrades still trying to move forward in the teeth of the Roman barrage. More turned to flee, and then their resolve broke completely and the entire force was streaming back up the slope, leaving hundreds of their stricken comrades in the bloodied snow.

'Cease shooting!' Cato yelled. 'Cease shooting!'

One by one the bolt-throwers fell silent and still, and then Cato turned to his cohort. 'Blood Crows, to the front! Form line and prepare to advance!'

The Thracians surged through the gaps between the weapons and jostled into place. As soon as they were ready, Cato drew his sword and pointed the tip at the fleeing enemy. 'Advance!'

The line edged forward, tackle chinking as the horses' hooves plunged into the soft snow. More snow fluttered in the cold air, mingling with the breath of men and their mounts. Cato gave the order to increase the pace to a trot, and the line grew slightly more ragged as the Thracians struggled to keep their horses moving at an even speed. Ahead lay the bodies of the enemy, scattered on the ground amid the shafts of the bolts that stuck up at every angle. The Blood Crows slowed as they picked their way through, the riders using their spears to strike down those natives who yet lived. Then they had passed beyond on to open ground and spurred their mounts on. In the last fifty yards, Cato drew a sharp breath and cried out the order to charge, and the

Blood Crows galloped after their prey. They caught up with the first of the enemy and the bloodletting began with almost savage abandon as the cavalry stabbed about them with their spears, impaling one man after another.

Cato did his best to stay at the head of his men, hacking with his sword and sharing their wild exhilaration as they shattered the enemy's will to fight and routed the natives. They had reached the top of the slope before he was aware of it, and at the ridge he looked up and reined in, aghast. On the far side of the hill, no more than a mile away, marched the rest of the enemy's army. There was no organised column such as the Romans used, but scores of large groups of men, the vast majority on foot. Most carried bulging slings, no doubt filled with their marching rations, Cato thought bitterly, his stomach aching with hunger. The rest of the Blood Crows halted along the ridge, while the surviving natives streamed down the far side of the hill. It was the first time Cato had seen the Druid–led army in its entirety, and he estimated that there were at least fifteen thousand of them in clear view, with more emerging through the distant loom of falling snow. More than enough to chase down and destroy Quintatus and his exhausted and starving men.

Thraxis edged his mount alongside his commander and let out a low whistle as he saw the native horde. 'Fuck me . . . We're in deep trouble, sir.'

'Thank you for your strategic assessment, Trooper,' Cato remarked. He took a last look and tugged on his reins to turn his horse away. 'We've done all we can here. Let's go . . . Blood Crows! Fall back!'

The Thracians swung about and formed up in a column

of fours. Cato led them back down the slope, around the fallen enemy, to where the legionaries were waiting. Macro greeted him with an expression of warm delight, rubbing his hands together briskly.

'Fine work! The lads on the bolt-throwers gave them a real drubbing. Pricked their confidence very nicely indeed.'

'Indeed.' Cato turned in his saddle and pointed towards the centurion commanding the battery. 'Set them alight. Make sure they burn properly and leave nothing for the enemy, then get your men back to the main column. Macro, same for you. We're done here. Get moving.'

'Yes, sir,' Macro replied with terse formality and strode back towards his colour party, bellowing for the Fourth Cohort to form line of march. The crews of the bolt-throwers scurried over to the braziers to light brands, and returned to their weapons to set the small piles of kindling alight, before feeding more combustibles to the small flames licking up. The pitch smoked before catching, and soon the first of the weapons was blazing, dark acrid smoke curling into the air. Once the last of them was on fire, the centurion gave the order for the men to withdraw, and they marched off with Macro's cohort in the direction of the main column.

Cato lingered for a short while to make sure that none of the bolt-throwers would escape destruction from the flames and then turned to Decurion Miro.

'Start sowing the caltrops. No need to concentrate them, just a wide band across the tracks we'll be leaving.'

As the rest of the Blood Crows pulled back a hundred paces, their comrades began to scatter the iron spikes. Cato looked up at the falling snow. It would soon cover any indents left by the caltrops, though it was not settling fast enough to obscure the route taken by the Romans. Some of the enemy were bound to suffer crippling injuries when they trod on the vicious little spikes. Enough to slow their comrades down and make them proceed very warily. All of which would buy the Romans badly needed time to keep ahead of their pursuers.

Once the final caltrops had been laid, Cato turned the cohort to the east and gave the order to advance. Behind them the hungry flames roared as they eagerly devoured the wooden frames and sinewed springs of the bolt-throwers. Cato glanced at the spectacle with a sense of foreboding. There would be no repeating the ambush when the enemy closed up on them again. Next time it would be down to hand-to-hand fighting, blade against blade, man against man. And for all the fine training and discipline of the Roman army, the men still needed rest and food. Both of which were going to be in increasingly short supply in the days to come.

CHAPTER TWENTY-EIGHT

'Poor bastards,' said Macro as he looked along the long strip of shingle. To his right were the stragglers from the column, the walking wounded, the hungry and the exhausted, plodding along through the snow and ice. A handful of centurions and optios were moving along with them, shouting at them to get moving, and beating those who needed it to stir them into making an effort to pick up the pace. Some, however, had given up and sat where they had slumped to the ground, staring vacantly, too weary to care any more about the authority and threats of their superiors.

But they were not the men to whom Macro was extending his pity. He was looking at the line of corpses stretching along the shingle, amid the flotsam of the wrecked ships that had been carrying the injured to safety. The shattered hull of a warship lay on its side on some rocks a short distance out across the rough grey sea, while sections of other ships rocked in the shallows as they were buffeted by crashing waves.

'They must have been caught in a storm and driven on to the shore,' Cato concluded. 'As you say, poor bastards. The wounded stood no chance. Nor the crews, in all likelihood. But I doubt they'd have been much safer if they had been with the column.'

Two days had passed since they had ambushed their overeager pursuers. The snow had fallen intermittently ever since, creating more drifts that slowed the pace of the march. Fortunately the same snow had hampered the enemy, who had been content to merely keep up with the Romans and made no further attempt to attack, other than the odd harassing sortie carried out by cavalry against individual soldiers or small groups who had ventured too far from the main column as they attempted to forage for food in the villages and farmsteads that the army marched past. There was seldom anything to be had. The inhabitants had disappeared entirely, taking with them their valuables, and their winter provisions. Cato guessed that they had been ordered or coerced to leave nothing for the Romans and their food supplies had either been hidden – easy enough given the snowfall – or simply destroyed. No rations remained and many of the mules had already been slaughtered, and the path of the army was littered with abandoned carts and wagons, discarded kit and those who were too tired to go on and had accepted whatever grim fate the enemy might visit upon them. Of the ten thousand men who had set out on the campaign, Cato doubted that even half remained, thanks to losses in combat and straggling.

The men of the rearguard detachment had held together well during the past two days, mostly down to the iron will of their commander. More than two hundred of Macro's legionaries were still marching behind the cohort's standard, while the Blood Crows numbered nearly a hundred still on their mounts and as many marching on foot. Cato had not let them string out along the way, but had kept Macro's legionaries in column while the Blood Crows led their horses along the flanks to rest the beasts as much as possible and prevent them from developing saddle sores. There was little feed to be had for the horses either, just what could be gleaned from the bottom of the emptied grain pits and barns they passed. Some of them were weakening badly, and two had already been slaughtered after being unable to continue, their flesh shared out amongst the men.

For his part Cato felt the hunger badly enough, but it did not bother him as it did those he commanded, as he was constantly distracted by the need to drive them on. There were times, plenty of them, when he thought again of Julia, and what it was to live in a world without her. It was tempting to let such thoughts deaden his soul and banish any last trace of hope. But instead he fixed his mind on the welfare of his troops. It had been impossible for him to save Julia, but he could save these men: Macro's bearded, gaunt-faced legionaries, who still carried their marching yokes, much lightened by the discarding of unnecessary kit, and stood stiffly to attention at roll call at dawn and dusk; and the Blood Crows, who looked after their mounts before themselves as far as they could, and chased off enemy raiders who came too close to the tail of Quintatus's army. But now they were flagging, and Cato feared that soon he would no longer be able to count on their innate pride in their units and their willingness to defend the standards that had led them into so many battles under his command. All men could reach a point where authority mattered no more and simple, raw self-survival reigned supreme in their hearts.

Looking at the two units now, drawn up in a line reaching from the shingle to a steep crag-topped slope facing the enemy, Cato wondered how much longer he would be able to hold them together.

The Druids had halted their force half a mile behind the rearguard some while ago and had remained there since. Just as they had the last two times Cato had been forced to turn and make a stand to allow the stragglers and some of the slower vehicles to catch up with the rest of the column. Their refusal to attack was perplexing him. In their place he would have harried the Roman troops every step of the way and given them no respite. Eventually, hunger and exhaustion would have broken them and all that would remain was to mop up the survivors. So why were the Druids seemingly content merely to follow Quintatus and his force?

'I'm getting a little tired of this,' said Macro, as if reading Cato's thoughts. 'Why aren't those bastards getting stuck in? They know we have no bolt-throwers left. They could sweep us aside just like that.' He snapped his fingers to emphasise the point and then cupped his hands together and breathed hard into them a few times. 'It's getting colder still, isn't it?'

Cato nodded. 'Much colder.'

The night before had been the worst so far. A blizzard had closed in round the army, the wind howling over the tents and stretching and straining the guy ropes. Several of the Blood Crows' tents had been blown down and it had been impossible to erect them again, forcing the men to crowd in with their comrades to see out the night. The dawn had revealed the army almost snowed in, the long tent lines weighted down by snow that had also drifted up against the sides. It had taken hours for the men to dig themselves free, and get the column on the move. Any water that had been left out overnight had frozen solid, and even the water in buckets inside the tents was iced over. Nor had the temperature lifted much during the day, the sun remaining invisible behind a dull overcast.

Macro cracked his knuckles and stared towards the enemy. 'This has got to be as difficult for them as it is for us, surely?' he hissed.

Cato thought a moment. 'Maybe. But they have food, and they are used to the mountains and know how to shelter in them. They're hardier, too. Most of our lads come from Italia, Gaul and the provinces around the Mediterranean. They won't be as used to this as the enemy. I'd say the natives are coping with it better than us. They are defending their homeland. That always lends heart to a cause.'

'Not to mention that they've got us on the run and can scent blood. That also helps.'

'Very true.'

Both were silent for a while before Macro began to punch his fist into the other hand. 'Now they're taking the piss . . . Speaking of which.'

He strode out in front of the line, his gait still a little stiff from the wound. He continued for a hundred paces across the well-trodden snow and then stopped and planted his vine cane in the ground. Reaching under his tunic, he fumbled for his cock and waited a moment before unleashing a stream of urine in the direction of the enemy.

'Useless shower of piss!' he bellowed across the open ground. 'That's all you lot are! Fucking Druids! I eat 'em for breakfast and shit out the remains!' The men of the rearguard roared with laughter at his crude challenge and joined in with their own mockery and jeering.

At first there was no response from the enemy. Then one of the Druids stepped forward a short distance in front of his men and reached into a bag at his side. A moment later he raised something in his hand and held it out for all to see. Cato did not have to squint hard to realise what it was. A severed head. To remind the Romans what fate awaited them.

Macro, having emptied the last drops from his bladder, tucked his cock away and turned and strode casually back towards his men. They chanted his name in a rising tone, ending in a rousing final cheer and then some laughter, which gradually faded away. Macro reached down to cup snow to rub between his hands, then grinned at Cato.

Cato smiled. 'Nice try, Macro. But I doubt they're going to take the bait. Whatever it is they are planning, they'll do it when they are good and ready. I just wish I knew what it was.'

'Maybe they're just scared witless by the thought of taking on our boys in a stand-up fight.'

Cato gave him a look. 'I don't think for an instant that is a serious suggestion.'

'If not that, sir, then what?'

Cato shrugged. 'We'll find out soon enough, I fear.'

He waited until the last of the stragglers still walking had disappeared over the brow of the next rise, and then dismissed Macro and his cohort. He allowed them a half-mile head start before the Blood Crows followed on. They approached a man hunched in his cloak beside the route. He had abandoned his marching yoke and his helmet, but still wore the heavy lorica armour favoured by the legionaries, and Cato drew aside, waving his men on.

'Soldier!'

There was no response from the man, who just stared blankly out along the shingle at the bodies and the remains of the ships that had been wrecked there.

'On your feet!' Cato said loudly. When there was no response, he slipped down from his saddle and stood directly in front of the man, blocking his line of sight. The legionary blinked and then looked at Cato with a surprised expression. He was an older man, with thick dark hair and a straggly beard. There was grey at his temples, crow's feet around his eyes and white scar tissue across his brow and on to his cheek. A veteran, then. Someone who had served many years on the frontiers of the empire and taken part in numerous battles and skirmishes in the name of Rome. A man who should know better than to give up and accept death at the hands of his enemies without a murmur.

As soon as he saw that he was confronted by an officer, the man struggled up and stood at attention, swaying slightly with fatigue.

'That's better,' Cato said mildly. 'What's your name and unit?'

The soldier frowned, as if struggling to recall, then snapped, 'Marcus Murenus, Second Century, Eighth Cohort, Fourteenth Legion, sir!'

'Well then, Marcus Murenus, you have lost contact with the rest of Legate Valens's lads, haven't you?'

'Yes, sir . . . I— I don't know how. I was with them, marching. Then . . . then here just now. What's happened?'

'You're tired, Murenus, that's all.'

'Yes, sir. So tired. So hungry.'

'As are we all. But there'll be plenty to eat soon. You've heard, I'm sure, that Legate Quintatus has sent men ahead to organise a convoy. It'll be with us any day. Why, it may well be in camp this very evening. Think about that!'

He saw a desperate gleam in Murenus's eyes, and the legionary nodded.

'So come on. Get back on the road and rejoin your unit, eh? Let's go.' He gave the man a gentle push.

Murenus lurched forward a step and stopped. 'I . . . I don't think I can, sir.'

'Nonsense. Just put one foot in front of the other.' Cato hesitated a moment and then reached into his side bag and fished for one of the two slim strips of salted meat he had left. He held it out to the legionary. 'Here. Eat this and give yourself a little strength.'

The man tried not to take the meat too eagerly. 'The gods bless you, sir.'

Cato felt slightly embarrassed by the man's evident gratitude and just nodded in acknowledgment. 'I'll see you in the camp later on then, Murenus. Remember, just keep moving and don't stop.'

'Yes, sir.'

Cato smiled encouragingly and then drew himself back into the saddle, his stomach churning at the thought of food. He clicked his tongue and urged his horse into a trot, riding along the line to resume his place at the head of the Blood Crows. When he glanced back a little later, he was pleased to see that the legionary was walking at a slow but steady pace as he chewed on the end of the strip of meat.

They passed several other men sitting or lying in the snow, quite evidently alive, but Cato realised he could not stop for them all without putting himself, and therefore his men, at risk, and he forced himself to ignore their fate. As they reached the crest, he paused to look back. In the distance, the vanguard of the enemy army appeared, spilling through the gap where the Roman rearguard had stood earlier. His gaze shifted to Murenus, and he saw the legionary turn to look, then shuffle to a halt. For a moment he was still, and then he slowly slumped to his knees and sat hunched over. A heavy sadness settled in Cato's heart at the sight. Then he steeled himself, turned away and continued forward, to catch up with Macro's cohort a short distance ahead of him.

As he entered the camp at dusk, Cato was instantly aware of a change in the mood of the men. There were still hundreds of stragglers stretching out behind the rearguard, and most did their best to pick up the pace as the last line of defence between them and the enemy marched by. The work on the ditch and rampart was not as far advanced as it should have been. The soldiers were working lethargically, despite being driven by their officers, while others were slowly erecting their tents. Several lame mules and horses were being butchered outside the headquarters tents, and even the blood was being collected to thicken the thin gruel being prepared for the senior officers.

An optio guided the rearguard to their tent lines, and while Macro's men downed their yokes and retrieved their tents from their carts, the Blood Crows shared out the last of the remaining oats and then fed and watered their horses.

There was a listlessness in the beasts as well, Cato noted, as he watched them standing where they were tethered, heads weighed down by hunger and weariness.

'This can't go on much longer,' Macro observed quietly. 'Within a day, or two at the most, the column is going to start falling to pieces. Even our lads will be losing the will to go on, whatever I threaten 'em with.'

'If that happens, we need to be ready for it.'

Macro turned to face him directly. 'What does that mean?'

Cato glanced round to make sure that they were not overheard. 'It means that the rearguard needs to stay together and fight our way out, by ourselves if need be. If every man looks to his own safety, then we're all dead. We'll have to keep discipline tight for as long as possible.'

'Yes, sir. I'll do my best.'

'I know you will.' Cato punched him gently on the shoulder. 'I will be counting on you.'

Macro rubbed his nose. 'We've watched each other's backs plenty of times before and been through every shit storm the gods have thrown at us. What makes you think a little bit of snow and a surly mob of Druids is going to cause us any particular trouble?'

Cato laughed. 'That's the Macro spirit!'

Macro grimaced. 'What else am I supposed to say? That we just give up and die? I just hope that Quintatus has enough backbone to see us through this. Him and the rest of the senior officers. Be interesting to hear what they make of things at headquarters tonight.'

Cato silently surveyed the camp before he replied. 'Yes, it will.'

Once both cohorts were bedded down for the night and the watches set and passwords given, the two officers made their way to headquarters. There was none of the customary sound of small talk and laughter from the tents they passed. Instead, a resigned silence hung over the camp.

'At least it's cleared up for a while,' Cato commented, indicating the sky. Only a few shreds of cloud lingered against the stars, and a full moon hung low over the mountains, bathing the snowy landscape with a silvery glow. 'The other side won't be able to give us any nasty surprises during the night.'

Macro looked in the direction of the enemy and saw the dull orange smear along the ridge to the west of the camp. 'Like you said, they don't need to come and get us. Just wait around until hunger does the job for them. They don't have the balls to stand up to us in a fair fight, the bastards.'

Cato considered pointing out that if the positions were reversed, he would adopt exactly the same strategy, now that he had worked out the enemy's intentions, but he was in no mood to debate the issue. He was too tired. At least the legate's bodyguard was on form, snapping neatly to attention as they approached the entrance to the largest tent. They were amongst the first officers to arrive for the briefing and stood towards the front, close to the brazier that provided the light and heat inside the tent. The rest filed in in ones and twos, the last a while after the change of watch was sounded. Cato studied their expressions and demeanour and saw the same lethargy he had observed amongst the ranks earlier.

The camp prefect had been waiting for the officers to arrive and now went to inform Quintatus. The latter pushed through the flaps that led to his private tent and his sub-ordinates stood to attention.

'At ease, gentlemen.'

The officers settled down again and there was a stillness as their commander gathered his thoughts. Cato thought for a moment that he saw a haunted look in the man's face, but then Quintatus cleared his throat and addressed them calmly. 'I'll deal with the routine issues first. According to the day's strength returns, over five hundred men failed to reach their units by dusk. Some may arrive at the camp during the night, but it'll only be a handful. We lost two hundred the day before. Tomorrow I'd be surprised if we lost any fewer than a thousand men to straggling. Of those in camp, the Twentieth Legion has two thousand five hundred and four effectives, the Fourteenth one thousand one hundred and eighty. Most of the auxiliary units can scarcely muster more than half their men, and we have over six hundred wounded to convey in our wagons and carts. The only cavalry unit we have left that is ready for combat is Prefect Cato's Second Thracian.' He paused and pursed his lips as he watched the reaction of his officers. 'The situation is critical, gentlemen. The army is starving and bone-weary. In another day or so it will be too exhausted to fight. We need to do something if the column is to survive. Any comments?'

There was a pause before Legate Valens spoke. He was sitting with one leg stretched out, splinted and bandaged after a fall from his horse. 'Could we not attempt to hold out here until Glaber and the relief column turn up with supplies? Failing that, we move on a day's march and then wait. If need be, we can cut a path through the enemy army to open the way for Glaber.'

Quintatus looked pained, then shook his head. 'I'm afraid not. There is not going to be any relief column, and no food. For the simple reason that Glaber never reached Deva.'

Around Cato the other officers stirred anxiously. Quintatus waited until they had settled again. 'Glaber was ambushed and killed, along with most of his escort, a day's march from here. The three men who survived rejoined the column just after dusk. It seems Glaber ran into another native army. Mostly cavalry. Which explains why the force following us has made no attempt to engage us in battle. They have been waiting for their friends to march round our flank and block our retreat. A very neatly worked trap indeed, I think you'll agree. It seems that my choice is now to either march on another day and engage those who killed Glaber, or remain here and wait for them to come to us. Either way, we'll be surrounded when the fighting starts.'

Valens took a quick breath. 'I say we stay put. Let the men shelter from the cold and save their energy for battle. Besides, we'll not lose any more to straggling that way.'

'That's true,' Quintatus conceded, 'but they will still be starving and we'll be another fifteen miles further away from any of our fortresses on the provincial frontier. And the enemy may simply sit on their heels and wait to starve us into submission. I, for one, would prefer to try and cut our way through the blocking force and attempt to reach the frontier. But I am open to suggestions, if anyone has any to offer.'

He paused and looked round at his officers. There was no immediate reply, and then Tribune Livonius stood up. Cato and the others turned towards him, curious to see what wisdom a junior tribune might offer his vastly more experienced comrades.

'Begging your pardon, sir, but another course of action does occur to me.'

'I'm all ears, Tribune.'

'Well, sir, as you know, I've been mapping the campaign as thoroughly as I can . . . well, that is, *we* have.' He indicated Hieropates standing next to him, who bowed his head modestly as his master continued. 'That entailed taking reports from patrols sent out to scout the terrain on either side of the line of march. Quite often such patrols covered a lot of ground, so we were able to extend the scope of the map accordingly, depending on their reports and—'

'Look, this is all very fascinating, Tribune, but we're in a fix. I need solutions, not presentations to the cartographers' guild. What is your point?'

Livonius's face flushed and he swallowed nervously before he continued. 'I think I recognise this place, sir.'

'You think? How?'

'I went out with patrols from time to time, and on one occasion we came to a defile that led through some crags before opening out to the sea quite close to here. We made notes and came back the same way. There was no question of using the route, since it was impassable to wagons and any other wheeled traffic. But men and horses could negotiate it easily enough.'

Quintatus took a step closer to the tribune. 'Where is this defile? Could you find it again?'

'Oh yes, sir. It's no more than a mile from here, between two of the mountains. I could point it out to you easily enough, given the moonlight.'

'Later. Tell me what's on the far side of it. Where does it lead?'

Livonius concentrated a moment. 'There's a valley between the defile and the route the army took on the way to Mona. No more than fifteen miles' march. And from there, it's mostly easy ground back to Mediolanum. Well, it was before the snow began to fall, at any rate.'

Quintatus had been listening intently. Now he thought through his options and turned to the rest of the officers. 'We have three choices, then. We march and fight. Stay and fight. Or we try to escape the trap and head into the mountains.'

Valens shook his head. 'I don't like the sound of the last, sir. The going is bad enough here. It'll be worse in the mountains. We'd be abandoning the shelter of the camp to take our chances on the word of this youngster. It's too much of a risk.'

His superior gave a short, mirthless laugh. 'It's a risk versus the certainty of destruction if we stay here and make a stand, or the likelihood of being annihilated if we march east and try to fight our way through before the main enemy force falls on our rear.'

'There's another problem, sir,' said Cato. 'Something we would have to consider.'

The legate rounded on him. 'And that is?'

'If this defile is not suitable for our wagons and carts, then what do we do with the wounded? We might be able to use the remaining mules and horses, but they're in a poor state and would not get far with such a burden. Besides, there are too few of them. We might save the walking wounded, but there would still be hundreds who would have to be left behind. And we know what the Druids like to do with their Roman captives . . .' He let the thought sink in so that none of the other officers could hide from the implications. 'We can't leave them behind alone, or at least alive.'

Macro's eyes widened. 'Now hang on, sir. What are you saying? We top our lads and do a runner?'

Cato took a deep breath. 'If we want to save the rest of the column, then what choice do we have? If we stay and try and fight it out, the wounded will die anyway. At least we can give them the chance to make their own decision when the time comes. And for those too badly injured to help themselves, the surgeons can do it as painlessly as possible.'

'By the gods, sir. That's no way to treat our comrades. These are men we have fought with—'

'Prefect Cato is right,' Quintatus intervened. 'If we leave the camp, then we have to leave behind those too badly injured to walk.'

Valens coloured as he leaned forward and tapped the thigh of his splinted leg. 'That's easy for you to say, sir. I hope you'll explain your thinking to all the wounded.'

'I would not abandon the commander of a legion to the enemy. We would find a way out for you.'

Valens glared back. 'Save me while the others are left behind to be butchered? I would never allow myself to be so dishonoured.'

'Nonsense, man! I am thinking of the damage to the reputation of Rome if you were to be taken alive by the Druids.'

'Trust me, sir. I would not let that happen.'

The two legates stared at each other for a moment before

Cato interrupted the confrontation. 'Sir, if I may make a suggestion?'

Quintatus tore his eyes away and faced the prefect. 'What is it now?'

'If we make good our escape, the enemy will soon guess what is up and come after us, once they've dealt with the wounded left in the camp. If we want to buy ourselves some time to get a decent head start, it would be better if there was some effort to defend the camp, to make it look like the army is still within the palisade.'

'Anyone who remains will die.'

Cato nodded slowly before he responded. 'Someone has to, whatever you decide, sir. I suggest we ask for volunteers, and then draw lots for the rest.'

'The rest?' Valens snorted. 'How many men did you have in mind, Prefect Cato?'

'Enough to make it look convincing, sir. Five hundred men should put up a decent show and hold the camp for a few hours at least.'

'Five hundred men . . .'

'Yes, sir.'

No one in the tent spoke for a moment. It was Quintatus who finally stirred, straightening his back as he addressed his officers. 'As I see it, there is only one choice that allows us to save as many men as possible. Men we will need to form the core of a new army to complete the work I have started on this campaign. There's a full moon at present. But there are clouds coming down from the mountains. The army will leave when it is darkest. Each commanding officer will ask for volunteers to remain behind to defend the camp. If necessary, we will draw lots to ensure that we have adequate men to maintain the illusion that the army is still in the camp. I will not ask officers above the rank of centurion to participate in drawing lots.'

Legate Valens raised his hand and interrupted without being given leave to speak. 'If you'll pardon me, I don't think we should exempt any officer, except yourself, of course, sir. After all, we wouldn't want someone of your rank falling into the hands of the Druids either. As for me, I will remain in camp to take charge of its defence. It will set a good example when we ask for volunteers.'

Quintatus considered this for a moment. 'Very well, if you are sure.'

'I am.'

'Then we'll need to act fast. Every unit commander is to brief his men on the plan, before he asks for the names of those who will remain. If we need more men, I will send word of how many each unit will be asked to contribute. After that, all units are to form up ready to leave by the southern gateway. Tribune Livonius will first establish where exactly the entrance to the defile is, directly we have concluded this briefing.'

Livonius looked startled, but then took a deep breath and nodded. 'Yes, sir. I'll find it.'

'You'll have to, Tribune. If you do not, then we're all dead men.'

CHAPTER TWENTY-NINE

Cato's bleak expression instantly told of the news from headquarters.

'How many does he want?' asked Macro.

'Ten from each cohort.'

'On top of the volunteers? We've already given up fifteen volunteers as it is. And one of them was Portillus. He's a good officer, and now he's going to get himself killed.'

Cato sympathised with his friend, but there was no avoiding Quintatus's order. 'Ten more is what he said. It's up to me to decide whether to select them or do it by lot.'

Macro craned his head so that he could read his friend's expression more clearly by the flickering flame of the oil lamp. 'And what have you decided? If you select them, there's enough malingerers and bad apples to go round. We could fill the quota without too much effort. It would save the best men.'

Cato had rehearsed the arguments in his head as he made his way over to Macro's tent. It was true that the logical choice was to pick those men whose deaths would be the least loss to their cohorts. However, the moral burden of choosing them was too heavy for Cato to endure, even though he was angry with himself for what he considered to be mere sentimentality. Officers were required to make difficult choices, or else they had no right to be officers in the first place. But there was something innately immoral about choosing men to die in this way. It could only cause bad feeling amongst the comrades of those who were picked, and that would poison the fierce elan of the men who served in the army's rearguard. It was better that blind fate determined who would live and who would die.

It would not be so easy for the wounded, who lay in the tents closest to headquarters. They had each been given a dagger, and the surgeons had gone from man to man to explain the quickest and most painless way to inflict a mortal wound. Most had resolved to end their lives by their own hand, but Cato knew that some would lack the heart to do it, and those poor souls would have to endure whatever torment the Druids chose to inflict on them.

'I will be selecting them by lot,' he announced. 'That goes for the Blood Crows. I will leave the choice of what happens in your cohort to you.'

Macro tilted his head slightly to one side. 'That should really be your decision, sir.'

'Why?'

'It goes with the rank.'

'It does,' Cato agreed wearily. 'That's why I am requiring you to decide. They are your men, Macro. Your responsibility. Either way, Legate Valens wants them up at headquarters as soon as possible.'

'Fair enough. I'll deal with it. By lot.'

'Good. When we're done, I want the rearguard formed

up and ready to march. The legate has ordered that half the tents stay behind, to help give the impression that the army is still in the camp. It means the men will have to double up, but at least it will halve the baggage. Which means we'll have the spare mules to eat.'

Macro laughed drily. 'There's always an up side.'

Cato smiled back. 'I'll see you once we're done.'

They saluted, and Cato strode off towards his cohort. The men already knew what was about to take place and were formed up in their squadrons, while Decurion Miro added coins from the cohort's pay chest to a nosebag. Once he had counted out the plain bronze coins, he added ten more, in almost the same size, of silver and gave the bag a good shake. Cato approached and turned to address his men.

'There's no time to waste on speeches, lads. The drill is this. The squadrons come up in turn for each man to take one coin each out of the bag. We'll start with Harpex and his lads; last to go will be Decurion Miro and his squadron. I'll go first.'

So saying, he turned towards Miro and the latter held up the nosebag. Cato placed his hand inside, stirred the topmost coins with the tips of his fingers, then closed them round one and drew it out, raising it up for all to see.

'Bronze! Harpex, you're up.'

Cato stepped aside and let the decurion lead his men to the bag. Each one took a coin out and held it up as the result was called out. It took until almost the last man before the first silver coin came up, and the Thracian froze in shock for a moment before accepting his destiny, bidding his comrades a brief farewell and stepping to the side to await the fate of the rest. The five remaining cohorts took their turn and more of the silver coins emerged, until at last there was only one remaining as Miro's squadron came forward. Each man extracted a coin from the dwindling number left and held it up.

'Bronze . . . Bronze . . . Bronze . . .'

As it continued, Cato could see the growing anxiety in the decurion's face by the light of the moon. And then there was just Miro and Thraxis left to draw, and the officer hesitated before holding the bag out to the standard-bearer.

'You first.'

Thraxis pressed his lips together, then reached in and quickly picked a coin out. He could not help a relieved expression as he held it up.

'Bronze!'

Miro looked at him in horror, then, as all eyes turned to him, placed his trembling hand into the bag and pulled out the last coin as if it were a poisonous serpent. 'Silver . . .'

He lowered the coin back into the bag and dropped it at his feet before looking helplessly at Cato, who forced himself to keep his expression impassive as he turned to the men who had picked the silver coins. 'That's the way it goes, lads. But remember, you have served with the Blood Crows. Do the cohort proud and you will be remembered. Hold the enemy off for as long as you can, and take down as many of the bastards as possible.' He clasped hands with each man in turn, and lastly with Miro. 'Goodbye, Decurion. It's been an honour to serve with you.'

Miro opened his mouth to reply, but no words came. He swallowed and tried again, in a low, pleading tone. 'Sir, you need me. Who will command the squadron?'

'I will take care of them for you.'

'But they need me, sir. They're used to me. We're comrades. Lose me and they'll not fight nearly so well as they did.'

'I am sure they will fight to honour you, Decurion. As will I.'

Miro leaned forward and lowered his voice further. 'Sir, I don't want to stay here. I don't want to stay here and die. Please don't order me to. Tell Valens you're a man short . . . Please, sir. Please.'

Cato tried to pull his hand free, but the decurion held on desperately. Cato felt sickened by the man's open display of his loss of nerve. He hissed furiously, 'Pull yourself together. Right now. The odds were the same for you as for everyone else, but Fortuna chose you. Accept it and get those men up to headquarters. Go . . .'

Miro's grip weakened for a moment and Cato took his hand back swiftly. 'Carry on, Decurion Miro. Do your duty.'

Miro hesitated and looked round, his jaw trembling. There was a terrible silence before Thraxis stepped forward. 'Permission to change places with Decurion Miro, sir!'

'What?' Cato was nonplussed. 'What did you say?'

'I'll swap places with Miro, sir. Like he said, the cohort needs him. Let me have a crack at those Druid bastards instead. I fancy teaching them a lesson.'

Cato was about to deny the request when he saw the desperate glint in Miro's eye and realised that the only way he would fight was if someone dragged him kicking and crying to the enemy. It would be unsettling for those that remained and set a terrible example. He swallowed his reluctance and turned to face Thraxis instead. 'Are you sure about this?'

'I am, sir. It'll be a chance to take down some of those Celt bastards before I starve to death. Be worth it.'

'If that's what you want, Thraxis.'

'Yes, sir. It is.'

Cato nodded, full of admiration for the man. 'Very well. But there's one last thing before we part.' He stabbed a finger at Miro. 'Give Thraxis your helmet and your medal harness. Now, unless you want to stay and fight at his side.'

Miro did not need to be asked twice and hurriedly handed over the most visible signs of his office to the standard-bearer. Thraxis made to give him the standard, but Cato intercepted it. 'I'll take charge of that. Miro, I am demoting you to the ranks and placing you on the mule team. Even that is more than you deserve. Get out of my sight.'

Miro recoiled as if he had been slapped in the face, then backed away sheepishly and turned to walk off into the night. Cato turned his attention back to Thraxis.

'For what it's worth, I am giving you a field promotion to decurion. You will be in command of the contingent of Blood Crows that remains in the fort. I know that you, and the others, will uphold the name of the cohort. And it's been my personal honour and privilege to serve with you. You might have been a bloody moody servant at times, but you're a fine soldier.'

Thraxis grinned in the moonlight. 'And you're a good officer, sir, but a fucking pain in the arse to look after.'

They shared a brief silence before Thraxis turned to the others who were remaining to fight and die with him. 'Blood Crows contingent! Attention!'

The small party stiffened, as freshly as if they had just arrived on parade. Thraxis marched to the front, took his place and paused before giving the order. 'On the word, quick march! One!'

As they headed towards the centre of the camp, one of the other men raised his arm in salute and called out, 'Thraxis! Thraxis!' The chant was instantly taken up by the rest of the cohort, and then Cato joined in too, shouting as loudly as he could until the ten men had passed out of sight.

When the cheering had diminished, he turned to his command and looked them over with pride and a certain fondness. Barely a handful of the men remained from the unit he had first encountered on his return to Britannia.

'There's not much to be said,' he told them quietly. 'Let's just make sure that their sacrifice is worthwhile. We'll return to the province, rest over the winter, and then come back in the spring to avenge Thraxis and teach those Druid bastards a lesson. That's all. Now form squadrons and prepare to march.'

Tribune Livonius and his servant had marked the route to the defile with javelins to which small strips of dark cloth had been attached. They had taken advantage of the terrain to ensure that as far as possible Quintatus and what was left of his column would not be observed. The chosen path started from the lowest corner of the camp facing the mountains, and followed a shallow vale down which ran a stream. Then it skirted a belt of trees, which screened the opening to the defile. The legate waited until a band of clouds obscured the moon before giving the order to move out. The rearguard stood aside while the rest of the army crept out of the camp and moved in single file along the line of markers. If the enemy happened upon the trail the following day, it might be mistaken for the passage of a small contingent, rather than the broad swathe of footprints created by a large force. The men moved in silence, black shadows against the dull loom of the snowscape, watched over by the officers to make sure that no one uttered a word or made any unnecessary sound. The horses and mules were muzzled and led gently by their riders and handlers, who kept a comforting hand to the beasts' flanks as they paced through the snow.

When the last of the column had passed out of the camp, Cato took a final look at the sentries on the palisade, and the other men who had gathered to quietly watch their comrades depart. Macro sensed his uneasy mood.

'Despite what I said earlier, you were right. This is the best of a bad situation.'

'I know. I just wish it was not such a waste of fine men. They deserve better.'

'At least this way they get to die as they lived, fighting with a sword in their hand. Save your pity for those who are going to freeze to death, or perish from their wounds, or sickness, or an accident. There are many ways death comes to a soldier, sir. This is one of the better ends. Trust me.'

Cato knew his friend was right, but it did not make the leave-taking of their comrades any easier. He drew a deep breath and gave the order as loudly as he dared. 'Rearguard . . . advance.'

Macro's legionaries led the way, leaving the fort in single file, followed by Cato at the head of the Blood Crows, each man on foot as he guided his horse along the narrow path carved through the snow by the men and beasts who had gone ahead of them. As the last men left the camp, the gate closed behind them, shutting the defenders in and giving them a few hours' respite before the coming of dawn and the fate that awaited them. The men at the rear began to collect the javelins marking the route as they reached each in turn. Snow began to fall in flurries, just enough to begin settling over the path the Romans had taken, but not enough to conceal it.

The night air was freezing, and Cato felt it chill his throat as he inhaled. Apart from the soft, crunching footfalls of those ahead and behind, the night was quiet and still, and Fortuna continued to favour them with an obscured moon. When the Blood Crows reached the treeline, however, and worked their way round towards the narrow gap between the rocky slopes and crags that divided the two mountains, the moon began to edge into a clear sky, silvering the feathery outline of the nearest clouds. The increase in the illumination was startling, and Cato felt horribly exposed before he realised that any observer would find it nearly impossible to distinguish the cohort from the background of the trees. They continued on, making good progress over the compressed snow that had been packed down and provided firm footing.

As the trees gave way to open ground littered with small boulders, Cato saw Macro's legionaries seemingly disappearing into the cliffs. Drawing closer, he realised that there was a gap wide enough for five men to march into. On either side, moss- and snow-covered rocks rose up and engulfed the sky, and the air was damp and musty-smelling. The passage soon began to narrow and the ground became uneven, and Cato reflected that Livonius had been right. There was no way that any wheeled vehicle could negotiate this route. Looking up, he saw that the sky overhead was a shade brighter. He turned and saw more light through the mouth of the defile and knew that dawn was fast approaching.

He drew his mount aside and let his cohort pass one by one. At the rear of the unit came a small string of mules carrying what little feed Cato had been able to glean from the camp. Miro led the animals by without daring to look round and meet the prefect's eye.

Cato watched for a short while longer as the sky continued to lighten and a pink bloom rose across the eastern horizon. That was when the distant note of a Celtic war horn brayed thinly. The signal was taken up by others as a swelling roar rose like the sound of surf breaking on a far-off beach. It seemed the enemy's patience had been exhausted and they were not prepared to starve the Romans into surrender. The Druids and their warriors wanted blood instead, and the honour of telling their grandchildren of the part they had played in annihilating a Roman army.

Cato tugged the reins of his horse and strode quickly to catch up with the tail of the column.

'Make way!' he ordered Miro curtly, and the former decurion hurried to get his mules off the path as the prefect hurried by. As he reached the rearmost squadron, Cato called ahead. 'Pass the word to the legate: the enemy are attacking the camp . . .'

CHAPTER THIRTY

Once the remains of the Roman army had cleared the defile, the units re-formed and began marching along a narrow valley that meandered east and south for several miles. As Valens had anticipated, the snow was lying more deeply here, and the men at the front of the column had to wade knee-high before a path was broken for those that followed. On everyone's mind was the fight being waged for the camp. Once the enemy had forced their way in, it would all be over very quickly. When that happened, the Druids would know they had been deceived and would be sniffing for the trail of their prey at once. It would not take them long to find what was left of the path through the defile and come after the Roman column again.

The enemy was not the only matter plaguing the minds of the soldiers trudging through the snow. Some had not eaten for nearly two days and had to endure a constant twisting ache in their stomachs. At least their thirst was easily slaked by handfuls of snow. But the hunger ate away at their strength and endurance, and the men, already weary, had to force themselves to keep going, one step after another.

It did not take long for the first of them to fall out of the line of march. Their officers bawled at them to get back on their feet, and if shouting did not work, they resorted to punches and blows from their vine canes. It did the trick for some, but others just curled into a ball and took the beating, no longer caring for the authority of their superiors or even the pain inflicted on them. Those men were eventually left to their own devices and remained where they sat. There were others who remained in the line of march, but only at the cost of abandoning their kit, and soon the route was littered with mess tins, spare clothing, entrenching tools and even full marching yokes, so that their former owners had nothing left but their weapons and whatever food and drink remained in their haversacks.

It broke Macro's heart to see soldiers, particularly his beloved legionaries, so dispirited that they willingly tossed their belongings aside against the blandishments of their officers. He watched his own men carefully, ensuring that his officers kept them moving and that they did not dispose of any kit. It was easier for the Blood Crows, who had horses to carry their belongings and who therefore had only hunger and tiredness as their constant burdens. Cato found his thoughts turning repeatedly to food, even at the occasional expense of his grief over Julia's death. Each time he had to force himself to put such thoughts aside and keep his mind on his men, watching to make sure they stayed closed up, offering words of encouragement to those who needed it, and forever looking back down the trail for the first sign of the enemy.

At noon, as close as Cato could estimate the time in the overcast, the legate halted the column to allow the men to rest and the stragglers to catch up. It was too cold to sit, and the men stood shuffling their feet and rubbing their hands, and trying to stay as warm as they could.

Macro came striding up.

'Bracing weather, eh?'

Cato, who had a lithe build, tended to feel the cold more acutely than his friend, and he struggled to stop his teeth chattering as he replied. 'Does nothing ever bother you?'

'Oh yes! Tarts with the clap, honest politicians, and anyone who cheats at dice. Cold you can get used to. Even in Britannia. But hunger? That's different. I could murder a haunch of venison right now, soused in garum and served with a thick onion gravy.' Macro stared into the middle distance as he continued his reverie, until a rumbling from his belly drew his attention back to his present situation. 'Sorry about that. Not very helpful.'

'Not helpful at all,' Cato agreed. 'I'd eat anything right now.'

He looked down the line to where Miro was tending to the animals. 'I think we'll slaughter the mules tonight. Half to the Thracians and half to your boys. Won't be much meat to go round, but maybe we'll have time to boil it to make it tender enough to eat without breaking our jaws. At least the men will have something to warm their insides and put a smile back on their faces. And we'll see what we can save for tomorrow night.'

Macro shot him a quick look. 'You're thinking too far ahead, sir. We've got to get through this one day at a time. That's what you need to fix your mind on, if you want to live.'

Cato thought a moment and gently rocked his head from side to side. 'Wise words, I suppose. I'll let you know if I live until tomorrow night.' His tone became serious. 'How are your men doing?'

'The lads are fine. Only a handful have dropped out so far, but you'll have seen that for yourself. Of course they'd eat their own mothers given half a chance. But for now they'll do as they are told, if that's what you mean.'

Cato looked round guardedly. 'That's exactly what I mean. From the amount of kit I have passed already, I'd say that only a handful of units are still in good enough shape to put up a decent fight. If it comes to it, the rest of the column will be depending on us. And we will be able to cover the retreat only for as long as we can retain discipline over the men and give them the heart to fight. It's on our shoulders, Macro.'

'I know, sir. Nothing much changes in this world. We seem to find ourselves up to our necks in trouble wherever we go. I'd swear someone had cursed us both good and proper.'

Cato laughed and then dissolved into a coughing fit. Before he could recover enough to reply, there was a shout from the rearmost squadron of the Blood Crows.

'Enemy in sight!'

Both men turned to look down the valley. Several figures on horseback, barely more than dots against the white backdrop, were galloping towards a mound less than a mile away. When they reached it, they paused to survey the Roman column. Then one of them turned and sped back the way they had come.

'Didn't take them long to find us,' said Macro. 'Now we're for it.'

Cato immediately called to one of his men and sent a

message to the legate to inform him that the enemy had been sighted. Then he turned back to Macro.

'If that's just a scouting party, it will take time for them to report back and for the enemy to come after us. We'll have a day's start on them.' He paused and gritted his teeth to stop them chattering. 'If, however, they are an advance party, riding ahead of their army, then we are in trouble.'

'Trouble? As in we-are-completely-fucked trouble, you mean?'

Cato arched an eyebrow and glanced at him. 'You put it so eloquently, but yes.'

Word of the sighting spread through the Roman column, and the soldiers turned to gaze back at the distant enemy. Cato watched their expressions and saw fear in many of their faces, deadpan resignation in others. Hardly a man spoke. A short time later, the muffled thump of hooves caught his ear, and he turned to see Quintatus riding down the side of the column towards him, his horse kicking up a fine spray of powdery snow. He reined in as he reached Cato and squinted for a moment.

'I count eight. Have you seen any more of them?'

'Just the man they sent back to report on us, sir.'

'So very soon they'll know exactly where we are. Damn.' The legate lowered his head in thought. 'We're still two days' march from Mediolanum. Maybe as much as three days in these conditions. We'll have to push on as swiftly as we can. I'll get the column moving again at once.' He looked up at Cato. 'No more stopping until we make camp. Anyone who falls out is to be left behind. Understand? We cannot afford to waste time and effort on stragglers.'

'Yes, sir.'

'And you'll have to be ready to turn and fight if needed.'

'I understand. The army can rely on Macro and me, sir.'

'Good. Then may Jupiter, best and greatest, watch over us and guide us to safety. If you see any more of them send word to me at once.'

'Yes, sir.'

Quintatus turned his horse around and spurred it into a gallop as he made for the head of the column. Macro watched him and then clicked his tongue. 'I do love a commander who leads from the front, just not so much when we happen to be retreating.'

Cato smirked. 'So it's down to us to lead from the rear, then.'

The column continued its advance down the valley. A few miles later it merged with another, larger valley, and Quintatus turned east. All the time, the enemy horsemen shadowed the Romans, always keeping a cautious distance. As far as Cato could see, there were no other tribesmen in sight beyond the scouts, and he prayed that Fortuna would finally show them sufficient favour to allow them to stay ahead of the enemy.

As they turned east behind the rest of the column, Cato looked round at the landscape and frowned. 'I recognise this. We marched through here on the way to Mona. I'm sure of it.'

'Are you certain, sir?' said Macro. 'Under all this snow. Things are bound to look different.'

'I'm sure of it,' Cato insisted.

A short distance ahead, they came across two legionaries

struggling to hold up a comrade as they staggered along. Cato stepped out of line to address them.

'What's the problem here?'

The men made a feeble attempt to stand to attention in front of an officer, and the soldier in the middle winced as he tried to hide his pain. One of his companions coughed to clear his throat and explained, 'It's Atticus here, sir. He can't feel his feet any more. He can't stand on his own.'

'No?' Cato forced himself to adopt a hard expression. 'Let's see. Step away from him. Do it now.'

Reluctantly the pair did as they were ordered. Once the last steadying hand had been removed, the legionary swayed for a moment before his legs gave out on him and he slumped into the snow with a sigh. Cato stood over him. 'Atticus, you have to march on your own two feet. You cannot put your comrades at risk by making them carry you. Do you understand?'

The soldier rolled his head slowly. 'Too . . . tired.'

'Atticus! Atticus! Look up!' Cato leaned over and shook his shoulder roughly. The legionary's eyes blinked open and it took a moment for him to focus. Cato thrust his arm out towards the enemy scouts. 'You see them? Very soon, thousands of their friends are going to appear, eager to run us to ground and cut our heads off. If you can't march, then you are dead. And if your comrades carry you, then they're dead as well. Rome cannot afford to lose any more men. So you'll get up and rejoin the column, or you'll sit there and die. Your choice.' He turned to the two legionaries. 'Get back to your unit. On the double!'

They looked uncertainly at their friend before Cato glared at them, defying them to disobey, then they turned away and hurried off. He gazed back down at Atticus and felt his guts twist in pity. It had been hard to make his comrades leave him, but necessary.

'Atticus, do what you can to keep moving. If you can't move, take your sword out and use it on the enemy or on yourself. Do not let them take you prisoner.'

The legionary nodded wearily and muttered, 'No prisoners.'

Cato straightened up and strode across to Macro, who had been watching the scene.

'I had to do that, Macro. So not a word on the matter.'

'Me? I know better.'

They marched on, cold, starving and with increasingly aching feet that made each pace a private torment. As the light began to fade and the shadows started lengthening, they approached a narrow gorge in the distance, and Cato immediately realised it was the scene of the opening confrontation of the campaign. The irony hit him like the worst of jokes. From here the Romans had marched on Mona full of confidence and in the expectation of a swift victory. Now they were slinking back to their winter quarters like whipped, emaciated dogs, looking back with the haunted expressions of animals that expected nothing but another beating. He took another long, hard stare at the gorge and then turned to Macro.

'Take command. I'll be back as soon as I can.'

'What?' Macro looked round. 'What's up?'

'Just keep the men going,' Cato said, climbing on to his horse and feeling the bones of its shrunken flanks as he urged it forward.

By the time he had closed up on Quintatus, the head of

the column was already passing through the gorge, and the legate and his staff officers had stopped to watch the men trudge by. At the sight of Cato, a brief look of alarm crossed Quintatus's face, and he called out, 'What's happened?'

'Nothing, sir. There's still no sign of the enemy.'

'Then why, by the gods, did you come tearing up like that?'

Cato realised that his commander was on the edge of exhaustion, his nerves clearly almost as badly worn as those of the rest of the men. He took a calming breath before he responded. 'You remember this place, sir?'

'Of course I do. This is where we were delayed by the enemy at the start of the campaign. Thanks to your dilatory progress in ousting a handful of natives.'

Cato could not resist a slight frown at the accusation. 'Precisely, sir. And now we have a chance to pay them back in the same coin.'

Quintatus thought briefly, and then looked into the gorge, where a cohort from the Twentieth was passing between the sheer walls of rock that let up to the crags on either side. 'You think we could hold them here?'

'Yes, sir. I am certain that the rearguard could manage that. For a day, maybe two. Certainly long enough for the rest of the army to reach Mediolanum safely. Provided we have every spare javelin and every bow and stock of slingshot left. Give me that and I will give you a day's grace.'

The legate chewed his lip. 'A day's grace may just save thousands of lives. Not mine, though. When word of all this gets back to Rome . . . Never mind.' He wearily shook off the train of thought and nodded. 'Very well, Prefect Cato. You will have all that you need.'

★ ★ ★

Cato halted the Blood Crows on a rise that obscured the enemy's view of the gorge while Macro and his men hastened forward to help make preparations for its defence. Loose boulders were piled into place to block the route and then built up into a makeshift parapet, leaving a gap just wide enough for a man to lead his horse through. Javelins, arrows and bows were stacked inside the gorge along with the remaining caltrops. One century was assigned to fortifying the approaches to the top of the crags, blocking any goat trails and easy routes with sharpened stakes and other obstacles, while another group heaved more boulders into position close to the edge of vantage points overlooking the entrance to the gorge that would have to be taken by the enemy when they came in pursuit of the Roman column.

The light was fading when Macro sent word to Cato that the defences were complete, and the Blood Crows were ordered to the rear. Cato remained alone for a short while, watching the enemy, who had closed to within half a mile. They regarded him in turn, then cautiously began to edge forward when they realised that one Roman hardly constituted a danger. Cato let them come within two hundred paces before turning his mount and trotting towards the gorge. By the time he reached the defences – the last man to pass through before the gap was filled – fires had been lit within the gorge and on the far side, and up on the crags. A rich aroma of roasting meat filled the air, and he felt his stomach lurch with ferocious appetite as Macro came up to greet him, brushing past the men posted to keep watch.

'Spit mule is on the go, and the legate's found a few wine

skins to hand round. He's already in his cups.'

'Quintatus is still here? I thought he'd have gone ahead with the rest of the army.'

'Think he wants a final word with you before he buggers off back to Mediolanum. Any last requests, that sort of thing, no doubt.' Macro shrugged. 'It's not as if it means anything. But I'm grateful for the wine, at least.'

'No doubt.'

Cato dismounted and handed his reins to one of the Thracians as Macro jerked a thumb back in the direction of the enemy. 'Any sign of 'em yet?'

'Just the scouts. But the rest of them can't be too far away now. I just hope we have a chance to rest the men before they attack. Right now, though, I am so hungry I could eat a horse.'

Macro clicked his tongue. 'Sorry, I just thought it would be quicker to cook a mule.'

They walked through the gorge, emerging by a large fire that lit the snow-covered rocks on either side with a warm orange glow. The torso of a mule had been pierced by a lance and was being roasted over the embers to one side. Meanwhile, soldiers sat hunched round with strips of meat stuck on the end of their javelins to hold over the flames, and several wine skins were being passed from man to man. Legate Quintatus was standing to one side with a cheery smile as he held his hands out to warm them. He looked up as Cato approached.

'Ah, Cato! There you are. Join the happy crowd.'

'Happy crowd?' Cato muttered, exchanging a glance with Macro. It was an odd phrase to describe men who would shortly fight impossible odds, but he guessed it was the drink talking. As he stepped up to the legate's side, he found a wine skin thrust into his hand.

'Take a good swig,' said Quintatus. 'It's from my estate in Campania. It may not travel well, but it has travelled far.'

Cato nodded his thanks and took a modest sip, not trusting his weariness to cope with drink. 'No sign of the enemy army yet, sir.'

'They're coming . . .' The legate pursed his lips. 'You can count on that. But we're ready for them.'

Cato smiled to himself at the inclusive nature of the comment, but wished that his superior would take himself off and leave the rearguard to themselves. The Blood Crows and Macro's legionaries had fought side by side for many long months and had established a strong bond under the command of the two officers. It would be a shame for the legate to intrude too long on what might be their last night together in this world.

'The lads will hold them back as long as possible, sir. And we'll make 'em pay a high price for getting past us.'

'Yes, we will,' Quintatus said deliberately.

'You're staying here?'

The legate breathed in deeply and nodded. 'What choice have I got? If I return with a defeated army, the emperor will want my head. If I stay and fight, then I may win a little glory for myself and preserve the honour of my family name. But don't worry, I shan't interfere with your command over these men. You have earned that. You and Macro both. It's just a damn pity that Rome will lose the services of two such fine officers. Who knows, by some miracle maybe I will survive to enjoy the acclaim. Either way, at least the rest of the army stands a good chance of making it to safety.'

'I hope so, sir. I hope we all share that miracle. Stranger things have happened in my experience.'

'If it wasn't for this damned early snowfall, we would have crushed the Druids.'

'It wasn't the snow, sir. It was the entire timing of the campaign. Winter is no time to venture into the mountains.'

'But I had to do it all the same. Time was short,' Quintatus insisted.

Cato reflected a moment. He was inclined to temper the criticism of his superior, but there was no point in worrying about it now. They were all doomed men. What did it matter what he said?

'*Your* time was short, sir. You wanted to win some glory before the new governor arrived. This was about adding lustre to your reputation, gambling with the lives of the men you took into these mountains with you. Isn't that the case?'

'I admit it was a risk, yes.' Quintatus paused and stared into the flames briefly. 'A grave risk. And I am prepared to pay a high price for it by staying here.'

'A price you also made the rest of us pay,' Cato said firmly. 'I'd be surprised if a third of the army returns to Mediolanum. Even the rearguard has suffered badly. Macro's cohort is down to two hundred effectives, and I can barely scrape together a hundred men of the Blood Crows. They deserve better.'

Quintatus turned to stare at him. 'Yes, they do,' he replied softly.

The men chewed their meat like ravenous wolves, tough as it was. As soon as the meat began to warm their bellies, their spirits returned. Their voices rose, and jokes and snatches of song echoed back off the walls of the gorge. Flickering flames cast giant shadows on the snow and rock, and Cato felt the warmth of their camaraderie more intensely than he ever had before. As for Macro, he enjoyed the wine more than was perhaps good for him, and looked forward to the coming battle with a glint in his eye and a cruel grin on his lips as he chewed on a tough strip of mule meat.

It did not take long for the mood to break. No more than three hours after sunset, one of the lookouts on the crags cupped his hands and called down to those around the fires, 'They're coming!'

CHAPTER THIRTY-ONE

'To your posts!' Macro bellowed, jumping to his feet. 'Stand to! Prepare to receive the enemy!'

The men around the fires dropped their food and wine skins to snatch up their weapons and armour and rush to their assigned positions. Macro and his legionaries took their place behind the rock barricade. Legate Quintatus drew his ivory-handled sword from its silvered scabbard and shouldered his way through to the front to stand beside the centurion. The latter regarded him with a frown and the legate chuckled.

'Take it easy, Macro. This is a centurion's fight, not a legate's. These men are yours to command. And I will follow your orders.'

Meanwhile, the Blood Crows divided into two parties and ran up the sides of the hills to the top of the crags. Cato went to the right and joined the men scrambling up through the snow, soon feeling his lungs and muscles burn with the effort of such violent exercise while suffering the debilitating effects of exhaustion and hunger. By the time he reached the uneven surface of the same crag he had scaled only weeks before, his heart drummed in his ears and he was gasping for breath. He crossed to the edge overlooking the approach to the gorge. The sentry who had alerted the rearguard was standing in the light of the crackling fire. The glow illuminated a nearby stack of javelins, bows and arrows.

'Where are they?' Cato gasped.

The Thracian pointed down the valley, and even in the starlight Cato could see a dense black tide sliding over the ridge a mile back. Ahead of the main force was a screen of cavalry, half as far away. As more of the Blood Crows gathered on the crags, some of the men muttered ominously.

'Quiet there!' Cato snapped. 'Save your breath for the battle.'

He looked down the slope that gave out on to the valley floor. The steep sides reduced the effective front to the width of the gorge and the two routes up to the crags. The advantage in that respect was with the defenders, as Cato had anticipated. Furthermore, Macro's preparations had been as thorough as time had allowed, and rocks and sharpened stakes blocked the access to the top of the crags. Boulders of a more manageable size had been stockpiled near the edge, ready to throw down on to the natives. Not that it would change the outcome of the struggle between the massively unequal forces, but Cato was confident that the enemy would suffer heavy losses before they broke through the gorge and annihilated the defenders. Even though there was no moon, the dim starlight on the snow revealed the barbarian forces clearly. They would not be able to surprise the rearguard with any discreet attempts to flank the position.

The Thracians continued to watch in silence as the enemy army flowed slowly across the ridge and approached the gorge. For the first time Cato could fully appreciate the scale of the forces the enemy had gathered to crush the invaders who had attempted to humble the Druids. Then it hit him – there was no way that Quintatus's ambitions could ever have been realised against such odds. The campaign had been doomed from the very start, in every way.

The enemy cavalry stopped a quarter of a mile from the gorge, at the extreme range of a bolt-thrower, and Cato smiled to himself. Clearly their experience of the weapon had left them feeling the greatest respect for it, and they were not taking any chances in case the Romans still retained a few pieces of their formidable artillery. The horsemen drew aside as the infantry followed up and halted. A moment later, a group of cavalry detached and advanced, walking their beasts forward. No doubt to determine the strength of the force that opposed them, thought Cato. He had no intention of accommodating their plans and turned to the Thracians.

'First squadron! Out with the bows and prepare fire arrows.'

The men set down their shields and spears and took up the bows, bracing one foot on the end and grunting with the effort needed to flex the arms of the bow enough to slip the bowstring loop over the other horned end of the weapon. Then they set to work wrapping linen wadding around the arrow shafts before drenching them in oil. By the time they were ready, the enemy riders had picked their way to within fifty paces of the mouth of the gorge. From there they would be able to see the outline of the barricade and Macro's men against the backdrop of the fire at the other end of the gorge. But they would have no idea of the strength of the Roman forces. It was time to shake them up.

Cato's lips twisted into a cold grimace. 'Light the arrows and prepare to shoot!'

The Thracians dipped the arrows into the fire until the wadding caught, then hurriedly notched them to the bowstrings.

'Draw!'

The bows creaked slightly as the men pulled back the strings and the flames licked from the wadding.

'Shoot!'

The arrows flew out in a fiery arc, brilliant in the dark night, and dipped down towards the horsemen. Most landed in the snow and were either extinguished outright or glowed like stars, casting small pools of light about them. Two struck their targets. The first pierced the rump of a horse, and the pain of the impact and the scorching of the burning wad caused the animal to buck and leap around, eventually throwing its rider before letting out a shrill whinny and running off into the night. The glow of the arrow was visible for a long way as the horse bolted along the side of the enemy host and down into the valley. The second projectile struck a man in the neck, and he flailed at the shaft, trying to extinguish the flame, even as blood coursed from his opened veins. He toppled from his saddle and squirmed weakly in the snow.

'Pour it on!' Cato encouraged his men, and they lit more arrows and shot them towards the enemy until they had dashed back out of range, leaving a handful of their stricken comrades behind.

'Cease shooting!'

The last arrows were loosed, and Cato turned to his

grinning men and gave them the thumbs-up. 'Nice work, lads. That'll have unnerved them, and they'll be wary when they make their first attack.'

The defenders did not have to wait long. A mass of infantry detached themselves from the enemy host and advanced towards the gorge. As they came on, the force began to divide into three prongs, the two outer ones heading for the slopes leading up to the crags on each side while the main thrust made for the gorge itself. Once again the fire arrows rained down, with more from the crags opposite, and Cato could well imagine the demoralising impact the blazing missiles had on the enemy as they trudged through the snow.

A short distance from the mouth of the gorge, the enemy gave vent to a tremendous cry and charged forward. Macro turned his shield towards them and rested the flat of his sword against the trim as he called out.

'Make ready javelins!'

Behind the barricade there was a short gap between Macro's first line of defenders and the rest of the legionaries. Those at the front of the reserves shifted their grip on their javelins, angled their arms back and waited for the order. Macro allowed the enemy to enter the gorge and close to within twenty paces before he barked, 'Loose!'

He was dimly aware of the veil of dark shafts that flew over his head, crashing and clattering amongst the onrushing tribesmen, skewering some of the dark shapes and knocking them down. More javelins were hurled, adding to the casualties, and then the enemy reached the hastily planted stakes and caltrops and more went down, pierced by the iron spikes, or shoved on to the points of the stakes by those pushing from behind. Despite the casualties, the attackers charged on, right up to the barricade, where they began to strike out at the Romans.

'Keep your shields up!'

Macro saw the dimly visible shaggy features of a tribesman rear up in front of him as the man tried to clamber over the rocks. He struck out, taking the native deep in the throat, then twisted the sword violently from side to side and ripped it back. The man fell away and another took his place, stabbing at Macro's face with a spear. He blocked it with his shield, absorbing the frenzied impact as his foe lunged again and again. Then he angled the shield up and the point glanced off overhead. The warrior was holding the shaft of his weapon tightly and lurched forward with it into Macro's reach, and the centurion stabbed him in the chest. It was a winding rather than a deeply wounding blow, and the Briton stumbled back, gasping for air as he staunched the blood flowing from his torn flesh.

For a brief moment no one opposed Macro, and he risked a glance to either side. To the left, Legate Quintatus let out a triumphant cry as he split a native's skull with his finely sharpened sword. Beyond him, Macro saw one of his men thrown backwards off the barricade as a javelin, snatched up from those unleashed on the enemy, was hurled back and caught him squarely in the face, smashing his cheekbone and plunging on into his skull. As his body fell, another legionary climbed up to replace him.

A swift movement drew Macro's attention back to his front as another warrior made for him. This one wore a Gallic helmet, chain mail and a shield, marking him out as a nobleman. Like all of his caste, he knew his business when it came to fighting. He blocked Macro's first strike with ease, and countered with a series of blows that drove the Roman back from the barricade. Taking advantage of that, he climbed up and thrust his shield against the centurion's. Unbalanced, Macro wavered as he struggled to stay on his feet, and for an instant he pushed his shield to the side to stop himself falling, and exposed his body to his opponent.

The nobleman hissed and drew his sword back to make the fatal thrust. Then the point of the legate's sword clattered into his helmet, jerking his head violently to the side and dazing him. Before he could recover, Macro threw his weight behind his shield and slammed into the man, sending him flying back from the barricade to crash on to the tightly packed mass of enemy warriors desperate to get their chance to fight the hated Romans and take their heads as trophies. There were several bodies slumped before the barricade now, and a handful of legionaries had fallen too. The fight raged on in the darkness, illuminated by the glow of the fire behind the Romans and the pallid gloom of the snow.

The enemy's progress up the slope towards the top of the crags was just as much of an effort as it had been for the Blood Crows climbing from the other side. At the same time, they had to endure the steady barrage of fire arrows and rocks hurled down from above, and Cato noted with satisfaction the number of bodies littering the snow as the natives struggled to close on their tormentors. They reached the first of the obstacles set up in their path and had to pause and uproot the stakes and move aside the boulders, all the time being pelted with arrows and rocks. Several more were struck down before the way was clear, and then they threw themselves up the final stretch of slope to the top of the crags.

'Over here! On me!' Cato yelled, as he rushed towards the larger boulders perched on the edge of the rocks over-looking the approach to the crags. He braced his feet and strained to shift the first of the boulders. It began to move, and then one of his men added his strength and it moved easily and rolled over. One more shove was enough to send it tumbling down the slope towards the enemy, knocking the first man aside before crashing into the next and sending him flailing down the slope, then hitting more of the natives and causing others to leap aside as it continued on its way. Cato and his men sent more boulders tumbling down, break-ing up the attack, and then readied their shields and spears and stood ready to receive those of the enemy who reached the top of the crags. The stiff climb had exhausted the tribesmen, and they struck out desperately at the Thracians lined up and waiting for them. A score of them fell very quickly to the Blood Crows' spears, and their bodies added to the obstacles impeding their comrades trying to follow up.

Cato stood to one side, watching. He noted that the enemy had stopped lower down the slope and fallen silent as their courage and determination to defeat the Romans wavered. Now was the time to strike. Drawing his sword, he took up his shield and forced himself into the front rank of his men as he drew a deep breath to issue the order. 'Blood Crows, with me! Advance!'

He stepped down the slope, shield up and sword pointed forward, his men in line with him. They had the advantage of the high ground and the reach of their spears, as well as being fresher than the enemy, and they drove them back with ease. Some fell to spear thrusts; others tumbled back against their comrades and were caught there, unable to avoid the bloodied points of the spears before they were stabbed in turn. The Blood Crows worked their way down the slope, steadily rolling up the enemy attack until at last the resolve of the native warriors broke and they turned to scramble away, desperate to escape the ruthless Thracians. Cato followed them up for a short distance before halting his men and ordering them to return to the top of the crags. At the same time, he saw the first of the enemy who had gone into the gorge falling back, streaming across the snow until they were a safe distance from the legionaries holding the barricade.

'Round one to us, lads!' he called to his men, and they raised a cheer. It was picked up by the men on the crags opposite, and a moment later by those down in the gorge, while the enemy engaged in the first attack retreated in fearful silence.

The natives attacked twice more during the night and were repelled each time with heavy casualties. The second attack exhausted the last of the fire arrows and javelins, and the Romans suffered more casualties as they were faced with fresh troops each time. Having failed to break through on the third occasion, the enemy withdrew to await the coming of dawn. Cato took the opportunity to make his way down to the gorge to see how the Fourth Cohort was faring. Macro greeted him by the embers of one of the fires around which the wounded had been placed. The dead lay in a line further off.

'How's it going up above?'

'We've held them well enough,' Cato replied, 'though I'm down to ten men. If dawn reveals just how thinly the Blood Crows are spread, then our friends won't hesitate to take us on, and this time we won't be able to hold them back. In which case they'll have the high ground and will be able to force your lads out of the gorge. Once they have us in the open, it'll be every man for himself. How's the Fourth coping?'

Macro stretched his shoulders and cracked his knuckles. 'We were doing fine until that last attack, and then the boys took a hammering. I've got no more than sixty men still on their feet, and most of them are carrying a wound, apart from being ready to drop. Looks to me like the next time round it's going to be over.'

Cato made a non-committal noise. 'And the legate?'

'Taken a spear wound to the thigh. It's been dressed but he'll not be running anywhere soon. Looks like he's not going to have any choice in seeing through his decision to make a last stand. That said, he's been a plucky bugger. Saved my neck once, and has downed several of those bastards. Given time, I might have made a decent legionary of him.'

'Then it's a shame he's a legate rather than a legionary. Would have saved us all a lot of trouble.'

'True enough. But he's got guts plain enough. More so than most of his class.'

Cato looked round at the casualties lying in the snow. Some were moaning pitiably; others lay in silence, either staring up at the stars or clamping their eyes shut as they dealt with the pain. He saw the cohort's surgeon, Pausinus, stopping by one man whose jaw had been cut clean through and was hanging by shreds of flesh as his body trembled violently. Pausinus had a scalpel in his hand, and as Cato watched, he made a nick in the injured man's throat and blood pulsed from the wound. The legionary began to stir, and the surgeon held him down firmly until he was no longer struggling, then rose to his feet and moved on to the next man.

Macro had seen that his friend was watching. 'I've given him orders to put the worst cases out of their misery. He reckons he can do it with the minimum of pain and they'll go off quickly. Better that than fall into the hands of the Druids. Those who are capable have been given a sword or dagger and I've told them to fight from where they lie, or take care of themselves when the enemy gets through the barricade. They know the score.'

'Fair enough. It's for the best.'

The two friends regarded the scene for a moment before Macro turned to Cato. 'Do you think we've bought enough time for the rest of the column?'

'I should think so. We've delayed the enemy until the morning, and they'll have had a night in the cold as well as many injured to deal with. And they'll be running short of rations too. I doubt they'll be keen to set off after what's left of our lads until they've rested. Besides, they've defeated us, and driven us out of their land. It would be foolish to lead hungry, tired men too far from any means of supply, as we've had to find out the hard way.' Cato's exhausted mind struggled to gather his thoughts. 'We've won an extra day for the column. Enough time to get clear of the mountains and reach Mediolanum safely.'

'Good for them. Though that's not going to help us much.'

'Macro, my friend, we're beyond help. You understand?'

'Of course! I'm not a bloody fool.'

Cato laughed. 'I never thought you were. So this is it, then. The end.' He paused awkwardly, not quite sure how to express his valediction to his closest companion.

'It's not the end until it's the end, lad,' Macro responded firmly, shrugging aside the comment. 'I'll take the bastards on with my bare teeth if I have to. When I go out of this world, I'll go fighting to the last.'

'I cannot imagine you doing any different.'

They exchanged a sad look, and then Cato clasped his friend's hand. 'Goodbye then, Centurion Macro.'

'Goodbye, sir.'

Cato turned on his heel and made his way back up to the crags. He climbed slowly, preserving his strength, and as he did so, he saw that the sky was already lightening, with a clear day in prospect. A shame, he thought. This was the weather the Romans could have used many days ago. Fate seemed to have a wonderful sense of humour at times. He reached the top and crossed to where the survivors of the two squadrons posted there stood to greet him, noting that Miro was still amongst them, bloodied but determined-looking.

'At ease. Save your strength for the enemy, eh?'

He smiled at them, then moved to the vantage point from where he had observed the tribesmen during the night. Already he could see more clearly than shortly before. Hundreds of bodies were strewn across the snow in the mouth of the gorge, and heaped up along the approaches to the crags. The enemy had suffered more grievously than he had thought, and while he took a professional pride in the performance of the rearguard, he well knew that the Druids would seek to avenge the fallen in whatever cruel way they could.

The light continued to strengthen, as did the glow along the eastern horizon. Then, just as the first rays of the sun flooded over a distant ridge, a war horn rang out, followed by others, and the enemy began to advance yet again, gradually increasing their pace until they let out a great cheer and burst into a sprint as they raced into the mouth of the gorge and up the sides of the slopes.

This time there was just a handful of rocks left to throw at the tribesmen, and only a few were put out of action before they reached the top. The Blood Crows still had the advantage of not being breathless, and of holding the high ground, but Cato could see that they would not be able to fend the enemy off this time. He drew his sword and took his place in the centre of the line as the Thracians, weary and grim-faced, lowered the points of their spears and braced themselves. There was no loud clash of shields as there was when two sides met on the level, just the steady arrival of one warrior after another, taking his place opposite a Thracian and starting a duel.

Cato was confronted by a hard-breathing cloaked figure with a kite shield and an axe. As the tribesman went to raise his weapon, the prefect plunged forward, shield smashing into shield with a loud thud that sent the man back a pace, at the same time punching his sword into his foe's armpit, driving the point through his ribs and into his heart. A savage twist of the blade and a wrench freed the point, and bright blood gushed from the wound. Cato stepped back and readied himself for the next enemy. On either side the Blood Crows blocked blows with their shields and thrust out with their spears. As before, more of the enemy fell than the Thracians, but now there were no men to replace the gaps, and the line was forced to draw closer together to hold their position.

Then the inevitable happened. Two warriors managed to work their way further up the slope and round the flank of the Blood Crows' line, where they fell upon a Thracian as he was fighting the man to his front. Caught between attacks on two sides, he hesitated before turning to face the men above him. The opponent he had been duelling with charged into his shield and knocked him to the ground, and the two warriors uphill fell upon him, hacking brutally with their swords. He struggled to rise, but the blows carved through his arms and neck and he fell back helplessly.

Cato had caught the incident during a quick glance and knew that his men must fall back and try to link up with the legionaries to give a better account of themselves before the end.

'Blood Crows! Retreat! With me!'

He slashed with his sword and cut deep into a warrior's shoulder, then turned and began to run back across the top of the crags to the route leading down to the rear of the gorge. His men raced after him, pursued by the tribesmen, who were still labouring for breath following the steep climb. They reached the slope and began to scramble and slither down, while behind them the enemy cheered as they saw that the Romans were on the run.

A short distance from the bottom, Cato looked up and

saw some of the legionaries falling back from the gorge, and heard more cheers echoing off the cliffs on either side. He felt his heart lurch with anxiety as he realised that the tribesmen must have broken through the barricade. Then he saw Macro supporting the legate as he withdrew, surrounded by a small group of legionaries and the Fourth Cohort's standard, and he knew that it was all over. As he reached the even ground at the foot of the slope, he turned to his men. 'It's every man for himself now. Good luck, lads!'

He ran towards Macro, intending to join his friend for the last stand. Some of the legionaries were running for the horse lines instead, desperate to escape the coming slaughter, and Cato could not blame them. Then he was aware of a figure charging in from the side, and just had time to check himself and half turn before the warrior slammed into him and knocked him over, the impact driving the breath from his lungs. He released his grip on his shield and thrust himself up, raising his sword just in time to block the blade swinging down towards him. He heard the clash and scrape of metal on metal, he saw the sparks and realised in an instant that he had only deflected the blade. Then there was a blow to his brow, as though he had been struck by a white-hot bar. Instantly blood poured from the gash and over his eyes, blinding him.

'No, you bastard!' Miro's voice rang out, and there was a deep grunt and someone fell into the snow at Cato's side. Then he felt a hand pulling him to his feet.

'Come on, sir. This way!'

Cato was dazed and stumbled along, guided by the Thracian. He reached up and wiped the blood from his eyes, glimpsing the chaotic scene as the enemy poured out of the gorge and fell upon the surviving Romans. He was thrust inside a group of legionaries and there was Macro, looking at him anxiously. 'Cato, my poor lad.'

'I'm all right.' Cato's voice was thick with fatigue and concussion. 'Lost my sword. Give me another.'

Then there was Quintatus, grimacing in pain from the wound in his thigh. He stared at Cato. 'Get him out of here, Macro,' he ordered. 'He's no use to us. You two have done enough. Rome will need you again.'

Macro opened his mouth to protest, but the legate thrust his arm towards the horse line and shouted, 'Go! Get the fuck out of here now!'

Cato shook his head. 'No . . . I will fight . . .'

Macro sheathed his sword and dropped his shield, and took Cato's arm. 'Sorry, my friend. You heard the legate. Miro, give me a hand here.'

'No!' Cato shouted, struggling to pull himself free as more blood covered his eyes. He heard Macro's voice close to his ear.

'Sorry about this.'

Then he felt a blow to his head, and everything went black.

'Miro! With me.' Macro sheathed his sword and ducked to brace his shoulder against Cato's midriff before rising to lift his friend on to his shoulder. He stepped forward, out of the circle of legionaries, and strode quickly towards the remaining horses, while Miro kept close to his side, ready to ward off any attacks. By the time they reached the horses Cato was stirring again, mumbling incoherently as the blood oozed over his brow and covered his cheeks. Macro manhandled him into a saddle and placed his hands on the saddle horns.

'Hold on to these, Cato.'

He was gratified as he felt his friend's fists tense around the smooth leather-covered posts that held the riders in position. Then he looked to his own mount, pulled himself into the saddle and took his reins, as well as those of Cato's horse, before he turned to Miro.

'Come on! Don't just stand there. Mount up!'

Miro took a step towards the nearest remaining horse, and then stopped. He turned back to Macro and shook his head. 'I'm staying. You go, sir. Save the prefect.'

'Don't be a fool!' Macro snapped. 'The three of us stand a better chance.'

'I'm sorry, sir . . . This is for Thraxis.' Miro hefted his shield, raised his spear and paced swiftly towards the melee spilling out of the gorge, then broke into a run as he cried out: 'Blood Crows! Blood Crows!'

Macro took a firm grip on Cato's reins in his right hand and urged his mount forward, trotting after the other Romans who were fleeing along the valley. He increased the pace to a steady canter, making sure that Cato was steady in his saddle. He was recovering consciousness but blinded by the blood caking his eyes as he grimly held on to the saddle horns to keep him in place.

A short distance ahead the track entered some trees and Macro slowed to take one look back at the gorge. The Fourth's standard rose above a dense swarm of tribesmen. He could just make out the glint of a handful of legionary helmets and the plumed crest of Quintatus, then the standard toppled out of sight, and there was a brief glint of a Roman sword thrust towards the heavens. Then it was gone and the natives let out a savage cheer as they waved their fists and bloodstained weapons wildly in the air.

With a leaden heart Macro turned away and spurred his horse on into the trees, blocking out the sight of the scene. All that remained now was to carry out the legate's final order and save Cato.

CHAPTER THIRTY-TWO

Three days later, at noon, the sentry on the western gatehouse of the fortress at Mediolanum was rubbing his hands and wriggling his toes in his boots. There had been heavier snow over the last day than any before, and a thick blanket covered everything. The shingled roofs of the barracks blocks stretching out in neat rows behind the wall were gleaming white and unblemished, and piles of snow lined the passages between the buildings where fatigue parties had cleared the ground. A futile effort, as the snow merely covered it anew. Smoke trailed from the openings in the barrack block roofs as the men inside huddled round their fires to keep warm.

The barracks were crowded with extra bodies, the remains of Quintatus's column, who had started to appear out of the blizzard over the preceding two days in a steady stream of stumbling, exhausted, starving figures led by Camp Prefect Silvanus and Tribune Livonius. Less than three thousand of them, a third of the army that had set out to humble the Druids and their allies. Many had abandoned their kit and kept only their cloaks and whatever other clothes they had to wrap around their bodies. As they arrived, they were given shelter and warmth beside the fire-places, and supplied with food and drink, which they devoured greedily. Some just sat staring mutely into the middle distance, too traumatised to accept that they were safe and their ordeal was over.

Nor were they the only new arrivals at the fortress. A few days earlier, Didius Gallus and some of his retinue had taken up residence in the headquarters block while the freshly appointed governor tried to take stock of what his interim predecessor had been up to. There were rumours spreading of Gallus's fury about the campaign to rid the empire of the final nest of Druids. Legate Quintatus would be severely disciplined and sent back to Rome to explain himself to the emperor, it was said. Few were under any illusions about how that confrontation would end. The legate's days were numbered.

The sentry was not having much luck keeping warm, and decided to pace to and fro across the tower in order to keep his feet from going numb. He tried not to think about the long hours he was required to get through before he was relieved at the change of watch. Not for the first time, he wondered at the wisdom of attempting to tame this wild island with its barbaric inhabitants. His home was Hispania, and he longed for the warm shores he had left behind when he had chosen to serve in an auxiliary cohort that was sent to join the army in Britannia shortly afterwards. That had been a bitter joke of the gods, he reflected sourly, and they had continued to get their laughs at his expense ever since.

He crossed to the front of the tower and looked out into the driving snow once again. It was hard to see anything more than a hundred paces away from the fortress, and for all he knew, the enemy could be out there, watching and waiting. Though if that were the case, he smiled to himself, they were even more stupid than he had been when he had decided to join the army. No man should be abroad in this weather.

He broke off from his thoughts and leaned on the wooden rail of the tower, squinting into the snow and blinking away the flakes that landed on his eyes. There had been a movement, he was sure of it. A fleeting glimpse of something darker against the white of the winter landscape. Then there was a fresh gust of wind and he saw more clearly. Two figures walking slowly towards the fortress. The sentry hurried across to the hatch leading down into the tower and called down.

'Optio! There's someone approaching the fort.'

Inside the tower, the optio stirred within the folds of his cloak. He was sitting close to a grate where a small fire burned, giving off enough smoke to make the air in the room acrid.

'More of ours, or theirs?'

'I can't tell yet, sir.'

'All right. I'll have a look.'

The optio went across to the small shuttered opening that looked out over the approaches to the gate. As he slipped the latch and drew in the solid timber cover, a blast of icy wind and snow made him curse. He peered out and saw the men approaching. There was no sign of anything that might reveal an enemy ruse. He watched a moment longer as one of the men tripped and went down on his knees and the other bent down to help him back up. Then he closed the hatch, slipped the catch back in place and made his way down to the squad room at the base of the tower where the rest of the section were taking shelter.

'Get the gate open, boys. Some more stragglers coming in.'

'More?' One of the men raised an eyebrow. 'Thought we'd seen the last of them.'

'Apparently not. And there may be others. Let's go. Move yourselves!'

The men grumbled as they got up and emerged from the door beside the gate. They lifted the locking bar from its receivers and made to open the gate, but the snow had drifted sufficiently to make the task impossible.

'Fuck,' the optio growled. 'Clear that away!'

He stood by, arms folded, as his men used their hands to remove enough snow to draw one of the gates back and create an opening. Then he stepped outside cautiously. The two men were now no more than twenty paces away, and he could see from the medal harnesses revealed as a gust blew their cloaks aside that they were both officers. One, the centurion, was shorter than his comrade, and his beard was thick and curly where it protruded from the hood of his cloak. The other was taller, his head swathed in a strip of cloth. His face looked gaunt and was stained with streaks of dried blood. They staggered forward across the causeway over the ditch, and the optio went forward to help them.

The taller officer held up his hand. 'No . . . need. We can manage.'

'Yes, sir.' The optio stepped aside as the two walked stiffly past him and into the fort. Then he followed them through the opening and gave the order for the gate to be sealed again before turning to the new arrivals. 'Come inside, sir. There's a fire on the second level, and I have some food you can share.'

There was no mistaking the gleam of hunger in their eyes before the taller officer nodded. 'Thank you. We'll do that. Then we must report to headquarters.'

'I'll send a man to the governor to tell him you're here, sir.'

'The new governor?' The two officers exchanged a look. 'Already?'

'Got here a few days back, sir. Who should I say you are?'

'Prefect Cato of the Second Thracian Cavalry, and this is Centurion Macro of the Fourth Cohort, Fourteenth Legion. I was in command of the rearguard of Legate Quintatus's army.'

'The legate hasn't come in yet, sir.'

'He won't. He's dead. What about our men? Have you seen any men from our units?'

The optio thought a moment. 'Only a handful, sir. Twenty or so. That's all.'

He left the two officers alone while he sent a runner to headquarters. For a while the new arrivals sat in numbed silence. Then Cato let out a sigh and his shoulders slumped. 'That's too bad . . . Too bad. Then we are the last of them, Macro. They're nearly all gone. It's the end of the Blood Crows. I've lost everything, Macro. My men . . . And Julia.' He sat heavily on a stool and shook his head.

Macro eased himself down beside his friend and leaned his back against the wall, letting the tension drain from his body. He took long, deep breaths as his body warmed.

'The Blood Crows will always be remembered, lad. Always. By every one of the men they gave their lives to

445

save. I can't begin to imagine your sorrow over Julia, but she will live on in your son. Try and take comfort in that. You still have Lucius. I am sure he'll be a fine boy. And a man you can be proud of. Hold on to that, eh?'

Cato opened his eyes and stared at Macro bleakly before he forced himself to nod. 'I'll try.'

They sat in silence for a while longer, warming themselves and accepting the offering of the optio's food and wine. It was enough to take the edge off their appetite before they had a proper meal.

There was a blast of cold air as the door opened and a heavily muffled figure entered the gatehouse then quickly shut the door behind them. He flipped his hood back and lowered the scarf that had covered his nose and mouth as he quickly looked round the room and fixed his stare on the two officers. Approaching them, he took out a stylus and waxed tablet from the folds of his cloak and addressed Cato,

'Excuse me, sir. I'm Tribune Gaius Portius. In charge of supplies here. I was just told the final contingent of the Fourth Cohort of the Fourteenth and the Second Thracian had arrived. I need to draw their rations. But I can't seem to find the men.'

Macro's lips parted thinly. 'You have found them. That's us.'

Portius frowned. 'I don't understand.'

'We are what's left of the rearguard. And we'll have our rations, thank you. Right now I could eat for the rest of the lads and come back for seconds. So you see to it. You get back to headquarters directly and you make sure there's a bloody feast waiting for us when the prefect and I get there.

446

A feast fit for heroes. Understand?' Macro glared at him and the young tribune wilted.

'I— I'll see to it, sir. At once.'

He bowed his head, put away his writing materials and pulled up his hood before leaving the gatehouse.

Macro settled back against the wall with a contented expression. 'Thank the gods for army regulations. Rations for each cohort, and enough to go round, for once.' He gave Cato a nudge. 'We'll eat our fill and toast the lads.'

'Yes. Let's do that. We'll honour the men.'

'And while we're waiting . . .' Macro sat forward and rummaged in the bottom of his waist purse before pulling out the small box containing his lucky dice. He took out the dice and kissed them before turning to the auxiliaries sitting around the room.

'So, boys . . . I'll need plenty of coin for wine at headquarters. Who fancies a game?'

AUTHOR'S NOTE

From the earliest conflict between Rome and the various Celtic nations, the Romans were vexed by the Druid cults who continued to be at the heart of the ongoing resistance to Roman expansion. From what little is known about them it is apparent that they were an educated elite who were revered amongst the tribespeople of Gaul, Britain and Ireland. As such they provided a unifying influence that the Romans – from Caesar onwards – were determined to eradicate. Like all imperial powers, Rome understood that it is never enough to destroy the enemy's armies. You also have to destroy the ideological ties that bind the peoples you conquer and reforge and impose new ones that bind those you have conquered to your world view.

It is likely that part of the planning for the Claudian invasion of Britannia would have dealt with the suppression of the Druid cult as a means of establishing and then strengthening Rome's control over the native tribes. Divide and conquer has always been a strategy adopted by imperial powers and Rome was no different. If Rome could remove the Druids from the scene then one of the most powerful forces that helped to cement opposition to the invaders would be dissolved, and the tribes would be easier to control as a result.

The difficulty for the Romans was that the Druids could move freely between the tribes and were fairly elusive. However, it soon became known to the Romans that the spiritual home of the Druid cults was the island of Mona – modern Anglesey – with its sacred groves and gory trophies of the Celts' enemies. If that could be taken, the Druids wiped out, and every trace of their existence extinguished along with them, then a blow would be delivered to the native tribes from which they would never recover. As a consequence, the man who achieved this end would win a great deal of popular acclaim. And if there is one thing that we know about Roman aristocrats, it is that they lived their lives with one eye firmly focused on posterity.

The historical record, patchy as it is, shows that Governor Ostorius died in office, probably as a result of the strains of trying to subdue the remaining hostile tribes of Britannia. There was a brief interregnum before a replacement governor could be sent out, during which the mountain tribes of modern Wales sorely tested the Roman forces and defeated one of their legions. This is the raw material out of which I have fashioned Cato and Macro's latest adventure. Knowing what we do about Roman political culture I could well imagine a scenario whereby an army commander would take charge of the province and grasp the political opportunity that presented itself, with the prospect of finally eradicating the Druids' influence. He would need to act swiftly, and recklessly, but the potential gains would be priceless. So it was with the hapless Quintatus, and I have depicted the possible story of an ill-starred campaign that left Britannia in a very vulnerable position when the new governor, Aulus Didius Gallus, arrived on the island to take up his office.

The challenges facing Didius were considerable. The mountain tribes had triumphed over Roman forces and were now more determined than ever to continue their resistance. Opposition to Rome in those tribes still beyond the frontier, and indeed some of those within it, was bolstered by the setback, and the Druids were still as influential as ever.

For Cato and Macro, exhausted though they are by the rigours of the campaign they have just survived, there will be little rest now. The frontier is aflame and the Roman position in Britannia is more precarious than it has ever been, not least because of the political games being played out back in Rome where the future of the new province hangs in the balance. Only when the aging emperor, Claudius, finally dies will that be resolved.

A BRIEF INTRODUCTION
TO THE ROMAN ARMY

The Fourteenth Legion, like all legions, comprised five and a half thousand men. The basic unit was the *century* of eighty men commanded by a *centurion*. The century was divided into eight-man sections which shared a room together in barracks and a tent when on campaign. Six centuries made up a cohort, and ten cohorts made up a legion, with the first cohort being double size. Each legion was accompanied by a cavalry contingent of 120 men, divided into four squadrons, who served as scouts and messengers. In descending order, the main ranks were as follows:

The *Legate* was a man from an aristocratic background. Typically in his mid-thirties, the legate commanded the legion for up to five years and hoped to make something of a name for himself in order to enhance his subsequent political career.

The *Camp Prefect* would be a grizzled veteran who would previously have been the chief centurion of the legion and was at the summit of a professional soldier's career. He was armed with vast experience and integrity, and to him would fall the command of the legion should the legate be absent or *hors de combat*.

Six *tribunes* served as staff officers. These would be men in their early twenties serving in the army for the first time to gain administrative experience before taking up junior posts in civil administration. The senior tribune was different. He was destined for high political office and eventual command of a legion.

Sixty centurions provided the disciplinary and training backbone of the legion. They were handpicked for their command qualities and a willingness to fight to the death. Accordingly, their casualty rate far exceeded other ranks'. The most senior centurion commanded the first century of the first cohort and was a highly decorated and respected individual.

The four *decurions* of the legion commanded the cavalry squadrons, although there is some debate whether there was a centurion in overall command of the legion's mounted contingent.

Each centurion was assisted by an optio who would act as an orderly, with minor command duties. Optios would be waiting for a vacancy in the centurionate.

Below the optios were the legionaries, men who had signed on for twenty-five years. In theory, a man had to be a Roman citizen to qualify for enlistment, but recruits were increasingly drawn from local populations and given Roman citizenship upon joining the legions. Legionaries were well paid and could expect handsome bonuses from the emperor from time to time (when he felt their loyalty needed bolstering!).

Lower in status than the legionaries were the men of the

auxiliary cohorts. These were recruited from the provinces and provided the Roman Empire with its cavalry, light infantry, and other specialist skills. Roman citizenship was awarded upon completion of twenty-five years of service. Cavalry units, such as the Second Thracian Cohort, were either approximately five hundred or a thousand men in size, the latter being reserved for highly experienced and capable commanders. There were also mixed cohorts with a proportion of one third mounted to two thirds infantry that were used to police the surrounding territory.

AN INTERVIEW WITH SIMON SCARROW

Learn more about the Roman world in this interview with Simon Scarrow . . .

It's been ten years since the Roman army landed. Can you give us a summary of what the achievements had been up to this point? It's clearly been uphill work! What successes have the Romans had in civilising the wild island?

It is important to remember that the main reason for the invasion of Britannia in AD 43 was political rather than military. The new emperor, Claudius, desperately needed to cement his authority in Rome, and what better way to do that than conquer the island that the great Julius Caesar had failed to subdue nearly a hundred years earlier? Fortunately the previous emperor, the madcap Caligula, had concentrated an army on the coast of Gaul for the same purpose, so the groundwork for the invasion had already been done. Some twenty thousand legionaries and as many auxiliary troops were deemed more than enough for the job and landed unopposed. However, the native tribes who had not already thrown in their lot with Rome were quick to respond, and a brief, but bloody, campaign ended in the defeat of the Catuvellauni and the surrender of their capital of Camulodunum.

Emperor Claudius had raced to the scene just in time to claim the credit for the victory and was quick to award himself a triumph back in Rome and to name his son Britannicus in honour of the event. The celebrations were somewhat premature, however, as the 'conquest' related only to the south-eastern region of the island. In the years that followed, Roman control gradually expanded into the south west and northwards as far as modern-day York and north west to the mountains of Wales, though not without considerable cost and the constant need to put down minor uprisings in supposedly pacified territory. The principal foe of the Romans, King Caratacus, managed to evade capture and continue to lead the resistance for the best part of a decade before he made the mistake of throwing himself on the mercy of Queen Cartimandua of the Brigantes, who promptly handed him over to the Romans (events covered in the previous Macro and Cato novel, *Brothers in Blood*).

At the time *Britannia* is set, the Roman forces were leaderless following the unexpected death of Governor Ostorius Scapula, and were awaiting the arrival of a replacement. At the same time, the death of Scapula had galvanised the tribes resisting Rome into continuing their struggle. And so the long war of attrition continues . . .

The operation on Macro's wound – the 'progressive extraction' – is horribly believable. What sources have you found for medical

practices of the time, and how did you make the experience so vivid?
By the first century the Roman army had a fairly well
developed system of medical care for its troops, borrowing
from the experience of Greek armies who had pioneered
many of the necessary treatments. It is worth mentioning
that the great Greek physician Hippocrates had been quite
explicit in advising would-be surgeons to get experience of
treating battlefield wounds if they wanted to refine their art.
For the novel, I relied most heavily on the references
to Celsus, who provides in *De Medicina* a comprehensive
description of how to treat exactly the kind of injury that
Macro suffers in the novel.

From the point of view of the patient I am indebted to
personal experience of a skiing accident I suffered in my
youth when the edge of a ski sliced through my thigh and
severed a muscle there. I was lucky not to cut through
any major blood vessels, or for that matter my scrotum.
Fortunately I went into shock and that provided the basis for
Macro's experience. As did the shock wearing off and having
to endure the ministrations of an Italian army medic who
pitched up without any anaesthetic or painkillers. Over the
course of an hour or so he sewed the muscle back together
and then sewed up the wound, and I can vouch for the
discomfort that entailed.

*The soldiers complain a lot about being posted to Britannia. What
posts were considered the worst, and why, across the Empire? And
what ones did the men really want to get – and why?*
Generally speaking, the more established the province, the
cushier the posting was considered to be. Provinces like
Egypt, Syria and Spain provided some of the finest comforts

of the civilised world, together with a usually docile population. A soldier posted to such a place could live out his career in relative comfort with minimal exposure to the risks of warfare.

By contrast, the provinces on the fringes of empire tended to offer far fewer comforts, and in northern climes the soldiers also had to suffer the hardships of bitter winters. Perhaps the modern tradition of complaining about the weather is something we have derived from our Roman forebears!

It's fascinating to see the cartographer at work. What information do we have on the extent to which maps existed, how reliable they were, and how often the army was relying on maps that were being drawn as the legion advanced into enemy territory?

Given that Roman military offensives were carefully regulated affairs where consolidation of ground won was an important consideration, it was vital to pay close attention to the logistics of supplying the advancing columns, as well as supporting the garrisons left behind to guard the lines of communication. That meant having an accurate understanding of the distances over which the army campaigned. Maps were drafted accordingly. However, as far as we know from the scant surviving evidence, Roman maps tended to feature few geographical features and concentrate on the distances between forts, towns and so on in terms of the number of days it would take to march between them.

How would fitness levels across the legions compare with those in the modern British army?

That's a difficult question to answer! There's a wide range of fitness levels across any army in any age. Today's SAS soldiers are phenomenally fit and their training pushes them to the absolute limit of endurance, in order to make the men aware of how much they can achieve within their 'normal' duties. As far as the Roman army goes, those men too were drilled hard and pushed to the limit, with the result that they could march around eighteen miles a day, in their armour, while carrying their kit on a specially designed yoke. At the end of the march they would then have to construct fortifications around their camp before they could erect their tents, cook and prepare to sleep.

Having consulted Roman re-enactors and worn such kit for a few hours myself I can imagine how fit a legionary must have been, and I think that they must have been some of the toughest, fittest soldiers who ever lived.

Could you give us more information about the sport of harpastum and how it developed?
Sports like harpastum had origins similar to those of football in Britain. They began as largely unregulated games with often unevenly numbered teams played over makeshift ground. There are a number of sources who describe the sport and most of them concur that it was a pretty tough game where violence and injury were common features. The exact rules are no longer available but we do know that the leather ball was round and hard and about the size of a football. In terms of appearance, harpastum would probably look like a game of rugby played by an unruly mob of paras on the way back to barracks after a night on the town.

Cato takes charge of attempts to rescue the crew of ships lost in the stormy weather around the coast, when so many men are lost in the icy sea. Which do you think was more dangerous in the Roman military – the life of a soldier or the life of a sailor?
Either career was fraught with risk, and the sea has ever been a grave danger to those who have ventured across it. But it should also be remembered that the Imperial Roman navy was primarily a maritime police force and was rarely engaged in combat. The last major fleet action fought by the Romans was the Battle of Actium at the end of the civil war that saw Augustus emerge as the de facto dictator for life, and founder of the first imperial dynasty. Accordingly, the main hazards of a life in the navy were the elements, whereas soldiers faced action on the battlefield as well as the usual hazards of army life: injury, illness and disease.

Cato won't see his son Lucius till the boy is months or even years old. How do you think the boy will react when he finally meets his father, and might Lucius also choose a military career?
He might, if he survives the high infant mortality rate that was a feature of life in the ancient world. If he is lucky, Lucius will meet his father very soon, although he will be too young really to understand much about the encounter. In time he will learn of his father's considerable achievements, and those of his comrade and close friend, Macro, and he will be proud of his father and hope to emulate him in due course. Who knows? He might even end up with his own series of novels!

If you could travel back to any time of your choice throughout history and live there at least for a while, where and when would you choose, and why?

If I could avoid it, I would at all cost. The risks and sheer discomfort of most of human history would be almost impossible to imagine. However, if you were to hold a gladius to my throat and command me to make a choice . . .

I wouldn't mind a few days in ancient Rome sometime during the first century. To witness a chariot race, or the excitement and barbarity of a day at the games, would be to better understand the Roman character. Also, I would love to sample some Roman cuisine – especially garum sauce. But I'd have to pack a large pack of Imodium to cope with such a diet . . .

THE ROMAN EMPIRE SERIES

The Britannia Campaign

UNDER THE EAGLE

New recruit Cato arrives in Germany in AD 42 to serve as second-in-command to fearless centurion Macro in the notoriously tough Second Legion of the Roman army. It's not long before orders to invade Britain are received and the long march west for this most brutal campaign begins...

THE EAGLE'S CONQUEST

It's the summer of AD 43 and the Emperor Claudius's invasion of Britain is underway. But the Roman army is desperately outnumbered by the savage Britons. Centurion Macro, his young subordinate Cato and the rest of the legions must rise against the enemy, and so a treacherous battle commences...

WHEN THE EAGLE HUNTS

Britannia, AD 44 – Camulodunum (modern-day Colchester) has fallen to the Roman army. But victory is short-lived as the family of the leader of the fierce Second Legion has been taken hostage by a dark set of Druids. Cato and Macro are their only hope, but they must race against time to find them.

THE EAGLE AND THE WOLVES

AD 44 – As the Roman army continues its quest to conquer the ferocious Britons it is weakened by its own split forces. Outnumbered, the Romans must recruit natives to fight under the eagle, and Macro and Cato must train them fast before they and their comrades are destroyed by the enemy.

THE EAGLE'S PREY

The Roman army's long campaign against a ruthless Britain has been a far bloodier and lengthier fight than the Romans predicted. But now, in AD 44, the Emperor Claudius needs a victory. A battle against the barbarian leader Caratacus could finally be the triumphant end that Macro, Cato and the empire they fight for desperately need.

Rome and the Eastern Provinces

THE EAGLE'S PROPHECY

It is AD 45 and the fate of the empire hangs in the balance. Pirates have captured scrolls that, in their ruthless hands, could destroy Rome. Centurions Macro and Cato may no longer be part of the Roman army but they must now follow orders to join the navy if they are to recover the scrolls before the empire falls.

THE EAGLE IN THE SAND

AD 46 – The eastern provinces of the Roman Empire are under threat. Centurions Macro and Cato have arrived in Judaea to restore order to the Roman troops whose indiscipline has meant control of the region is starting to crumble. The local revolt is gathering strength – the Roman army must return to its full force before these provinces are lost...

CENTURION

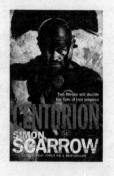

Unrest in the eastern provinces continues in AD 46 – Rome's old enemy, Parthia, prepares to unleash its might across the border into Roman protectorate Palmyra. Macro and Cato are posted to Syria in a desperate quest to protect the empire. A battle that will test their courage and loyalty begins...